THE FOX'S TALE

Jay Sherfey

ISBN: 978-1-964462-01-1 (sc)
ISBN: 978-1-964262-02-8 (e)

Rev. date: 04/23/2024

PROLOGUE

Some gardens failed while others flourished. The one belonging to Anna Forrester in the suburbs of Auburn, fifty miles west of the northern capital, Dover, flourished. Where she wanted flowers or shrubs to grow, they did. Weeds never broke the soil seeking the sun. Everything bloomed as if by magic.

Anna's talent ruled the dirt beneath her feet, not magic. She absorbed or projected energy, sometimes unaware she did so. Wrapped in a thick, dark purple, wool coat, she walked her garden deep in the clutches of winter, oblivious of the icy cold. Hopelessly distracted, she struggled to understand the politics threatening her family. A plan needed consideration, an escape strategy, should the situation devolve into horror. She and Robert, her husband, showed surprising clairvoyance in their published writings from thirty years earlier. The long-term results of the gathering of power north of the Aquitaine River had the opposite effect of what those in power one hundred years ago promised. The sons and grandsons of those powerful men who ruled from the marbled halls of the capital would not willingly give up power. It would have to be ripped from them for the good of all.

The small white stones of the path crunched under her boots. She walked among the many plants, shrubs, and trees; her children cut back and made ready for the spring sure to come. The sun may rise earlier and set later, but the politics on the ground had changed. Anna no longer felt assured. Sides had not gathered yet. It was, however, only a matter of time. Their home in Auburn, once unassailable, struck her as vulnerable.

Anna and Robert Forrester, she eighty-four years old and he about to celebrate eighty-eight years in this world, had threatened none of the elite thirty years ago; patted on the head like children who declare they have found something new. Their warnings about the weakening of the energy projectors had gone ignored. Treated as pariahs who advocated for a basic civility from an age long gone, the established order ignored them.

The clamor of voices from the rooms of power in the capital leaked lately. She and Robert might become a target; a new generation of challengers of the status quo referred to the Forrester's published work.

Anna stopped before a line of ever-green trees: sentries against a caustic wind tearing at the gentler occupants of her flower beds. A bit of green just beyond the tree's branches caught her attention. It called to her. Kneeling, she gently lifted the infant leaves like touching a born baby's hand. The dark green furry appendage wrapped around her finger. Anna smiled. The sudden shimmer and transfer of energy caught her by surprise.

Gently relinquishing the feather hold on her finger, she pulled back her hand. Anna stood and felt her legs complain. Looking up, the sun poured through the trees, lighting her face. It had been over her shoulder when she touched the fresh growth. She knew of only one plant that might come up with a weak sun and intense cold: a plant projecting energy instead of demanding it. Robert needed to know.

Anna stretched and turned toward the house, scanning the windows for his office on the second floor. She saw him looking out at something, having an animated discussion with himself. Two steps toward the house and she collapsed, all energy evaporated from her body. She wondered as consciousness melted away if Robert would notice.

Her dream tore a path through everything she considered settled in her life. Awareness made the dream cognitive for a few moments before she awoke. Reluctantly, Anna came fully aware.

She lay in their bed, warmed by the hearth with its glowing embers. Robert must have discovered her and brought her inside. She smiled at the thought and sat up. Next to her Robert looked to be asleep, propped up on a few of pillows with a thick book open on his lap: his chin on his chest. The rustling blankets, however, woke him.

"What happened?" he asked, concern in his expression. He wiped the sleep from his eyes.

"He's coming, Robert." Anna pulled back the covers and left the bed. She crossed the room and sat at her vanity.

"Okay," he said, confused, watching her lean into the mirror and smooth something out on her face. "Who… exactly?" He wondered not for the first time if his wife might have lost her mind.

"Titus told us." Eyeing her reflection in the mirror, she picked up a brush and applied it in easy strokes to her thick silver hair.

"What… Titus?" Robert closed the tome and climbed out of bed, pulled on his housecoat, and went to the hearth. He placed logs on the glowing embers. The flames burst forth with little effort and devoured the fresh fuel. He turned back to his best friend, his love, and worried. "What could you possibly mean?"

"He's coming, Robert. The earth goddess is real." She stopped brushing her hair and stared at the mirror. "From the south, from a great family, change will come forth."

"Titus is long discredited, and they banned his writings. More myth and foolery was Titus." He studied her carefully, listening for illogical thought: something a crazy person might say. "Besides, there are no great families in the South. They are all here in the North."

"I have had a sign, and I do not refer to Titus' philosophical writings. I refer to his earlier intellectual treatises. He had it right." She put the brush down and spun on her cushioned seat to face her husband. "The goddess stole my energy yesterday evening. It was a sign. An exchange occurred, but nothing clear has come from it… yet." She smiled.

Robert knew better than to ignore such signs. This had to be taken seriously.

"Let's dress and have something to eat in the library. You can tell me all that you remember and what you suspect is happening."

Anna pushed the heavy library door open. Ancient hinges complained like her knees sometimes when she straitened up after hours in her garden. Robert entered the library and went to the furthest corner.

"We are fools for keeping this." Surrounded by books, he ran his finger along the thin, golden frame. Reverently, he placed both hands on the frame and lifted the ragged document, imprisoned behind thick glass, placing it face-up on the desk.

With the coffee steaming in its silver pot and the butter melting on bread, they sat in deep brown leather chairs around a low circular table.

"'The spirit will arise from a great family, from the South, from the least of us. The earth goddess is real'," read Robert. "Short on details."

"It is a case of comprehending what I have experienced with the words here." Anna looked unnerved. Her eyes moved back and forth, looking for agreement but expecting an argument. "He is definitely coming. I have experienced a deep, earth energy discontinuity."

"From the South?" asked Robert. He leaned back in his chair with closed eyes, overwhelmed by the thought of a southern uprising. *Everything will change,* he thought. *What will happen to us?*

"Yes," stated Anna. She looked at Robert, concerned, when he stood up and walked to the window without comment.

"When will his presence be felt?" asked Robert, rocking back and forth, heel to toe.

"I do not know," said Anna, frowning. "Spring or summer may bring more than warmer weather."

"The only way this can happen is through the slave trade." Robert spoke the last few words with obvious venom.

"Yes."

"We have to decide what to do next, of course," said Robert, concerned about running down a false trail but unwilling to deny his soulmate's experience.

"Most families we might call 'great' are in Dover." Anna sat with her hands firmly on the chair's arms. "The capital, regardless, is the place to start. We will need allies. Old friends will have to step up and old enemies will have to agree things have changed, forcing the action I advocate."

"Advocate?" Robert returned to his chair. "What do you want to happen?"

"Revolution, my dear, of course."

CHAPTER 1

Jack Fox stepped out of the retched cold along Snakeport's docks into Gracie's place, then paused just inside the door to scan the storeroom. Alone for the moment, he pulled a dirty rag from his pocket to wipe at the blood and snot, which had partially frozen on his upper lip. Working swiftly to remove the evidence, Jack wiped his nose, folded over the cloth, and wiped again. When the rag came away with no new streaks of red, he spat on it and scrubbed his scabbed knuckles and the dried blood between his fingers. Fearing the worst, he opened his oversized brown canvas coat and raised his gray cotton shirt, both showing holes and rips. Expecting an oozing cut, Jack instead found clear, undamaged skin. A big grin spreading across his face, he stuffed his shirt back into his pants and headed to the back of the shop, the bloodied rag back in his pocket.

Jack waited patiently, glad not to be freezing or bleeding. The storeroom smelled of pine tar, wood smoke, and a not unpleasant mustiness. His eyes roamed shelves full of rope, block and tackle, tools, all sorts of bladed weapons, anything valuable to the shipping business: land or sea. Daylight filtered through small, dirt encrusted windows above the shelves, offering enough light for Jack to find his way around the many barrels, large and small, piled three and four high. It was like making a get-away from trouble through Old John's Square, zipping around its many twenty-foot pillars that circled the open area where public hangings took place.

At the back of Gracie's, the well-worn, dark wood counter stretched cleared of clutter, unlike the rest of the shop. A brass rail ran along the floor in front of it. Jack stood one foot on the rail, his hand pulling through his short, brown hair; long hair was a liability in a fight. Flakes of dried blood drifted to the floor.

From behind a stack of whiskey barrels, a tall, attractive woman appeared. "At last," said Gracie. The sleeves of her purple, full-length gown rolled up to the elbow, exposing rose and dragon tattoos on either forearm. Tattoos did a good job of hiding her scars, Jack knew. A white apron covered much of the dress's front, and a piece of leather held back her long, dark hair. She carried a burlap bag over her shoulder.

Heaving the bag onto the counter, Gracie emptied its contents and lined them up. From the apron's pocket, she pulled a small notebook, rifled through the pages, and settled on the one needed. She scanned the list in the left and lightly touched each item with her fingers. Once done, she leaned forward and smiled at Jack. The notebook slapped down on the counter, ready for his review.

"You ain't forgot your letters?" She eyed him suspiciously.

Jack trusted this woman. She stood like a rock, consistent when chaos raged in the streets. Gracie and his mother had been good friends helping each other survive in Snakeport, the Snake, as the locals called it. With a well-earned business reputation—not always legal—his benefactor was the only adult who did not back-stab friends or business associates. She kept faith with agreements, both big and small. Jack glanced at the tattoos as he picked up the list, knowing it wouldn't be surprising to discover a dead man for each scar. Her talent with blades earned her a high level of respect: if you couldn't defend yourself in the Snake, you died.

"No, ma'am." Jack read better than most and confirmed the order providing a week's worth of food and necessaries matched the goods on the counter. He frowned at the last three items.

"Now, now." Gracie reached down behind the counter and brought up three bottles. "Ya got no right to…" She paused, then sighed. "Well, ya do… but ya shouldn't." The three bottles of rum went into the bag, along with everything else. "I known too many chained to the grog. Nothing to do about it. The hurts too deep."

She took back the notebook, picked up a pencil, and made a few marks. "Just make sure," said Gracie, a look hard as steel. "Ya be a dodger and stay safe. Can't fix it." She stared at him, looking for a sign of understanding. "There ain't no fixin' a rummy."

Jack nodded, knowing better than to argue, but there never was a time when he did not duck and dodge from trouble. She made the same point every week. His mother drank to live. So, what? He kept his mouth shut and patted his inside pocket, checking on the small package and the knife.

Gracie reached out and captured the boy's chin between her thumb and forefinger. "Too scrawny by half, Jack." She turned his head left, right, up, then down. "Hmm." Her hand released his chin, but quickly grabbed his hands. "So… whose blood?"

"Not mine." Jack pulled his hands from hers and crossed his arms, stuffing either in an armpit.

"Good." She patted his cheek in a comforting, soft manner. "What happened this time?"

"Some boys from the quarry went after Spunk and Mini," said Jack, making his case. "It was five on two."

Jack paused as a righteous anger filled him.

"Tell me." Gracie crossed her arms and leaned back on the shelves, both hungry for a good story but thinking Jack might not be long in this world. "Spunk can take care of herself."

"Not with three holding her down and the fourth with his hands under her shirt and…". Jack stopped. The look on Gracie's face said, *I want the whole truth.* "Okay, okay." Shoving his hands into his pockets, and standing straight, he began.

"I woke up early this morning. It was barely light outside…"

Jack climbed out of bed in the same clothes worn every day. Washing took time and money: a luxury for him and his clothes. He shared the hovel with his mother. The space under a corner floor-board made a good hiding place. Quietly, he went to it and lifted the board, revealing a hidden stash. One of two cloth wrapped items found its way reverently to an inside coat pocket. Replacing the slat, Jack stood, shivered, and went to the pot-bellied stove, long dead-cold. Taking a piece of wood from the stack behind it, a flint, and the razor-sharp knife used last night to cut near rotting meat from the bone for supper, he produced thin, dry strips that would fire easily. In short order, as sparks arced from the steel and flint, a flame caught. The burning kindling and the log found their way into the stove. As the fuel popped and crackled, he added more. The iron door clanged shut.

"I made sure that the place warmed up enough for her," Jack told Gracie.

… the meat turned out edible, barely so. It filled him up and did not make him sick: another luxury. Jack put the knife and the flint back in the drawer where he found them.

Today was market day. It took Jack to Gracie's—a good start, no matter what. He checked on his mother. A quick glance over the gray sheet hung on a line across the room for privacy did the trick. A lump beneath dirty covers faced the wall, snoring.

"I came here after checking the other side of the curtain."

"Keep going," said Gracie, nodding. She knew all too well about Jack's mother. "Get to the blood-letting."

"I slipped out the door…"

… escaped the familiar scene. He cared about his mother, but knew she collapsed into uselessness until her head cleared and she regained the ability to put a few words together that made sense. Besides, it was market day!

Bitter cold met him outside, but the air came fresh, blowing in from the ocean side. He pulled his coat closer, took a deep breath, then bounded toward the shortcut through Old John's, getting to Gracie's quickly. The gallows stood ready to do its job, another acolyte due this very day. Jack paid little attention to the rope and noose swaying in the breeze. The shout, a cry, brought him up short at the first alley beyond the square.

"The biggest boy's hand crawled up under the girl's shirt. Time stopped." Jack freed his hands from his pockets. "When I saw the girl trapped on the barrel was Spunk." A fist pounded the counter. "I don' let friends fight alone!" His arms dropped to his side, and he shook his head. "I don' recall rightly everythin' that happened next," he mumbled, keeping his eyes from Gracie's.

… he stopped thinking and plowed into the big boy's knees from behind. Surprise was an ally. His target fell backwards. Jack rolled from under his legs to the left. Coming up fist first, he slammed the boy holding down Spunk's legs hard. Teeth cracked, and the boy slid to the alley cobbled stones. With Spunk partially free, Jack felt no longer needed. She fought like an evangelical warrior. Jack watched as her muscled legs in acrobat-ballet fashion shot up and locked around the neck of the boy clamping down on her right arm. She squeezed without mercy.

Jack confronted the fifth boy, whose hands chained Mini in place against his body. The young girl half her assailant's size struggled, her burlap doll with red stitched eyes and smile still in her grasp.

The boy kept his hands away from the girl's mouth as she fought. Bloody teeth marks marked both hands. With Jack in the mix, Mini became a liability. Her attacker grabbed her under her arms, lifted her small body, and tossed her aside. She crashed into a stone wall, then went to the ground unconscious. Her doll dropped beside her.

"He pulled a knife from his back pocket," said Jack.

Gracie's eye's widened, excited. Her hands signaled, like a mother enticing a toddler to come to her, "Get to the point."

"I bashed his head," he said, looking down, unwilling to say more.

… the flash of the blade forced him to stop, but hesitation was death. Jack struck. Quick as a viper, he moved left, intending to get within the knife's reach to trap it, then break an arm or slam his knee into the boy's groin. As fast as Jack moved, the knife struck faster. It sunk to the hilt through the coat. It sliced left and right. The searing pain of a razor-edge slash to his stomach came and went. Jack pushed through the initial shock and got inside the boy's reach. He applied an all-out head butt to his face.

"Ya should 'a seen the blood spurt over his lips," laughed Jack. "The fool's flattened nose sent his eyes rolling up. The body hit the ground like a sack 'a potatoes."

"And Spunk?" asked Gracie.

"Spunk hammer-kicked herself free." Jack said with a shrug.

"Jack!" cried Spunk. Her captors bloodied, or near dead, she rushed to her friend, fearing the worst.

"What the hell…" yelled Jack in the alley. He felt no pain. No Jack Fox blood flowed. He looked at his punctured coat, then up at Spunk, not knowing what to say.

"So, you're okay?" Spunk, relieved, dressed like Jack with similar short hair, took a step back.

He nodded, wondering how he survived.

"Ya sure?"

"Yeah, I just…"

Her punch landed squarely, snapping back his head. He stumbled back a step as she screamed, "I can take care of myself!". She went to Mini as the little girl scrambled on her knees to her doll, cradling it gently. Slowly, with Spunk's help, she got to her feet. The girls made a hasty retreat from the alley and disappeared around the corner.

"You're welcome," mumbled Jack, and wiped the blood flowing from his nose with the back of his hand. The knife that should have claimed Jack's life caught his attention. He picked it up, cleaned it on his pants leg, then pocketed it. The quarry boys stirred.

"I left the alley, saw no sign of the girls, then turned to your place." Jack challenged Gracie to find the story he left out. Surprised when no argument came forth, he said, "Why'd she hit me?"

"So, you took on five larger boys all by yourself and saved the ladies in distress?" Gracie only raised an eyebrow, and smiled at his question, then packed the bag.

"No. I just helped is all. Spunk did most of the fightin'". Jack, hands back in his pockets, lightly kicked the brass rail, keeping his eyes on the ground.

"Okay, Jack," said Gracie, patting the full bag. "Let's settle accounts in the office. Shall we?" She came around the counter, the silk dress swished, then she disappeared behind the barrels.

Jack followed, shocked she'd let his selfless actions go without comment. She led him into a small room with a heavy, ornate desk, several chairs, and a small stove. A pot of steaming coffee filled the room with its fresh brewed aroma. Gathering up her apron, Gracie removed the hot pot and filled two mugs on the desk.

"What're you now?" Gracie put the pot back on the stove. "fourteen, fifteen?" She patted the apron back in place, handed the boy his steaming mug, then sat at her desk.

"Maybe," Jack shrugged. The black coffee warmed him as his hands wrapped around the hot clay mug and he sipped. Settling back into the chair, Jack enjoyed this luxurious moment. This morning would find him energized from the coffee—on top of the world. Gracie's stare grabbed his attention.

"To good business." She raised her mug. Jack did the same. They drank. When done, Gracie rested her elbows on the chair arms and asked, "What have you got for me?"

Carefully, from his inside pocket, Jack produced a paper-wrapped piece and set it gently on the desk. Gracie snapped it up and unwrapped it with great care. From a scrap of white marble, Jack had teased out an eagle, wings spread, extracting a fish from the water.

"This Mr. Fox," said Gracie slowly, amazed, "will square us right enough." She held the sculpture in the light from the window above. The splay of primary flight feathers—so delicate yet so powerful—awed her and stole her words. A finger slid over the scales of the fish snatched from the water.

"You like it, right?" Jack asked hopefully.

"I ain't seen nothing like it." Her focus moved slowly from the eagle to the boy in front of her. "It's a marvel, Jack," she said simply. "You, my boy, are a marvel."

Jack gave her a cheeky grin in return. Her young protégé, he knew he offered her a gold mine for the care of him and his mother. Steady customers would pay ten times the value of the food she provided.

"Ya keep this talent of yours quiet. Just you and me, Jackie." She sat back in her chair, weighing her next words. "Ya know how things are in the Snake? You and what ya can do would be worth a good bit of coin. There are some, as would sell you to a slaving family in a flash."

Jack nodded. He'd heard the tales.

"Ya stay a dumb boy, not good for much, but scrounging around the docks and things will be just fine." Gracie stood, gently picked up the statue, and placed it on the shelf above her head. "More coffee, Jackie?"

He held out his near empty mug eagerly.

"Did all the quarry boys live?" She smiled.

He nodded earnestly. "Yes, ma'am."

"Good. We don' want no trouble with the quarry." She stared into her coffee for a moment. "You are almost growed up, Jack." Gracie paused, then looked up. "I may need you for other work."

"Sure. Whatever ya need." Jack blurted.

Gracie drank her coffee. She returned to the storeroom and loaded Jack with two bags of provisions.

"This second goes to Spunk. Tell her ol' Nanna that I ask after her."

"I will." Jack hoisted the bags over his shoulder and set out. He gave no further thought to the fight or to what further things Gracie might need.

No profit presented itself in dwelling on such matters.

CHAPTER 2

THE DOOR CRACKED OPEN ENOUGH FOR A HAZEL EYE TO IDENTIFY who might be there: friend or foe. Jack watched the eye disappear. The door opened further, telling him he had permission to enter. Once inside the shack, before he could put down the sacks, a small ball of energy, all arms, legs, and flying hair, crashed into him. Mini threw her arms around Jack's waist and held on tight. She still had her doll in her hand.

"Who's there?" called a crackling, weathered voice from the other room.

"It's the blasted hero of Snakeport!" yelled Spunk from the kitchen.

The shack next to the town cemetery had three rooms. Spunk and Mini slept in the front room while their grandmother, Nanna, slept in the small room off the kitchen, closer to the stove on cold winter nights.

"Hush Cindi. Take your blessings where ya can," Nanna said crossly, then turned her attention toward Jack and smiled. "Come and give Nanna a hug." The pots and pans banged around in the kitchen as Cindi, Spunk's real name, controlled and vented her temper.

"Don't call me that," came from the kitchen—not loud enough to carry, but Jack heard it. Call Spunk by her given name on the street and you were in for a fight. No one called her that, but her grandmother. Cindi was her mother's name, and Spunk rejected anything and everything coming from her parents, who had abandoned her.

Jack looked down at Mini, who looked at him with a smile warm enough to melt the ice on the northern wastes. He dropped his sacks, pulled her arms from around his waist, and swept her up in a bear hug. The little girl, strong as all things that survived in the Snake, applied her wrestler's grip around his neck. Jack waited for her to lean back, and when she did, she placed her hand on his cheek.

"You're welcome." Jack knew what Mini's gestures meant. She did not speak; no one understood the malady, nor did anyone try to find out. Doctors were few in the Snake, and expensive besides.

He put her down, pointed to the bag, and she took it to the kitchen. Jack went into the other room to pay his respects as Mini dragged the supplies to the next room.

"Ah, Jack Fox." Nanna sat in an old rocking chair with her swollen legs up on an old crate. She had long white hair she kept in one long braid resting over her left shoulder. She reached out to the boy; the cross patched, multi-colored quilt fell from her. Cocooned in a thick purple sweater with more layers unseen, her arms enveloped the boy. On his knees next to her chair, Jack felt happy to be captured in her welcome.

"Gracie asks after you," said Jack when she released him.

"I'm fair ta middlin," nodded Nanna. "You," she said and jabbed her finger into his chest, "did somethin' good." She looked toward the room where pots still banged on the wrought iron oven. "That girl can be a right fool on a time." Jack nodded. He noted the long-barreled revolver handle sticking out from under the blanket. This woman, not as strong in her old age, was not feeble; feeble, put you in the grave across the road.

"I says," winked Nanna, speaking loudly, "if ya help with dinner, that ya got a right to eat it." The answering iron on iron battle stated the unwelcomed message found an unfriendly ear. "Go help where ya can."

The elderly woman pulled her quilt up. "Ya could make it a bit warmer!"

"So go out and get more wood!" shouted Spunk.

"Tha' girl," chuckled Nanna as she drifted away, both worried and, Jack knew, immensely proud of her granddaughter.

When Jack came into the kitchen, he saw the axe on the table.

"Ya can go up into the hills after you check in on your ma," stated Spunk. "We need enough to get through the next few nights." Jack nodded, picked up the axe, slung his bag of basics over his shoulder, and left without comment. Mini waved to him as he left; Jack smiled back at her.

The cemetery rested an hour's walk from Gracie's and the woods then another hour's walk north close to the quarry where Jack collected the scrapped stone for his carving. It made no sense to go back into town to drop off his load. Jack emptied the bag just outside the kitchen door. The empty bag would allow him to carry more wood.

An hour later, sweating from the brisk, uphill walk, Jack gathered and trimmed large, discarded branches left over from the harvesting of the bigger trees providing the raw material for the ships' masts and other accoutrements. Time passed quickly as the ax swung and sweat poured from his body. Finally, he packed his burlap bag with as much as would fit without tearing the material, lifted it over his shoulder, and started back downhill, a second load cradled under his other arm with the axe clenched in that hand.

He stumbled a step or two under the load, kicking up wood chips. The whole ground seemed to react by shimmering with a sudden iridescence. Startled, Jack dropped the axe and logs, trying to keep his balance.

"Sonuvabit…!" he yelled, letting go of the bag. Fuming, Jack stopped and breathed deep controlling his temper. *Nothing bad*, he thought, *just lost my footing*. He stacked the wood he dropped and reached for his axe, but the glimmer came again next to the axe blade.

A small dark green leaf attached to a fragile stem grew an inch from the blade; it flashed. Jack pushed the axe head away and leaned closer, then gently lifted the leaf, amazed to see anything green in the depths of winter.

It curled around his finger's top joint.

"What? Who?" Jack stood up certain seconds had passed but felt the bone-ache from being in one position for hours. He did not know what happened or what he thought he heard, but what he saw shocked him; the sun hung in the wrong part of the sky than when he turned to walk back with his full load only moments ago. Late morning had become late afternoon.

Jack shook his head, bewildered, but put the episode out of his mind. Thinking about what you could not control wasted time. He put himself in order, reloaded his burden, and headed back.

Behind him, unnoticed, the leaf glinted one more time, then wilted away. The stem pulled back into the soil.

Spunk nodded when Jack arrived out of breath, put the axe in the corner, and stacked the weeks' worth of wood along the kitchen wall. The dinner was ready. Nanna, plate in hand ate in her chair in the other room. Mini sat at the table where three plates waited to be filled. A lit candle threw small light about the room as the gray sky gave way to the night's black.

Eating became a quiet affair: a matter of focus and getting enough. Enough, they had this night. Jack caught Spunk's signal to help her with the dishes, which he did without complaint. He scraped what little stained the plates into one bucket while Spunk wiped them down with a wet cloth wrung out from another full of water. Spunk did not say a word. She kept sneaking a look at him; Jack sensed an explosion coming.

"What?" He turned to her, wanting to settle whatever aggravated her. "Ya got somethin' on your mind. Let's hear it."

Spunk picked up a towel slowly, looking thoughtful, and wiped a plate dry.

"How come you're not dead?" She put the plate down and tossed the towel on the counter. "I know what I saw." She paused, scared to ask. "Are ya djinn, Jack?"

"Don't know." He had asked himself the same question. Did he have some magic in him that the northern people had? "Seems like it, though. Can't explain what happened with that knife." The part about the sparkling leaf he kept to himself.

"Shut up about it! Tell no one," commanded Spunk. She grasped his forearm hard. "They will hurt you or take you away." Not clear who "they" might be, Spunk and everyone else in Snakeport knew a power existed, and it watched.

Jack nodded.

The North stole the djinn from the South and left the southern country poorer: a place to despoil for its natural resources. The marble slabs from the many quarries in the south traveled north to grace their buildings. Almost a hundred years had passed since that civil war, but the South had not recovered economically or emotionally.

"I heard the same from Gracie 'bout my statues." He shivered, afraid of losing what little he had. Jack went around Spunk and picked up the dinner plates, walked them to the shelves, and stacked them up.

"Gracie knows," said Spunk quietly. She knew of Jack's talent before anyone and had benefited from the selling of it. When Gracie took over, a steady stream of supplies came every week. This kept their families fed and safe. "Say nothing about the knife, even to Gracie. She's got it tough enough."

"It be too quiet!" shouted Nanna. "Might think you two had hands on each other!"

Spunk and Jack looked at each other, then laughed aloud at the idea.

"Well then, make yourselfs useful. Put more wood in the stove! I am a fright, chilled!"

Jack and Spunk nodded, acknowledging their agreement to keep their talk a secret. Jack put more fuel in the stove then he and Spunk joined Nanna.

"Tell us a story about the war, Nanna." Spunk took comfort in her grandmother's stories of how things were and might be again. Jack sat on the floor next to Mini, the girl already asleep. He pulled the worn blanket over her shoulder and tucked it. Spunk took the stool next to her grandmother.

The old woman smiled. She soaked up the attention and felt proud of these youngsters who proved themselves not to be fools.

"There was a time," Nanna began, "when the law meant somethin' in the Snake…"

* * *

Jack left shortly after Nanna fell asleep in her chair; the stories had gone on a long time. A history he could hardly imagine. Snakeport offered little schooling. It covered basic reading, writing, arithmetic, and local history, but the idea of Snakeport sixty years ago surprised him. Images rummaged around in his mind during the hour-long walk home in the dark. The djinn had gone north or disappeared, but the city sheriffs kept the streets safe, and judges provided a consistent and equal level of justice. Schools collected students and educated them. Without the djinn power for support, however, the outnumbered sheriffs slowly over time looked the other way and with them the judges who decided to survive than stand up for the law. Money spoke louder and louder as time passed. Learning from the street became far more important than anything offered in the classroom.

Jack and Spunk had watched as Nanna, after a long silence, nodded off.

"I'm off to home," said Jack, gathering up his bag. Spunk nodded and went to the door. She held it open, then watched him disappear into the night. "Take care, Jack," he heard her whisper.

With bag in hand, he reached his home and opened the front door, finding it in total darkness. His foot banged into a bucket which sloshed half full. Only one bucket usually by his mother's bed used as a privy when ice cycles hung over the roof's edge would be in his home.

"Dammit." He moved the bucket to the side, out of the way.

Closing the door and latching it, Jack moved carefully in the dark to the kitchen. He laid down the groceries and went to the drawer where he found a candle and striker to get the fire going. From the fired kindling, he lit the candle and placed it on the table. Its weak light revealed his mother sitting, watching his every move.

"Oh." Jack turned away from her and placed the flaming pieces into the stove. "I thought you would be asleep."

"Hoped I would be asleep more like," said his mother, sober for the first time in days. Her eyes followed her son. She hated herself, loved him, but the desire for alcohol consumed her.

Jack ignored her words but felt afraid of his mother's uninhibited anger. The fire caught. More wood from the stack behind the stove banged as it dropped on the smoking pile. He leaned down and blew on the fuel. The flames grew. Winter's cold invaded from outside, but an emotional chill flared from his mother. Strategies on how to handle what she might throw at him whizzed through his thoughts. He stood up, closed the iron door, and waited, but not for long.

"Abandoned your mother, you did." She had not moved, seemed no bigger, but her resentment filled the room. "Where'd you go? With that tart, maybe sticking it in now that you're older. You men are all alike."

Jack did not say a word. He picked up the burlap bag and placed it on the table. He unpacked a few items, then purposefully placed one of the three bottles in front of her. Jack glanced at her, then looked away as he continued to unpack provisions. If all went well, she would be quiet and give in to her true hunger.

"You want something to eat?" Jack held out a loaf of bread. "Maybe some bread and butter to start?"

"What I need is a clean glass." She grabbed the bottle and pulled it closer to her: a cherished possession. The flickering light from the candle obscured her features. The room and Jack's mind existed in dancing shadows that may or may not hold a bit of truth as the flame grew and revealed his mother's smile.

"You know where they are," said Jack tersely. *Get up, damn you, and get it for yourself.* He hated her smirk and detested her weakness. Without thinking, he started to the shelf before she spoke.

"You get it."

In a last act of useless defiance, Jack slammed the glass down in front of her. He left the kitchen, hefted the pail by the door and dumped it in the latrine out back. After Jack found his pallet. It had been a long day. He fell asleep thinking of the knife and his ultimate defeat at his mother's hand. He heard the cork squeak and the glug as liquid filled a glass.

Gracie's words came to mind, "You can't fix a rummy."

CHAPTER 3

The candlelight from many sconces about the room overpowered the winter's gloom with help from the fire burning in the dining room hearth. The playful, flickering light, however, did little to lift the mood of the five sitting at the large mahogany table.

Gracie sat silently with her hands in her lap, but saw everything. Her other three associates watched one of their members devour the dinner provided by their host.

Reginald Lakeland, their host, held court at the head of the table drinking dark red wine from a pewter goblet. He grinned, watching his guest make a mess. "Edward," said Reggie. His long brown hair tied back with a black ribbon, he swirled his wine, amused. "You have the most atrocious table manners."

Edward Blogger stopped mid-bite into a haunch of pork and turned to Lakeland. He tore away a mouthful, chewed noisily for a moment, snorted something from his hooked nose, then turned to the servers standing along the wall.

"More meat… and potatoes." Grease trickled from the corner of his mouth. "Lakeland, ya're always cheap with what ya offer." He used his sleeve to wipe his mouth, then straightened the wig of long brown curls on his bald head. Since his stomach extended out, blocking any view of his feet, a line of food and drink ran down the front of his shirt looking like a mountain stream splashing over rocks. The napkin remained neatly folded beside the plate; gravy dripped over the edge to the tablecloth.

"It is, however," laughed Lakeland, "your favorite, Edward." Lakeland took a drink. "It's free." Lakeland, the exact opposite of Blogger, was civil to a fault, with an athletic physique and an amount of charisma. He charmed people and claimed an aristocratic ancestry, which meant nothing in the Snake. It begged the question, though no one cared to ask, of what he had done to be condemned to life in Snakeport.

"Make fun as ya wish at my expense," scowled Blogger. "But I will have my day. Just you wait…"

"Yes, Edward. We know." Lakeland cut him off. "What of you, my dear? Not hungry tonight?"

"I will eat," said Gracie, "after we conclude our business." She smiled sweetly at Lakeland, who nodded. The business at hand put a damper on this evening's mood. Blogger's behavior acted as the evening's entertainment.

"What of you Thomas? Will?"

"I agree with the good lady," said Tom Haggard, who sat across from Gracie but next to Blogger. When standing, he looked like a preacher all in black with a long coat, stick thin, and eyes sunk into a harsh face. Eyeing his neighbor in disgust, he moved his plate aside.

William Biggs looked like a shorter edition of Lakeland. He, however, was a sea-rat imprisoned on land until the winter and her killer storms passed. "Let's get on with it. There's things to be done tonight."

"Right then." Lakeland reached under his seat and brought out a leather-bound folder. He opened it, then stood, turning a page or two. "We are suffering our usual dead-of-winter, low income. Mrs. Hargreaves is doing a might better than the rest of us." He looked up at Gracie. The question hung in the air.

"It's been said," accused Blogger, "that ye're playing in the arts. High-quality statues, as I heard."

Gracie demurred. She sipped her wine and kept silent.

"Well?" demanded Blogger.

"The details," said Haggard, "are not any of our business. Does the lady pay her fees our little venture demands or not?"

"To the penny," stated Lakeland, pointing to the ledger he had pulled from the file and opened.

"Then," Haggard nodded to Gracie, "there is no argument."

"I says we have a problem." Blogger grabbed the napkin, attempted to clean up, failed then tossed it on the plate. He pushed back his chair, maneuvered his girth to the edge of the seat, then stood and pounded the table. "She is holding out on us, plain and simple."

The three men stared at Blogger, not knowing what to do. They all cheated on their mutual agreement, but never grievously so. Nothing of this issue bothered the men other than the Blog.

Gracie ran her finger around the rim of her goblet. "We are all aware of each other's business." She spoke softly, but with an angry edge. "I have stumbled onto something of value. I didn't hide it like some." She stared at Blogger as she lifted her wine, using it to point at her nemesis. "I intend to protect it. It is mine, and I won't let anyone steal it from me."

"Now, now Mrs. Hargreaves, no need to threaten." Lakeland leaned forward on his hands.

"Tell the Blog," Gracie said with disgust, "to stop threatening me."

"Agreed," called out Will Biggs. "Don' need to pick holes in each other's coats."

"Times is hard this time o' year," Blog calmed and fell back into his chair. "Why shouldn't we all share in this newfound wealth as was writ in our charter?" Blog sat up straight and surveyed the angry faces. He smiled, becoming the ideal of reasonableness.

"Like ya share with those snatched kids you ship north?" Gracie disliked Blogger from the beginning and had grown to hate him. Trade in humans, especially children, fired her rage. If she could prove it, she would have had Blog killed for such evil.

"Sharing revenue to balance stupid decisions by any member is not part of our charter." Lakeland waited patiently for an argument from Blog.

"I gambled. I lost is all," complained Blog. He looked around the table and saw no sympathy from his associates. "I need some help to get even, if ya know what I mean?"

"So," stated Tom Haggard coldly, "you want our charity? Perhaps you should sell your membership in our enterprise to cover your losses." No one spoke, but all eyes hung on Edward Blogger to clarify his situation or lie: his first tendency. The ridiculous notion Lakeland or any of his guests fell on hard times went unsaid.

"Don't need nor want no charity," grumbled Blog. He pouted, whispering obscenities only he could hear.

"Are we done with this unfortunate complaint?" demanded Lakeland. Blogger, seeing no support for his position, nodded. "Good." Lakeland turned the page on his log, went to the side table, and pulled the quill from its inkwell. He signed the page, then went to each member one by one. They signed agreeing to the current situation as defined by the figures in the log.

"I adjourn our meeting." Lakeland slapped the log closed, then picked up his goblet and drained it.

"I'm off," stated Blogger, surprising his business partners. He struggled to his feet, straightened his wig, brushed what dribbled food he could from his front, then left without a word.

"If I were to guess," spoke Will Biggs, looking at the door through which Ed Blogger just exited, "our Edward is up to something." Will stood, went to the hearth, rubbed his hands together before the flames, then said, "He just ain't smart enough to keep his mouth shut. Too full of hisself I would say."

"I think Mr. Biggs has a point." Lakeland looked over to

Gracie. "Mrs. Hargreaves, would you like an escort home this evening?"

"My dear Reginald," said Gracie, "thank you for the consideration." She rose and went to the sideboard, picked up a plate, and filled it. "You, Tom and Will are true gentlemen. I can, however," she twirled the carving knife then sliced meat from the bone, "take care of myself."

* * *

Edward Blogger never forgot or forgave slights: real or imagined. On a stool behind his desk covered with papers and shipping logs, two planks set across two barrels, he studied the three men standing before him. They came highly recommended by his shippers, who moved street urchins grabbed by Blogger and his men north. Demand for slaves by the northern rich grew steadily. Dressed as ordinary Snakeport citizens in the brown pants and blue or green jackets, the three waited patiently for their pay master to speak.

"Mrs. Hargreaves is not ta survive what will look like a robbery." Blogger scratched his armpit through the white stained linen shirt. He sat atop his stool with his pants half undone to maintain a level of comfort hard to find with his protruding stomach. "You've been to her shop and got a good sense of the place."

The three nodded.

"You ain't from around here and I don't need to know from where ya hail. I need ya to act quickly and right smartly. Ya got my coin in your pockets. Ya don't want ta disappoint."

"The boys and me," said the tallest, called Main, "aims to be of value to you. Consider this an action in good faith for more work to come?"

"Ya get this job done right and ya can count on more." Blogger caught the deadly calm in their eyes and thought the high cost, money well spent. He needed to be rid of this annoying woman. "Soon then."

"Done and done," said Main. The three turned and left. The Blog stared after them.

"Goodbye, my poor Gracie," said Blogger, a smile on his face. He picked up the quill from the inkwell and made entries describing his latest haul heading north.

CHAPTER 4

The campfire crackled. Flames reached high. Piercing cold ruled, and the three bearded men cradling their tin cups of steaming coffee complained.

"Don't see no reason we should be out here." The man drank. The firelight accentuated his short, curly, dark hair and rugged features. "Strikes me that the Blog is just 'afraid of his own shadow.'"

"As long as you got his gold in your pocket, Stan," said Main, short for Germain. "You stand where he says, sits where he says, and piss where he says." The first time a fool called him Germ, the man lost part of a finger and earned scars on his face. Few argued with Main since then.

"It's bleedin' cold out here," said Randy. The youngest of the three, with rugged features and a beguiling smile with no visible scars. Often underestimated by his enemies, Randy destroyed anyone in his way. "Stan's got a point. We got coin. Let's pay for a more advantageous situation." He set down his tin and pulled his wool scarf wrapped around his head tighter over his ears. "Ole Stan the Man and you, Main, owe that Snake dung Blogger nothin'."

"Gold is gold boys. This is to be a very quiet, very secret thing." Main took a gulp of his coffee. "We pay for a room, then someone who might talk says we was here. 'Sides, this ain't so bad. Could be a whole lot worse." Main stood stretching. His unbound, long brown, knotted hair had not seen soap and water in some time. He scratched his beard and looked down on his compatriots. "Business is business. There's a job to do."

"Yeah, but you ain't been working the quarry like me," said Stan. "I'm sick a this. Sick a their food, their clothes, everything.

Time to get back north as far as I see it." Stan looked up at Main, then down. "I don' my part to fit in."

"And ya will, Stan." Main moved close to his partner in crime, bent down, and slapped him on the back. "This little bit of business will take no time. You'll be home fast as death by the rope."

"Goin' to wear my lucky shirt and socks for this job." Stan stared at Main, ready for an argument.

"As long as you hide it, ya can come in a dress for all I care." Main looked forward to getting away from Stan after this job. He thought him unpleasant. "Now, let's go over it again." Main sat.

"I checked out the warehouse when I bought a load of shipping equipment," said Randy. "She's not much on the protection angle. Shops wide open. Should be easy. It's a woman, after all. How much trouble can she be?"

"Got three ways in and out," added Stan. "We go in at the back tomorrow night. She'll be alone according to Blog. He wasn't totally worthless."

"Right," said Main. "Nice and clean, boys. The woman dies then…"

"Still don' see why we can't go with guns." Stan stared into the flames, thinking. "Would be a lot easier armed as not. She ain't gonna just stand there nice and pretty for us to do her in."

"Surprise is the ticket, and we don't need any ears detectin' what we're about." Main shook his head since he had already covered this topic. "A band of robbers would be quick and quiet." Main shook his head in frustration with his team. "Only desperate men would attack Hargreaves. They wouldn't have the money to have guns, Stan. It's gotta look right, like I said more than a few times."

"What about…?" Stan started.

"No," said Main. "No guns even with a promise not to use

'em. We kill the woman with blades or hammers or whatever we have on hand."

"Then what?" questioned Randy.

"We," smiled Main, "remove Blog. Grab his snatched boys and girls and sell 'em at the border all nice and neat."

"Double cross," smiled Stan, forgetting his complaint. "I like it."

The three raised their tins and toasted their plan. It would all start with a quick death for Gracie.

* * *

Gracie ran a tight ship with her business and engaged in a full inventory of her shelves and barrels. Everyone knew to stay away from Gracie's on inventory day, the third Thursday of every month. Her dinner, mutton and taters, steaming on her desk, went ignored. In a simple, gray cotton shift with her hair tied back and shawl over her shoulders, she neared the completion of the lists. With the last stroke of her pen, Gracie smiled and shivered. The little heat coming from her office, nor the candle in her hand could cure the cold.

She turned to the faint sound of splintering wood echoing from the farthest end of the floor. Placing the ledger and the candle on the nearest barrel, she pulled a sabre from the nearest shelf in front of her. The metal scraped as the blade escaped its sheath. She walked across the floor and around the barrels to her office. The pistol lay in the lowest drawer of her desk. Gracie slipped it from its leather holster, then went back into the store. She waited in the shadows.

"Come on, you bastards," she whispered. The gun shook slightly in her right hand, the sabre in her left. The hammer clicked as she pulled it back. She calmed. Alone against an unknown enemy, Gracie strategized, not caught completely unprepared. *If there are over six with pistols,* she thought, *I'm in trouble.*

Gracie heard them as they came in the back door at the far end of the warehouse and climbed the six steps to the main floor. The candle left burning on the barrel would light up her targets. It sounded like two men moving toward her. She set the sabre down on the floor and grabbed a knife from the shelf next to her. The blade flew across the room and into the office. It sounded like a fork or knife dropped. As they moved toward the office, the shadowed figures came into the light of the candle. Calmly, Gracie raised the gun, aimed carefully, and fired.

Main watched as Randy splintered the backdoor with a crowbar. When the door swung open, he stepped back to let Stan and Randy take the lead.

"She like as not heard," whispered Main. "Now, she might be scared and dithering about what to do, or maybe not." He looked around, then sighed. "You two go in here. I'll get in by the other door."

"Right." Randy handed him the crowbar. "We'll wait a bit for you to get ready."

Randy led the way with Stan close behind. They climbed the steps into the shop slowly. The wood creaked beneath their weight. On the warehouse floor, they took positions behind the barrels on either side. They waited, giving Main time to get in position. The distant candle flame flickered. After a time, they moved forward, closing on the light but keeping out of direct sight in the darker parts of the floor. With no sign of their target as they closed on the candle, Stan signaled to Randy to halt. The clatter of silverware ahead and to the left, the office, gave them confidence to move ahead. With Main coming from the opposite direction, they would have her trapped. Stan waved Randy forward.

The first bullet ricocheted off the barrel's metal stave next to Randy, causing him to jump to the right. The second round went through Randy's lung and out his back. He slid to the floor, the blood beginning to flow. Shock shut him down. "Not fair, dammit. Not fair." Stan heard him utter before losing consciousness.

Stan reassessed the situation, cursing Main for not letting him have a pistol. Somewhere in front of him there stood an armed, angry woman who knew how to shoot. She either had four shots or two shots left, depending on the weapon. He saw Randy, who had slid down to the floor into the candlelight beyond help. No longer worth his consideration.

"Where are you Main?" Stan whispered. He stayed put and made some noise to distract their prey. This might give Main a chance to move on her. He pressed against a stack of barrels, causing them to wobble slightly. The third bullet missed him by a few inches.

"Good God, she's good. Main, you are such an ass." Stan moved to safer ground among the barrels further from the candlelight. "If I get out of this, you and Blog are so dead."

"You bastard!" cried a woman's voice.

A muffled call for god's grace came next. Stan stood moments later and smiled, sure that Main had the woman in complete control or had killed her. The bullet speeding toward him pierced his shoulder, spun him around, and wiped the grin from his lips.

When Gracie saw the silhouette near the barrel seconds after she pulled the trigger, she fired her second shot. Without a second thought, she turned to her back, holding the weapon out, ready to pull the trigger. Even though the entry had been recently boarded up for replacement, she felt exposed. No target presented itself. She calmed and returned her attention back to the attackers on the shop floor. The legs sticking out in the dim light confirmed her riddance of one of these low life scum.

"Three, maybe four," Gracie whispered, emboldened. She swept the revolver across the field of fire before her. One laid flat, most likely dead; the second froze somewhere in front of her. The third and fourth she would deal with as the strategy unfolded before her. Only two ways in and out existed with the third blocked.

The block and tackle flew in and out of the candlelight from her right, striking her shoulder and tangling Gracie's gun hand.

She had shifted her position, barely avoiding a direct hit to her head by the thick wood pulleys. She released the revolver, freeing her hand from the tangled rope, and pulled her dagger from her belt at her back, then reached for the sabre on the floor ready for the close attack. The knife blade pressed tight against her wrist and the sword point balanced on its tip hidden behind a fold of her dress. She looked helpless.

The man, Gracie guessed, was huge and came at her fast. With no escape possible, she stepped out into the open.

"Come to die, fool."

Her assailant saw a woman standing weaponless with her back to a wall of barrels. From behind her skirts, she raised the sabre. The dagger she held unseen. Her survival depended on the shorter blade. The man kept coming. He held a cudgel in his left hand with nails pounded into its thickest part. He swung the weapon at the last possible second, batting the sabre away, and crashed into the lady. His right hand closed tight on her neck, cutting off her breath.

Gracie did not panic. She'd given her attacker the sabre as a target. His evil grin turned to surprise as the blade slashed over his arm across his neck, just under his ear. Blood spurted.

"Oh, god," said the man, bringing his hand to his opened neck. He stepped back, then slumped to his knees.

Gracie pushed him over and swiftly rummaged beneath the rope and wooden blocks for the revolver. She freed it, stood, and aimed where she expected she would be if she wanted to strike from safety. The hammer struck. A bullet exploded from the barrel. A surprised grunt told her she had fired true.

"You can die here or not!" Gracie yelled, then waited. "Two are down, maybe dead or soon to be!"

"Well…" said a voice to her front. "Ya have the better of us." A man shuffled about, then stood in the candlelight: an easy kill.

"Let's hear those blades hit the floor." Gracie too far away to make out his face kept the revolver trained. His voice sounded familiar, but she could not place it. When the weapons clattered on the boards, she breathed easier.

"Gather up your friend there and get out."

"Well… I got this hole in my shoulder which might make it a might difficult…"

Gracie fired another shot that chipped the wood next to his right foot.

"You can die with him," she pointed with the pistol to the man dead at her feet, "or you can live."

Stan moved slowly, but deliberately, to Randy. The man lived, but only just. He gritted his teeth against the agony of his shoulder and dragged the limp body back the way they came in.

Gracie let her gun hand drop to her side. It was over: only three to fight. She survived. For a long time, she trembled uncontrollably, which her business mind found annoying: a block to getting anything done. In her office, she drank directly from a brown bottle of rum. It shot a throat-burning shock to her system. She regained control, cringing as the liquor went down.

"Time to gather the team." Gracie took another long pull on the bottle. Only one fool would try such a thing. "Blog is a dead man."

CHAPTER 5

SPUNK STARED OVER THE LEDGE BETWEEN HER KNEES, MAKING sure the man lying face down twenty feet below on the shelf of scrap rock did not move. The body lay headfirst, pointing down the hill of broken marble. Holes showed in the soles of his boots.

Freezing weather crept back to Snakeport over the week since Jack presented Gracie with the marble eagle statue. Nothing much changed in the Snake except for the attack on Gracie and the coming counterattack on Blogger's outfit. Life and the battle-dance went on.

"You see the bottle?" asked Jack next to her. His legs dangled over the edge too. Looking out to the horizon where the dark blue night sky turned lavender, he knew the sun would start cresting soon. The quarry men would pass by about the time it peeked over the trees. They needed to be long gone by then.

"Yeah. Looks real natural-like." The lifeless hand was grasping the neck of the broken liquor bottle. What Spunk could not see worried her. "What about…".

"The slash across his neck I plugged nice and pretty and all the other cuts with razor sharp bits of stone that are all over the place." Jack looked at her, wondering why she was fretting. "The fool got drunk as the quarry workers tend to do and he fell like as happened before."

"Yeah, yeah. I just worry 'bout Gracie." Spunk looked up at Jack. She witnessed too many hangings, one of the few reasons for the Snakeport citizenry to socialize, but she stopped going. No one she cared about would climb those wooden steps if she could do anything about it.

"Don't bother yourself. There ain't no tracks leading back

to her." Jack stared at the body and changed the subject. "He's dressed like he's from 'round here." He paused, thinking. "But somethin' ain't right. He sure ain't missed too many meals. Maybe he's from up north or west."

Spunk followed his gaze. Jack recalled how she knelt close to him and watched as he took out his fine, sculpting tools and shaped the stones just enough so they would make the killing look like an accident. She did not flinch when he shoved the knife-like shard deep into his neck. They spread pig's blood on the stones since the body had already bled out before they moved it from Gracie's to the scrap heap.

"I would guess he ain't from 'round here," said Jack. "Who in the Snake without an army would ever make an enemy of Gracie?" They sat in silence with their thoughts.

The fool paid the price for trying to rob and then attack Gracie at her place, thought Jack. Their benefactor came away with a few fresh scars but defended herself with deadly capability. Gracie called in a few men to clean up the mess to avoid any official investigation. She gave Jack and Spunk the job of taking the body in the dead of night to the scrap heap and making sure the body of evidence told the right story.

"We should go," said Jack. He stood and went up into the trees where the hand drawn cart waited. Spunk followed. The walk back downhill into Snakeport would be a good deal easier with less dead weight, even with the load of wood they gathered on the way. If anyone stopped them, they would see a couple of kids hauling firewood: a common sighting.

"Gracie tells you everything," said Spunk, a touch of jealousy in her voice. "What happened?"

"What always happens." Jack looked at his friend with a frown. "The Blog got greedy, and Gracie took care of business."

Halfway back to Snakeport, Jack and Spunk stopped to

repack their load of wood, so nothing fell by the wayside. Logs kept falling off the stack whenever they rolled over a stone or into a pothole.

"That should do it," said Jack, leaning against the wagon next to Spunk. The arc of the sun barely crested the horizon.

"Yeah," said Spunk, breathless with the effort. She slid close to Jack, contacting his body. He turned to her at this unexpected closeness. *This is different,* he thought excited.

"We should get go…"

Spunk's kiss cut off Jack's words. Shocked at first, not sure what to do, he melted into the kiss, placed his hands on her waist, and pulled his friend close. He felt her arms wrap around his neck. Their lips parted barely as their eyes locked, seeking honesty and a caring one for the other. Their lips came together stronger, firmer. When the kiss ended they held each other.

"We have to get back," whispered Spunk, pulling back and staring into Jack's eyes.

"We do." Jack raised his hand and cradled her cheek. This felt right, and he didn't want it to end.

Spunk smiled. Unlike other times, his advance would be an invited set of hands exploring her body: a tenderness she craved. She pulled back further and placed her hand on Jack's chest.

"I guess," she said, "I should say thanks for the things you've done to help Nanna and us out." She leaned in and kissed him.

"You're welcome," said Jack when she pulled away.

"You want to commit?" asked Spunk, looking away, her heart beating fast. It was a big thing to ask, and she didn't want to see his hesitation.

"Committed." Jack put his hand over hers on his chest. His lips found hers one more time.

They broke, then nodded to each other, turning to the task at hand.

* * *

"We found a younger man's dead body in the alley near here." Lakeland sat across from Gracie in her office near mid-day three days after the attack. Impeccably turned out, he wore a black, long coat with bright, brass buttons, knee-high, polished boots, and a nobleman's black walking stick in his left hand. With his hair pulled back and held with a gold clasp, he looked appropriately dismayed by the attack on Gracie. "My men removed him."

"I am grateful," said Gracie in the same dress and shawl from the other night.

They turned to the door when a sudden clash of metal on metal erupted on the shop floor.

"Enough horseplay, ya useless pee-wits!" commanded a Valkyrie voice. "Stack them rifles correct-like!" The sound of running feet and the scrape of metal on metal gave proof to the correction ordered.

"Thank you for arranging for Mrs. Congress to join us." Gracie pulled the shawl tighter as though taken by a sudden chill. "Her wisdom and skills are a great comfort to me."

"Nanna? That, my dear, was a pleasure." Lakeland brought the scented kerchief in his hand to his nose. "She helped me when I landed in the Snake." He caught Gracie's eye, then looked away. His brass tipped walking stick moved back and forth on its point: a nervous habit. "You did well. Feeling well enough?"

Gracie stood, allowing her shawl to drop off her shoulder. The ugly bruising climbed over her shoulder to her neck, where the imprint of fingers showed clearly. She went to the office door, called out, "No interruptions.", pulled it shut, and returned to her seat.

"With Blogger soon to be done, I will feel considerably better and safer." She smiled. "You turned down the trade in children, as did I."

"Yes. It is an ugly business and not one for the likes of us," he stated without hesitation. He sensed Gracie's need to have his confirmation. "I cannot, however, join you in this action against Edward."

"I have not asked you to do so," said Gracie, the smile slipping away. "We need to work out how we break up the Blog's holdings and find another partner for our membership."

"What have you done with the other body?" asked Lakeland. Any loose ends posed a problem to their organization.

"It is, shall we say, well placed for discovery and misdirection."

"And the third assailant?" Lakeland looked around the office, settling upon the eagle sculpture. *Exquisite*, he thought.

Gracie rose from her chair again and gathered two goblets from the shelves, plus a dark bottle with heavy black wax over the stopper. As she set it on the desktop, she said, "I know all too well to avoid trouble with the local officials."

"My people are looking," Gracie confirmed. She set the cups on the desk. The corkscrew proved too difficult for her, given her wounds. Lakeland got to his feet and finished the job. Her most winning smile returned to her face as she lifted the bottle and poured. The room filled with the heady vapors of long, aged wine.

"You, my dear Reggie, will enjoy this." Gracie handed him the goblet, then picked up hers, raising it to toast. "To out-living the bloody bastards."

"Hear, hear." They drank together.

"Ah," said Lakeland, allowing the wine to sit on his tongue before he swallowed, "an excellent vintage." He emptied the cup. "More, if you would be so kind." Lakeland watched as the dark red wine filled the cup. "We must remove this third participant. The quicker the better."

"I will finish it in short order." Gracie sipped her wine. "Hiding in the Snake is a most painful challenge for my enemies."

* * *

The man, unconscious, laid flat on his back on the pallet. Jack Fox stood over him and frowned, more worried about where he would sleep this night. The bloody bandages wrapping the shoulder needed changing. The smell from the wound filled the room. Hard experience told Jack where things headed if no local mid-wife would help. No doctor ever ventured into this more poisonous part of the Snake. He checked on his mother, looking over the sheet wall, and found her passed out as expected beneath the covers. The empty bottles stood guard, lined up on the floor. He shook his head, glancing back and forth between the two adults in the room.

"Damn it," he whispered harshly. He knew he had Gracie's third attacker on the floor. Although the front door always remained unlocked, Jack thought it likely that his mother knew she had a bleeding man in the house. The man had committed to her and fathered Jack. It had been years since he last saw him. The simple task of finding Gracie's last attacker and killing him just got complicated.

Jack considered his options. The path of least resistance demanded a quick slit of the throat and a dumping of the body off the docks. Things would get back to normal or near normal. He might also consider waiting to get more information: who, where, what, and how. Killing may be the easiest but not always the best way to go. Right and wrong never played a part in his thinking: the weight of the Snake's dog-eat-dog reality made itself felt as Jack thought it out. He decided and moved.

Jack went to the sink and from the drawer next to it drew the razor-sharp knife. The last full bottle of rum he grabbed from the table. Again, he stood over the man, staring at the dried blood.

"Well, ya just goin' to stand there, boy?" The man's blue eyes locked on Jack's.

"Not much to be done," said Jack, controlling his surprise. He nodded at the bandages then thought, *One quick cut just below the ear.*

"I see." The man pushed himself up to lean back against the wall, wincing with pain. "Seems like you and your ma are doin' fine."

"You ain't," said Jack coolly. The knife pointed down and tapped against his pants' leg. "Ya come here to die?"

"Now that ain't no way to talk to your poor, sick pap."

"No pap to me!" Jack fired back. His anger boiled. "Where ya been?"

"Ha!" the man coughed. "Sound like your ma. 'Course she ain't been all that talkative." The steadfast son studied the prodigal father. Jack watched as he grinned, then grimaced. The wounded man reached over with his right arm and hugged the left tight. Time passed; the pain seemed to ease.

"Must hurt some," stated Jack.

His father's head came up to find his son's dispassionate expression. The boy, he realized, a child of the Snake, thought nothing of taking his life. He groaned softly and said, "I need some help."

"Ya got gold or silver?" His father's suffering meant nothing to him.

"Yeah, I can help ya and your ma. I got some coin right here." From beneath the pallet, the man produced a purse that clinked as he tossed it to Jack with his good arm. It hit the boy's leg, then fell to the floor with the solid clatter of heavy gold.

Jack did not react to the sudden riches tossed his way. The knife's point rose to target the man's neck; the sharp side of the blade faced up. Jack advanced.

"What're ya doin'?" cried Jack's father. He saw death coming for him. "Ya got the gold. What…"

"Shut up, ya worthless…" Jack mumbled the last word and went to his knees, slid the blade under the foul bandages. "Ya don' wanta move or I just might cut somethin' ya don't want cut."

The strips of bloodied cloth fell away easily, but the wound reopened. His father grunted when the scabs tore away. Blood trickled from the hole. Jack pulled the cork from the bottle with his teeth and flooded the wound. Before his father could scream, he dragged him forward harshly and soaked the exit wound at the back.

The man fell back when released in shock, breathing hard, barely conscious. Jack stood, went to the stove, and returned with a lit taper. The flame ignited the rum. An intense blue flared for a short time, then went out. His father screamed, then passed out.

Jack cut a few lengths from the sheet separating the room and bandaged the shoulder. He soaked the new strips of cloth with the dark liquid. The half empty bottle sat on the floor in easy reach of his father. When finished, he stood back and examined his handy work. Maybe his father would live, maybe he wouldn't. Glancing over the sheet, his mother slept undisturbed. He looked down on his father and shook his head.

"Damn you!"

Jack reached down and swept up the purse from the floor, and stormed out of his home.

* * *

"Jack Fox!" called out Nanna from behind the bar at Gracie's place. Six freshly cleaned and newly loaded revolver cylinders lay to her right. Five more partly dismantled pistols waited for her attention on the left. "Got something on yer mind, do ya, Jack?" She asked, shocked by the boy's grim demeanor.

When he shouldered through the front door to Gracie's, the last person Jack expected to find sat behind the bar yelling out orders. The men moving through the storeroom, some of whom he knew, did not surprise him. Jack pulled up short. Stared at Nanna as though she had no reason to be here, then eyed the weaponry surrounding her. He passed the stacked rifles and came deeper into the shop.

"There's to be a great comeuppance, Jack." The old woman smiled. She picked up a cylinder and started ramming an oil cloth into a chamber. The powder, lead ball, grease, and cap laid out in a line for loading after a thorough cleaning of the six-shot pistol. "Gracie's inside," she nodded to the closed office door, "having words with his lordship." She held up the cylinder, checking her handiwork. "Ya look a might sour, dear boy." She fixed him with her stare. "What's eatin' at ya, Jack?"

The closed door annoyed and angered him. Jack swung back to Nanna, who waited patiently. He released a long-held breath and trudged further down the aisle, around the bar, and plopped down on a barrel next to her. He couldn't be upset with Nanna.

"What do ya know 'bout my father?"

The old woman threw her arms around the boy's shoulders and pulled him close. After a moment, she leaned back and asked, "Ya seen your dad, did ya?"

"He's bleeding all over my bed," said Jack, nodding. His anger returned. He stood up, escaping Nanna's hug.

"It's a'right, Jack." Nanna grabbed his hand and squeezed.

"My ma's just a lump on the bed." Jack's breathing became faster and shallow. "I did what Gracie needed done. I…"

"Done enough as far as I can tell," said Nanna. She reached

over and picked up a knife and flung it at the closed door. It thumped into the hardwood and vibrated.

Gracie flung open the door moments later. "No interruptions, damn ya!"

"We got your third," said Nanna. She patted Jack's arm. "This young man," she looked up at Jack, who studied the weaponry on the bar to avoid Gracie's displeasure, "needs a few answers. He does."

Gracie's anger standing in the doorway dissolved when she saw Jack next to Nanna. She apologized for her outburst, went to the boy, hugged him, and took his hand. She pulled him into the office, cocked her head abruptly for Lakeland to get up, and sat Jack down. The door remained open.

"So, this is your sculptor?" Lakeland stood next to Gracie as she sat behind her desk, looking Jack up and down.

"Yes," said Gracie, focused on her young protégé. "He's something special."

"Extraordinary." He held the statue close and studied it. His fingers lightly ran over the bird's marble feathers. "Truly remarkable." Lakeland put the sculpture back in its place on the shelf. "Now, to business."

"Tell me true, Jack," started Gracie, "about the man's wounds." When Jack told her, she turned to Lakeland and said, "I'll be damned, Stan Fox."

"I can have my men pick him up, if you wish."

"Yes. Tuck 'em away someplace secure," said Gracie. "My men will be busy with getting ready for Blogger."

"Any material you need from me…" followed Lakeland.

"Stan Fox! Who the hell is Stan Fox?" Jack looked from one to the other. His anger rose at being treated like he was not in the room . "You're going to do what, exactly? What do you expect me to do in all this ya got planned?"

Gracie and Lakeland stopped talking and turned to Jack.

"Stan Fox is his real name," Gracie told him at length. "I first met him when your mother brought him around. She said Stan came from northern parts but never provided more."

"There are," said Lakeland, clearing his throat, "families up north, strong with the djinn power. Foxhall, Folfox, and others." He paused a moment with the kerchief at his nose again. "Children not strong with the power in a powerful family either come south or work menial managerial jobs for that family."

"Why come south?" asked Jack, still wondering if he had any of this power.

"Weaklings are often done away with," stated Lakeland. "Not unlike things in the Snake. 'Ey Jack?" He smiled and winked at the young man.

Jack did not smile; he did not like his lordship, but Gracie needed him for reasons he did not question.

"So, I might have a father from a djinn family with no djinn power of his own?"

"Might," said Gracie, who had turned to glance at the eagle sculpture. She wondered if there might be something more to Jack, then turned back and asked, "You have a problem with your father turning up dead."

"Yeah, I do," said Jack, remembering the body on the marble scraps. "I coulda killed him, but I didn't think it the best plan." He sat forward, gripping the armrests. A dead Stan Fox provided no answers to any of his questions about the family he left in the north.

"Just how many men have you killed, Mr. Fox?" asked Lakeland with a toothy grin.

"Killed?" Jack slowly turned to Lakeland. "None I know of." He fixed the man with an icy stare. "A fare number went to the ground in some fights. Ya know how it goes in the Snake. 'Ey

Lakeland." As Lakeland took a step forward, obviously angered, Jack added, "Meaning no disrespect, sir."

"Boys, boys," laughed Gracie. "Let's deal with what we must now." Gracie stood and placed a consoling hand on Lakeland's shoulder. "We leave your father alone for now. We focus on Blogger. Your only job, Jack, is to cover the shop while me and my men handle our dear Edward." She looked expectantly at Jack. "You, Spunk, and Nanna will be our rearguard."

Jack nodded. He caught Lakeland's amused expression. He let the insult pass and wondered if Lakeland came from a northern family: disowned, cast out, and down here.

What's so great about the north, anyway?

CHAPTER 6

The gun barrel at Edward Blogger's right temple concerned him. Forced to sit with his arms out, palms down on the wooden planks, he sought a way out or a sympathetic face. His constantly moving eyes found neither. His untouched dinner steamed at his left hand; he felt a loss: a great calamity. Two lit candles on the desk and the light from the hearth left no doubt in his mind about his unfortunate situation.

Gracie stood before Blogger's desk, a pistol in her right hand and eight armed, angry men behind her. The hem of her dark purple gown touched the floor, darkened and heavy with blood. Blog's men, surprised in the middle of dinner, died scrambling for their weapons or ran away. Cobble stones outside of Blogger's front door ran with blood.

Gracie had one bullet left, having killed five of Blogger's men as she fought side-by-side with her force. Nineteen shot by Gracie's loyalists lay bleeding or dead out in the street.

"Well, Edward," said Gracie sweetly, "here we are." She pulled the hammer back on her pistol. "We can do this one of two ways." Gracie raised the gun. "Quick and relatively painless or slow and very painful for a time."

"What do ya want?" Blogger could not believe he would die tonight. Losing to a woman disturbed him even more. Something would happen to favor his position.

"When and where is the next shipment of children heading north?"

"Probably already headin' to the river." Blogger smiled, but abruptly stopped. "So, yer a bit late."

"Where are the children kept until they get moved on?" Gracie felt the powerful need to shove the barrel of her gun into the Blogger's mouth, then watch the back of his head decorate the wall behind him.

"Now, why would I tell you that? Yer goin' to kill me one way or the other."

Gracie scowled, and at that, Blogger felt the tables turning ever so slightly—he might have some leverage.

Gracie nodded to the man holding the pistol to the Blogger's temple. He holstered his weapon, then turned and picked up a hammer and two long, thick iron nails. He tossed them on the plank. They hit the wood with a loud bang.

"If you don't, these good men will nail your hands to the plank. Then I," Gracie slid the hunter's knife from the sheath at her back, "will remove your nether parts." The razor edge of the blade flashed in the candlelight. "Then," she looked at him with false pity, "you will at least be entertaining, if not as informative as I had hoped."

"They go to the Downs first!" Blogger screamed. He had seen the grisly outcome of what Gracie threatened. She would do it. "Always go there first from the Snake." No one lived in the Downs: a swamp, long thought to be a haven for bad, sickness-causing vapors and evil spirits. "They will get moved to Heathrow before heading to the river. Maybe in a week if they catch enough. Another week to gather those from other places."

He gulped and stared at Gracie, wide-eyed. "If ya get to Heathrow with a few hundred well-armed men about that time, ya might save a few of the little blighters before the slavers kill 'em. If they can't have 'em, nobody gets 'em as far as they's concerned."

"Well, I guess we won't need the hammer after all." Gracie smiled.

"There's a secret partner working with me. Someone from the Snake. Never could fig're out who."

"Thank you, Edward. You have been helpful." She pulled the trigger, the cap sparked, and the bullet exploded from the barrel. Blogger's heart suffered the lead intrusion poorly.

"*Damned, woman,*" flashed in his mind, then the world melted away.

Gracie stared at her long-time nemesis and wondered about the hidden partner to the child slave trade stalking the Snake. Blog's description could be almost anyone of a hundred men with whom she had connections. She ordered her followers out and made sure no telltale signs remained that might incriminate her.

"Let one of Lakeland's team know I need to meet with him," commanded Gracie of the man nearest her. "Sooner than later." He nodded.

Maybe Lakeland can be a help to ferret out this silent demon.

* * *

"We know the rules, Stan," said Lakeland. Stan Fox laid on a cot in a large storage shed owned by Lakeland close to the docks. Lakeland paced back and forth, his black walking stick in his right hand. "I'll make you a deal."

"I'm in a lot of pain," coughed Stan. With no stove in the room, the cold dominated. "I don't 'ave much choice." He shivered.

"Always quick on the uptake, Stan." Lakeland stopped and looked down on his prisoner.

"I want Jack." Lakeland waited, expecting a father's outrage.

"So, take him." He touched his shoulder wound and winced. It healed though the burning left scars and it still hurt. "Can I get someone to change the bandages?"

"The boy can sculpt," said Lakeland, looking for a reaction.

"Yeah. What of it?" Stan, looking under his bandages, wanted a doctor to look over the holes in his shoulder.

"Who in your loving family up north showed this talent?"

Lakeland grabbed a small wooden crate, stood it on end, and sat. The brass tipped stick wagged back and forth on its point in his right hand.

"My sister had the talent," he answered.

"Would you say," said Lakeland, his black gloved hand pointing at Stan, "that she projected with strength?"

"By all that's holy, yes." Stan grinned, remembering his sister and how she manipulated matter in a projected energy field. He stopped abruptly, checking his wound, realizing what Lakeland implied. "Ya don't think…"

"Doubt it. He's your son after all and his mother's a drunk," said Lakeland. "The boy would be worth a huge amount of money in the trade with only the suggestion of energy competence. If you get where I'm going?"

Stan glowered at him. "Why do ya need me for any of this?"

"It's time for you to go home and stay there… and maybe be my eyes and ears north of the Aquitaine." Lakeland got to his feet. "Keep an eye on your son."

"Ya snatch him, send me north, and I'll do what I can." He looked at Lakeland. "Never much liked the slave trade." He rubbed his shoulder. It throbbed. "But there's other trade that might be worth your while."

"Then we understand each other?" Lakeland nodded, rose, and paced again. "By the way," he stopped, "I also have family in the north. They will be watching."

"Ha! They always watch. Damn 'em all to hell." Stan sighed then said, "We understand each other completely."

"Good. You will see the doctor later today." Lakeland pulled a scented handkerchief from his coat's inside pocket. He held it to his nose. "I will have a stove brought in to warm you up." Lakeland smiled.

"I'm grateful." Stan closed his eyes, suddenly exhausted.

Lakeland made the arrangements for his new partner's comfort, then headed to an appointed meeting place.

Lakeland, behind his bodyguards, watched from horseback at the side of the road. He smiled, watching the urchins from the streets of Snakeport and other places in the South move north in horse-drawn, caged wagons. The dirty children, hungry, beaten down, but defiant, stared at the men on their magnificent horses with their polished buttons and obvious wealth.

He shared the slave business with Edward Blogger as a very silent partner. He felt nothing for these children. With the Blog eliminated, Lakeland realized that he would have to give up these significant profits or find a substitute partner. Lakeland trusted the Blog's weaknesses. A trust never betrayed. Finding another uniquely suited partner, where he could safely isolated himself from the dirty work, would take a long time.

It would not work for him to be known openly as a child slaver. Mrs. Hargreaves would do her best to destroy him. She could be an exceptionally energetic executioner when betrayed. For self-preservation, he would have to stab his long-time associate in the back. He enjoyed her, even liked her, but gold shined brighter.

As the last of the ten wagons passed, he pulled the reins. His troupe followed. Lakeland considered his options.

"One more play," whispered Lakeland. "One more special shipment."

CHAPTER 7

"We should walk the walls," whispered Spunk, not sure she wanted to just yet. The half-moon wrapped Gracie's place and the surrounding streets in a mix of light and shadow. Her hand on Jack's cheek, she thought that Gracie's attack on Blogger must have ended. They could relax.

Jack and Spunk faced each other, their guns lying on the ground at their feet. The cold bit, but neither paid it any attention. He placed his hands on either side of her waist and pulled her close. He looked deeply into her eyes. It occurred to him they possessed a beautiful, lighter brown color with flecks of gold. Her lips, slightly apart, overwhelmingly demanded to be kissed. Jack tilted his head slightly and leaned in.

"Committed," he whispered and kissed her long and tenderly.

"Oh, Jack," gasped Spunk when their lips parted. She clung to him, leaning her head on his shoulder. "If we're quick about it, we can complete our…" She looked up at him longingly.

"No," said Jack. "We do our job, then meet back here, then get inside out of the cold." Jack hugged her tight, never wanting to let go. These unknown feelings crushed his logical mind, but things had to be done to keep Gracie safe. "I don't want quick." Jack released her. They stepped back and picked up their weapons. "We do our jobs then…"

"Nanna sleeps like a cat, ready to jump." She pulled back the pistol hammer and spun the chambers.

"I think she approves." Jack winked at her. "We will be quiet, but not quick." He caressed her cheek. She smiled.

They both turned at the sound of metal crashing several streets away, followed by barking. After an angry shout, a brief whine, and a slammed door, the world returned to quiet. Jack nodded to Spunk and turned left to walk the perimeter of the warehouse, checking for enemies. Spunk turned the other way, doing the same. They held their pistols up with the triggers back, ready to shoot.

Jack's whole body tingled. Their kiss was the most intimate, most erotic thing he had ever experienced. It flooded his mind. He walked blindly; the memory of soft lips and a warm body pressed against his. Jack stopped, lowered the gun, and leaned against the wall.

"Think." He shook his head. "Do your job." Jack stood next to the newly boarded-up entrance his father had used to enter the shop. He checked his weapon, making sure all firing caps remained in place, then moved along the wall, staring into the few alleys stretching away to the docks. He and Spunk patrolled the perimeter for the fourth and last time. With no trouble the first three times, they gave into the insatiable ache to touch each other. Jack shook his head again and focused.

Movement down the last alley, three houses down, caught his attention. The wind off the bay picked up. Jack stepped away from the wall and moved to get a better view of what he thought he saw. The shadow moved again. Jack crouched, pointing the gun at the silhouette. The shadow of a tri-corn hat and a sabre moved out from behind a scraggly tree. Jack remained low as he dashed for cover closer to the alley entrance at the first building. He peered around the house's stone foundation. The man, Jack assumed, shrunk back behind the tree.

His palms damp, Jack checked his weapon again. This might be the night he killed his first man. Shivering, Jack closed on his target, staying low and hiding in darker shadows. The gun shook slightly in his grasp. He stopped and leaned against a water barrel.

Calm down! Jack chided himself. He peered over the barrel.

The man disappeared. Scanning to the left and right, scared that his enemy had moved to sneak up on him, Jack froze.

"I missed you," whispered a voice softly close to his ear.

Jack dropped flat on the ground, spun, and shoved the pistol into Spunk's grinning face. Laughing, she grabbed the gun barrel and pushed it aside.

"Damn it!" Jack pulled back the weapon from Spunk's grasp and wiped the barrel as if she had somehow contaminated it. "Are ya crazy!" he hissed. "There's a man over there with a sword. Didn't ya see 'im?" Slowly he turned over, got to his knees, and searched for his target.

"Ah," whispered Spunk. "Ya mean the baker's scarecrow?"

"What?"

"It's only been hangin' from the dead tree in his backyard for years now." Spunk stood. "Ya never seen it?"

"I guess not," said Jack, getting to his feet, embarrassed.

Together, they walked into the baker's yard. They watched the wind have its way with the straw man in a tricorn hat with a wooden sabre attached to an arm. The frayed bit of rope around its neck held it to the long, dead tree.

"Shall we see," said Spunk, "if Nanna's asleep yet?" She wrapped her arms around Jack from behind.

Jack did not answer. He took Spunk's wrists in his hands and escaped her hug.

He felt stupid not knowing about the scarecrow. *What am I doing?* Suddenly more nervous than when he thought he might have to shoot a man, he slipped his hand in hers and picked up the pace to get inside where warm blankets waited, and they could start a slow voyage of discovery.

* * *

The fire burned low, and the chill edged into Gracie's office.

Nanna shivered and woke up in the padded chair near the stove. She searched the room for trouble. The quiet bothered her. She stared through the open door to the warehouse floor. Trouble ready to spring from a quiet trap haunted her. Her hand gathered the handle of the pistol in her lap. Her knees popped as she lowered her legs from the crate to the floor.

"Where are those damn kids when ya need 'em?"

She reached down, felt around the floor, and found the cane. Leaning it against the chair arm, Nanna unfolded the layers of blankets about her and pushed herself up on to her feet. With the gun in one hand and leaning on the cane with the other, she shuffled toward the warehouse floor. At the door, grateful that her swollen legs did not cause her pain, she scanned the darkness and listened intently. The first sign of trouble, a whisper, came from the other side of the bar. Holding the gun out before her, she closed on the danger. She had survived so long in the Snake by shooting first and asking questions later. She stopped when the cane tapped against the brass rail.

"Like this Jack." The hushed words filled the darkness.

"Better?" a second voice whispered.

"Oh… yes."

The old woman smiled, relaxed, and aimed the pistol at the floor. She shook her head. *Those two should have found each other like a man and woman a long time ago.* As quietly as her condition allowed, she returned to the office. As she passed the threshold, she closed the door.

"Need their time is what they need."

Nanna placed the gun in her chair and leaned the cane against the crate, then slowly moved around the room, gathering a few pieces of wood and a bottle from the nearest shelf. With a few well-aimed breaths on glowing coals, the new wood caught. Back in her perch swaddled in the blankets, Nanna laid back her head staring at the ceiling. As the room warmed, she could not be sure if the heat from the stove or the fiery liquor she swigged from the dark green bottle took her back to a better time.

"Oh, Robbie, do ya remember?" Nanna called out to her husband, who died of a fever a decade earlier. "Not much older than us." She tilted the bottle and swallowed. "Not much older at all." Her eyes moved to the closed door. "We had a time, didn't we? Oh yes, my dear. You and me, Cock Robbin. We made somethin'."

Lost in her memories, the woman drifted off unafraid as her Robbie gathered her up in his arms.

CHAPTER 8

Jack worked carefully on the marble statue. A candle on his empty dinner plate provided light. He had captured Gracie's face well. The folds of the gown proved more difficult than expected. Jack set down his tool and stared at the eight-inch block, searching for the best way to solve his problem.

The knock on the door startled him. Nothing good in his experience ever came from such a visit. He rose from the table and checked his mother, who sat up in bed, her head drooping. She mumbled something incoherent. The knock came again, and Jack moved to the door and opened it.

"Jack Fox?" asked a little boy, maybe eight or nine years old, to Jack's eye.

Wary, Jack nodded, then stepped outside and looked up and down the dirt street. It was too dark to see anything. Somewhere in the distance, men laughed, and a dog barked.

"Come quick. Spunk needs you," said the child, who dashed away.

"Hey!" called Jack, "Wait!" He closed the door behind him and charged after the boy who stayed ahead of him.

At Old John's Square, Jack caught up and grabbed the boy's shoulder, pulled him back, and turned him around. "What's the trouble?" he demanded. The child pointed. Jack turned to the gallows steps where someone sat. He let the boy go. "Who are you? What do you want?"

As Jack moved to get a better look at the person, he heard a footfall behind him. Before he could turn, the ground came up.

* * *

"Gracie Hargreaves!" echoed from one end of the warehouse to the other. The coarse command demanded a response. Gracie, weeks after her successful raid on Edward Blogger, stormed out of her office.

"Who the hell dare's…" Gracie stopped short when she saw the person calling her out. "Lilly?" Jack's mother stood before her, obviously upset and stone-cold sober. Her knotted, uneven-cut, brown hair needed a wash, as did the soiled, green dress she wore. She worked hard to hide the shakes that came with her addiction, pulling the coarse wool shawl tighter.

"Where's my son?" Lilly Fox advanced on Gracie, angry but intimidated at confronting her meal-ticket. "Jack ain't been home in days." Nervous, her eyes bounced around the shop, then settled on her longtime friend. "What have you got 'im doin'?"

"Come back into the office." Gracie waved her hands for Lilly to follow. "We need to talk, private-like." She kept an eye on her friend to make sure she came along. "I sent my men out to find Jack days ago," Gracie said, taking a seat at her desk. "I know you don't much like Spunk, but she led a special group who would carry the search to the river." Gracie stared at the ledger open on her desk. After a silent pause she said, "Like you, I don' know where he's got to."

"I can't get along without my Jack," moaned Lilly. Tears appeared in her eyes.

"Did ya know Stan came back?" Gracie said coldly. *Still thinking of yourself, Lil?*

"Yeah," she said, her eyes fixed on the floor. "I knew 'bout Stan." Lilly sat down and rocked back and forth in the chair, ignoring Gracie's criticism. She looked up, then glanced higher at the liquor bottles on the shelves.

"Now, Stan's gone missing and with 'em seems to be Jack, too." Gracie's fingers tapped on the desk. "Somethin' is going on, but I can't tell what just yet." Gracie watched as Lilly licked her lips and stared longingly at the shelf. She shook her head, then asked, "Did Stan say anything to you about Jack?"

"Stan never paid no attention to Jack," whined Lilly. "Do ya think the slavers got 'im?"

"I pray not," said Gracie, shaken by the thought. "He knew how to take care and what to avoid."

"So," stated Lilly in what appeared to be a moment of clarity, "someone ya trust, maybe, sold 'im out with Stan's help." She locked into Gracie's eyes. "Who have ya been trusting that might not deserve it?"

"I trust no one except for a few who could not do such a thing."

"Are ya sure?" Lilly sat forward. "There're some snakes that smile in your face as they rob ya blind."

Gracie just stared at her, and after a long pause, she watched Lilly slowly reach into the folds of her dress, then produce a roughly carved piece of stone and set it on the desk.

"I found this on the table along with Jack's tools." She sat back and looked up at the ceiling, trying to remember. "Seems like I recall someone calling for Jack to come quick."

"When was that?" asked Gracie, reaching for the unfinished piece. Surprised, she saw herself emerging from the marble. Lilly noticed the catch in her throat like she might cry as Gracie studied the bit of stone.

"Don't rightly know." Ashamed, Lilly stood to go.

"I will send a man around to help you, Lil," said Gracie. "In the meantime, I'll keep looking."

"My poor Jack," cried his mother, stumbling out of the office. She needed to get back to her place, back to the bottle by her bed.

Gracie watched her go.

* * *

The thick mud clawed at the heavy iron-bound wagon wheels. Four horses complained, huffing and snorting as their hooves dug and slid into the sodden road. A whip cracked, and harsh voices yelped; the slaver wagon made slow, forward progress in the early spring, heading north. It bounced and slid into ruts and holes. Two of the three young, barely teenage, caged passengers with terror-stricken eyes wrapped their arms through the wooden crosspieces. The third in the cage, unconscious, slammed back and forth across the wagon bed.

At the river, the horses calmed; the wheels rolled easier over the even, wooden planks of the long bridge. Thick cross beams creaked beneath the weight; the water below flowed noisily around the massive tree truck support pillars. On the other side, the decaying road continued occasionally made better by stretches of six-inch tree trunks laid side-by-side across the worst parts. The slaver drivers knew the rough road would become better and reached the buffer region between the two states. Suddenly, as when a flame comes to life in the dark revealing the room, the road became hard and smooth. The ride no longer threatened to break bones or crack skulls.

"Ya think he's dead?" asked the girl, looking at the unconscious boy's back. She released her hold on the cage. She tucked her bare feet beneath a ragged, thread-bare blanket. "Can ya tell? Is he dead?" She sat back against the cage.

"Might be," said her fellow prisoner. He had settled into a corner with his arms hugging his knees. His covering also providing a low level of warmth to his exposed feet. "There's blood comin' outa his ears." The boy's head rest on the cage edge facing away from the girl.

"The bastards won't make their money on this one." She smiled. *He's better off dead, anyway.* She stretched out her leg and stuck her toes into his lower back to make sure. "Serve these cow turds right to lose somethin'."

"Where'd they get ya?" The boy focused on the body, looking for any reaction.

"Farming country north of the Snake," said the girl, filled with sudden anger, despair, and defeat at the same time. "Dad decided he could give up a useless daughter to save the rest." She lashed out and poked the body harder. As much as she prayed that the men who grabbed her would suffer, she abruptly changed her mind; this boy had to be too tough to give up, so she could find the will to go on.

They both jumped when a moan erupted from the lips and the body turned over on its back. Blood dribbled from his nose over the lips.

She abandoned her corner and went to the kid's side. Her hands ran over his body knowingly, feeling for broken bones. Accidents on the farm happened regularly, and you had to move quick to keep the damage to a minimum. The blood congealed dark red, but his blue hands, feet, and lips concerned her more. She grabbed his wrists and shoved his hands down the front of his pants. She grabbed the burlap wrap left unused in the corner and wrapped the fabric around his feet.

"Help me move him away from the sideboards," she commanded.

"What good is that?" asked her companion. "Besides, I'm freezing." He pulled the cloth closer about him.

"His head gets banged anymore, and he's dead," she said, her words clipped. "It's winter. It's cold. You're used to it. Get over here." The girl said nothing about the warmer feel to the air north of the river.

"What's your name?" she asked. "I'm Hattie."

"Berg." The boy came away from his corner. "My name be Berg."

"Watch his head, Berg."

Together, they centered the body in the middle of the wagon bed. Hattie folded her thin blanket and placed it under his head. Berg returned to his corner and pulled his piece of cloth around his shoulders.

"Where ya from, Berg?" Hattie knelt by the unconscious boy's head. She gently lifted the eyelids and gasped. He had demon eyes, red where there should be white. Hattie had seen this before: not a good sign.

"The Snake," grumbled Berg. "I worked the quarry." He stared at the boy's face as Hattie wiped away the blood from his lips. "I know this one," he stated angrily. "This here's Jack Fox."

* * *

The slaver wagon after hours on the smooth road pulled up in front of a square brick building: a northern medical outpost. Two of the slavers hauled the unconscious teenager out of the cage, threatening Hattie and Berg with a beating if they interfered. The men took the body inside and slammed him down on a metal table. One slaver left to watch over the other two while the other remained to deal with the northern doctor.

"Should be dead," said Doctor Peppers. "Looks like the back of his head was stove in." The resident physician at this remote university clinic, in his white garb, examined the boy on the shining metal table. He lifted an eyelid, held it, and dropped in close with a lighted tool. The irises did not respond.

"Ya, but…" The driver shifted his weight from one foot to the other. Aggravated with the possible financial loss. He expected hell to pay if this child wound up dead. "Not dead or likely to die, Doc?" asked the driver.

Peppers looked up, noted the concern on the man's face and almost laughed. "There's bleeding inside his head." He turned back to his patient. "I can't tell for sure what is going to happen. He may be healing or dead in a minute or two." Peppers shrugged.

"When are ya goin' to know for sure?" asked the driver.

Standing up, Peppers laid the tool on the counter next to the table. He considered the risks and the options that would interest the slaver who watched his every move intently.

"My best recommendation," said Peppers, "is to leave him here. Deliver the other two, then come back. He will either show signs of recovery or he will be dead."

The slaver rolled his eyes, took off his tricorn hat, and swiped his fingers through his thinning salt and pepper hair. Pointing his hat at the doctor, he said, "Ya ain't goin' to sell 'im an' cheat us?" He placed his hand on the holstered pistol. "Won't do at all, not at all."

Peppers waved his left hand and the space between him and the slaver rippled like hot air over a campfire. The driver crashed back into the wall. His breathing became hoarse, gasping like he slowly choked.

"Where, sir, do you think you are?" Peppers dropped his level of energy. "I have no interest in the slave trade, only healing those I can." He walked up to the man and pulled the weapon from the holster. "Not much good is it," said Peppers, looking down at the gun in his hand. He pulled back the trigger and spun the cartridge while the man pressed to the wall passed out. "Well, there you go." He put the gun back in the holster. The slaver slumped to the floor. Peppers went back to his patient.

Running his fingers through the boy's short hair, looking for obvious damage to the bone structure, his hands came away wet. He turned the boy over on his side and pushed back the hair at the back of the head.

"Well, I'll be damned." He saw a line of small holes and liquid oozing out. He placed the boy on his stomach. His immediate supervisor needed to be consulted. This special case the university might want to explore.

The driver regained consciousness minutes later and got to his feet. Sheepishly, he approached Peppers, who sat at his desk across the room writing his report.

"Meaning no disrespect sir," he started, "I'm sorry for me hasty…"

"Think nothing of it, my man," interrupted Peppers. "I have no intention of cheating you or your higher ups." He reached down into a drawer and pulled out a canvas bag. "Will two hundred cover us for now?"

"Yes sir. Thank you, sir," said the driver, relieved. "We'll be back in a week." He found his hat on the floor and placed it back on his head. He grabbed the bag and left the clinic.

Peppers followed him and watched as the two men mounted the wagon. The girl in the cage stood clasping the bars and stared at him. As the wagon moved out, she yelled, "Don't give up, Jack! Don't let the bloody turd win!"

The doctor knew his patient never heard her words: a desperate appeal. He turned into his office, closing the door behind him. Very curious and deeply concerned about the boy, Peppers double checked what he thought might be happening.

"So, Jack. What are we to make of you?"

* * *

"I read your report. What has happened between then and now?" asked a gray-haired, short, heavy-set man. He drank from his mug of coffee, considering Peppers critically. The two physicians sat across from each other at Pepper's desk.

"The cranial structure which showed considerable flattening at the back of the head has now taken on a more curvaceous, more normal appearance." Peppers knew he must keep to the provable based on observation. His superior, Doctor Byron Shephards, had come a long way in a short time to examine his patient: a slave. The doctor's reputation preceded him. Peppers had heard that Shephards never argued with the data. He shivered. His superior suffered stupidity poorly and was unforgiving in his analysis. Pepper's career hung in the balance.

"Your analysis?" asked Shephards.

"The boy is healing himself. That would explain the fluid flowing from self-inflicted holes in his scalp to relieve the pressure on his brain." Peppers paused. He did not want to go where the data led. "Based on these observations," he swallowed, "he is one of us." Shephards' lack of a reaction to his comment unsettled him. He added quickly, "I must ask you to examine my patient to correct my analysis."

"Has he gained consciousness, if only for a short time?"

"No, sir. No signs of consciousness." Peppers looked appropriately obsequious.

Shephards nodded agreement. He leaned forward, lifted the ceramic, gilded coffee pot, and filled his mug. He stared into the black drink, thinking as he poured the cream. *We have either an explosive situation or…* he stirred the mixture then sipped from his mug, *a mystery to be kept quiet as the university sorts it out.*

"I see," added Peppers, "that it would be a troublesome matter if he comes around."

"Do you see, doctor?" Shephards did not arrive at the remote clinic without knowing with whom he would deal. Peppers' career followed the normal routine. The senior physicians, however, recognized a rising star in the medical arena. Shephards placed his coffee on the desk, looked to the left at the body on the table, and stood. "You are near the end of your time at this clinic?"

"Yes."

"I will need you at my lab and hospital." Shephards looked at the resident physician, making sure he grasped the importance of this case, "with this boy."

"I understand," said Peppers, suddenly overwhelmed by the invitation to work at the most prestigious medical clinic in the North.

"Okay, then… Let's have a look." Shephards stood and went to the examining table. He went to the left while his protégé took his place on the right. The elder physician examined the body still on his stomach. With his left hand, he pushed the hair back.

"Sticky with proteins. No surprise." Shephards looked closer. "The pressure relieving holes have sealed."

"Yes." Peppers looked from the back of the head to Shephards. "That started only hours ago." He paused. "You see what has confused me?"

"My dear doctor," Shephards chuckled. "There is no confusion here. He indeed is showing signs of an energy manipulator trying desperately to survive."

"Well sir, if that is the case, what do you suggest I do?" Peppers, well-schooled in the environment of a South from which nothing good comes, pleaded with the experienced doctor.

"He goes north, of course." Shephards walked away from the examining table. He exerted a small amount of energy to warm his coffee as he stood by the desk, sipped from the cup, then sat. "He must become the property of the university without question."

Peppers remained at the table, following Shephards with his eyes.

"You, of course," said Shephards, "must come with your patient. He is a mystery and politically dangerous. Wouldn't you say?"

They jumped when the boy on the metal table groaned and moved his head.

"What did he say?" asked Shephard.

"Sounded like…," The young doctor swallowed and turned back to the boy. "It could have been 'committed'?"

CHAPTER 9

"I SEE WHAT YOU'RE SAYIN', BUT THINK ON WHO YOU'RE TALKIN' about." Tom Haggard, dressed as always in austere, preacher black, stared at Gracie in her office. He stood before her desk, refusing the offered chair. "We four have been in business, good business, for a while."

"Yes, Tom. But that is all in the past now." Gracie appreciated Tom for his forth-rightness. She and he shared similar approaches in their business dealings. Tom, the preacher she found amusing on most occasions, but not today. "There are witnesses."

"Ya killed Edward." Tom confronted Gracie. "Now ya want to take down, Reggie? Where's the proof?"

"Someone dear to me has gone missing, Tom." Gracie looked at the carved eagle on the shelf. "Edward trafficked in the slave trade. Ya may not have been sure, but ya suspected. I knew and acted accordingly." The vapor from the steaming pot on the pot-bellied stove caught her attention. "For goodness' sake, Tom, have a seat and something to drink." She needed no more enemies.

"I won't argue about the slave trade. I killed any number of them over the years." Acquiescing, showing his faith in Gracie, Tom relaxed, looked behind him and pulled the chair forward, and sat.

"Coffee or something stronger?" Gracie lifted the pot, filled her mug, then offered the same to Tom. He waved her off.

"Stronger, please." Tom stared at his shoes.

"You're a good man, Tom Haggard." Gracie took a glass, long stemmed and fluted, from the shelf next to Jack's carving. She filled it from a bottle readily at hand. She faced Tom and held out the drink.

"Thank you." Tom eyed Gracie suspiciously. He drank, closed

his eyes with abject pleasure. "I appreciate your efforts," he stared at the flower-like challis. Shades of green in the stem came and went as he twirled the glass. He took a deep breath, released his hold on the ornate stem and looked Gracie in the eye, "but… taking on Reginald Lakeland is perhaps a mountain too high."

"I hate this, Tom." Gracie returned to her seat. "I counted on Reggie, but he betrayed me in a most hurtful way."

"Proof?"

"I have witnesses, but…" she smiled, knowing that witnesses bloodied or witnesses untouched would not be believed. One tortured, and the other paid off. "If you are willing, I can show you."

"I'll consider it." Tom needed another drink and nodded to the empty glass. Gracie refilled it. Tom knew the game began, whether or not he liked it. "Gracie. Can we stop the moves on the chessboard? I know what you want. How it impacts my business is the point." He drained the cup and pointed it at Gracie, about to speak, but she cut him off.

"If I commit to making you whole, however this issue turns out, will you be a witness to the crime?"

"In writing?" asked Tom.

"Yes." Gracie maintained eye contact with Tom. She had to assure him of her commitment.

"Then, done," he said. "I will be where you wish me to be to see the truth of it." Tom stood. "My licensure will be in contact with yours tomorrow."

"You will have the agreement and the evidence," said Gracie. "Can you travel tomorrow night?"

"Tomorrow?" Tom asked, raising an eyebrow.

"Slavers waste no time getting their product heading north." Gracie raised her mug. "To the truth Tom Haggard. To the truth."

He gently set his empty glass on the desk, then took Gracie's hand. With a shake of the hand the agreement made, he added, "I will be where you wish."

Gracie nodded and stole a glance at the majestic eagle frozen in time on her shelf.

* * *

"We want this one." Peppers studied the slavers who returned for their property. "What is your price?"

"Well, let me consider," said the man whom the doctor had smashed against the wall on their first meeting. "There's time and effort to account for and then the value of the body itself." He rubbed his chin, thinking as fast as he could.

"The university has need of a body to examine completely," said Peppers.

"Well sir, and meaning no disrespect, he's a fighter and still alive," said the slaver crossly.

"He is damaged goods with limited value and remains on the edge of survival," said Peppers. The boy's body laid out on the table, easily seen.

"We might settle on a thousand in gold."

"Let's say twelve hundred and nothing more is said about it?" Peppers saw the glee on the slaver's face with the extra gold. It sealed the deal. He laid the canvas bag of coins on his desk.

"Done and done, sir." The slaver laid his hand on the bag.

"Put your mark here and we are agreed." Peppers placed the paper in front of the slaver, who scratched out an unreadable signature.

The slavers left, heading south. The doctor wrapped the body on his table in a comfortable blanket and tucked him in gently.

"Couldn't have the fool believe you're on the mend, could we Jack," said Peppers, tossing the tranquilizer syringe he had used in a wastebasket by the table. "Everyone is happy now… for the moment, anyway."

* * *

"Twelve hundred!" yelled Lakeland. He slapped the table. Lakeland held forth in the back room of a local tavern in Snakeport: The Golden Heron. The ugly side of his business demanded secrecy if he wanted to be safe. Owner of the establishment where proof lay in the document graveyard in city hall, he paid no business fees or taxes. "I thought, Mr. Chelmsford, that your men adept at negotiation. I expected thrice the amount for the boy." He sat forward, hands white knuckled on the table's edge, on the brink of losing control and cursing the man.

"Two things, Lakeland." Chelmsford stood and leaned across the dark wood, invading Lakeland's space. "First, the boy showed significant damage when we picked him up, like tossing a sack of potatoes into the wagon. Second, my driver had an energy user negotiating terms. A doctor, no less, saying the boy might never stand on two feet again. We don't deal with those kinds of people. We agree to control the damage, if you take my meaning." Chelmsford, the preeminent, practical businessman, stood six feet tall. His beard balanced his receding chin, giving him a stronger looking jaw. In his line of business, looks mattered.

"Who took the boy in the alley?" asked Lakeland, his anger dissipating.

"Boyd and Watson."

"And the elder Fox?" Lakeland sat back, considering a new strategy.

"Only to identify and as a guide. Boyd and Watson caught the boy and brought his body along."

"Crushing his skull?" Lakeland pulled a notebook from the

bag next to his chair. He opened it, set his inkwell and pen, then, taking the pen in hand, scratched an entry.

"The boy was not about to cooperate," stated Chelmsford. "Perhaps our boys used a bit too much force to bring him down." Chelmsford paused a moment. "You said get the lad. We got him."

Lakeland and Chelmsford, cut from the same cloth, stared a challenge at each other. Both dressed richly, both handsome enough, and wealthy from earnings in selling children, neither could intimidate the other. Lakeland turned away first.

"The fools hit him too hard." Lakeland sat back and accepted the obvious. "The other two went where?" He could accept the disappointment if the other delivered more than expected.

"Well," said Chelmsford, smiling broadly. "The girl fetched twice what we expected. We left her not far away from Hempstead: a very wealthy family, as I understand it. The boy went for a bit more than we had hoped in Dover."

"So, we did alright," said Lakeland, grabbing the two bags of gold, lifting them, and placing them with the others along the wall behind him. "The boy is a disappointment, but… things are what they are. He is dead or driving others to violence, as was his want."

"Agreed," stated Chelmsford. He straightened up and took a step back. "We have more shipments to consider and gold to collect."

"Yes." Lakeland got to his feet and went to a side table to pour wine for the two of them. "I believe it is the last we will hear of Mrs. Hargreaves' protégé, Mr. Jack Fox."

CHAPTER 10

THE HEAVY BRONZE DOORS SWUNG OPEN. JACK, SUPPORTED BY his ever-present Doctor Peppers, hobbled into the sunshine on an early, warm spring day. They stopped at the edge of the wide granite porch. The fluted, many-stepped, stone stairway led to the street and sparkled in the daylight. Jack stared in awe: the landscape clear and clean. Trees, tall with thick trunks, lined the sidewalks; people talked in small groups in the shade of new leaves, lay about in the small grassy field, or walked purposefully with heads down. The paved avenue stretched as far as he could see, with many storied stone buildings on either side: buildings taller than any in Snakeport. The clear blue sky held not a cloud.

Jack, eyes wide, watched a horseless, shiny, metal vehicle with glass windows move effortlessly around the circle in front of the university clinic. The doors opened by themselves and people stepped out onto the sidewalk while others waited patiently to board the vehicle. When the doors closed, the wheels moved like magic as far as Jack could tell.

"How is this possible?"

"It is the way of things here," said Peppers, amused by Jack's reaction to life in a northern city. A month had passed since Jack arrived in the college town. The young doctor, like Jack, stood in awe. Jack, however, amazed him. His patient took a fatal blow to the head, healed himself, and here he stood. He sensed the unease among his superiors that a southerner, a slave, shared their abilities. Peppers had come to respect and consider Jack a friend. He watched Jack's amazed reaction, so precious, suddenly turn to anger.

"This isn't right." Jack's jaw clenched. "These are the reasons we hate you," he hissed.

"What could you possibly mean?" asked Peppers. "This is not even the largest of our towns and cities." The doctor considered his patient suspiciously. "Why would anyone hate me?"

"Our struggle to live in the South pays for this," argued Jack through gritted teeth. "There's an old woman with swollen legs, hobbling around, struggling to keep going for her grandkids' sake." Jack turned to Peppers. "You could heal her in a blink."

Peppers arched an eyebrow at the young man. "Yes." He paused, knowing how weak his words would sound. "I had nothing to do with what happened in the past and what the government is doing now."

"The sky is so blue here," said Jack, ignoring his shadow. "No choking smoke from wood or coal fires. We can't build above three stories. There is no time to sit around in the grass talking. All our trees go for fuel to keep warm or cook. Have you ever worried that you might go without a meal?"

"No," said Peppers quietly. "I have never been south of the river."

"Take me inside," said Jack, turning away from the opulence. He waved his hand dismissively. "I can't stand the injustice of it all."

A minor tremor erupted from the porch, down the steps, up the avenue, and life on the street stopped. A few seconds later, people belatedly ran to the trees, seeking safe ground. The horseless vehicles jumped an inch off the road surface. Peppers watched as Jack shuffled unaided down the hall back to his room, unaware of what happened on the street.

Peppers' head snapped back and forth between Jack staggering down the hall and the chaos out in the street.

"This won't go over well," he said. The hammer would hang over his head and come down hard if blame came his way. Peppers dashed down the stairs, running to the right toward the medical school. He had to talk to his mentor, Dr. Shephards. He needed a good defense.

* * *

Four men huddled in the corner of the Hempstead medical school's library while other authorities, in robes of red or black, stood or sat around the long, dark, heavy wooden tables in two columns of five. Shelves, stuffed floor to ceiling with books, surrounded the open space where students would normally study at this time of day. The audience and jury, the local authorities, represented the city, university, and student's parents. Their citizens complained; something must be done. The assault on their happiness, on their children, a week earlier, would not be tolerated.

"This is most unusual," said Dean Camden, the president of the school. Thick, white unruly hair framed a weathered face. Thick-lensed glasses corrected his blurred vision, but he steered the university on a steady course, away from danger with his clarity of thought and his analytic mind. It cut through the fog of specious arguments and Dover politics. Broad shouldered with an ample gut, Camden wore the purple robe of his office, and expected force to be applied for a formal ruling to the government's liking. The informal meeting met to gather data on the incident: nothing more. Politics, however, shadowed everything these days. He glanced at the three men standing nearby and listened intently prior to the start of the inquest.

"It does not have to be thus," said Dean Rockman, the Dean of Students. "He is just a slave." Taller than the surrounding men in the green robes of his office, he looked down on Camden and Dr. Shephards. He smiled, closed lip. It looked unpleasant. "What do you say Laudon?"

"A slave's life is of little consequence," agreed Max Laudon, the government's representative to the university. He wore the black, long-tailed coat of his government office. It did not fit his thin physique very well. His square, ruddy face with eyes red tinged avoided direct contact. Laudon detested meetings held before lunch.

"That might be a very foolish tack to take," said Shephards, the medical school's Director of Graduate Students. He knew the "holier than thou" Dean of Students all too well and the capital's mole in their midst, supporting him.

"The boy is a fly on the breakfast table ready to be swatted." Rockman brought one hand down on the other. "With what consequence?" He chortled. "A slave dies." He raised his hands above his head overly dramatically. "Who is going to complain about the death of a slave?"

"No one," said Laudon firmly.

"The slave might," said Shephards.

The hum of talk stopped when Jack and his doctor entered the room.

Camden went to the librarian's desk in front of the tables and sat waving the two newcomers to come forward. Shephards stood behind the president on the right, Rockman and Laudon on the left. The others either found seats or stood at the back.

When Jack and Peppers reached the desk, they sat in the two chairs placed especially for them to the right. The quiet of a tomb descended on the gathering.

"Let's get this started," said Camden, who rapped his knuckles on the desktop. "By what name is the subject called?"

"Jack," said Peppers, turning to the school's president.

"What name did you go by in your former life?" The thick glasses focused on Jack.

Peppers told Jack there would be a hearing concerning the energy released into a public space. He worried when Jack decided matter-of-factly, they would either kill him or let him go. The boy's lack of concern in the outcome jolted him. As the silence stretched, he nudged his friend's shoulder.

"My name is Jack Fox." Jack looked at the man sitting at the desk. He examined the men standing behind him. Turning to face the audience, he said, "My father was Stan Fox. His family in the north found him to be a useless piece of dung and I don't disagree."

"Do you know why we are gathered here?" asked Camden, ignoring Jack's lack of decorum.

"The doc here tells me some disruption on the street." Jack smiled. He could not be certain if what had happened came from him. If it did, he would gladly claim it.

"Your name doctor if you please," followed the president.

"I am Claymore Peppers, sir. I am a graduate medical student finishing my clinical work," said Peppers.

"Tell us the history of the issue before us." Camden, more than anyone in the room, wanted to know the details.

"The first time I saw Jack…" Peppers told the story, leaving nothing out.

"I would concur with Dr. Peppers' chronology and facts of the case," said Dr. Shephards, stepping forward and addressing the room.

"So, Dr. Peppers, you state for the record," asked Camden, "that you had nothing to do with the energy release?"

"None, sir. I am not that capable. Healers seldom can exert such power." Peppers sitting ramrod straight held the school president's eyes.

"Very good," said Camden. "May I take it, Dr. Shephards, that you agree?"

"Yes." Shephards turned to Jack. "That it came from this

young man is the only possibility that aligns with the data we have."

"Mr. Laudon," asked Camden, who turned and looked up, "what is the government's position?"

"I have only just taken this matter under consideration, sir." Laudon took a step forward and glanced at the tables of men before him. "It is too soon to expect a response sent to the capital on the subject."

Jack let out a laugh.

"Something funny, young man?" Camden leaned forward with a stern look.

"I've seen his sort." Jack glared at Laudon disgusted, then at Camden. "Action of any sort becomes confused when drink clouds the mind."

The room went silent. Laudon stepped back, furious at the verbal assault. Jack just made an enemy.

"You realize," said Camden, "that your life may end depending on how things go?" Camden sat back. "You might take this more seriously."

"Kill me or don't!" Jack's anger at the threat rose in him like it did on the porch. "The Snake couldn't do it, but if you can, then do it. I am not afraid of you or death." The rumbling from the tables behind him caught his attention. He stood and turned to face them. Peppers tried to pull him back into his chair but failed. "You think yourselves so civilized. How good can you be when slavery is acceptable? You're all hypocrites." Books fell from shelves and slapped on the floor as if thrown.

"He's like a toddler." Camden stood up, annoyed. Someone had not sealed the doors after the meeting began. Curious citizens entered the library and joined those standing in the back. As a few more tomes dropped, he forgot about the newcomers and considered Jack, shaking his head slowly.

"A dangerous toddler," called Rockman. "We cannot tolerate this."

Jack sat down bewildered and looked at Peppers to explain what they meant.

"You did it again," Peppers whispered. "Not much energy, but everyone in the room and a few textbooks felt it."

"In my capacity as president of this university," stated Camden, "the case has been made that the boy here, called Jack, is an energy projector. He is untrained and dangerous to those around him." Camden paused, giving his next words considerable weight. "Dr. Peppers will take responsibility for Jack and remove him to a place where he can receive the rudimentary training in control of the energy he possesses."

The room erupted in calls for eliminating the threat. Angry epitaphs flew at the purple-robed man: never show a slave such leniency.

"Quiet! Quiet! There will be order!" Camden banged on the desk with his fist. The room calmed. "If this boy cannot be trained, then we will let the government decide what should be done. We will monitor his progress, or lack thereof, week to week." Camden hit the desktop again. "I will give three months for this activity, no more." The president walked over and stood next to Jack. "We will evaluate his status as a slave at that time. This is my decision. Make it happen." Camden then smiled down at Jack and wished him a whispered hope for success. He targeted the exit and swiftly marched down the aisle between the tables and left the room. Rockman and Laudon followed on his heals waving their hands extolling him to reconsider.

"Claymore?" asked Jack, grinning at Peppers.

"Call me Peppers or doc. Otherwise, I'll let the government have you." Doctor Peppers frowned at Jack.

"Could be worse." Jack stood up and watched the train of robes leave the library. "Ya can only kill me once. Right?"

"Well…"

* * *

"This is not right," said Anna Forrester, unhappy. They traveled to the capital. She and Robert quickly settled matters about the upkeep of their home while they were away. In the event they did not return, their employees, former slaves who truly ran the place, would own it. The trip took weeks longer than expected as friends happily put them up and wanted them to stay longer. "He won't be in Dover."

"We need to consult with the Chief Inquirers." Robert stared out at the passing landscape. It grew greener as the temperature rose the closer they got to the capital. They expected it. The atmospheric lens high over the capital maintained by energy projectors kept the capital always in an early summer environment. "If Dover is the wrong place," he said, turning to Anna, "where should we be looking?"

"I think," Anna began, hesitating, "he will be somewhere they will recognize his abilities." She could not look at her husband. Their high-risk venture depended on her assertion that someone special approached. "After Dover, let's go to Hempstead. We will find him or signs of him there."

"A guess?" Robert arched an eyebrow.

"A logical conclusion."

Robert nodded, smiling. He had earned his various degrees attending the university in Hempstead. It would be a homecoming, more pleasurable than their staying with good friends over the last weeks, making their way eastward. They may be on a wild goose chase, but he would very much look forward to spending time on his old stomping ground.

"Don't take this the wrong way, my dear," said Robert, "but what do you expect to happen if you encounter this special person?"

"Underestimated, thought useless, by the powers that be," Anna stated. "He will, however, be immediately recognizable to you and I." She paused. "Maybe to a few others." She smiled as Robert nodded.

"So, get in and out of the capital quickly, then on to Hempstead." Robert still had a few friends among the Inquirers who would not feel threatened by Robert's desire to study the slave trade as a follow-up to his outdated, published works on the issue. He would breathe easier having a signed license from the Board of Inquirers to do some research. That the research might undo the state as it currently existed need not come to light.

"Yes." Anna smiled. "The sooner, the better."

* * *

Two days after the hearing a sullen Peppers with a smiling, carefree Jack in tow entered a classroom with forty, fidgeting, four to seven-year-old children who sat behind desks in five rows of eight. The number of girls matched the number of boys.

"Get serious," said Peppers, gripping Jack's forearm. "This is your first day of school or trial, and I will be with you every step of the way to keep everything on the up and up. These little kids will have ten years to finish," Peppers poked his finger in Jack's chest for emphasis, "you have only three months. If you don't do well, you die." Peppers relaxed when Jack nodded, losing the grin. They sat on stools at the back of the room.

"They're so little," said Jack.

Peppers returned his attention to the children. "Yes, they're young. We try to separate those who can from those who cannot as early as possible."

"Why?" asked Jack, surveying the rows of youngsters. Every desk had an occupant with long hair and dressed in colorful, high-quality clothing: the boys in shirts and pants, the girls in dresses or knee-high pants and loose-fitting blouses. Green pants and cloth shoes or boots dominated the style of dress, either yellow green of new leaves or a dark, late summer forest green. Jack saw no value in complaining about the wealth of the North any longer: no point. He kept his anger bottled up. "I don't see the good of it."

"The point is," said Peppers, he and Jack on their stools, "to waste less time with those who cannot manipulate energy versus those who can." Peppers watched as the teacher entered the room, her arms ladened with a thick stack of paper. The children who stole glances or boldly stared at the two at the back of the class, sat up straight, and focused forward on the woman. She wore a light blue pants suit in accordance with her profession. A blue ribbon held back her brown hair.

"So, what happens to late bloomers like me?"

"How do you know you're a late bloomer?" Peppers turned to Jack.

"I did not know that I might be what you say I am when younger," whispered Jack, watching the teacher rifle through her notes at the desk. He thought she might be pretty, but looked worn out. "Would I have been told that I didn't belong?"

"I don't know," said Peppers. He felt uncomfortable with Jack's constant questions. Nervous hands patted down the black, long-tailed coat with imagined creases.

"Welcome children." The teacher smiled at the class. "My name is Miss Stewart." She paused a moment to write her name on the slate board. The chalk scratched and screeched across the surface. Jack and the other students grimaced. Miss Stewart turned around and dropped the chalk on the desk. "Today will be a short, simple day for you." She picked up the papers on her desk, walked to the head of each row, and handed pages to the first student in every row. "Take one, then pass them back."

The task took moments. Jack did not get a paper. He looked down at his clothing. Compared to the teacher, children, or Peppers it looked decidedly poor. His gray over-sized shirt matched the pants: too big for his frame.

"Please fill out the form and answer the questions as best you can." Miss Stewart walked up and down the aisles, making sure each student had a writing implement. She pulled a small notebook from her jacket pocket and started writing; Jack went ignored. Before completing the walk along the last aisle, several children folded their arms on their desks and rested their heads.

Miss Stewart studied the two at the back of the room for a moment and looked disappointed. She shook her head and muttered something. Jack stared back at her. She returned slowly to the first row of students and started the passage among the desks again.

As she passed Jack, he felt the urge to sleep. He yawned.

"Wait!" hissed Peppers, just loud enough for the teacher to hear. "Do the job they pay you to do."

The teacher had taken several steps up the last row, but stopped and turned.

"I am not a fool, Miss Stewart," said Peppers. "You are being excessive with this subject." Peppers pointed to Jack. He stood up, went to the woman's side, and whispered. "If this is not done per the rules, I will report you."

If looks could kill, Peppers would have dropped to the floor. Miss Stewart raged in a controlled, stiff way: her arms tight at her sides, her hands fisted. She fumed, but returned to her desk without speaking. More children fell asleep at their desks. Some heads hitting the surface with a clunk. Jack's need to nod off faded.

"What exactly is happening?" he asked, confused.

"Self-defense is the earliest measure of ability." Pepper returned to his stool. "This program forces a student to do what they do not want to do: fall asleep. It's simple and safe." Peppers watched Miss Stewart intently. "She used excessive force on you, so you'd fail early." He expected righteous outrage, but Jack simply nodded.

The Snake demanded you do whatever you needed to win and live another day. Jack made no judgement on the woman: now a known enemy. Miss Stewart, to Jack's way of thinking, acted in her own best interest. Civility, right and wrong, had nothing to do with it.

"Thanks," said Jack, turning to Peppers. "You shouldn't have done that." Only civilized people can argue about injustice. To his way of thinking, neither the North nor the South could claim to be civilized.

"What!" gasped Peppers. "I made sure the test was fair and so you move to the higher classes if you are able. We need to know what you can do."

"It doesn't matter, my friend." Jack looked at Peppers and felt a strong connection, a bond between genuine friends who never lie to each other nor hold back the truth. In a different life, he and Peppers would be brothers or the closest of friends.

A week passed with simple projection exercises and more tests. Peppers decidedly avoided any effort to keep the training fair. The training and discovery moved to a higher level at the start of the second week.

"It's basic projection," said Peppers in answer to Jack's

question. "Listen to what she is saying. Stop arguing. There is a point to all of this."

Half of the children, those who succeeded in the week before, filled the same classroom. As instructed, boys and girls stared at their hands. Brows furrowed in the attempt to make visible lines of light connect their fingers. If done right, a spiderweb of light would appear.

"I don't see the point," said Jack. The fine, bright lines appeared almost immediately, but the pain forced him to snuff them out. "Somethin's not right. I can't hold it," he whispered. Not wanting to admit failure, his hands disappeared into his coat pockets.

"Just do it," hissed Peppers. He scanned the class and saw a few children with the filaments of light easily seen.

"I did, damn it." Jack whispered. Something had gone wrong. He wondered if the teacher worked against him again.

"Well…" Peppers raised his hands with fingers spread. "And?"

"It hurt too much. Like my hand might burn away." Jack stared at Peppers, who stepped back shocked.

"I didn't see any light. You're sure it happened and caused the pain?"

"Damn it, Peppers." Jack's anger bubbled over. "I did what she asked. You watch the kids. You missed the lines of torture." He looked away, sick of Peppers' anxious face. "Either believe me when I tell you something or hand me over to the judges as a failure."

"Sorry, Jack." Peppers saw the teacher coming toward them. "I have no question about your abilities and, most important your ability to control them. It has to be visible to everyone else."

"Show me," demanded Miss Stewart. She stood, arms crossed, with her usual stern expression. This nobody would not turn her world upside down. Hatred of every success caused a different pain.

"I will, but for only a brief time. It hurts." Jack pulled out his hands and concentrated.

"You think you are soldier material, slave?" She snorted, then grabbed Jack's hand, looking for trickery. Her timing could not have been worse.

Jack reacted to the unwelcome contact. The web of light glowed for an instant.

"Damn it!" growled Jack, feeling the burning in the bones of his hand.

Stewart refused to accept the truth and paid a price. The energy imparted to her stole away control of her body. She sank to the floor.

"Foolish woman," said Peppers, going to the floor beside her to ease the fall. He placed his hand on her forehead and pulled energy from her overcharged system. "You're getting better at control. I siphoned away enough energy to just about kill her." Standing up, he moved next to Jack. "We should just let her sleep."

"I did what?"

"You didn't kill her, which is an improvement." Peppers went to the front of the class and faced the children. "I am a doctor. Your teacher is fine and will join us in a while. This gives all of you time to practice. Please do so." He smiled at the class, then returned to Jack's side.

"Do we make a break for it or stay put?" asked Jack.

"We stay." Peppers sat on the stool, the teacher at his feet, and said, "We are not criminals. Her testimony will say you tried to kill her. We, however, did not run but sat tight waiting and took care she was not seriously hurt."

Jack nodded, then asked, "What did she mean by soldier material?" Peppers stared at Jack, then looked away. "Later."

That evening in the crowded dining hall over a hot meal, Jack asked Peppers about Miss Stewart and what she said. Jack set down his tray at one long table. Northern students at the other end scampered tripping over themselves to get away from the diseased, low-life southerner. Peppers frowned. Jack laughed, taking a seat.

"She will make a formal complaint," said Peppers, angry at the shunning of his charge. Slowly, he placed his dinner on the table, then took Jack's pewter cup of water and drank as the northerners watched. "I will argue the other side of the matter." He raised the cup in a toast to his countrymen, then sat. "I think you will be allowed to continue."

"You mean, they won't kill me." Jack stuffed a piece of meat into his mouth and chewed appreciatively. He watched as his friend replaced the cup on his tray.

"These fools think you are a pestilence." Peppers shook his head in disgust, then looked at Jack, "No, they won't kill you. Dean Camden is on our side. They may want to turn you to dust, but he will not let that happen." Peppers considered the vegetable dangling from his fork.

"Tell me about the soldier thing that Miss Stewart said."

"Okay," said Peppers, looking worried. "Soldier rated projectors can manipulate a larger amount of energy than someone like me." Peppers pushed his food around on his plate, considering what to reveal. "I am a doctor because I can micro-manage small amounts of energy to get around the body to help people get better. A soldier would simply explode body parts about the room."

"So, I got less control than you, but greater energy at my disposal?"

Peppers looked up from his plate to see his friend's fork

pointing at him. He put down his, picked up his cup, sat back and drank.

"Maybe… but I have not seen that lack of control yet." Peppers could not say with any surety exactly what level of energy manipulator Jack might be. The discovery excited and concerned him. "I guess we will see how the training goes."

"What does the soldier class do?" asked Jack, stuffing his mouth. He chewed, then swallowed. "You're not at war."

"Soldier class energy projectors create the winter lens over the capital. They are powerful and stand guard on our northern border."

"Northern border?" Jack stared at Peppers. "What's going on up there?"

CHAPTER 11

Gracie stood at the open door of her warehouse as the sun, not yet over the horizon, lightened the dark. She held a large mug of coffee and breathed deep the clean, damp air of a new spring day. It would not be long before the usual wet, cloudy mornings gave way to dry, sunny ones. She would not, however, complain about the damp. The day would be warm.

"Good mornin' to ya, Mrs. Hargreaves." The greeting came from an old, bent man passing by on his way to the dockyard. He carried his wooden toolbox by a leather strap over his shoulder.

"Mr. Slythe." Gracie raised her mug. "I am glad to see you."

As a child scrounging the dock for food, she often ended up at Mr. Slythe's work bench. The stacks of large iron tools and the wooden ships under construction towering above amazed the eight-year-old. She remembered a day long ago. It changed everything for her.

"Well, my girl," said a younger Mr. Slythe to Gracie. "I may have a job fer ya. Are ya willin'." The large hammer and wrench clanged together as he tossed them onto the bench. "It ain't easy." He eyed the girl on the burlap bundle. "Might be, no promise here, but I might get some money for ya."

Gracie nodded. She pulled a bit of leather from her pocket and tied back her long, dark hair.

"Here." Mr. Slythe pulled an apple from his pocket and placed in her hand.

"Eat first." He winked at her.

That day she returned home with coins in her pocket and caulking-tar ground into her underclothes, arms, and hair. The clothes and skin cleaned up well enough, but the hair required the barber's sheers. The dress survived, safely abandoned on the burlap. Small arms fit under and around the huge support beams to seal open seams overlooked. Her knees bled, then scabbed over from crawling in and out of the ship's superstructure. It turned out to be steady work and set her on her course of self-reliance that made her a force, twenty years later, to be reckoned with in the Snake.

"How is your family?" asked Gracie, grinning at the memory and proud of that eight-year-old. She had learned some excellent lessons from this man.

"Doing well enough. Thank 'ee." Mr. Slythe stopped and turned to Gracie. "My youngest has done the wise thing at your behest. I am grateful." Mr. Slythe's son agreed to an apprenticeship at Gracie's urging to work in Tom Haggard's shipping office.

"Glad to hear it, Mr. Slythe." Gracie sipped her coffee and noted that the old man looked more haggard than usual. "You feeling alright, sir."

"A bit off my feed," he said, placing his right hand on his stomach. "Nothing to worry on."

"Mr. Slythe," she ordered. "You tell Mr. Cain that I want you to be seen by Miss Waltham. You can't work if you can't eat, sir."

"Thank 'ee, Mrs. Hargreaves." The man bowed to Gracie, turned down the street, and walked to the shipyard.

"Tell the baker," she called after him, "when you finish with Waltham that you need something. Tell him to charge me for it." Gracie raised a hand as Mr. Slythe waved acknowledgement.

A satisfied smile turned up her lips. She ran a good business, but something more. A business savant, already well off, she needed a semblance of civil life in Snakeport regardless of profit. Mr. Slythe and his family ended up on her list of the many she helped to succeed.

Taking one last sip of coffee and scanning the street left to right, her eyes settled on legs outstretched where the rest of the body laid hidden behind a rain barrel. Gracie paid for many eyes to watch and keep her informed. Her informants identified this man as an enemy agent.

"Still spying on you?" asked Tom Haggard as Gracie claimed her desk seat.

"Tom." She shook her head in disbelief. "They are doing exactly what I expect. Is it a feint to take me off guard or are they truly inept? What do you think, Will?"

"He fears you," said Will Biggs. He sat with his elbows supported on the chair arms. His hands, with fingers entwined, rested against his chin. "I sit here trusting Tom's report and my work with you, madam. But… I am not happy with this venture." His hands came away from his face, separated, and dropped to the armrests.

"You saw, Tom?" asked Gracie.

"I saw. Your agent brought us to the slave trade gathering place." Haggard said nothing else. The silence filled the room. Tom stared at Gracie.

"We need," she started, "a new business agreement and…"

"No!" Tom hissed.

Gracie jolted back at Tom's sudden aggression and saw Will unaffected by the outburst, as if he expected it.

"No agreement," demanded Tom, "until these vermin are dead. I saw. I want war on these depraved…" Haggard could not, at first, find the words to state his outrage. He calmed and said, "Kill them, Mrs. Hargreaves. Kill them all."

Tom Haggard brought forth an unexpected well-laid out plan to deal with the issue. At this time of the rolling year, the greatest number of children disappeared. Tom would be at that yearly gathering. Gracie and Will agreed, pledging both wealth and foot soldiers to the cause. Tom and Will left late in the afternoon. The slaver war had begun.

"They got three out there now," said Spunk, showing up after dark, as usual. She slumped into a chair in Gracie's office.

"All Lakeland's men?" asked Gracie, who stood when Spunk entered and gathered glasses and a bottle. Gracie noted the tear streaks on her dirty face. The girl lived in the field now, guiding Haggard, identifying Lakeland's men, or looking for clues to find Jack.

"Yeah. I followed them." Spunk took the offered glass, gulped down the wine, and held it out for more. "Stupid northerners from what I can tell."

"You did well with Tom and Will, showing them the way of things." Gracie smiled and filled the glass.

"Thanks." Spunk sipped the wine. "Any word on Jack?"

"Nothing more. His father betrayed him. Our Jack got hurt, not conscious when they carted him away." Gracie sat.

"We taking down Lakeland?" Spunk changed the subject. Gracie witnessed the struggle as Spunk tried to let Jack go, but finding it hard to do; she focused on the matters at hand which kept her alive.

"Yes, in time." Gracie considered her protégé. Unlike Jack's mother, Spunk never accused her of putting Jack in a position to be taken. The girl simply wanted to have a hand on the hilt of the knife plunged into Lakeland's heart. "He is not Blog, but keeps a step or two ahead in planning. I, we, must be careful."

"Do you think he knows about me?" asked Spunk. She did not want any trouble splashing over onto Nanna and Mini.

"He knows you are with me, but… he is one of those stupid northerners." Gracie finished her drink and poured more. Spunk leaned forward to have her glass topped off. "For some reason, northerners think little of their female citizens."

"Think little of southern anything."

"They got a power we don't," said Gracie. Jack's sculpture

grabbed her attention. "Maybe… just maybe that's about to change." *Jack is not gone, only delayed for a time.* Gracie clung to this belief. She would not tolerate the thought of Jack Fox dead.

* * *

Gracie commanded fifty men at the Downs. They followed her as a matter of faith: rank meant nothing in the southern army. They fell in line behind Haggard's three companies, with Will Bigg's fifty bringing up the rear. The two hundred and fifty men marched in single file, skirting the edge of the swamp. Frogs croaked, birds called, and animals screamed or whined, blocking the sound of the army's approach. The night deepened. Tom Haggard stopped the line and went back to meet with Gracie and Will.

"Okay," Haggard said, drawing a diagram in the dirt with a stick. "My one hundred men will move here, cutting off any escape." He scratched a straight line to the top of the diagram. "You two will line your men up directly opposite and fire, driving them our way."

Gracie and Will nodded their understanding.

"How much time," Gracie asked, "will you need to get into position?"

"The same time, it will take you two to crawl through the swamp and start." Haggard smiled. "Tell your men to move quiet and when they stand, remember to shoot low."

"Good luck, Tom," said Will. They shook hands. Will watched him also shake Gracie's then head off. "We will be well disguised, covered with swamp mud when we stand."

Gracie laughed nervously. "Time to get moving."

One hundred men waded through the murk, the water sometimes waist high.

"If I complain enough, will it get us out of this mess?" asked a man close behind Gracie.

"No," she whispered. "Now shut it and keep your rifle and bullets out of the water." Gracie raised her pistol.

They crawled over thick mud for the final twenty yards, then stopped. Only a few feet of brush hid them from the enemy. The line formed; men knelt, ready for the order.

"Check weapons," ordered Gracie. She waited a minute for the command to pass up and down the line, then looked over to Will, who nodded back. They rose to their feet.

The hundred men stood above the bracken, aimed low, and fired.

The enemy filling their dinner plates from the pots over dozens of fires dropped where they stood. Those who did not catch a bullet fled into the night directly into another hundred-man volley. Will and Gracie's men moved into the open and kept up their fire.

"Bayonets!" echoed from Haggard's side of the field.

"Cease fire! Cease fire!" called out Gracie when she saw Haggard marching into the campsite. She witnessed his companies releasing children from the wagons and summarily executing any slaver still alive. The battle at the Downs ended with every slaver dead, as promised. Lakeland's body was not among them. Five hundred children escaped the cages.

The three leaders came together at the broken slave wagons.

"Well done," said Haggard. "If I may say, you both look better in mud." He laughed.

Will and Gracie looked at each other, grinning.

Five hundred freed boys and girls milled about the camp, happily gobbling up any food offered by their rescuers. They ransacked the bodies for anything of use. Before too long, they let it be known they had no reason to go back to their lives in the Snake. Joining this army, ready to fight, struck these former slaves as a good idea.

Haggard ordered any child over the age of twelve or a height of four feet into the ranks. The rest found use as couriers or sent to whatever home they had. The army tripled in size.

The second battle further west along the Aquitaine went the same way. Surprise won the day. No slaver made it out alive to warn the other groups. Another seven hundred escaped their chains and demanded the right to fight.

The army's numbers increased further, with men and women from the towns and ports of the south picking up their rifles to end the evil trade in their children. What started out as a battle at Snakeport and its immediate environs became a southern call to arms in opposition to northern theft of their children.

Gracie Hargreaves walked the line in full view of the enemy at the third battle close to the mountain country far to the west along the Aquitaine. Wearing brown pants with the legs stuffed into the top of her black leather boots and a dark brown waistcoat over a loose-fitting white linen shirt, she stopped to look at the fortifications. Two hundred yards away, the enemy waited behind thick logs over rifle pits and mounds of dirt. Slaver rifles aimed her way. She worried but showed only confidence to her men, who crouched behind their makeshift defenses of fallen trees, piled rocks, and stacked limbs. If it could stop a bullet, a soldier took cover behind it.

"Get yourself kilt, you will, ma'am," said a young recruit, looking up at her from behind his cross-hatched tree-limb shield.

"Need to know you thick headed farmers and such learnt something 'bout not getting killed." Gracie smiled down on the boy whose clothes might be worn, but his weapons and how best to use them never concerned her. Her pride in the battalion showed in her calm manner. "Name soldier?"

"Yes, ma'am. Hank, ma'am." He and his mates up and down the line, who could hear the exchange, chuckled. They had confidence in their commanding officer; they liked her.

"Where ya from Hank?"

"Out Middleton way, ma'am." Hank rose to his knees, proud that the commander would stop to talk to the likes of him.

"Heard folks out your way are the devil's own fighters."

"Yes, ma'am." Hank went quiet, uncomfortable with Gracie's attention. He pulled his rifle close across his chest and patted it. "Those slavers ain't got no chance, ma'am. No chance at all."

"Good man," said Gracie. Her five hundred men strung out along the edge of a forest prepared to assault strong defenses after crossing an open field. They needed to see a fearless leader willing to die with them if required. She walked on giving and reveling in the comradery of soldiers' insults. The orders to charge into the enemies' rifles would come soon enough.

"Colonel Hargreaves?"

"We're alone, Spunk," said Gracie from her tent. Bent over the barrel-desk, she studied inventory reports on munitions, food, and bandages. Her coat hung on a nail from the tent's center post. Her revolver and knives within easy reach on her cot. "Just Gracie will do."

"The men are with us." stated Spunk.

"Men?" scoffed Gracie. "Men, women, boys, and girls." She studied the pages until satisfied, the pile of supplies supported her troops for this action. Setting them aside, she looked up at her aide. "Yes, their spirit is good."

The coffee pot on the field stove steamed. Gracie got to her feet, grabbed her metal tin and signaled to Spunk to do the same. The strong black coffee helped her stay focused.

"This action will differ from the other two." The colonel returned to her field chair.

"Yes. No surprise. I expect there'll be dead and wounded," said Spunk on her feet, staring into her cup. "Course, we got extra stuff to fix 'em up."

Gracie nodded. She prayed that Tom, who grudgingly accepted the command as General Haggard, had the right strategy. The first two actions against the slavers turned out better than expected.

"A rider is coming, Gracie," said Spunk, setting down her coffee.

The horse charged up to the tent and stopped with the rider, handing a pouch to Spunk.

"With the General's compliments, Colonel Hargreaves should have her men ready to demonstrate when the sun touches the treetops." He tipped his hat in salute when he saw Gracie take the pouch and pull the paper he needed to return. She signed and handed it back.

"Tell General Haggard morale is high. We are ready and able."

The rider nodded, then dashed off to pass on the message.

"Get the sergeants." Gracie pulled the coat from the hook, strapped on the holster, and sheathed the two knives. With a hand raised to block the sun's glare to check its position, she figured the step out onto the field remained a few hours away. "Tell them we are going with my strategy. It might be strange, but maybe it'll save a few." *Maybe we can do more than just demonstrate in front of the enemy.*

"Yes, ma'am." Spunk saluted and left to get the sergeants.

Four hundred men and women, boys and girls, in two lines of two hundred stepped out on the open field with Gracie in the lead on the right. With rifles on their shoulders and Gracie with her revolver in hand, the line moved to within one hundred yards of the enemy's fortifications. She turned her back to the enemy and waved her arms to signal the next action.

Fifty men rolled inch thick, thigh high wheels of wood up to the front line then beyond about fifty yards in front of the enemy. They spun the shields around and crouched behind them while the front line came up, aimed, and fired. The enemy finally responded. Lead whistled high with only a few bullets chipping the wooden cover.

"They're firin' high," called out voices along the line. Laughter erupted.

"Forward," ordered Gracie.

With the shields hefted by leather straps, the soldiers dashed forward again, cutting the distance in half. Those who had reloaded before the order to advance hunkered down behind the shields. Twenty-five on the far right fixed bayonets. The other seventy-five of the front line stood and fired. The slavers aimed more carefully this time. Their barrage tore at the shields. The second line, still at the hundred-yard mark, took aim and let loose a hail of bullets. As the enemy ducked beneath their fortifications, but before they could reload, the twenty-five led by Gracie charged the dirt mounds. They climbed, slipped back, but staggered their way up the loose dirt.

"We got 'em boys!" yelled Gracie as her revolver exploded into the face of a slaver, leveling his rifle at her. In short order, the twenty-five cleared the defenses and cut down the defenders with bullets or bayonets. Replacing the empty cylinder quickly, Gracie reloaded and commanded half of her squad to move further into the trenches to expose the rifle pits.

"Like shooting fish in a barrel, it is," shouted a soldier.

Gracie watched the rest of her command assault the slaver fortifications and take them. She heard the weapons fire in the distance as Haggard made his assault. Nearly five hundred troops rolled up the enemy line, driving the slavers into the waiting arms of Haggard's forces. She halted her advance and waited for word from the commanding officer.

"Go back down the line, Spunk," she commanded. "We will hold here. I want to know about casualties."

"Yes, ma'am." Spunk swung her rifle over her shoulder and trotted back the way she came.

"Mr. Hodges," called Gracie to another sergeant, clearing the rifle pits. "Collect the weapons and ammunition from the enemy."

"Aye, ma'am," he called. "C'mon lads, there's a job to do."

The rifle fire became sporadic not long after, then ended. Gracie stood and walked out of the trenches with a few soldiers, men and women, at her back. They approached tents and wagons of supplies. Hundreds crowded the slave wagons in the distance as soldiers broke the locks and opened the cages.

"Get guards on those supply wagons and start up as many cooking fires as you can." Gracie knew it would not be long until chaos reigned as the freed children fought over any morsels of food they could beg, borrow, or steal. "I want the most recent recruits to go out ahead and start telling those kids what will happen."

"Aye, ma'am," erupted from several men and women close by. The calls for action echoed back and forth across her command. A line of boys, rifles in hand, formed out in front of the wagons; a line of fires started up with pots and pans made ready to feed hundreds; and a line of men moved the supplies from the wagons to the cooks.

"Sergeant?"

Spunk came up to her side.

"Five dead. Ten wounded." Spunk waited for further orders.

"Let's find Haggard," said Gracie, satisfied with what she saw as the former slaves rushed her position. The boys held, and someone brought out tin plates given to each with a spoon if they lined up at the cooking fires. "Find out who ordered those plates to be distributed. We will need more officers soon."

"Yes, ma'am." Spunk made a note in a small pad pulled from her back pocket.

Gracie looked over the field, knowing she would have to provide for another five hundred or a thousand hungry but committed soldiers. *More officers, more guns, more wagons, more of everything to keep a large army in the field,* she thought. *More important, what will we do when the North comes?*

CHAPTER 12

"Yes, yes, exactly," stated a tall, middle-aged man, watching his four pupils force their will on the energy they projected. "Amazing, Mr. Jack. Amazing, indeed." Mr. Willis, his salt and pepper hair cut short and dressed more like Jack than his northern students, taught the more gifted young men and women moving through the early training process. Four participants jumped this way and that about the large open courtyard, sweating mightily to keep their shields facing oncoming assaults as Mr. Willis hoisted projectile after projectile at them.

Jack, still the oldest, tired of whirling about. He encircled himself completely and stood still in the middle of the yard, adding more energy where necessary. Nothing impacted his shielding.

"Stop," called Mr. Willis. "Look at what Mr. Jack has done." He walked from the corner into the center of the courtyard to stand next to Jack. "I want all of you to do the same or get as close as you are able."

After repeated attempts, the task exceeded the other's capabilities.

"Enough," called Mr. Willis. "Tell us, Mr. Jack, how you performed this manipulation."

The three students gathered around Jack, awaiting his insight. Awed by his shield that still shimmered.

"I… I don't know. I just did it," said Jack, embarrassed.

"It does not work that way, Mr. Jack." Mr. Willis crossed his arms, annoyed. "We learn from each other. How did you do it?" Willis commanded.

"I remembered a time… the cold. We had no wood to burn."

Jack stared down at the floor and shuffled his feet, not wanting to describe how poor he lived in Snakeport. "I put on every stitch of clothing I had, then pulled down the sheet that made our one room into two and wrapped it tight around me."

"Interesting," said Mr. Willis, intrigued.

"I just wanted to feel warm. The shielding became my blanket." Jack looked up at the faces, seeing the total lack of comprehension. They had never experienced such deprivation.

"Very good." Mr. Willis waved Dr. Peppers over from his bench under a tree in the yard's corner. "This completes the exercises for the day," he said to his students. "Please consider what you have just heard. What experience might allow you to project a wall of safety about yourself?"

Peppers closed the book he read, marked the page, stood, and walked over. The students, bent at the waist in deference to their teacher, went to gather their belongings and set out for home. Peppers looked at Jack questioningly. *What did you do this time?*

Jack shrugged.

"Is there a problem, Mr. Willis?" asked Peppers.

"No." Willis stared at Jack and said, "You may drop the shield now, Mr. Jack." The effervescent air surrounding Jack disappeared. "Were you aware that it still held?"

"No," said Jack. "Is that wrong?"

"No." Willis turned away from Jack to Peppers and leaned close. "He is much more than a southern oddity." He clapped Peppers on the shoulder. Turning to Jack, he said, "You have a visitor. They wait in the library. Tomorrow, Mr. Jack, more challenges are in store."

"Yes, sir. See you tomorrow." Jack watched Willis cross the yard. "Now what? Another hearing?"

The last hearing before the University's president sent Miss

Stewart back to her classroom but Jack forward to Mr. Willis's class of talented students. After a month with Mr. Willis, who called all his students by Miss or Mister, Jack's talent became clear, and his projecting control grew exponentially.

"To the Library," said Peppers.

"Did you know about this?"

"No."

They walked in silence out of the building down the street to the medical school library. The bright sky and cool weather blessed the town. People crowded around outdoor food booths on the common, waited for the horseless caravans on sidewalks, or absorbed the sun while lying in the green grass. With only a month to go until the final decision on whether he would die or live as a member of the projectors club, Jack enjoyed and took pride in what he could do. What more might be in store clawed at him as he absorbed the training, developed new skills, and discovered on a personal level what it meant to be a projector.

At night, when he could not sleep, the room sparkled with energy. Light from the hallway passed through air lenses of varying thickness and cut to focus light on books Jack devoured. He laughed at Peppers' reaction when the books delivered one day were ready to return the next. Good food, a comfortable place to live, plus training and learning the magic his hands shaped increased Jack's confidence. Undoing the hegemony of the north, though he had no set plan, remained a focus.

"At last," called out an old woman who rose from her chair as Jack and Peppers entered the empty library. The aged man sitting next to her examined both with a stern expression. Pepper's eyes followed the silver-haired women, unbent by time, as she pulled a small flowerpot from a bucket-sized bag, and placed it on the table: a short stem with soft, bristled leaves on either side and a bit of growth showing at the top.

"You haven't forgotten what happened among the trees in the cold?" she asked Jack, ignoring Peppers.

"No, ma'am." Jack recalled the stolen hours gathering wood for Nanna. "How did you know about that?" He came forward, cautious of her silence, and kept a wary eye on the woman while feeling a familiar pull from the small leaves. Without hesitation, his index finger lifted a fragile leaf; it wrapped around the joint. The woman did the same with the other. Instantly, the air around the two became a kaleidoscope of color like stained glass windows folding then unfolding.

"What is happening?" asked Peppers, awed by the sheer power. It looked like time stopped within the ever-changing colors revolving about Jack and the woman who ceased to move. They became statues.

"They are in a place unique to her talent where very few others can go," said the old man. "She calls it the gift from the earth. I appreciate the energy produced," he raised his hand to the riot of color produced, "but…". His logical mind rebelled against his wife's demand for belief in some ephemeral goddess or other.

"She calls it?" Peppers could see the two figures outlined in pinpoints of flashing light. "The earth-gift is a myth?" He turned to the old man. "Who are you? What are you doing here?"

"I am Robert Forrester, and this is," he raised his hand toward the energy display, "my wife, Anna." He dropped his arm and looked at Peppers. "You are?"

"Doctor Peppers and that," Peppers similarly raised his hand showing the two encased, "is Jack Fox." He dropped his arm and asked, "earth-gift myth?"

"Call it whatever your logical mind allows." Robert rose

from the chair. "When they come back to us, they will need a safe place to recover."

"I am sure we will find accommodations," said Peppers, unable to stop staring at the display. "Well, what do we do now?"

"We do nothing but wait. It will likely be some hours before they break the connection." Robert exerted an effort and the doors to the library closed by themselves, sealed against any intrusion. "Tell me, doctor, what has the boy been doing in Hempstead?"

Peppers described all that had happened up to this time, how Jack's abilities rose to military grade. His true power remained a mystery, but his control and insatiable desire to learn astounded the doctor.

"After this," Robert nodded to the vibrant colors exploding around his wife and the boy, "he will be different."

"How?" Peppers demanded. "Will he be more dangerous?"

"He," said Robert, leaning back against the table looking off to the side, "will be a greater power with self-control… I hope." The last two words he whispered. Aloud, he said matter-of-factly, "or dead."

Peppers collapsed into a nearby chair, dumbfounded.

Robert turned to him, patting his pockets as if seeking something. "I have other matters needing my attention while I am here." He found the letter from a friend, picked up his bag, then said, "Recruiting must start immediately."

"Recruiting?" asked Peppers. "Recruit who for what?" The doctor stared at Forrester, confused.

"I apologize, Doctor. Peppers, isn't it?" Robert turned to the doctor. "Well, Doctor Peppers, my wife is determined to change this world, restore it to an earlier, more just time. The boy is an integral part of the effort. He cannot, however, do it alone."

"Jack has little good to say of the North, our current way of life."

"What do you expect with an inflexible, established order?" said Robert. A grin crossed his lips. He had quoted a line from one of his papers. Maybe he felt redeemed or deathly afraid that he might be right. "What, again, is the boy's full name?"

Peppers who stared blindly mumbled, "the blood on the many battlefields." He looked up. "Just Jack Fox."

"Jack Fox," repeated Robert softly. "Well, this Fox will have a tale that must be told when this is all over."

CHAPTER 13

"Prime Minister Dowler is weak, waffling, and lacks confidence," said Edward Sedgwick, the North's Minister of the Interior. "He is, in fact, exactly what we wanted." The rotund minister stood at the small counter, pouring himself a snifter of brandy. Late morning sun poured into the cavernous office through the floor to ceiling open windows. White sheer curtains ruffled in the cool breeze. Just under six feet tall, Sedgwick's shaggy white hair highlighted the ruddy skin of his face. He lifted an empty glass inviting his friend to share his brandy.

Daily doses of alcohol became part of Sedgwick's routine later in life, after his wife's death ten years earlier. Her loss left a hole too big in his soul. His superior ability to manipulate energy proved useless. He numbed the pain with drink. The game of politics gave him purpose. The riskier the better, where his abilities came to bear on outcomes that pushed all other considerations to the side. Brandy controlled the sudden feelings of anguish. Life and death politics took it away completely.

"Did you inform him of this?" asked the Minister of War, Rupert Higgins, sarcastically. He waved off the proffered drink so early in the day. "The fool thinks he is politically astute. He is, in fact, a lazy, self-indulgent fool who will lead us where, Edward?" Where Sedgwick proved soft, Higgins held like a rock. He possessed jet black hair and goatee, a soldier's physique he worked hard to keep, and years of field experience sparring with the barbaric people on the northern border.

Higgins, friends with Sedgwick since they trained together as young officers, also commanded superior energy abilities. He gave up on family like his friend when death in childbirth took his wife and child. He had cats instead of brandy or whiskey:

four torturing his furniture. When not pampering his furry companions, he played the power game to the fullest for the same reasons as his friend. He and Sedgewick, brothers on the battlefield, shared fate's indifference and chaos in their personal lives: they had each other's back.

"He leads nowhere," laughed Sedgwick. "He will follow whatever course we set him on. All we have to do is make sure we or our supporters are the last to whisper into his ear." He returned to his desk and sipped his drink. "The good Colonel Martell has been waiting outside. We should get his report."

"Yes, yes." Higgins waved his hand impatiently since no preparations started for the coming clash with the peoples on their northern border. "I need more resources, Edward. The Colonel needs more recruits. You know what we are facing up there."

"Let's hear it from the horse's mouth, shall we?" Sedgwick waved his hand to the armed man at attention by the gold gilded door. "Corporal!"

The tall door opened, the Colonel's name echoed down the hall. A tall, slender man with graying hair strode down the carpet to the minister's desk. His uniform gleamed; his military short hair and clean-shaven face highlighted his preference for military precision. The intelligence officer, hat cradled in his left arm with eyes pointed at a spot on the far wall, saluted the ministers, and waited.

"Please, Colonel," said Sedgwick, "take a seat." He finished the brandy in one gulp. "Your report."

"The greatest short-term concern is to our south," said Martell.

"South?" Higgins shot forward, surprised by the news.

"The supply of workers from the south has stopped," said the Colonel.

"Details, Martell if you will," commanded Sedgwick, considering his empty brandy glass. Considering this new twist and its potential impact on his plans, he rose from his chair and doubled the pour of brandy. "When was this item a known quantity?"

"Confirmed late last night, sir." The officer opened his coat and pulled several folded sheets from an inside pocket. "A force of southerners has killed their fellows involved with the gathering of workers for our needs. There are fewer replacements for the gold mines and the fields producing our food supply. We are not in any immediate danger, but if left unaddressed, there will be shortages."

Sedgwick returned to his desk, sat back, swirled the brown liquid, and stared into the glass. The silence stretched. Funny, he thought, how we call the children delivered into slavery workers. Semantics always made the immoral more palatable. "So, the rate of loss of workers in the mines and fields continues unchanged?" By loss, he meant the number of dead from the hard labor and dangerous conditions.

"No change."

Sedgwick nodded. "How are our recruiting numbers?"

"Soldier-quality boys continue to be a problem." Martell leaned forward and set the papers down on the minister's desk unfolded. "We have enough for now to cover one front. Probably not two if the South moves against us."

"You need a live field-training exercise, Colonel. I am sure you agree, Minister Higgins?" Sedgewick placed his drink on the desk and waited for a response.

"I do. Field experience is badly needed," said Higgins. Both ministers created commissions to study the decreasing number and strength of energy manipulators in the general population. Both commissions started with the published work of Robert and Anna Forrester from thirty years ago. The latest output on the subject recommended politically unpalatable answers to the question. Nothing from these commissions became public.

"If, Colonel, you send, say, fifty soldiers, a mix of veterans and new recruits, plus whatever support persons you need to remove this southern nuisance, would our northern border be in jeopardy?"

"Not a significant draw down. Asking for five hundred would have required planning and options for dealing with a surprise attack along the northern front."

"Ha!" laughed Sedgwick. No one considered any barbarian assault against their northern border a surprise. Their northern enemies did nothing quietly: horns blaring, drums beating, hours of drinking to build up courage, then a crazed all-out assault. "Prepare your troops. They need to try out their projection defenses and assaults in an actual battle. This southern rabble needs to be reminded why they should not be a bother to their betters."

"Yes, minister," said Martell.

"Now," added Higgins, "what has happened in Hempstead, if anything? I refer to the Forrester's doings."

"There is a minor eruption over some southerner having our abilities." Colonel Martell turned to Higgins. "My spies have reported nothing of interest beyond the usual college bombast over something out of the ordinary. It is likely all smoke and mirrors. As for Robert Forrester, there is nothing of consequence. He received a pass to study whatever at the college."

"This 'whatever' being what exactly?" Higgins caught Sedgewick's eye. "He has a history of being a troublemaker."

"No reports of consequence, sir."

"Monitor Forrester, Colonel." Minister Sedgewick sipped his brandy. "In his time, he caused more than a few political headaches, shall we say."

"When can you move against the South, Colonel?" asked Sedgwick.

"A few weeks of practice and…" Martell stopped and focused on his boots.

"Something else, Colonel?" Sedgwick did not tolerate hemming and hawing very well.

"We will need weeks to teach our boys how to ride horses, Minister."

"Horses?"

"Our vehicles will not pass on southern roads or through rough terrain," said Higgins. "Horse travel is the only way to move swiftly in that country."

"Ah," nodded Sedgwick. "So, in a month, you will be ready."

"Yes, sir," confirmed Martell.

"You will have the necessary funds to do what needs to be done, Colonel." Sedgwick winked at Higgins. "Which is why my good friend, the Minister of War, insisted on joining today's meeting." Sedgwick raised his glass to Higgins and finished it. Silence filled the room until the snifter hit the desktop.

"Then, gentlemen," said the Minister of the Interior, "we are finished."

Sedgwick remained at his desk after the meeting ended. He took a deep breath, released it slowly, and allowed the wave of silence to carry his thoughts where it would. Sara's face, smiling, surprised by his unexpected return from the front, a happy memory, found its way around the politics of the moment. Her hands had been kneading dough. Flour dusted her dark hair, arms, and clothes. A cloud of it puffed into the air when she ran into his arms; his major's uniform patterned with white splotches when they broke apart.

"Edward," she whispered, wonderfully happy to see him. He

heard her whisper clearly, like she stood next to him. Sedgwick choked and cut off the moment from twenty years ago. It hurt too much.

Pulling himself out of his seat, he went for a refill. As the liquor poured, the minister glanced at the many framed awards and accolades that covered the wall. The small, plain paper, half hidden by the bottles, attracted his attention.

"Damn!" yelled Sedgwick when the glass overflowed. He slapped the cork back in place, shoved the bottle into its slot, and using a towel, gathered up the spill. He leaned over the glass after tossing the towel aside to sip enough to allow him to return to his desk without leaving a trail of drips on the floor. Without thinking, he had pulled the plain commendation from the wall.

Once again in his chair, his wife's memory slid beneath the turbulent waters of recent matters as its partner bubbled up: this new memory fashioned the key to his and Higgins' success.

Lieutenant Howard Dowler, never comfortable in his own skin and much less willing to seek help or companionship among his fellow officers, had orders. A far north village needed to be cleared: move the population to an internment camp. A simple task, thought Major Sedgwick, who made some false assumptions: Dowler would research the village in question, read the reports, understand the goal, and not be a total moron. Dowler did none of these things.

The population cleared from their homes milled about in the town square. Women and children with a few old men eyed Dowler and his men suspiciously. To the Lieutenant's way of thinking, the order to clear meant kill.

As the soldier's shielding weakened to allow an attack by energy projection, crossbow bolts came from three sides. Shields snapped back to full energy. The people in the square attacked their murderers with knives. Civilians died with their weapon's hilt deep in their enemy's chests.

"Give the order to pull back. Our position is not tenable!" yelled the platoon sergeant. He watched exasperated as Lieutenant Dowler froze. "There is no value to this ground. Give the order!"

"This is not my fault," stated Dowler, aghast at the bodies of his men bleeding out. "I had orders…"

"Screw the orders! Pull back!" Three feathered arrows disturbed the air close to the sergeant's head. A fourth struck Dowler in the shoulder, knocking him off his feet. Confused and scared, he had not maintained his shield strength.

The sergeant immediately took command and called for the remaining men to withdraw. The attack strengthened, but the platoon escaped without further casualties because of the sergeant's quick assessment.

Major Sedgwick took the sergeant's report on what had happened that night.

"You dragged the lieutenant to safety, saving his life?"

"Yes, sir, I did." The man hesitated for a second, then added, "He whined about the pain the whole way and cursed me for being a coward in the face of the enemy. I am thinking I should have just left him… sir."

The major scanned the papers, witness reports, on his desk all confirming the sergeant's story. There would be no politics undermining his command. He ignored the man's last comment and stood, saying, "Thank you, sergeant. You may attend to your regular duties." Sedgwick returned the non-com's salute.

The rage of politics took over the whole situation. Dowler, based on the many witnesses, had acted in a manner unbecoming of an officer. The general officers should order a court marshaled. Family connections, however, would overcome the culture of the military.

Major Sedgwick had then made a face-to-face report to Colonel Higgins on the issue and its likely ramifications on the army.

"Major, I appreciate the clarity with which you see this episode." Higgins had said, pulling papers from the drawer of his desk. "They will honorably discharge the errant lieutenant into his caring family's arms. The army will be better off, and the government will have no complaints."

Months later, the commendation in its simple frame had arrived along with a furlough that took the Major home to his wife's smile.

Sedgwick let the reward for making the correct political move drop on his desk and drank. He and Higgins both retired from the army as general officers ten years later. Dowler suckling at his family's bosom played at politics with success during that decade.

The Minister of the Interior smiled, thinking of how he and Higgins recruited Dowler.

"You are ours, you weakling, you pandering sonofabitch."

CHAPTER 14

"He has not recovered," said Robert Forrester to his wife. Her condition concerned him. The dark circles under her eyes and the unsteadiness when she had tried to stand were not normal. Worried, he looked her over as she sat up in bed among the embroidered pillows in their apartment.

Anna had been transported to the Forrester rooms. Neither she nor Jack would recover before the library opened to the public. Peppers arranged for Jack to be hauled back to his room in the medical school.

"Something," Anna started in a low voice. Her movements and gestures, as if she pushed against an opposing force, came slow. She swallowed, grimacing as though fighting off a swollen, sore throat. "Something happened beyond my awareness."

Robert leaned in closer. "What does that mean, Anna?"

"It means, my dear unbeliever," Anna smiled and caressed Robert's cheek, "that she came to us."

"Who?" Robert took her hand and cradled it in both of his. In his mind, he answered his own question. He wanted proof, not metaphysics.

"I cannot say that she spoke to me." She looked away at the open windows at the bright blue sky; a white cloud crawled across the window. "I, it would seem, acted as the bridge. She wanted the boy. I must talk to him as soon as possible."

"Yes, yes," said Robert. "You will as soon as the boy regains consciousness."

"I think you might have told me, but I forget," continued Anna, "how long has it been since we gathered in the library?"

"Five days, my dear. The energy radiation ended abruptly, the two of you collapsed, and the plant withered." Robert massaged her hand, his brow furrowed with concern.

"Almost a week," sighed Anna. "Does the boy look like me, done in?" "No. He flounders and flops in his bed doing battle with himself, or so it seems. He cries out every so often." With no food or water for days, the boy's stamina amazed Robert. At least Anna drank when a cup touched her lips. All attempts failed to supply the boy with sustenance.

"Robert, I saw him, really saw him," said Anna, turning to her husband. "The anger that boy carries is beyond our experience. The pain…" She stared in silence for a moment. "Of course, she will either help him or not. We will have to see." Anna looked up at Robert.

"So, you think…" started Robert, shaking his head, unable to accept Anna's tendency to bring mysticism into their frame of reference.

"The earth, Robert," she grinned beatifically, "through a glorious little plant, the earth met us."

As Anna made her pronouncement, Peppers stood among a team of assistants assigned to help the doctor with his only patient. They focused on the door to Jack's room fifty feet away at the end of the hall and spoke in whispers, as if keeping vigil at a deathbed. Peppers, his friend in bed down the hall crying out with sudden flurries of air punches and sobbing, realized that Jack walked in a different world.

The sudden mighty crash and subsequent cracks in the wall and ceiling of the corridor startled the medical experts in the hall. Plaster rained down with chunks of wall or ceiling falling on the men. They hunkered down with hands over their heads. More mighty hammer blows rocked the building. Shouts and complaints screamed from tenants below and echoed along the empty hallways. When it felt like the entire building would soon come undone, it stopped.

Peppers swiped the white dust off his clothes and out of his hair as he approached his patient's door. Stepping around the debris, he grasped the doorknob. The door swung open easily. Peppers stared in disbelief.

"You're," he choked, clearing his throat of plaster, "up?"

"I'm leaving, Peppers." Jack sat up straight in his chair surrounded by a few bags holding his accumulated belongings from his time in the North. The room showed no damage: the bed made; many bottles and glasses and plates of day-old food and drink gone; no stink of an unwashed body in a sick bed assaulted the nostrils.

"Leaving?" Peppers, in shock, could only repeat Jack's words.

"Right now! And you're coming along," stated Jack. He grinned ear-to-ear. "I have a few patients for you to see down south."

"Jack, we can't just go. They'll stop us for sure."

"Send a message through one of your men in the hallway to Anna Forrester." Jack ignored Pepper's fear of capture. "Tell her I've gone home."

"Do what…?" Peppers put his hand to his forehead, placing his other at his back like an old man forced to move his crippled body hastily to escape a burning house.

"Now, Peppers, now." Jack stood, picked up his bags, and stepped into the hall. He considered the mess. Twisting his head in a circular path left shoulder to the right, the cracks and chips reversed their path. Plaster rained up. The larger pieces jumped to their original positions. The house and all souls within found unexpected healing in a matter of seconds. "Now, Doctor Claymore Peppers!"

Peppers ran after Jack with hastily packed clothes and

belongings. Shirt arms and socks dangled out of the bags. When he caught up with him near the library, he expressed his reservations about their plan.

"We are both dead, which I assume you understand, if we must escape on foot." Peppers huffed and puffed, trying to catch his breath. "How exactly do we get out of here… safely?"

"In one of those," said Jack as they turned the corner and looked out over a field of vehicles. The size varied from bus-type to a single-seater.

"I can drive, maybe…" Peppers never needed to be a proficient driver living in cities his whole life. Nevertheless, he knew the basics. "How do we power it?"

"You steer. I power." Jack strode down the grassy knoll and walked down the rows searching for the right vehicle. "This will do." He patted a gleaming, obviously new, four-seater painted a forest green. "Load up and get in."

With their belongings jammed across the two back seats, Peppers behind the wheel, and Jack riding shotgun, they stalled. The "how" of road travel was not readily obvious.

"Well…" said Peppers, his white-knuckled fingers grasping the steering wheel. "Make it go." He stopped being stunned by his partner's sudden increased abilities. Circumstances demanded that he accept the new reality: go with the flow.

Jack sat quietly, considering his options. He had hoped the way these things worked would be apparent. He smacked his head, trying to loosen up a few pebbles of inspiration to solve the problem. Pulling or lifting the metal contraption into operation would consume a huge amount of energy. There had to be an easier way.

What now seemed a lifetime ago, he and Spunk leaned against a wagon full of firewood. Kissing popped into his head.

They broke apart, breathless and committed to each other.

Thereafter, the wagon rolled easily down the hill to Nanna's place as he and Spunk kept it from tipping on the rough path into town. Downhill.

The vehicle started forward slowly. Peppers applied the brake, looked over at Jack, who pointed forward. He eased off the pedal, and they pulled out of the parking space. With a few minutes' practice, in the field of carriages, both Peppers and Jack got the hang of their separate tasks.

"You have a map, right?" asked Jack.

"Yeah, in the back seat." It took them a long time, squabbling like two cantankerous old men, sure the other should have done a better packing job.

He and Peppers pulled into the remote clinic yard in the early evening. The current resident doctor welcomed his predecessor and his companion without alarm. The long trail in a four-passenger horseless vehicle from Hempstead to the clinic close to the river marking the border took ten hours. Jack had to be helped from the passenger seat. The effort to keep them moving forward exhausted his energy. He fell asleep as soon as he collapsed onto a cot.

Dawn remained some hours away. Only one day had passed since Jack and Pepper's left Hempstead. With four hours of sleep, Jack left a snoring Peppers to walk around the remote clinic where he first arrived months ago, barely alive. Slowly, his fingers ran over the examining table. Every drawer had to be searched in what had been Pepper's desk. No memory of this place remained, only a vague connection: a reaching out to his psyche. He felt driven, like an itch he could not scratch. It made him crazy.

Jack smiled as he stared out of the examining room's window into the courtyard and almost laughed out loud, remembering their griping over the map. A slavers wagon with a broken wheel leaned to one side in the far corner. The wagon's thick cage cross pieces touched something in his memory.

Is he dead? Move him. Is he dead? A girl's voice. Peppers said a girl named him as the slavers took her away. *Is he dead?* Maybe this pricked him into wakefulness and pushed him to search the clinic.

Jack's forehead rested against the glass. He closed his eyes.

"What is it?" Peppers rubbed his eyes and yawned.

"Trying to remember this place," said Jack.

"You showed up unconscious and left the same way," said Peppers. "What's there to remember?"

"The girl, I guess." Jack turned to Peppers, who nodded, remembering her.

"Did I tell you about the large transports rumbling through the night before we arrived?" asked Peppers hastily. He scratched his stomach and turned toward the kitchen. "I must find something to eat."

"No. Transporting what?"

"The resident recognized them as military." Peppers walked away to the kitchen, his stomach grumbling. Jack followed.

"Military?" Jack wanted to smash the glass bottle of milk Peppers found in the icebox as he gulped. Controlling his frustration, he hissed, "What made him think they were military?"

"Umm," said Peppers slowly. "He recognized the uniforms. He did a stint on the northern border." Peppers put the bottle back. He crossed his arms and said, "What? They had no interest in finding us. At least not with five troop carriers."

"Five! How many men?"

"That's what he said," shrugged Peppers. "Maybe fifty soldiers heading south."

"How many times," said Jack slowly, "did something like this happen when you practiced here?"

"Never," said Peppers, running his fingers through his unruly hair. "So… you think something is happening?"

"Nothing good." Jack left the kitchen calling, "Pack up. We leave as soon as we can."

"Mind if I eat?" yelled Peppers. He looked around the kitchen for a lamp. "A little daylight wouldn't hurt either, ya know!"

Two hours later, the carriage rolled up to the bridge. In the backseat, a large box of medical supplies sat in one seat. Jack expected to find the southern dead and wounded in desperate need of any help available.

"Okay," said Peppers, staring at the bridge and looking concerned at the river roaring around the bridge pillars. "What do we do? Is it safe, you think?"

"It's strong enough for this vehicle, which doesn't weigh all that much more than horses and a wagon." Jack noticed that the northern forces left their larger transports on the north side of the Aquitaine.

"Based on the piles of manure, they switched to horses," said Jack.

Peppers nodded and, with great caution, moved onto the bridge's wooden planking.

"You sure about this?" he asked.

"Yep," assured Jack. "Let's get across."

The bridge timbers creaked, and some platform boards cracked, but they got across safely. They kept to the road, but their progress slowed. The dry surface made the ruts and holes easier to see. Jack braced himself, his arm outstretched to keep from being thrown forward against the windshield. The road passed through a forest of massive trees which ended abruptly on a large, open field. In a distant corner where the thick forest started up again, they saw tents.

"Let's check it out," said Jack. "Leave the vehicle here."

They stepped out and approached the encampment. The air shimmered slightly with their defenses up.

Eyes high in the trees watched with great interest as two northerners, manipulating energy, moved toward the battlefield.

CHAPTER 15

The fire's flames burned high with sparks escaping into the night sky. Tom Haggard and his officers sitting on logs shared coffee from the large pot. The gathering was unusually subdued. Some stared into the fire, others stirred the dirt at their feet with a stick, and still others focused on the uncountable stars.

Haggard's first comments deflated a few egos. They had been lucky in their three engagements. Their luck, however, would change with an invasion from the North to stop the effort to end the child slave trade.

"They will come," stated Haggard, "we cannot stand against them."

"Sir," asked one of his younger officers named Smithers, "how can we lose? We are near five thousand strong now. Well-armed men, women, boys and girls ready to fight."

Haggard smiled kindly at the young man. "You are an excellent leader, Smithers, but what do you know of our battles a hundred years ago?"

"Little, sir," admitted the young man. "But aren't the northerners equally unprepared?"

"No," stated Haggard. "Do you think this is the first attempt to end the slave trade?" The General placed his coffee on the ground and stood. "Thirty years ago, four Northern soldiers walked into a camp of two hundred well-armed men and killed them all in seconds. The need for firewood put me and a few others in the forest out of harm's way."

"Tom," spoke Gracie, "I have heard the stories. A hundred of them would be a match for ten thousand well-armed men." She got to her feet. "What I know for certain is the unbridled arrogance of the northern men. Remember our business transactions. We are less than the dirt beneath their feet."

"Your point, Gracie?"

"They will come on us like we are too stupid to defend ourselves. They will use the known strategies, but their arrogance might give us an opening."

"You agree with young Smithers here?" asked Haggard, surprised. He reached down for his cup and tossed the remains into the fire.

"In part," said Gracie, so all heard her clearly, "and we watch them closely once they enter our territory. If they believe they are untouchable, then they will make mistakes. We will need smaller, quick attack groups armed only with blades."

"Still high risk but more practicable and… worth consideration." Haggard got to his feet. "We are done for now." He walked away from the fire toward his tent. "Gracie, a word if you will."

She followed him and just outside of his tent; he turned.

"I appreciate your thinking and level of detail. We are now a sizable army. How are your provisions? How long can you keep your regiment in the field?" Haggard turned and went to the field desk, picking up a pile of paper.

"I have enough money to feed my troops for another week, possibly two if we ration," responded Gracie. "There is enough of everything else."

"We need to send out patrols to gather supplies. It is not clear when the North will invade." Flipping through the reports, he stopped at one of greater interest. "It seems that Lakeland's holdings extended beyond the Snake. We will gather those and share them among our five regiments. Hold out as long as you can, and I will resupply you."

"I would think, Tom, we will see northern soldiers back on

southern soil soon," suggested Gracie. "After that, depending on what happens, we will be hard put to keep our forces together, especially when the food runs out."

"Agreed." Haggard sat at his desk. "Work with Smithers and Will Biggs on the patrols. We need to know if they have any weaknesses."

"Yes, sir. We will outfit our patrols with horses, so they can cover a wider range swiftly," said Gracie.

"One other thing." Haggard set down the paper and looked at Gracie, frowning. "Your shield maneuver, although effective, will not be a workable solution with an experienced force, which I expect we will see from now on."

"Yes, Tom," nodded Gracie, "I agree. A little more courage on the slavers' side, and it might not have allowed us to get up over the wall."

"Good. Nothing more to be said." Haggard reached into a bag next to the desk and pulled out a bottle. "Just maybe a miracle will happen, and we won't face annihilation."

Gracie saluted her superior, pivoted on her heel, and walked away before Haggard could invite her to share a drink. She needed action. Miracles had to be made by human hands in the South.

The invasion came sooner than Gracie expected. On receiving the reports of enemy movement across the bridge, she ordered Spunk and troopers from her command to move on the enemy. The plan required courage and decisions bordering on strategic art. Luck played a heavy hand in deciding the outcome. Gracie would ask for forgiveness, opting to avoid requesting permission if the action ended in her troopers' deaths.

* * *

As Jack Fox considered the broken-down wagon at the remote clinic and Gracie paced back and forth unable to sleep, eleven soldiers, dressed in northern light blue, entered the northerner's campsite coming from the forest through the line of tethered horses on the north side of the camp. A few sergeants moved about in the dark, preparing to rouse the troops. They paid little attention to what they recognized as the younger, newest recruits who had trouble sleeping through the night and went to the trees to relieve their bladders or vomit their dinners. They failed to recognize the four females in the group.

These sergeants died quietly; the blades sliced open arteries just below the ear. Frozen features captured their total surprise. The officers slept soundly in their larger tents, hearing nothing. The eleven regrouped around the fire burning low near the center of the camp.

"Remember, any of these dung eating djinn can kill all of us with a thought," whispered Spunk, squatting next to a body. She wiped her knife on the dead soldier's pants leg. "Don't think, just kill." She looked every trooper in the eye. "Be back here quick, then we set the explosives." Groups of two walked calmly to the larger tents and did their work among the officers. With the sergeants and officers out of commission, they regrouped, then laid out the tubes of powder and priming them with fuses. They lit their slow burning tapers to ignite the fuses from the burning campfire.

"Where's Tanner and Frank?" asked Spunk. The others looked at her blankly. "Shit," she hissed, "We got a live projector." She examined the explosives, then commanded, "Short fuse four and ten second fuses on the other twenty. Sal and Digger come with me. We got to find that tent fast. The rest of you spread out among the small tents and when you hear the first blast, light your fuses and toss the bombs, then get the hell into the forest."

Seconds later, Spunk felt a pull on her jacket and looked back.

"That's the one," whispered Digger, pointing. "I saw 'em take that one."

"I want a charge on either side of the tent. I'll drop two in front. We light them together, then run for the trees."

Time slowed for Spunk as the three of them stood in position, then lit the fuses. The tubes fell as if falling through molasses. As she turned, a bloody hand pulled back the tent flap, and an energy bolt shot out into the graying sky. Spunk ran. Sal and Digger dashed ahead to the right. A wall of searing energy chased them. The explosives detonated, lifted Spunk off her feet and threw her to the left. It saved her from the enemy officer's dying effort. She rose to her feet unsteadily, her uniform singed and smoking. Her ears rang as her other troopers gathered her up, pushing her forward. The dash to safety slowed as one of her men leaned over and grabbed a jacket collar, heaving a body up off the ground. He stopped long enough to hoist him over his shoulder, allowing the cauterized stump of a right arm to dangle, then continued on. The white dust fell snow-like on the morning air, forming a mound. Spunk wondered which soldier got cremated by the energy wall. No one looked back as a sequence of twenty explosions rocked the camp.

When the dying officer's tent exploded into a million pieces, flames burst out, and set the line of officers' tents ablaze. Chaos erupted. When the twenty other charges went off, many northern recruits died in their bunks or pulling on their boots.

Spunk's team melted into the surrounding forest, then stopped to catch their breaths and observe the enemy.

The sky lightened as the terrorized, inexperienced soldiers either froze, crouching with tears streaking their cheeks or shot energy in all directions cursing the cowardly southerners. The bursts of concentrated light killed fellow northern soldiers not fast enough to get out of the way. Finally, the survivors ran north, each man for himself.

"Three dead, one wounded," said Spunk, taking a moment to write in her notebook. She listed their names. *About twenty enemies turned and ran. The others are dead.* She snapped the notebook closed and slid it into her jacket pocket. Closing her eyes tight, she held back her tears and controlled the scream, wanting to burst out.

"Grab whatever has value. Gather as many of their scattered horses as you can." ordered Spunk calmly. "Get out of these uniforms and return to our lines. Be quick about it." She stepped from cover and waved her arms, signaling to the scouts in the trees around the site. Several young boys and girls dropped to the ground and joined the others hauling valuables. Others remained at their posts. An eerie silence owned the battlefield.

* * *

"The fools let them get in close," said Jack, stepping around the thick pools of dried blood. "No pickets, no fence, no sentries." He shook his head at the stupidity.

"I… I never…" Peppers grabbed his stomach and heaved for the third time.

"You'll have to get used to it, Claymore." Jack went inside one of the larger charred tents. *Fast, clean, no hesitation.* Back outside, Peppers sat on a log looking desperate, unable to process the level of killing. Jack joined him.

"C'mon, let's get back to the carriage and move on," said Jack, helping Peppers to his feet. When seated and wheels rolling, Jack said, "they have been watching us."

"What!" yelled Peppers, hitting the brake. "Those killers!"

"Peppers?" Jack turned to him slowly. "What do you think the northerners intended?"

"Yes, yes… but…" Peppers knew the bodies could have been southern boys; he wanted, however, to argue some point about northern honor in battle. Facing forward and lifting his foot off the brake, he said, "Let's just go."

The string of children, boys and girls, blocking the road a mile into the forest, stopped them.

"Well," said Jack, taking a deep breath and letting it out. "This is where I die or go home. You stay, I'm going to talk."

"Our funeral, I guess," said Peppers. "I assume you will go with shields down?" He looked at Jack. "I really don't want to discover what it feels like to get shot."

Jack opened the door, stepped out, and walked up to the children. He smiled, signaling thumbs up to Peppers since the many rifles aimed at him did not fire.

"I need to talk to someone older. Would one of you let them know?"

Five persons dressed in brown with either revolvers or rifles aimed at Jack stepped from cover: two to the left and three to the right. Jack faced the three to the right. They came close.

One rifleman lowered his weapon. He studied what he at first took to be a northerner. Tilting his head left, then right to get a good look, his thumb eased the weapon's trigger against the cap.

"Well, I'll be damned." He smiled. Jack smiled back, sure he had seen this soldier before. "Ya always was good in a fight with us quarry boys, eh Jack?" Planting the rifle stock on the ground, he leaned on it, then signaled the others to put down their weapons.

Jack remembered in a flash. He was the guy holding Mini in the alley who had tried to knife him so long ago.

The soldier called out loud enough for the other hundred soldiers ready to pour lead into the enemy to hear, "What we have here, ladies and gents of the Quarry Company, is Jack Fox!"

CHAPTER 16

"I had me a fine dream," whispered Nanna, stretched out in her chair in the house across from the graveyard. She patted Spunk's hand. "I heard our Jack and maybe saw his face, though I'm not so sure a that." Still in the many layers of clothes in the summer's heat and armed, as always, she looked up at her granddaughter, who grinned then looked over her shoulder. Jack stepped forward, then went to his knees.

"Can't be." Nanna's eyes grew huge. Her hands shot out and cupped his face, then went to his shoulders, making sure she could trust her senses. "The slavers? That poor excuse of a father? How?" A tear escaped from the corner of her eye. She reached out and demanded Jack to hug her.

"I've come home, Nanna. It's a long story which I will tell, but first I want you to meet my friend." Jack pulled back and waved Peppers forward. "He's a doctor, Nanna. He's going to help if you let him."

"No good doctor in the Snake." She eyed the stranger suspiciously as he came close. Without thinking, her right hand wrapped around the handle of the pistol beneath the covers.

"To be honest with you," started Peppers, "I'm from up north."

Nanna shot a questioning look to Jack, then Spunk.

"He's on our side, Nanna," said Spunk. "He's djinn, grandma."

"Well," said Peppers, "if I am to help you, madam, I need your name. I do not think I know you well enough to call you Nanna." He reached out and placed his middle finger on her wrist, checking her pulse.

"Congress be my married name," she said, staring at his hand, startled as it moved from her wrist to her legs, feeling her ankles through the blanket. "Cynthia be my first."

"Mrs. Congress, I need to examine you."

"What be your name, doc?" She grabbed the shawl that fell away when she hugged Jack and pulled it close.

"Doctor Peppers."

"First name, doc." She pulled the revolver from its hiding place and handed it to Spunk. "I think what you're gonna do puts us on first name callin'. Don't ya think?"

"Claymore, though I don't much care for it."

"Then I will call you Clay," said Nanna. She pushed herself up in the chair. "A happy memory to me," she nodded, "a boy called Clay."

"If Cynthia and I might have some time alone?" asked Peppers.

Jack gently pulled Spunk toward the kitchen. "Where's Mini?"

"She's over at Gracie's stitching uniforms and such for the war effort. Your ma is there too." Spunk leaned against Jack, wanting to hold on and never let him go.

"Oh, my!" called out Nanna from the other room.

"When will Gracie be there?" asked Jack.

"In an hour, most of Haggard's officers will be there, ready to hear what you have to say." Spunk looked back, wondering if the northern doctor could do any good. She put the revolver on the counter next to the sink.

"Let's go. Peppers needs time to do his job." They left the house, heading to Gracie's warehouse.

Jack and Spunk stepped out of the summer's heat into Gracie's place. The emptiness of the floor and shelves surprised Jack. Tables lined the far wall piled high with bolts of brown or tan cloth. Half-finished and finished pants, coats, socks, and other clothing lay folded ready for pickup. Near the office, an older woman and girl sewed pants' seams. Mini looked up as Jack approached. Her mouth hung open a second in disbelief, then she sprang from her seat and crashed into him, throwing her arms about his waist.

"I'm back," laughed Jack, delighted. He lifted her into a bear hug.

Mini crushed his neck, holding tight. After a moment, she loosened her headlock and leaned back. Her hand cupped Jack's cheek. The touch felt rough against his skin.

"I missed you too." Jack dropped her to the floor. Taking her hands, he examined her fingers. Calluses covered every finger pad. Jack stepped back when Mini pulled her hands away. "You've been working hard. Nothin' here to feel bad about."

Mini smiled but crossed her arms, hiding her hands. A moment later, she returned to her stitching, signaling Jack and Spunk to follow.

Jack stood next to the older woman, who never stopped pushing the threaded needle as Mini jumped to welcome him. He waited patiently for her to stop and decide to respond to her lost son.

"I'm trying to be a help," said Lilly Fox. She quickly looked up, then back to her sewing. Lilly studied a stitch intently.

"I can see," said Jack, feeling a deep sorrow for what might have been. His mother wore a sleeveless shift. The skin of her arms covered mostly bone, the muscles used mostly to tip the bottle and lift the cup. He thought she looked much older, like her life force bled away into some invisible, cosmic bucket.

"I don't drink when I am working," said Lilly. Again, she looked up, then turned away.

Jack went to his knees and gently took the needle from her hand and gave her a hug. He whispered, "I am glad you are helping." He patted her back, hoping she might show some sign of affection. It did not happen. Jack leaned back, then stood up. "I'm djinn, Ma. I will need to talk to you about my dad, his family, and yours."

Lilly nodded. She picked up the needle and thread.

"Okay," said Jack, placing a hand on his mother's shoulder. "I'll leave you two alone to finish what you're doing." He smiled at Mini, who grinned back, waving her arms as if performing some spell of her own. Jack nodded, comprehending her question. "Like magic."

"Let's wait in the office," said Spunk. "Haggard and his officers are comin' 'round." She addressed Lilly and Spunk. "You can leave early today."

Once seated side by side in the chairs before Gracie's desk, Jack took Spunk's hand as he scanned the office. Not much had changed. His eagle sculpture rested next to his unfinished statue of Gracie.

"You're djinn," stated Spunk. "We need to know what that means and how you can help us when the North comes south in larger numbers." She shifted in her chair to face him.

"As I told my traveling companion, I intend to see that the North is undone," said Jack grimly. The body count would be high, which bothered him. He prayed the trade-off, freedom over blood, meant more northern bodies than southern.

"How?" Spunk asked seriously. "I can imagine a pile of corpses all bled out on the battlefield."

Jack raised a hand, palm forward. Gracie's desk split in two. The motion of two fingers and the ragged edges of splintered wood came together and repaired.

"So easily?" Spunk pushed herself up from the seat, eyes wide. "I heard," she choked, "but never witnessed what djinn could do."

"No," said Jack. "It will be hard, very hard. They will have warriors of equal power on their side."

"Jack Fox!" yelled a familiar voice from the warehouse floor.

"In the office!" called Spunk.

Gracie appeared at the doorway and froze for a moment, her eyes teared.

"Come out to the street," she said. Her grin swept away from her face. "We have people who say you'll vouch for them." Gracie turned and headed for the door with Jack and Spunk hard on her heels.

In the street, several hundred soldiers with rifles cocked and ready to fire faced ten wagons of civilians. The air about the new arrivals, however, shimmered with shields. To southern eyes, northerners invaded the Snake.

Jack went to the middle of the street between the northerners and southerners.

"Jack Fox!" called a voice: a girl.

Jack turned toward the call.

Is he dead? Flashed in his mind. He moved down the line of wagons with Spunk close at his side. *Is it the caged girl who called my name from the slaver's wagon?*

A young woman climbed over the edge of the wagon and hit the street, running to Jack. Rifles followed her, intent on destroying and ending any violence to a southerner. Jack turned to the soldiers and signaled for them to lower their arms. The young woman stopped feet away from Jack. She laughed and cried at the same time.

"Thought I'd never see you again." She looked Jack up and down, then turned to Spunk. Without a second's thought, she threw out her hand for Spunk to shake. "This one," she nodded toward Jack, "looked mostly dead the last time I saw him. I'm southern, a slave no longer. Hattie's the name."

Spunk took the proffered hand and held it. In the few

moments of contact, she noted Hattie's better clothes, shinier hair, better hygiene, and serious eyes. "Welcome home, Hattie."

"Not home exactly, like Jack. But the Snake is close enough." She dropped Spunk's hand. Hattie pointed to the first wagon. "It was the Forresters who got me here with my useless former owner." She laughed, overwhelmed with emotion.

Jack swung around in time to see Robert and Anna coming toward them.

"I vouch for these people!" called Jack. "Stand down," he said to the soldiers, "and you," Jack waved to the people in the wagons, "can drop your shields."

The palpable collective sigh of relief escaped from hundreds of people.

"Well," said Robert Forrester, watching the rifles drop and the shields dissipate as his people climbed out of the wagons, "we have come."

In that instant, the sound of cavalry drew everyone's attention. General Haggard, accompanied by his officers, formed a line in front of the wagons. Some drew their side arms. Haggard dismounted and drew close to Gracie.

"Gracie?" Haggard pulled off his hat, ran his fingers through his hair, and looked out on the scene before him. "What's going on here?"

"Reinforcements, Tom, for the coming big battle." Gracie stepped close to Haggard. "Maybe," she said so only he could hear, "salvation."

* * *

"The problem," emphasized Forrester, addressing his northern followers at Gracie's warehouse, "is action and acclimation to a new reality." He, with Haggard and Gracie by his side, considered the audience of young northerners who abandoned a comfortable life for the challenge of sacrificing for a cause greater than themselves. The reality of life south of the Aquitaine, Robert saw, grated on some of his followers. They needed something to do for the greater good to aid their adjustment to a new life.

"I, General Haggard, and Colonel Hargreaves have discussed all that needs doing to prevent a complete collapse of the South when the full military might of the North invades." Robert closed his eyes and raised his right hand. "No… That's not it." He opened his eyes, paused, and captured as many eye-to-eye as he could. "I mean the death of all the people you met today. The death of those who only wanted their children to be safe."

"Professor Forrester," said a young follower at the back, raising his hand as though in school. "We are not fighters. We are students. We study, research, and document our findings. It's not clear how we can help."

"Exactly," said Forrester. "Your strengths are needed. The lack of intelligence on what happened a hundred years ago could be a disaster." Robert stepped up to the front row. "The General has agreed to give all of you the right to enter any house or building to discover archives and data about the earlier war. It is critical to the success of the South in the short term and the redemption of the North in the long term."

"Professor?" Gracie came forward. "If I may?"

"Of course," said Forrester. "Colonel Hargreaves, for those of you unaware of what has happened, has led thousands of men and women in the fight against slavery. Where do women," he stared at several women in the audience, "stand in the northern hierarchy?" He took several steps back and let that last word stew among the female participants.

Gracie nodded. "We will provide you with some old city maps, so you will not start blindly. We need your quick action to discover and document the long forgotten historical details."

She paced back and forth. "Do not be polite or understanding or civilized in your search. These are not civilized times." She stopped next to Forrester as hands shot up.

"Are we only talking about Snakeport?" called out a man in the front row.

"For now, yes. If your data calls for a search in other cities, then you go and find out what you can."

"What protection can we expect?" asked another long-haired man. "They will recognize us as northern."

"You will have soldiers with you at all times, but keeping your shields down would delay recognition of your northern connection," said Gracie. The rippling air here and there among the audience subsided. "You are a very special team, and we are grateful for your willingness to join us."

"We," called out a young woman who pulled back blond hair from her face, "can do this, but we have lost our workers who made things easier for us." She looked left and right at her friends, who nodded agreement. "We would like to have them back."

"If you mean your former slaves," stated Forrester, losing his composure, "then you can pay them to do the job. The Snake does not tolerate slavery, whining, or incompetence." Addressing the privileged group, he lifted his hands and said, "You will live or die on your own abilities. No quarter given, none asked. Look up the reference if you do not understand."

"I believe the Professor has made things clear," said Gracie. She turned to Haggard, who nodded his approval. "The professor will assign groups of you to different parts of the city to begin your work."

"Please line up at the tables." Forrester extended a hand toward four tables with soldiers sitting behind tall stacks of paper. "You will receive your starting points and maps. Remember… you may be the one to discover victory."

Long hours passed as southerners sized up the northerners and the northerners worried they might have made a mistake following Forrester. In the end, exhaustion pulled all to their bunks. The seeds of hope, however, had been sown.

The old woman brought Jack and Spunk to their room. She felt the need to describe the amenities available to the young couple: the large bed, the chamber pots under the bed should her guests need them, the filled water pitcher, and cups on a sideboard under the window. The night manager apologized. She could offer nothing stronger with the Slaver War underway. When satisfied with the job done, she set the candle on the side table, bowed slightly, and left, shutting the door behind her.

Jack and Spunk settled into the accommodations available at the only hotel in Snakeport, the Court. The first-floor design gave the building its name. What passed for the legalities in the Snake took place in the courtrooms at ground level. The rented levels above went to those with the money to pay. Wealthy defendants stayed in rooms above the courtrooms instead of the grungy, local sheriff cells: guilty or innocent made no difference. Money decided the issue.

Exhaustion decided whether they would fall into dreamless sleep or peel off their clothes and become physically reacquainted. Boots dropped to the floor, undone buttons, loosened tight clothes, and sleep leapt at them when their heads sunk into the down pillows. Spunk's smile blurred and his fingers lightly touching her cheek faded; dreamless sleep took them.

Bright daylight poured through the open window. Jack sat up, startled, then raised a hand to shade his eyes. It took him a moment to remember he came home. Turning away from the light, rubbing the sleep from his eyes, he froze.

"It is time we talked," said Anna Forrester, sitting on the

corner of the bed by Spunk. She smiled and placed her hand on Spunk's leg. "She will not awaken for some time yet."

Jack rose from bed and dressed, feeling the need to straighten and pat down his wrinkled clothes. Pulling on his boots, he followed the old woman out of the room to a small parlor downstairs. A pot of coffee and a plate of bread and butter sat on a table. They helped themselves, then sat across from each other.

"I did not," started Anna, "stay for the late-night part of the council meeting at the Hargreaves warehouse. Tell me what happened and what agreement you reached."

Jack gulped his black coffee and stood up to refill his cup.

"Too much and too little." Jack contemplated his answer. The northern presence at Gracie's place had become an event. At the start of Haggard's council, she and her husband, Robert, had sat side by side before a table where Haggard wearing the gold sash of total command of the army and his staff peppered them with questions on how the North would react and what these northerners offered in the coming fight. Jack had felt the same tension as when he had dealt with the University officers in Hempstead a lifetime ago.

"Haggard needs a workable strategy," Jack started slowly. "After you left, Robert discussed the details concerning his northern people who will scour the city for documents: the history of the last war. They are university types. This will appeal to them and keep them busy while they adjust to southern life. Apparently, they…"

"I know: the whining," said Anna. She buttered some bread and took a bite. "They are a pampered lot. The change will be difficult."

"Robert expects the invasion of the South will not happen until the far northern border is secure. This surprised many." Jack sighed and thanked the heavens for the South's time to prepare. "It falls to me to get our northern allies ready to fight and finding any others like me."

"A tall order," said Anna, shaking her head. "There may be other more important actions to take first." She set her empty plate on the sideboard and picked up her coffee.

"Like I said, Dr. Peppers, your Robert, and I start immediately to find others like me," said Jack. Staring at the floor not sure he wanted or could perform to expectation, it scared him that the South's success laid firmly on his shoulders. "The others will dig up any history on the previous civil war looking for some strategy we have not considered."

"Yes, poor Robert," said Anna, shaking her head. "He will work so hard to be of help."

"Poor, Robert?"

"Sometimes… he and other brilliant men lose sight of the solution right in front of them." Anna looked to the side. "It is frustrating when my husband cannot accept that other forces might help."

"You are talking about what happened in the library." Jack captured Anna's eye and held it. In the weeks since the episode in the Hempstead library, he had pushed the experience to the back of his mind. "Bits and pieces flash now and then, but… what do you recall?"

"Tell me what you remember first." Anna smiled. It made Jack uncomfortable, like he played a dangerous game where only she knew the rules.

"Gracie sat talking to me, much like we are now. I didn't much care about what she had to say." Jack looked out the window as soldiers marched down the street. *The walking dead*, he wondered.

"And…" Anna nodded at Jack, who just stared back. "This is important, Mr. Fox."

"She said my desires were small. That I did not think big

enough for the gifts I had received." Jack felt betrayed by this image of the woman, more a mother to him than his actual mother. "I hold myself back. I had much more to learn from everyone."

Anna took another sip of coffee and kept quiet.

"Isn't undoing the northern hold on the South, big enough? Ending the slave trade in children isn't enough?" Jack's hands became fists and pounded the arms of the chair as he spoke.

"How old are you?" asked Anna knowingly.

"The dream Gracie told me," admitted Jack, surprised by the question. "She said I'm sixteen and my birthdate is on the summer solstice. Why is that so important?"

"The woman in this vision took on the identity of someone you trust and gave you a truth about yourself." Anna stood. "Let's take a walk. You can help me become more familiar with Snakeport."

Arm in arm, Jack led the way to Old John's Square. A wind off the bay cooled the air, keeping the usual stink from the docks at bay. The gallows remained but seldom used. Any convicted when given the choice between the rope or the war to end the slave trade declared for the cause.

"So," asked Jack as they passed among the columns, "who was she really?"

"The Earth, a goddess."

"I don't believe in god or gods."

"Of course, you don't," said Anna, patting his hand. "You believe in power, and that is where we will start. In time, you will come to know her as I do."

"What do you mean by a start?" asked Jack.

"There is not enough food. The army will starve soon. You and I will fix this problem." Anna looked up the street where the wagons that brought her to Snakeport still stood in-line. "Take me to Robert, then you must return to your young lady."

"Where did they put you up?"

"At the Lakeland mansion." She felt the surge of emotion in Jack as he stiffened at the mention of the name.

"Yes, yes, he has not finished his part in this story. Gone north, I would expect where he will tell the ministers about the south." Anna fell silent as they walked, then added, "He thinks he knows about you, but he does not. You are the unknown in all of this. Together, we will find out who you are."

"I'm Jack Fox," he insisted. *And that's pretty damn good enough.*

"For now, dear, for now."

CHAPTER 17

"Cowards?" asked Minister Higgins. Casually dressed, he tapped his fingers on the desk in his library and studied his intelligence officer, Colonel Martell. Two candles on the mantelpiece cast the only light. A cool breeze tossed shadows about the room as the flames flickered, then stilled.

"No, sir. Just ill prepared and poorly led." Colonel Martell, impeccably turned out in full uniform, sat cross-legged before his superior. The data gathered over the last days lay in the many page report delivered to Martell at headquarters near midnight.

"Ill prepared?" Higgins raised his finger, delaying the colonel's answer. He waved the house servant in and watched him place the silver coffee service on the side table near Martell. The tall clock in the hallway chimed twice as the servant left closing the door. When alone, Higgins said, "Help yourself."

A golden colored cat jumped up on the table and sniffed the coffee creamer. Higgins smiled as Martell hesitated. His hand scratched behind the ears of a second cat, a tabby, on the floor by his side.

"To be honest," said Martell uncrossing his legs and leaning forward to fill a cup when the cat jumped to the floor, "based on the information we gathered from the survivors, the officers failed to follow the minimum requirements for a force in enemy territory. Our arrogance and belief in our superiority defeated us." He held up the pot offering to pour for his boss.

"The southerners?" Higgins declined with a wave of his hand.

"They knew they stood no chance in a direct confrontation." Martell sat with the cup and saucer, then sipped the hot coffee. "They took a calculated risk and won."

"Won how, Colonel?" asked Higgins skeptically.

"No witness reported gun fire. Explosions went off everywhere, but no sergeants or officers showed themselves." Martell shrugged. "The leaders were dead long before the explosives went off. Killed by surprise: knives, maybe." Martell looked at Higgins. "A well-planned surprise attack."

"I see," Higgins sighed. He trusted his intelligence officer. "Next steps?"

"We invade with a larger, more experienced force with deadly intent. We do not make the same mistakes." Martell gulped the coffee, then refilled his cup.

Higgins empathized. His intel officer looked weary. Higgins prayed the coffee would rejuvenate both of them. It must have been a long two days for the Colonel traveling swiftly from the capital to the border to interview the soldiers, then back. The minister smiled when Martel almost jumped as his large male black cat rubbed against his leg.

Martell noted the slight grin on Higgin's face, smiled back, then reached down and stroked the black cat's back; he would have his adjutant brush his uniform free of the black hairs.

"What worked last time?" Higgins, not roused from a deep sleep in decades to address such an emergency, shook his head. He made the realization that any decision put forth tonight might very well spell the end of the northern way of life, with much killing on all sides. The history of the civil war he knew well, but the Colonel had a talent for finding the right angle of attack.

"Back then," started Martell, "the southerners matched us, but we had undermined the southern projectors willingness to fight using spies and family connections to weaken their resolve." Reaching out to pull a napkin from the tray, he draped it over his lap, drank, then balanced the cup and saucer on his leg. "It no longer applies now. They have no energy projectors. It will be easier to crush them this time, as long as we are not stupid about it."

"Yes, Colonel," said Higgins, raising an eyebrow eager to pursue the subject to some reasonable conclusion. "We cannot be stupid. So, what is our backup plan if there are southern projectors?"

"They have none as far as I know, but if they do, they cannot have many." Martell finished his drink. "With no training or soldier-quality combatants, the outcome is a certainty."

"You are sure?" Fingers tapped a steady tattoo. Higgins watched Martell stand and refill his cup. The napkin slipping from his lap falling to the floor.

"I know how long it takes to train our recruits." The colonel added sugar and stirred. "The same will be true for them." He bent and retrieved the napkin.

"And if they manage, however unlikely, to improve on our process?"

"Then our victory will be costly." Martell paused, considering his answer, then stopped as the golden cat jumped into his lap and claimed his knee as it sniffed out the creamer on the silver tray. The Colonel balanced his cup and saucer in one hand while he gently lifted the animal with the other. The cat landed on the floor gently as he said, "We send an overwhelming force and assume they can meet us projector to projector, which, of course, they cannot."

"And the northern border?" Higgins turned to the candles on the mantelpiece and allowed the mesmerizing flames to capture his attention. On a deeper level, the minister developed a strategy that might be the better option. He looked about his feet where cats had plopped down. Smiling Higgins grabbed the cream from the tray and placed it on the floor. His furry companions, in their well-rehearsed fashion, pounced on the silver cup according to the usual pecking order: males first.

"That will be for you and others to decide," stated Martell.

"Either we let the southerners do as they will and maintain our stand against far northern invaders or we confront the southerners, kill most of them, then return to our northern outposts." The Colonel looked at Higgins. "I believe I have covered the only viable options."

"Timing?" Higgins pulled his attention from his cats and focused on Martell. He stood and placed his palms on the desk.

"Move as fast as we can on the South," said Martell, startled by Higgins intensity, "then move faster to fortify the northern border."

"What if we reverse that strategy and move decisively against the barbarians to the north first and let the southerners have their way for a time?" The minister came around his desk to pour his own coffee. He could not sleep anymore tonight as he worked the details of his plan.

"First," insisted Martell, annoyed, "we have become too used to thinking of the far northerners as simply barbarians, easily routed, easily destroyed." He held Higgins' eyes. "Their strategies and fighting capabilities are more sophisticated. It will take time to stabilize the front. Our soldiers do not face barbarians," he stated, anger rising. "They face well led, trained warriors."

"My apologies, Major," Higgins filled the Colonel's cup before replacing the pot on the tray. "I did not mean any slight to the army. I want to know what would happen if we addressed the far northern problem first." He returned to his desk.

"The general population must prepare for sacrifice." Martell calmed, then put down his coffee. He felt the effects of the caffeine and comprehended where this new strategy would lead, then pointed to the Minister and nodded, "With the northern border secure, we could move that overwhelming force south without worry."

Higgins smiled at Martell's last comment. "Victory, Colonel," he said enthused.

"Victory," echoed Martell.

* * *

"I find this rather distasteful." Howard Dowler, the northern Prime Minister, considered his Ministers of War and the Interior. He passed his hand over his bald pate. "Such low things should not have any say in our matters."

"Agreed, Prime Minister," said Sedgwick. "However the rudeness of this sort might be, we need to know what they know about the southern defenses and any preparations."

"We are currently cleaning out the towns and villages north of our border to allow a large force to go south. This is the time to gather information and get it right. Consider what happened weeks ago to our small force." Higgins' ignorance of the southern methods that resoundingly defeated a stronger force tortured him. The sting of failure opened him up to political attack.

"But," whined Dowler, "why meet with these… empty shells?"

"As expendable spy masters, Prime Minister." Sedgwick cringed when Dowler got stuck in his childish this-just-isn't-fair complaining. Unlike his ministers, Dowler's battlefield experience lasted barely a year. Bailed out by better politically placed family members, Dowler discovered he had a knack for politics. Sedgwick needed to slap some sense into this man.

"Think about it, Lieutenant. We may need a force of these men to fight as the southerners' fight." Sedgwick got the reaction he wanted when he called up the Dowler's military record.

"You…" coughed Dowler apoplectic. His face contorted into a red rage.

"How will the people treat you," said Higgins following Sedgwick's strategy, "when they no longer can afford their way of life? What will they call you then? What do they think of you now as they give up their house slaves to work the mines and fields?"

"Not… not my fault!"

"Does it matter?" asked Sedgwick defiantly.

Dowler slapped the arms of his chair and stared at his ministers. Sedgwick knew he considered asking for their resignations. When the Prime Minister's head dropped, a clear sign, the man realized he needed these powerful supporters to stay loyal. Once Dowler surrendered, Sedgwick suspected he would get even when he and Higgins least expected it; something to consider after the southern problem found resolution.

"I do not want to meet with them. The dirty work is yours. Do what you have to do." Dowler grunted, then pulled himself up. On his feet, his size showed below his loose robes. As Sedgwick never turned down alcohol, Dowler never missed a meal and often made time in his day for extras.

"As you command, Prime Minister," said Higgins, with barely concealed contempt. Dowler's ministers stood together.

"What of those students and professors in Hempstead that went south?" asked Dowler, catching his ministers off guard. "Will that change your strategies?"

"We are investigating the issue, sir." Sedgwick smiled. "A hundred will not make a vast difference."

"Make sure it doesn't," said Dowler, feeling the impetus come back his way. "If I go down, you go down."

* * *

"Ya worthless. Good for nothin' non-projectors…" The big man with three chevrons on his light blue sleeve stopped, shook his head, then stalked up and down the line of one hundred men reloading their rifled muskets. "You are all dead!" He stopped in front of a man his own height but not as sturdy of build. "Pitiful! What exactly did I say?"

"Aim low, Sergeant," stammered the recruit.

"Did you aim low, turd?"

"Not low enough." The recruit almost fell when Sergeant Clifford snatched the rifle from his grasp.

"This man is too stupid to be in this outfit!" shouted Clifford. He stepped back from the line. "Southern scum will cut you fools down!" The sergeant turned toward the distant targets, shouldered the weapon, and fired. A large can labeled with a picture of peaches flew into the air. He went back to the recruit and tossed him the rifle.

"One more chance. Reload, turd." The sergeant marched up and down the line waving his hands, screaming at the soldiers. The official letters to their loved ones describing their stupid, wasted deaths sat on the Colonel's desk.

"Aim… low!" He stepped behind the line. "Make ready!" Rifles came up. "Aim!... Fire!"

A few cans jumped off their pedestals. More important, most mini balls raised the dirt near the targets or chipped the wooden platform beneath them.

"Better!" called out Clifford. "Maybe twenty or thirty of you will survive the first volley! Reload! I want to see more bloody peaches in the air!"

On the hill overlooking the shooting range, Reginald Lakeland and his officers on horseback watched the training progress through binoculars. They had reviewed the exercises over several hours as company after company entered the field.

"Enough." Lakeland dropped his binoculars and turned his horse about. The other officers followed. Lakeland held the rank of colonel and commanded the force of several thousand non-energy projectors.

"What a mess," stated Major Stan Folfox. "Any idiot could see where this is going."

"Where might that be?" asked Lakeland. He disliked Stan,

now called Major Folfox. The man's ineptitude led directly to the coming war. Lakeland's part in misreading the pushback that came after Jack Fox's kidnapping also bothered him. If he had not underestimated Gracie Hargreaves or if the boy had died, none of this stupidity would be on his plate. Sedgwick, his boss, made it clear to him.

"The Slavers War started because of your kind's greed," Sedgwick had said, looking comfortable behind the desk at his home. Lakeland stood before him. Many late-night meetings lay ahead before this business ended.

Your kind's demand, ya old fool! Lakeland fumed. "It started --," he began.

"Whatever," interrupted Sedgwick. "The war is here, and we must respond. The prime minister agrees that a force of non-energy men should form for fighting and spying on the South."

"Why? You have enough projectors to level the South." Lakeland grew annoyed and wandered, not for the last time, why him and what Sedgewick wanted.

"With the war won, you will be a rich man to live either north or south." Sedgwick opened a ledger on his desk, then rustled some papers, searching for details. "We need riflemen and men who can easily move around in the south undetected. The prime minister is concerned we do not know enough about southern capabilities."

"How wealthy?" Lakeland shifted his weight from left to right.

"Very," stated Sedgwick. He dropped the papers in his hands and leaned back.

"How many men?"

"I would expect..." paused Sedgwick, scratching his chin. "Two or three thousand."

"Would we coordinate our movements and operations with the projector commanders?"

"Perhaps," said Sedgwick, aware that would never happen. The regulars had their standards. Working side by side with the untalented would be worse than fighting next to women projectors.

"I want Stan Folfox as my second," stated Lakeland.

"Folfox," chuckled Sedgwick. "An unfortunate twist of fate, wouldn't you agree? Reports from Hempstead provide a name to go along with the threat. What do you know about a teenager, one Jack Fox?"

Lakeland said he never heard of him, but cringed inside over the news of the boy's survival. Lost money triggered many anguished reactions.

"We need to know if he is a projector or a very lucky non-projector." Sedgwick pulled on the collar of the white shirt he wore, then unbuttoned the top buttons. More comfortable, his eyes scanned Lakeland. "I hope you are the man to lead this effort."

The silent judgement from the minister enraged the Colonel. His father's appraisal reenacted as the old man sentenced the eighteen-year-old Lakeland to be banished from family matters: make your own way or die. Fantasies about returning home to fling his great wealth and success into his father's face gave way to a wish for bullets and brains splattering the walls of the house in which he grew up.

Lakeland's thoughts returned to his forces. He applied spurs to get ahead of the following entourage, then said, "I'm not interested in the marksmanship of our men." His major came even with him. "The sergeant in that last exercise and others like him are the men I want for a special detail."

"I wondered when we would send eyes and ears south," said Folfox, who recognized the signal as Lakeland pulled away for a private conversation.

"I want you to set up the crews and target different southern sections." Lakeland did not like his second since he cost him everything he had built in the South. The man, however, knew his business and often provided an answer before Lakeland formed the question. "The job is to learn what they can as fast as they can, not get caught, and deliver what they find. Make it happen."

"Yes, sir," said Folfox. "I will sort the men into those who know the south and those who don't. The choices will be easier to make."

"Good." Lakeland removed his wide-brimmed hat and wiped the sweat from his forehead. "The invasion will not happen until the winter." He passed his gloved hand around the hat's inner band, then put it back on his head.

"Why so long?"

"Keep this to yourself." Lakeland looked at the major, who nodded. "Stability on the far northern border is taking longer than expected. Preparations to support a large force in the field are coming together slower than expected. Finally," Lakeland stared off to the horizon, "the bastards are scared."

"Scared of what? They hold the cards." Folfox, as all the untalented northerners, knew who Lakeland meant: the government.

"The unknown. All the paralyzing 'what-ifs'." The Colonel hauled on the reins. The column halted. "Is your son a projector?"

"Jack?" asked Stan Folfox, stunned by the question. "He has my sister's talent for carving. He survived what would have killed any other man." The major glanced back down the column, then turned back to Lakeland and said, "Yes. The odds are he has the power, or he is the luckiest sonofabitch alive."

CHAPTER 18

"Mornin' Doc," said Hattie at the door of the house across from the cemetery. "I was told you was helping out."

Peppers, half awake, eyed her suspiciously. It took a moment before he recognized her as the girl from the wagon at the clinic months ago. He opened the door and waved her in.

"I just wanted…"

Peppers touched his finger to his lips to quiet her. "My patient just fell asleep. It's been a long night."

"Sorry, doc," she whispered. "I just wanted to say thanks is all."

"For what? How did I help you?" asked Peppers confused. The slavers had taken her and the other boy. He did nothing to stop them.

"Maybe I should be angry and all, but I'm not. I'm glad you're here with us." Hattie smiled. "Maybe you should get back to sleep yourself." She noted the dark circles under his eyes. "If you can trust me, I can watch over your patient and wake you if there is any trouble."

"How would you know if trouble erupted?" tested Peppers.

"I been takin' care of folks for a long time. Helped some but others became too sick, and they died."

"Okay." Peppers knew he could not stay awake much longer and the girl, Mini, sleeping like a log in the corner, offered no help. "Check her breathing every hour. Do you know how to check a heartbeat?"

"Sure. That's easy."

"Good. Check her heartbeat when you look for her breathing. If it is irregular, I mean, skips beats come and get me."

"You eat anything recently, Doc?" Hattie looked to her left

into the kitchen, seeing no pots on the stove or food on the table. A handgun lay on the counter.

"Not important right now." Peppers stared at Hattie for a moment. "I'll be on the floor over there if you need me." He pointed to a pallet in the corner.

"Go sleep, Doc."

Peppers turned away and headed to his poor bed, which looked so inviting. He stopped and over his shoulder said, "You may have had more to do with Jack's survival. If he had suffered any more hits to his head, he would not have lived." Peppers yawned. "You saved him."

Hattie could have thrown her arms around him. She did not, however, know the doctor well enough for such a demonstration. Decorum still held sway in some parts of the South. The doctor rose in her estimation even if he claimed northern birth. As Peppers collapsed in the corner, she noted the little girl in the opposite corner breathing softly, then went to the old woman in the other room whose chest rose and fell normally. Hattie rubbed her hand against the cloth of her loose trousers warming the skin, then placed her fingers on the old woman's neck. The heartbeat was strong and regular. The kitchen became the next area of focus, where a large burlap bag of provisions laid in a corner.

"Well…" she unloaded the bag's contents on the table. "This shouldn't be all that hard."

After six hours of simmering, the aroma of ham and beans bubbling on the stove woke everyone. Hattie took the large stock of beans and the fresh meat, which would go bad if left uncooked, and made a meal for the four of them. The rest she put away according to her idea of an orderly kitchen and figured the bag provided enough for a week.

"I don' rightly know who ya might be," said Nanna when she felt fingers at her neck and found an unfamiliar face over her.

"I'm Hattie, ma'am."

"Not from 'round here?"

"From farming country 'bout halfway to the border." Hattie smiled at the elderly woman with dazzling eyes. "What name should I use for you?"

"Most young-uns call me Nanna." She looked around, expecting to find others. "Where's Clay?"

"Clay, ma'am?"

"My doctor or so he says," said Nanna. "The girl is one a my granddaughters. Her name be Mini. A course Spunk be my other. Away in the army, ya know."

"The doc is asleep, as is Mini, and I met the sergeant. She and Jack ought to come by sometime soon, I would expect." Hattie reached around and pulled the revolver from her waist, handing it handle first to Nanna. "Thought you might feel more comfortable with this in easy reach."

"Smart girl." Nanna grabbed the weapon and deftly hid it.

"What smells so good?" Peppers came to check on his patient. "How are you feeling, Cynthia?"

"Right better, Clay." She pulled herself into a sitting position and took his hand in both of hers. "Don' know exactly what ya did, but I'm a might stronger."

"Good." Peppers checked her. The swelling in her legs had subsided. "Hattie, here, kept an eye on you for me. Looks like she did a good job and made an excellent meal for us. So… let's eat."

"Help me, Clay," insisted Nanna. "I want to join y'all at the table."

As Nanna took a seat, Mini came into the kitchen, rubbing the sleep from her eyes.

"Clay," said Nanna, nodding at Mini, "this be your next patient. See what ya can do."

Mini ignored the talk and grabbed the plates on the counter

and handed them out. She kept looking at her grandmother, who had not sat at the table for as long as she could remember. Happy to stand by and let Hattie, a stranger to her, bring the pot to the table and ladle it out, she sat. Since the start of the Slaver War, strangers had routinely come and gone in her life. She felt no fear.

"I'll do what I can," said Peppers, blowing on a spoon full of steaming beans. He turned to look at the girl. "What seems to be the problem?"

* * *

"I agree. This is a suitable spot," said Anna Forrester. Early the morning after their walk in the city streets, she and Jack tramped up the well-worn path from Snakeport to the woods near the marble quarry while her husband and southern leaders held forth in the city, and the search for war documents got underway. He brought them to the fallen tree, decaying and providing a home to insects and food for new growth. "This is the place I first felt the connection."

Anna did not expect to find beauty. In many ways, the woods reminded her of the garden at home. "Let's stop here and see what happens."

"What do you expect?" asked Jack. He looked for the small plant with the glistening leaves but found only the regular green plants and dark earth in the forest. Only a day had passed since he escorted Anna to her rooms, then returned to the hotel to find Spunk waiting patiently: a return never to be forgotten. Clothes evaporated as arms and legs entwined. No thought or words got in the way, just pure desire. A total release in a shared silence. The memory made him smile.

"I expect nothing," said Anna. "I will kneel here. Kneel where you will, and we will start." The old woman went to her knees near the exposed roots of the fallen tree. Placing her hands palms down on the ground, she looked at Jack, waiting for him to find his spot.

"This kinda doesn't…" started Jack. Ready to argue about what makes sense, he felt the sudden urge to move to his left. The white petals of small flowers on long stems drew him. As he neared, energy drained from his body and he collapsed to his knees.

"She may come again, maybe not." Anna pressed energy into the soil, seeking the familiar connections unaware of Jack's condition. "If she does, it may be to one of us alone. We will see."

"What's happening? I.." questioned Jack, breathless. He pressed his hands to the earth to keep from falling face first into the dirt. Energy bled from him. He felt his strength wither. *Weakness gets you killed in the Snake.* Jack fought the draining of his energy: an ant standing as the ignorant boot snuffs out its life.

"I will never abandon you, my child."

The words flashed in Jack's mind. He shook his head, startled.

"This must be done."

"What must be done?" Jack's body relaxed, accepting the power guiding him.

"Time for you to find out who you are, Jack."

Memories flashed in his consciousness like letters from his past. He relived his life in all its ugliness and glory, unable to play defense, unable to look away.

"I'm hungry, ma," whined four-year-old Jack.

"Then you best get on out and find something to eat," demanded *Lilly, sitting at the table drinking rum from the bottle. The chair scraped as she rose unsteadily. "You think this is my fault, don't ya? Never really wanted you anyway," Lilly muttered. She grabbed*

the little boy by the scruff of his neck and dragged him to the door. "Don't come back without food." She tossed Jack out into the street. The door slammed shut.

Jack cried silent tears sitting next to the door with no idea what to do, scared to death.

Stan Fox yelled, "You're worthless, just like your ma." He hauled seven-year-old Jack down the street. "But I can get you hanged like you deserve." Old John's pillars came into view.

"What did I do?" screamed Jack, sure that his father meant to kill him.

"Where's my money?" demanded Stan as he threw the boy onto the street.

Jack cried as he put his small hand in his pocket and pulled out four copper pennies.

Stan snatched them up, then pulled Jack to his feet. "Turn around and face the wall."

Jack did as he was told.

"I could have you hung for bein' a thief," started Stan. "But a good whipping may do a better job." Stan undid and pulled off his belt.

Jack screamed, drawing a curious crowd. The belt hit his backside over and over.

"I'm leaving," yelled Stan, "and I'm takin' what's mine."

"Good," said ten-year-old Jack, almost as tall as his father. Growing up on the street and doing odd jobs for Gracie, he learned how to take care of himself and fight back. "Then you be going empty-handed."

"Don't sass me, boy," said Stan furiously.

"Ha," laughed Jack, then he became quiet with a stern face. "Get out before I kick you out."

Stan came at Jack in an uncontrolled rage. Jack side stepped the attack and, almost like magic, lifted the older man off his feet and slammed him into the wall. He then pulled Stan up by the lapels of his worn coat and tossed him out of the door.

Jack considered this one of his best and worst days.

Tears of loss and hopelessness ran down his face. A warmth like a coat thrown around a cold, abandoned child on the docks, a sense of total acceptance ensued. Paralyzed, Jack could only hold tight in the emotional whirlwind and let the force of reality and the emotions long suppressed pour out and take control.

"It was not your fault."

"Oh, God," escaped his lips in a whisper. Jack wanted to break contact: too much, too painful. *Tell me how to defeat the invaders! Not this!*

"Let go, my child, and you will have all that you need. You are not alone. It was not your fault."

"I am alone! I will be again when this ends." Jack gritted his teeth and tried to lift his hands. *"I will always be alone."* The surety of this flamed despair. Completely defenseless, he wailed.

Strong arms wrapped around Jack's chest and heaved him from contact with the earth. He cried out for it to stop. Time passed, and he felt the emotions calm. The silence but for the sounds of the forest filled his senses. He gave up.

"You're not alone, my boy," said Anna, hugging Jack as hard as she could; he stopped struggling. His anguished howling broke her from her connection. "I'm here. It's going to be alright." She maintained her hold on him as he lost consciousness. Letting him go, Anna arranged herself so Jack's head rested in her lap. "No more pain. You don't have to fix it all." She felt his grief, his anger, and his feeling of being trapped. She placed her hand on the ground to relieve the stiffness of old joints.

"*Thank you, daughter.*"

Anna smiled.

"Now my boy," she said, looking down on Jack's peaceful face, "we do great things."

CHAPTER 19

"Jack Fox... Jack, Jack, Jack," said Mini, supported in his arms. Then she laughed. Her hand on his cheek, she leaned close and whispered, "I love my Jack."

"Can't rightly stop 'er from talkin' up a storm," said Nanna, smiling while focusing on the task at hand. She stood at the counter cutting up rare, fresh vegetables for the stew bubbling on the stove. Hattie stirred as Nanna added a handful from the chopping board to the pot.

Jack stared at Mini, joyfully surprised and said, "I love you too".

When he and Spunk came to check on Nanna, the girl had jumped into his arms, as always. Cradled and eye-to-eye with her hero, Mini released her newfound voice.

"How?" Spunk placed her hands on Mini and leaned her head on her shoulder.

"Oh, that," said Peppers, coming from the kitchen, "a rather simple procedure." He stretched and yawned. "A little energy to remove some benign growths on her vocal cords." The open-mouthed, amazed expressions mildly annoyed him. "No big deal, I assure you."

Silence.

"Nanna fixed too?" asked Mini.

"Well, of course, but Cynthia's case proved a bit more complicated. I had..." started Peppers, but he never finished his thought. The chopping at the counter paused.

"I told you so," stated Jack emphatically. He let Mini drop to the floor and watched her take Peppers' hand.

"Yes, yes," said Peppers. "You had the right of it, Jack." He bowed in mock surrender. "I guess I will have to expect to be overwhelmed by the next thousand patients." He grinned down at Mini. "You, my dear, are a delight."

"We will have to fix up the old hospital," said Jack. "It won't be long until they line up."

"We have to prepare to treat thousands of wounded too," stated Spunk.

"Doc, get your ass in gear." Jack went over to his friend and put a hand on his shoulder. "You have helped my family. Help the others."

"Are you nuts!" Peppers looked around the room. "I am one person with stone knives and forks trying to save what?" He staggered. "The lines of people seeking relief will be tens of thousands?"

"Take Hattie with you," said Jack. "She knows her way around helping the sick and wounded." Hattie came up behind Peppers, all smiles. "Grab some of the university types and start teaching as fast as you can. I also need your help to find others like us."

"You think there are any?" Peppers looked over his shoulder at Hattie.

"I have it from a good source," said Jack, "that I am not the only one."

"Who? Forrester or his wife?" Peppers shook his head.

"A higher power." Jack turned to Spunk, took her hand, and squeezed. "A much higher power."

* * *

Robert Forrester, a determined agnostic, considered the young man before him. "My wife, Mr. Fox, described what she could of your encounter." They met as planned in Gracie's office; the old professor sat behind Gracie's desk. "We need to get down to basics. Whatever happened in the woods is not essential." He huffed, leaned forward in the chair, and slapped the table.

"What is important is how the army is to be kept in the field? What strategies do we create to confront thousands of energy projectors with the few on our side?"

"You worry too much." Jack on his feet walked around the room, thinking it good of Gracie to allow the free use of her space. He had never taken the time to learn about the things Gracie collected and considered important. The shelves held books he never noticed. The titles varied from obvious fiction to biographies. All possessed worn covers and yellowed pages. They looked old, maybe as old as Nanna. "Call me Jack, Mr. Forrester." He turned to the fuming man with his hands on his head as though keeping it from exploding. "May I call you Robert?"

"We cannot," Forrester insisted indignantly, "give up our futures to some fantasy earth goddess rising to save the South."

"Let's talk about strategy, then." Jack, who had pulled a volume from the shelf, put it back and took a seat. "Your wife, Anna, and I will use our energy to shorten the growing season immediately. There will be enough food for the army. Second, Dr. Peppers will get the hospital straightened out and start training new doctors, plus look for other energy projectors. You and your team of academics might search for projectors as they go about their investigations. Third, you and Anna are ancient and full of knowledge of the North and its weaknesses. Didn't you, in one of your publications, declare the North could not strip projecting from the South? It would return in time." Jack smiled. "Seems like a hundred years is about time enough."

"I…" Forrester stopped and calmed. "I feel like I am talking with my wife," he said, trying not to smile but failing. "Sometimes frustrating, but always enlightening." Forrester changed the subject. "Anna says you communed with the earth."

"Yes."

"I am not ready to throw my trust to something supernatural and yes, call me Robert or Professor." Forrester sat back and retrenched. "I avoid faith, preferring data driven knowledge.

"She is not supernatural." Jack gathered his thoughts, aware of the professor's position. "I call her 'she' because that is how I heard her voice. It would likely be something else to you. I felt Anna and read her thoughts as I did the goddess. I don't know how, and it doesn't matter, as you say." Jack leaned forward. "There is a connection across the land. It has mass like our brain has mass. There is purpose in those networks: a positive purpose." Jack looked down at his hands and flipped them palms up then down. "I am now a soldier devoted to that purpose. It is the North that has armed itself in opposition."

"There is a plan?" Robert asked with a curious tilt of his head.

"Whatever we decide," said Jack.

"It will come down to power against power," said Robert.

"Has it ever been any other way?"

"If they come in the next few weeks, we die." Robert stared down at the desk.

"Will they come that soon?" Jack stood up and walked to the shelf beside the desk. He took the unfinished marble carving of Gracie and slipped it into his pocket.

"No, thank goodness. They must deal with the threat from their north." He looked up at Jack.

"Tell me about the far northern threat. I know nothing of them. Maybe the enemy of our enemy is our friend." He touched the other shelves and examined them for clues to his most ardent supporter.

"Not likely," stated Robert watching the young man move along the shelves. "They have a way, not exactly energy projection but something that is a threat. Call them vicious killers ready to invade and expand their territory. Destroyers, their own towns and villages are torched, leaving nothing for the invading enemy."

"Not altogether unlike us," said Jack. "We both are ready to revolt."

"Yes," nodded Robert. "By the way, we have found some documents."

"Documents?" Jack stopped his search, wanting to hear more.

"Diaries," said Robert. "We will go over them with Haggard. They describe why the South lost." He watched as Jack nodded, then resumed his search. He reached for something on the shelf and pocketed it as he did the statue.

"I look forward to reading these histories." Jack came back to his seat. "So, the North cannot completely defeat their enemy in the Far North?"

"No." Forrester considered his observations of real-time events over a long life. "Much like they did not completely defeat the South." He shook his head. "What a singular waste of effort for such superficial gains."

"So, assuming they stay with the wasted effort strategy, what should we expect immediately?" asked Jack. "They know about you and the volunteers who came with you."

"If I commanded, I would send spies south to find out what we are up to." Forrester clasped his hands together and tapped them gently on his chin, thinking. "They might enlist those without energy talent. It's what I would do in their position."

"So, my father may have a part to play?"

Robert nodded slowly. "Perhaps."

CHAPTER 20

The upper echelon of officers and civilians congregated at Gracie's, then shuttled from one War Department to another, a table with a paper placard calling out its function: ten tables setup across the empty warehouse floor. Each office offered what new information they had and asked for help to accomplish the task before them.

"How long do we have?" Haggard sat legs crossed, serious, and worried about the shortfalls. To his right sat Gracie, the gold sash of a general officer around her waist, and Will Biggs, also in the general's ranks. To his left, he noted Jack, Spunk, Robert, and Anna Forrester. He let them know he expected them to be quiet and listen closely.

"Two weeks before the food and forage runs out," stated a young officer at the Office of Supply table. "We expect Jack and Anna will resolve the issue. They just have to get it done in two weeks." If the officer felt threatened under Haggards hard stare, he did not show it.

"It will be done," said Jack. "We go out to farm country tomorrow."

"What about ammunition and powder?" Haggard pulled a small notebook and pencil from his pocket.

"No shortages there or with uniforms, boots and the like. Food or the lack of it threatens us most."

Haggard nodded.

"General?" asked the supply officer. He waited patiently as his commanding general scratched notes on the page.

"Yes." Haggard looked up as he closed the notebook and put it away.

"Gold, sir, or silver. We need more, much more."

"We are aware of the shortage: food and gold." He paused, then said, "Everyone has to sacrifice." Haggard, Gracie, and Will poured their personal wealth into the effort to keep the army together in the field, ready to face the northern invasion. Unfortunately, the enemy never came, but still might. They neared bankruptcy.

"We can't take from those who have little to nothing to begin with. If you take my meaning, sir." The young officer and those sitting next to him nodded.

"Again," said Haggard, "we are aware. There will be coin, but it may take some time to get it. That's all I can say."

After gathering reports from each office, all with similar needs and complaints, Haggard and the team went into Gracie's office and shut the door.

"We are all dead," started Haggard, "if we do not change our strategy."

"We attack, Tom." Gracie knew when to gamble. The realities of their position forced greater risk taking. "We don't know when they are coming." She stood by the shelf next to the eagle, pulling what it needed from the water. "Robert, what are they thinking?"

"Based on what I know of the northern leadership and the way they work, I would not expect an attack until the spring. Their northern border is not stable. The leaders who count are practical men. They are risk averse." Robert, a superior energy projector in his own right, with little exertion, could end this southern affront to northern hegemony: just boil the blood of every person in the room. The thought flitted through his mind, then disappeared as his greater need to do the right thing took over.

"A flanking maneuver while the north dithers and frets," insisted Gracie. "Grab what we can from the goldmines located at the edge of the western mountains."

"Bold, General, but explain why this isn't incredibly stupid." Haggard and the others gathered around the desk as Gracie unfolded a map of the mountain country.

"This is how I see it," said Gracie, who then laid out the entire strategy.

"And what do you expect the mountain people to do?" asked Haggard. "Just let us pass through their country?" He rose and leaned over the map. "We know little of these people as we know less of the far northern folks." He ran his fingers over the many triangles showing the mountains of the west. "Why exactly won't they kill and possibly eat any team we send into their territory?" Everyone in the room grew up with parental threats of being sent to the mountains if they did not behave.

"They have made no move against us ever. We move into their land slowly, ready to talk or negotiate as needed." Gracie sensed the fear in the audience. Irritated, she said, "What damned choice do we have, Tom!" At her outburst, the room deflated. Seeing them grumble but nod, she added, "I want Spunk here," she extended her hand at the girl, "to lead this action. She will need to be promoted."

Gracie surprised Spunk only recently promoted to lieutenant after the fight near the bridge. Spunk rose to her feet and studied the map.

"I'll need a few days to get organized," said Spunk, confident in her success.

Later, after the meeting, she paced, waiting for her scouts to report. Jack had paired up with Anna and made ready to leave. Will Biggs executed his orders to outfit a few ships to patrol the coast. Robert took on the task of finding out when the invasion might come. Last, as the sun dropped behind the rooftops, Spunk reviewed the scouting reports. All was quiet along the river. She made ready to go into the mountains and figured that by the time she returned, if they did not get eaten, they would provide more answers. Jack and she would have to wait for another time to be together.

* * *

Spunk missed the warm southern air almost as much as she missed Jack and felt incomplete without him at her side. She exhaled, watched as the frost dissipated, and pulled her coat tighter. The slaver wagon rolled smoothly over the gravel pathways through the western mountains. She left Snakeport for Lancaster, leaving Jack and Anna Forrester to perform some sort of magic. Five days had passed since the line of wagons left Lancaster and crossed into northern mountain territory. The mountain people lived independently: not part of the North or the South. Once among the peaks, Spunk never lost the sense of being watched.

"Hey, how much longer?" said a boy sitting among the other twenty persons caged in the wagon. "I'm right cold and sick to death of jus' sittin'."

"When it's dark, Jimmy Nicks." Spunk placed her hands on the bars and studied the rocky slope, wondering if the tales might be true: mountain ghosts that ripped flesh and devoured people. "Stop your complaining. It's annoying."

"Beggin' your jumped up, high and mighty's pardon but…"

"Stop." Spunk turned around and stepped in front of the boy. "If you made this much noise in the trees, I'm surprised you aren't long dead."

"Ya never spent hours on a limb tryin' to get comfortable watching for djinn. A big, old, fat girl who looks a lot like you led us, but she never could climb like us little guys." Jimmy tried to keep a straight face, couldn't, and grinned ear-to-ear.

"And us too," said the girl sitting next to him. She grabbed the revolver at her waist and moved it to the other side to be more comfortable. "We girls got higher than you boys."

"An hour, Jimmy, should do it." The sun had long ago dropped behind the cliffs. "I'll need scouts for tonight's work. You ready?" Jimmy's teasing did not upset Spunk, who thought this must be like having a younger brother. She liked it. "You too, Heather."

"Me?" asked the boy with a surprised smile.

"After you eat, and the horses are well tended."

"Yes, sir," said both children together.

The train of wagons heading north looked like any other slaver convoy delivering product to the northern mines. Dressed to look like rag tag children for sale, the youngest soldiers rode in the cages while quarry men held the wagon reins or rode before and behind the wagons. The quarry men carried rifles while every disguised slave kept a pistol hidden within easy reach.

When the troop finally stopped, the wagons emptied in the waning light. Fires glowed behind folding tin screens to minimize the light and draw less attention.

"Heard tell of a small outfit led by a woman got in among the djinn and kilt 'em all." A big man spooned a mound of beans and bacon into his mouth. This southern man, Hilton, born and bred close to the mountains, guided them. The men and young ones around the fire glanced at Spunk as they shoveled in the food.

"Not all," said Spunk. "A few survived to send the message north." She reached for the cup of water at her feet, drank, put it back, then wiped her mouth on her sleeve. "Come south if you dare, but we're fighters and we'll kill the lot of you."

"It's said," Hilton nodded and scraped the rest of the food on his plate to one side. "That you is tight with Jack Fox, who accordin' to some is djinn." Never looking up with the edge of the plate against his open mouth, he devoured the last of the food on his plate. He licked the spoon, the plate, then stopped when he noted the quiet as all eyes around the fire focused on their leader.

Spunk set down her plate, stood, and, using a rag, lifted the hot pot of bacon and beans from the fire. Starting with Hilton, she doled out more.

"Yes, we are committed," said Spunk as she walked around the circle of men, women, and children.

"Formal like?"

"Yes." Her stated commitment to Jack and his to her stood as a formal agreement across the South. Preachers and ceremony belonged to the moneyed folks.

"Good." Hilton watched the leader of this expedition as she served the men and women around the fire. Ten such camp sites with mostly similar conversations spread out along the wagon train. "Makes me think. If Jack is djinn, could any of the rest of us be and not know it?"

"Maybe. Seems the Professor, the Doc, and Jack are trying to figure out who may be." Spunk put the empty pot on one rock cloistering the fire. "If you survived this long in the Snake or elsewhere in the south, maybe you got some djinn in you." She sat and lifted her plate to finish.

"Some of the young-uns called ya Sarge," Hilton in a show of respect, got to his feet and gathered the near licked-clean plates and the pot to wash. "If it ain't no trouble, what be your name?"

Spunk caught the nods of the men and women who did not know her.

"I'm Captain Tillotson now, Cindi Tillotson." Practical matters forced her to stop stamping her feet when called Cindi. "Y'all can call me what you will. I prefer you call me Spunk."

As the fires burned low, the questions ceased, and the camp bedded down for the night. Jimmy and Heather left to scout the way forward for a few miles.

"Wake me when you return," said Spunk. "Stay hidden as best you can." The children nodded. "Off with you." She followed their moves until they disappeared among distant boulders. It made her uncomfortable that the operation had met no problems: no blocks, no fighting. *Too easy.* Spunk slid down to the ground, leaning back against a wagon's wheel, tired but too worried to sleep.

"Spunk," whispered a familiar voice.

Spunk instantly faced the threat with a revolver out with the trigger cocked. Startled, it took several moments to assess the situation. Jimmie and Heather looked down at her.

"A might edgy there, ain't ya," said Jimmie Nicks, smiling. He watched her re-holstered the gun.

"Report," demanded Spunk, getting to her feet. She stretched and felt embarrassed that she let down her guard and slept.

"All clear, for as far we went. How far do ya think, Heather?" asked Jimmie, placing a hand on his fellow soldier's shoulder.

"Two miles easy, maybe closer to three."

"Good job," stated Spunk. "You two get some sleep. We start early."

In the morning, while it remained dark, the troops recreated the charade of slavers heading north. The children and any women climbed into the cages. As the sun brought the light, not a cloud marred the intense blue sky. The horses grunted as they pulled, wheels turned, men yelled using harsh language.

Hilton came even with Spunk in the cage and nodded. She knew he expected yet another uneventful day traveling in the western mountains. They would move slowly.

The large boulders across their path barely a mile from the camp brought them up short.

Spunk stared at the wall of stone and wished it away, but

the stubborn stone remained in its seamless squares, blocking the path.

"It weren't here, I swear," stated Jimmie Nicks, scratching his head. "Just the other side, the path splits in two. One on the left is a dead end. That other goes on and on."

"How?" questioned Hilton. He scowled. "Just how far did you really go? Maybe you rested a bit and fell asleep?"

"These stones were placed. They did not fall in a landslide." Spunk could almost sense the mechanical contraptions quietly settled on the other side of the wall with hundreds of men and women who did the job. "Get everyone out of the wagons. Find cover and set up your men and the children for an attack. Shoot anything that moves on the slopes or comes over this wall."

"Really?"

Spunk spun around, angry at any challenge in the heat of battle or the potential for battle. She would shoot any mutineers. Almost tripping over Hilton's collapsed body and finding both Jimmie and Heather on the ground, instinct took over. Her legs acted jumping free of the impediment of bodies, her finger warmed the trigger of her revolver as it sought a target, her mind worked overtime to analyze the tactical situation, so she might survive.

"Impressive, my dear. But totally unnecessary."

Spunk crouched, the business end of her gun pointing at the tall man with the long gray beard. She could not see his face hidden beneath the cowl's hood. He made no aggressive move, so Spunk quickly reassessed. The gun lowered but still held ready.

"What have you done to my men?" demanded Spunk.

"Men?" chuckled the man. "These adults and children sleep a stone's sleep: no dreams or worries to trouble them."

"Who are you?" asked Spunk. "Did you build this wall?"

"I am the Warden of the Western Mountains."

"The wall?" She stood up and checked Hilton, Jimmie, and Heather confirming they remained in the land of the living.

"Time for a talk," said the Warden, pulling back the hood. He grinned broadly. His intense, laughing gray eyes beneath bushy eyebrows and a head of graying hair gave him a disarming effect.

"So, talk."

"I do not rule here." The man pointed to the revolver. "Any talking will be among my people and your people, not just you and me. We must decide."

Spunk's gut said she could stand down and holster her weapon.

"Decide what?" asked Spunk, feeling churlish at the man's easy manner and obvious power.

"Whether or not we kill all of you."

CHAPTER 21

"My lords!" called Prime Minister Dowler. On a pedestal behind a mahogany podium he looked out over the gathering of peers: several hundred old men. Dowler scanned the sheets containing the speech prepared by Sedgwick. The first line on the page he underlined then scratched out the rest.

"We will lose this fight with the South!"

Sedgwick and Higgins, sitting with the other government ministers below the pedestal facing the audience, turned to each other. Their puppet went off script. Shaking their heads and angry at the weasel they created, fear crept into their hearts. Dowler needed them, but did he know they kept him in power? Scapegoats rarely survived long after losing office.

"Our northern border is not as secure as I want it to be. Why haven't we built a wall? We have the power. The State took your workers and sent them to the mines or the fields to keep food on our tables. The South has treacherously destroyed our force sent to help them settle their internal war." Dowler let the drama build and took the measure of the crowd. None of the hard times to come would be his fault. "Government agents, without my knowledge, made a mistake. Some have betrayed us!"

The yawning and side conversations stopped. Dowler possessed their full attention. The gathering took place every year in the cathedral-like Soldiers Hall, built after the war fought a hundred years ago. Some among the audience had fathers, uncles, or grandfathers who projected on the battlefield for the North. Others had forefathers who abandoned their southern roots and came north yielding to greater power: survival demanded it. Some, however, knew this day would come. The war ended nothing. It waited. It waited to devour their sons.

"We need your wisdom and effort to achieve the grand design of our fathers. We need you to correct the errors!" Dowler felt invigorated by the crowd's total focus on him. He wondered why he did not do this more often. Maybe some of his ministers held him back? "I try, my lords, to see a way out, a different path. That path needs you. You are this country's salvation!"

The foot stomping began at the back, pre-arranged by Dowler with a little transfer of land and title to families falling on hard times.

"Peace is illusive! Peace, we all crave!" Dowler placed his hands on either side of the lectern and dropped his head as if calling on a higher power for support. His head came up. "When all lands share the same bounty. When all lands accept the truth that energy abilities make the measure of a man, then peace will come. We need you…" The Prime Minister stepped away from the podium and using his abilities through his voice to echo from the walls, "We must make all lands in our own image. Then we will have peace."

The stomping swept through the old men across the floor until all brought their boots down resoundingly and clapped their hands.

"Whether these people, now our enemies, like it or not, we will tear down the walls separating our lands!" shouted Dowler, unaware he contradicted his earlier words but loving the intensity of the crowd. "No more walls!"

"No walls!" started at the rear. The chant moved in all directions among the old men, who wanted nothing more than to tend their fortunes and have their house slaves.

"No walls! No walls…"

* * *

"I am not sure what I am to do with you." Prime Minister

Dowler filled a plate from a buffet table in his office. "You recommend caution, but my gut forced me to take another direction which seemed to work with the peers. Don't you think?"

"You made quite an impression, Prime Minister," said Sedgwick. He watched Dowler pile the meat on his plate, then stop.

"My father, you know, did not know what to do with me after I retired from the army." Dowler set down his plate and turned to Sedgwick and Higgins. "He sent me off to be a low-level assistant to another peer. 'Politics' he said, 'seems to be your talent.' I hated him for sending me… no… he banished me from my family."

Dowler purposely, in a slow deliberate fashion, went to the bottles and taking up a snifter filled it with a strong, brown whiskey and held it out to Sedgwick. His minister took the glass and nodded his thanks.

"My Father, however," said Dowler, "did me a great service. I… I am very good at politics." He returned to his plate, lifted it, then walked to his chair. Slowly, Dowler lowered himself onto its cushioned seat. His fingers gently caressed a piece of chicken, lifted it to his lips, and devoured the morsel. "'You made quite an impression,' my father told me after some time with the peer whom he foisted me upon. Didn't welcome me back into the family, but those were the kindest words I ever got from the man."

Sedgwick and Higgins remained silent. Sedgwick ignored the liquor in his hand. They did not know where this train of thought might lead.

"I am Prime Minister because I aligned myself with sturdy, military types such as yourselves. Which is why I enlisted your talent in my rise to the office I hold. The peers are comfortable with you." Dowler continued to eat. "You, however, should not get comfortable with me. Remember, I rule."

Dowler's ministers kept silent.

"Now," said Dowler, convinced that he had sufficiently bullied these men, "what can we do to make me look good and how fast can we do it?"

CHAPTER 22

"Prove it," demanded Robert of Anna.

After many meetings at Gracie's, Anna provided a reasonable set of experiments to be performed in the Snake. Anna, with Jack's help, plowed energy into a half acre plot in the city between burnt-out three-story buildings. They produced three mature corn crops in two weeks.

Impressed, Robert suggested one other viable option. He asked them to grow another batch of corn but bring children, any twelve children, along. He might get the first data supporting his thesis that the projector power in the South lay dormant, not vanquished. Give the kids a taste of energy and see if they have the strength to respond by putting out more energy than the amount taken from them.

"Imagine a special liquid flows from your hands into the dirt that causes the corn to grow strong and tall," said Anna, smiling raising her hands as she uttered the last words.

The young boys and girls stood around the edge of the garden and did as ordered. On their hands and knees, with only a small injection of power from Jack and Anna, the kids projected into the soil. They became known as the "Dirt Eaters". The corn sprang up and matured in one day. Not one child collapsed or felt the need to sleep until the experiment finished. Then, as a group, they dropped to the ground. The Dirt Eaters slept next to the crop they brought in.

Jack hated separating from Spunk. Their individual talents, however, took them in different directions for the cause. He took on the job of driver and rode with Anna Forrester in the first wagon: one of many sent to gather provisions from as many local farms as they could find within a week's ride of Snakeport. The project to gather food for the army started out with two hundred children and fifty wagons when it left the Snake aiming north.

"How many does that make?" Anna put her hand on top of the wide-brimmed hat she wore keeping it in place as a warm wind blew. In the distance, a house and barn stood barely visible among a stand of trees. The fields on either side of the road cut, leaving only remnants of corn stalks as far as the eye could see.

"How many what: farms or kids?" Jack followed her gaze. "Looks like maybe twenty acres." He returned his attention back to the road. "Eleven farms of similar size so far… hundreds of kids." Jack stole a look behind him into the wagon, where fifteen youngsters ranging in age from five to twelve waited impatiently for the trip to be over. "We'll lose more of the hundred we still have." He expected some children to deplete their energy and return to the Snake.

An hour later, Jack pulled back on the reins when they came up to the house they spied earlier. The front door opened, and a man stepped out. Barefoot, he wore pants with holes in the knees held up with suspenders. More significant, he raised a rifle aimed at Jack.

"Jus' stay in the wagon and move on. We ain't got no more. Ya take our seed corn and we starve." No one moved. "Get off my land! Damn, ya!"

Jack dropped the leather reins and removed his thick leather driver's gloves.

"Mister, this is your lucky day. We come to leave your barn full." Jack stood and swung his leg over to stand on the wheel, then dropped to the ground.

"Looks like you brought mouths to feed." The rifle followed Jack, then the click of the trigger slipping into the firing position filled the silence. The children looking over the side of the wagon ducked.

"We don't want any trouble, mister. Just need to use your fields is all. We'll pay you for the opportunity." Jack reached into his coat pocket and brought out gold coins, which he held out in his palm. "My name's Jack."

The barrel dropped an inch. The man watched as Jack gathered the coins into a stack and held them up for him to see a promising future more clearly. He licked his lips, then eased the trigger from the firing position.

"Gold for field stubble?"

"No," said Jack confidently, stepping forward so the rifle touched his chest. He moved half the coins to his left hand, then held the rest up in his right. "Take them." Jack slapped the coins into the extended hand as the rifle's business end dropped to the ground.

"The rest is yours when we finish, Mister…?" Jack put the rest of the stack back in his pocket.

"Philpot's the name… Rasmus Philpot." Without thinking, Philpot leaned the rifle against the horse rail behind him and counted the money. "Unless ya got magic about ya, I don't see ya making much from my land so late in the year."

"Come watch, Mr. Philpot." Jack turned on his heal and signaled for the wagons to empty and everyone to take up positions. A hundred children lined the edges of the corn field keeping a fifteen-foot gap between them. The men dressed in butternut uniforms waited by the wagons. Their work and Philpot's would begin after.

Jack and Anna took their time walking over the broken stalks to the center. Taking a few steps back, they knelt, then placed their hands on the rich, dark soil. The children followed suit.

"What's all this then?" asked Philpot, watching intently. He walked to the nearest man with chevrons on his sleeve waiting among the wagons. His fist clenched, the gold sure he would not be allowed to keep it.

"Well, Mr. Philpot, if I heard your name correctly, djinn have returned south."

The man's eyes nearly popped out of his head as green stems broke through the soil.

"Well, I'll be damned."

The original Dirt Eaters repeated the Snakeport experiment with a hundred others on twenty or more acres at the first farms in the first week of Jack and Anna's expedition. The first hundred children returned to Snakeport, depleted of energy, with wagons overflowing with provisions. Before they could scurry away, Robert, now widely known as the Professor, swept them up and ordered them into the classroom. They became the first, whining all the way, to attend school in a generation.

"This can't be right," mumbled Robert Forrester. He stood before a room of thirty children in the dilapidated building. It had been a public school many decades ago. The pupils stopped complaining, sat up straight, wide awake, and eager to find out more about being djinn. Robert and his northern projectors, out of an abundance of caution, made a study of the building. It passed. The rooms upstairs became dormitories for his charges. Most had no homes and looked to the army as their way to a better future. This class gathered as one of three.

"Mr. Langston," called Robert to his assistant at the back of the room. "Could you push harder?"

"Professor, I am already past the limit we discussed." Langston, one of the graduate students who came south with Forrester, agreed to train any potential projectors they might find. Neither expected to find more than a handful. The young man with the ready smile and shock of black hair came to the front of the room when the Professor signaled him.

"Mr. Langston," called Robert, who pulled his assistant close and whispered. "We must be very careful and very sure of our findings."

"I understand." Langston ran his hand through his hair. "They all complained about pain when holding the web of light very long." He turned to the rows of children shaking out or massaging their hands. "How can they all be soldier quality?"

"How indeed?" Robert thought for a second. "Let's move onto the next round of exercises and push them as far and as fast as we are able." He watched as Mr. Langston left the room to gather up things needed for the next tests.

"Well, ladies and gentlemen," started Robert. The class broke into giggles and catcalls about who earned the title of lady or not. "You, my dears, are all djinn." He felt the pride palpable among the smiling faces, watching his every move. "Djinn here are called projectors in the North. Some projectors will become doctors, some will become builders, and others will become soldiers." Robert walked slowly down one aisle. "For the near future, until things settle, we will expect you to use your talents to battle the North. You are soldiers."

"Professor?" a girl near the front called out. "We gonna kill those that steal us?"

"Yes," said Robert. A truth easily understood. "Yes. You will fight to make sure no more children are taken." He watched as Langston returned and placed a stack of papers on the desk.

"You will now read and write some answers to questions."

"Professor?" called a boy from the back. "Some can't read nor write worth a damn."

"Speak for yourself, Dodger," fired another boy.

"Ya can read, Smitty, like I can pass gold out my ass." The class laughed, and the badgering and bullying began.

Such a large number of potential high-quality projectors

provided an unexpected twist and something for which they had not planned. Langston and Robert conferred in the corner quietly. They needed to distract the children with simple tasks while they exerted energy to overcome innate defenses. When they turned to the class, more than a few shoes and any other weapons at hand had flown across the room.

"Enough!" The room erupted with power, forcing each child back in their seat. "Mr. Langston and I will read the questions," started Robert, "then have each of you answer. If you can write your answer, then do it. If not, I will make a note."

If the kids can do it, thought Robert, jumping to the next supposition, *what about their parents?*

* * *

Peppers had collapsed on the broken-down leather couch in his office, exhausted. The demand on his time and abilities since he opened the hospital overwhelmed him. He could not believe the effort put in by Hattie day in and day out. With no projector ability, she did more good, in his opinion, than he. She created the respite he needed to deal with tumors, lung function, and heart ailments. Most walked away cured after his administrations.

What had been a decaying arboretum, Hattie turned into a garden catering to the medicinal plants which she knew. The broken windows in the roof and the structure rot only energized her efforts to get the medicines she knew worked. The first crop of pain killing extracts bought him time, as well as his patients' relief. She cajoled the workmen who replaced support beams and patches for windows: no glass available.

Peppers rose from the couch and stretched. As soon as he had opened the front doors to the old hospital, he recalled, they came; the line of men, women, and children snaked around the building.

In the first weeks, his energy to heal went to ailments not seen in the North in fifty years. Hattie then applied her herb remedies, while he found time to take breaks and catch his breath, then deal with the more seriously ill patients. He could not get along without her. Still, he would give his right arm for a fully stocked laboratory to deal with unfamiliar infections he encountered.

Brushing down the wrinkles from sleeping in his clothes, Peppers grasped his office's door handle and opened it. The usual crew of young women and men patiently waited to confer with him on patients with whom they did their best with few resources. The nurses stood and followed as he walked away. Peppers and his entourage stepped down the grand stairway to the second floor, where the wards of sick and dying stretched left and right down long corridors. Why no noises of the sick and dying? He headed toward the desperate ward where even his abilities failed to prevent death.

At the door to a room with ten beds, he saw his first patient, Cynthia Congress, sitting and reading aloud to the dying in their beds. He wondered how she got up the stairs. He listened intently at the door held open by an old shoe to allow the air to move. Her voice, quiet, carried throughout the room. As she read, he realized it was a children's story about magic and the defeat of evil.

"Doc." Hattie came up behind him and smiled when he turned to her, startled. "Sorry. We need you in the isolation ward." She glanced into the ward. "Nanna has come here every day for weeks."

"Does it help?" asked Peppers, amazed at the old woman's stamina.

"Seems to," said Hattie. "They sleep better. I think they see one of their own and take comfort from that." She placed her hand on his shoulder, pulling him. "Others need you now."

"Yes, of course," agreed the doctor. "Ladies and gentlemen, talk to me as we walk."

They passed down the hall as he gave out instructions until only Hattie stood at the top of the stairs.

"What is happening in isolation?" Peppers, with each stride down the hallway, stepped into his doctor mode: emotionless, deal with illness, and remedy it.

"Lung function has decreased in some. The fans applied by the nurses are not enough." Hattie referred to the young ones who waved fans to help the patients breathe and cool them down.

"How many?"

"Half."

"I will need some food and drink. I may be a few hours at this." Peppers could deal with pneumonia easily in northern clinics, but here, death defied him. It was impossible for him not to take it personally.

"Yes, Doctor," said Hattie. She took his hand and placed a fold of wax paper in his palm. "Swallow this powder when you cannot keep going. It will help." With a squeeze of his hand, Hattie turned away and hurried down the hall.

Peppers stared at the paper pouch and wondered, *Who is the real magician?*

CHAPTER 23

Spunk's riders and wagons with their occupants entered a long, wide tunnel. The path inclined downward, and sunlight passed through holes in the rock walls above their heads, giving them light. The Warden, with Spunk's hands on the reins, rode in the first wagon with Hilton alongside on horseback.

"This is a service entrance," said the Warden, "which will give you access to other tunnels heading east." He pointed to people waiting up ahead. "Those folks will guide your company to places to park the wagons and take care of your animals. Rooms to eat, sleep, and get washed up will be next door." When they stopped to allow the mountain people to take the lead, the Warden climbed out of the wagon, offering his hand to Spunk. "Does this satisfy your needs?"

"Yes," said Spunk, taking his hand and jumping to the stone floor. "Mr. Hilton," she ordered, "pass the Warden's message down the line. I don't want any of the mountain people shot by mistake." She watched as Hilton nodded and trotted down the line.

"In that case," insisted the Warden, "you and your second in command will join me for dinner. There is much to discuss." He noted Hilton's return, dismount, and surrender of the reins.

"And why exactly aren't we dead?" asked Spunk, pulling her hand from his.

"Had you been real slavers," he said matter-of-factly, raising an eyebrow, "you would have died where you stood. But… you were not." He shook his head and chuckled. "All those kids with guns in their belts gave it away." The Warden headed left entering a smaller tunnel heading upward with Spunk and Mr. Hilton right behind.

"I will show you to your accommodations. You will have a few hours to rest and clean up." The Warden looked the two travelers up and down and rolled his eyes. "You will need fresh clothes?"

"Thank you," said Spunk, embarrassed, slapping dust from her sleeves. "We did not plan on a formal dinner."

"We mountain people have no interest in your war with the Eng," the Warden stated emphatically. His guests looked refreshed after a few hours' rest and a chance to clean up. He surveyed the rich table settings and fine food. Satisfied, he turned to Spunk, waiting patiently for her response.

"You and your people are the first mountain folk," started Spunk, "we have ever met." She paused a moment, then considered the Warden with a serious expression, then said, "Our southern ignorance and laziness to find out about you almost led to our ruin." She spread her hands and surveyed the bounty before her. "Thank you for this, but I believe beneath the veil of tall mountains and impassable cliffs exist cities carved from and beneath the rock."

"Well said, my dear," said the Warden. He poured two goblets of wine and handed her one, smiled, and said nothing more.

"Eng?" asked Spunk.

"It is what we call those to our east. They are the Eng."

"And, I assume, there are Neng," said Spunk. She sat at a table set for six, a candelabra hung from the ceiling providing light.

"Now that is an interesting assumption." The Warden set down his wine and served the other three people: Hilton and two mountain people. The two well dressed mountain natives included a man and a woman. Of average height, they looked more muscular than Hilton. "We have a power of our own, so we are not Neng. For now, you and your people are Neng." The

Warden grinned. "So, you will have our help to end the slave trade, which we despise, but we will not engage on any battlefield."

"You allowed us to pass through your country," said Hilton.

"Yes. We laid traps if you were slavers. We have been waiting for the good people of the South, and here you are." The Warden took his seat at the head of the table. His compatriots nodded agreement with his comment. "If the southern people refused to fight for their own, why should we place ourselves in the way of destruction?"

No one said a word around the table.

"But… here you are taking a stand," said the Warden. "We will do all that we can to end the caged wagons passing along our roads." After serving his guests, he returned to the head of the table. "Please, dear people, eat."

During the meal, other persons entered the room with a harp and flutes. When the wine bottles stood empty and stronger drink filled small, fluted glasses, the musicians played. The instrumental music filled the room, flowing from energetic to mournful, then back.

"I… have heard nothing like it," whispered Spunk when the music ended. An accompanied ballad sung by a tenor started.

"I'm glad you like it, Captain," spoke the Warden softly. He leaned forward, then said so all could hear, "We will help you reach your goal and escape with no traces if you win. If you lose, we will help those who survive and find their way to one of our tunnels. Expect nothing else."

"Warden," said Spunk, whose liquor glass went untouched, "the help you offer is appreciated. I expected nothing, so we are already in an improved position with what you have done."

"Honorable, my dear." The Warden raised his glass to her and sipped. "Are all southerners like you?"

"I hope there are many better than me."

"We realize a single decisive battle is coming." The Warden put his glass on the table. "Before the coming fight return to us here. Bring the Source with you."

"The Source?" asked Spunk.

"You do not know what you carry: something we sense. A conversation with the Source, the instigator of these actions, would be something special for us." The Warden sat and stared at her.

Jack, she thought. "If possible, I will bring him."

"Then we are done for this evening." The Warden and the other mountain folk stood, bowed to their southern guests, and left. "Go prepare your soldiers." He said over his shoulder, climbing up the stairs. "Bring us the Source."

* * *

"Damn," whispered Spunk, lying flat at the cliff's edge. She studied her target through an old, cracked set of binoculars. Two hundred feet above the valley floor, she watched as a line of horseless wagons rolled into the fenced enclosure up to the buildings. Twenty people stepped out from the silver vehicles. The surrounding air shimmered enough for Spunk to see that more projectors than they expected would need killing.

"A problem, Captain?" asked Hilton, less of a guide with the mountain people showing them the way. He laid on the ground next to her.

"An unexpected complication, Mr. Hilton." Spunk dropped the binoculars and thought. "We will have to deal with over twenty projectors."

"I ain't much for suicide, if ya take my meaning." Hilton reached for the binoculars and studied the camp.

"We will have to watch them for a day, then attack smaller but manageable groups of them." Spunk immediately made further revisions to their plan.

"This will have ta be a night action," stated Hilton. "Daylight might kill us all."

"No. With this lot, daytime is the only way to win." Spunk smiled. She saw their victory so clearly in her mind's eye. "Given a choice, I don't want to die either." She patted his shoulder. "Stay here and observe. I will send others to relieve you."

Spunk pulled back from the cliff's edge, then stood and headed back down the path to the waiting soldiers. She stopped as commanded on her way back to the wagons by southern troops ordered to stand among the stones. She smiled as they demanded she identify herself.

"I need two of you to go up to the cliff and maintain a watch on the northerners." She heard the triggers ease from their firing positions. "Tell Mr. Hilton to join me." Spunk watched two children dash up the path to the cliff. The others went back to their posts. *Killing time again,* she thought without emotion.

Spunk made a mistake.

Action started in darkness, not in daylight. The scrape of the sharpening stone along the edge of her blades stopped an hour before daybreak. Clicking cylinders as the children checked their weapons filled the cavern where they had slept. Thirty minutes after Spunk started out through the tunnel, her soldiers moved out to take their positions along the paths the slaves used to gather their tools on the way to the mine.

The blade cut easily through the skin and viscera beneath the ear. Arterial blood spurted. The victim stared, eyes wide, and called out. His arms thrashed as he tried to get out of bed. Spunk chuckled and shook her head.

"No one to hear, my dear," she said. Spunk left the man to do what he would until he calmed in death. Careful to avoid any blood on the floor that might stain her stocking feet, her last best pair of socks, she went to examine her victim's things, dumping the travel bag's contents across the table. As with the first two projectors, an unexplainable curiosity compelled her to look through their personal effects.

From the start, Spunk embraced her good luck. The front fence went unlocked. She went to the house where her watchers had seen the men enter. Abandoning her boots beneath the first story window, she became a second story man, a thief familiar in the Snake. Silent action felt good to her. The first two men died in the same messy way, but Spunk also cut deep into their throats to minimize any cries for help. Laying across the chest of each man in the order she chose kept the noise of their flailing to a minimum. After the first two, out of habit, she moved cautiously down the corridor to the last door. The door swung open on well-greased hinges. Amazed at the sheer stupidity, she thought, *Do they ever learn? Are they so unaware?*

"Either way, dead is dead." Of course, she never faced a projector who saw her coming.

Spunk found nothing of interest among the personal items. None wore rings or had pictures of loved ones. Even the hardened crew with her had little keepsakes like a string around a wrist or a scratched sentiment on their gun barrels: make 'em bleed.

When she left the building, the first gun fire echoed among the cliffs surrounding the mining operation. As planned, her soldiers had joined the line of slaves heading toward the mine. Heads down, looking destitute and bedraggled in their worn clothing, they became one of the workers. As the projectors grouped, pushing the slaves to their tasks, they created their own kill zone, easy to hit. The revolvers came out and before any defense might be mounted; the bullets tore away the back of a head or a face. Only a head shot would do ordered Spunk. The children took their orders seriously.

The twenty new arrivals from two days before and the few projectors used to run the mining operation lay dead. The line of slaves, however, continued to the mine.

"Hey! Stop!" yelled Jimmie Nicks.

Spunk found him and his five-man crew, boys and girls, near the front of the line. Three adult bodies lay on the ground. The boy walked over to one of the dead, pointed his gun at the corpse, and pulled the trigger. The explosion echoed off the walls.

"See! They's dead and can't hurt none of you no more." Jimmie took a pick from the hands of the nearest boy and tossed it on the ground. "You ain't slaves no more. We's here to take y'all home." The silence and the lack of any reaction like the dead frustrated Jimmie.

"Jimmie Nicks," called Spunk gently. "Have your crew lead these people from the mine to the tunnel. If they want to keep their tools, then let them. I suspect freedom may not mean very much to them right now."

Jimmie and the other five crews guided over two hundred slaves, mostly children and teenagers. The occasional adult in the line with scars on his or her back from the whip followed along just as mindless as the younger set.

Further down the valley, a windowless house stood locked and secure. As promised, the Warden's people showed up and made quick work of locks. Inside wooden chests looking like caskets lined up one after the other across the floor. Holding a flaming torch high in one hand, Spunk pulled up the lid on the first crate. The light reflecting off the gold bars blinded her momentarily. She let the lid drop with a bang, left the warehouse, and went looking for the smelter.

"Time to clean house."

"IT DOESN'T MATTER," YELLED PRIME MINISTER DOWLER. THE echo in the large room of his mansion accented his surety. "Attack now, attack later. The outcome will be the same. We are the power. They cannot stand against us." He examined the attendees at his informal cabinet meeting, sensitive to arguments or naysaying of his ideas. The four well-padded leather chairs with high wide arms caressed their occupants. Dowler intentionally looked to their comfort, providing food and drink in his home. The Prime Minister's desired goal for tonight's efforts aimed at the discovery of those who remained loyal and those who would not and needed to be removed.

"Sir," spoke up Colonel Martell, "you are correct in a standard field engagement. One hundred of our men against ten thousand of their rifle-carrying soldiers and they lose. Should we count on this as the only possible confrontation?"

"If we march five thousand strong to Snakeport, what else can they do?" The Prime Minister did not belittle field officers with the credentials of Martell. He posed questions guiding the answers to his goal. "Surely they will try to stop us."

"They could just as easily burn down the city and the surrounding area, leaving our forces dependent on a long supply line easily harassed. When you have nothing to begin with, you have little to lose or mourn by setting it alight."

"I see." Dowler wanted to gather the entire northern force, supplemented with older capable civilians, and squash the South quickly. The movement of workers from households and schools to the mines and fields would support the country's needs for a while. It provided a patch, not the last fix. "So, Higgins," said

Dowler, turning to his Minister of War, "our northern border is safe finally after months of effort?"

"Yes, Prime Minister," said Higgins. "We can now concentrate our forces on the southern border." The reports from the northern border said the fighting had stopped. The savages had gone quiet, retreating further north. Exactly why Higgins could not extract from the pages. He would ask Martell to clarify the status of the northern border after tonight's meetings.

"Our launch will happen…?"

"Late winter," said Higgins. "It is possible they may be taken by surprise. We have not fought a winter engagement in centuries."

"How many men?" Dowler got to his feet and went to the side table and filled a small plate with fruit and sweetmeats.

"Five thousand is the estimate. More if the older civilians lend their abilities." The discussion with those older civilians came next when they joined their meeting. "Then we have the extra thousand non-projectors to fight fire with fire, so to speak."

"Rifles are worthless," said Dowler, returning to his seat and setting the plate on his chair's arm. "This thousand will be only good for distraction, if that. Cannon fodder is their best use."

"Their value will come in the time before the battle when the generals need solid intelligence on the enemy." Sedgwick spoke up. He had kept his thoughts to himself up to this point. "It is what we do not know that will cost us the most. That is how we lost the initial confrontation in early summer."

"What makes you think these men rejected by their families will be any more loyal to us?" Dowler drank from the tumbler of dark liquid. He placed the blame for the summer disaster at Higgins' feet.

"We offer them the rule of the South after our victory," said Sedgwick. "Of course, if all goes well, there will be little over which to rule." Sedgwick stared into his empty glass, then looked up as the surrounding men chuckled.

A liveried servant approached Dowler and leaned down to whisper in his ear. The Prime Minister nodded, then waved his man off.

"Gentlemen, the rest of our council has arrived." Dowler stood and waved a greeting to the ten silver-haired men who took places at the large round table at the other end of the room. "Let's join our lambs and pray we can turn them and their followers into wolves."

As the prime minister rose, an officer strode into the room and focused his gaze on the Colonel. He pulled a paper with the red wax stamp of a top secret from his pouch. Martell rose to his feet and took the offered communique. He broke the seal and read.

"This is confirmed?" Martell turned to Dowler and handed him the paper as the messenger nodded. Turning to Sedgwick and Higgins, he stated, "Ministers, we have a problem."

"Betrayed by our own!" hissed Dowler, crumpling the bad news in both hands. "I want you to round up all the families of those soldiers and… question them." Torture them until they spoke the truth struck him first. The Prime Minister eyed his spymaster and his Ministers of the Interior and War. "It is the only way this could have happened!" He had been on his feet, ready to engage the senior citizens when he threw his weight in the chair. Dowler cupped his forehead in his palm. "All that gold gone."

"No betrayal took place," Higgins insisted.

"I concur," said Colonel Martell, anticipating Dowler's outrage. When the Prime Minister slapped the desktop, he hardly reacted.

"Why damnit, do you concur?" said Dowler in a whining, sarcastic tone.

"Our vanished, assumed dead, men fought on our northern border for years. Given lighter duty they escorted the gold shipments. Never been south of the capital, so no turning opportunity."

"Then how did this happen, Colonel?" All three men turned to Martell. He had not allowed for such a bold move, but offered an answer.

"Like the summer attack, surprise."

"Surprise?" questioned Dowler. He threw the balled-up paper at Higgins, who caught it in his right hand and gently flattened it on his hip. His eyes quickly scanned the message.

"Prime Minister," said Higgins, "would you have expected an attack by non-projectors several hundred miles into our territory?"

Dowler's eyes shifted left, then right. He stood up, sat down, then grunted.

"Sir," interjected Sedgwick, taking the missive from Higgins, "we have fifty heads of powerful families gathering for our report. These men will take up the uniform in their later years and bring battalions to aid our cause." He leaned forward, holding up the paper. "Faced with this, they need calm, assured direction based on the facts."

"Facts? What facts?" Dowler climbed to his feet and went to the nearest window and looked out at the green fields of his home and the forest in the distance. He waited, worried, when no one spoke. A solution had to be found, but not by him. *Not my fault.*

"Reassurance," repeated Sedgwick, "and a plan to learn all that we can on activity south of the Aquitaine."

Dowler returned from his retreat to the window and nodded. "What is the plan?"

"Come," said Sedgwick, "I will give you our best advice, then we join the other guests."

The meeting with the whole counsel took place around the large table where the family heads must commit to a military solution. The Prime Minister at the head of the table raised his hands as though his audience had armed themselves with rotten food for throwing. After he noticed the strange looks aimed his way, he regained control of himself and turned the discussion of the lost gold, men, and slaves over to Martell.

"A winter attack is no longer viable," stated Colonel Martell. "Spring would be the earliest we might move against the South. A summer campaign might be the best option."

"Exactly, what happened at that mine?" asked Prime Minister Dowler, per their previous arrangement.

"We don't know with certainty," stated Martell. "The only clues are spots of blood on room and cave walls." The Colonel talked to the Prime Minister but looked to each man at the table. "An entire shipment of gold disappeared, as did several hundred workers. The guts of the smelter are gone."

"No tracks? Wagons laden with heavy gold coffers would leave ruts in the road." Artemis Folfox looked at Martell. Folfox took his military duties seriously. Like the Colonel, he came to the meeting in a simple uniform, but unadorned simplicity allowed him to project his personal power. "Have we seen anything like this before?"

"No, to both." Martell shook his head in frustration. "No tracks, no bodies, no gold, nothing." He paused for a second. "I have asked our researchers to find any reference to an action like this in the past."

"So, who sent the small troop to their destruction?" asked Dowler.

"No one," interjected Sedgewick. "A regular pick up with no reason to expect anything out of the ordinary."

"Has our hands-off agreement with the Mountain people ended?" Asked an old man with long white hair who sat with his chin on his chest and eyes closed.

"It is not clear how involved the Mountain people might have been." Martell stood and leaned forward on the table. "The walls and tunnels looked blocked, as they have always been." He tapped the tabletop with the palm of his hand. "The blood suggests that what happened to our younger recruits this summer took place again with veterans. Complete surprise."

"Gentlemen," said Higgins. "If we assume another bold southern gambit, it will force us to split our forces between defense and offense. Regardless, we need to recruit more men, train them, and restock our ranks."

"Thought we had," said Folfox.

The back and forth and the looking for blame went on for hours. Finally, Dowler called a halt to the counsel and reviewed their next steps. They agreed to meet again in a month when more data might be available. A conscription called for another ten thousand men to increase their forces.

Sedgwick and Higgins cornered Martell in the hall outside the meeting room after vows of support and ultimate victory fell flat.

"I hate not knowing what is going on," whispered Higgins.

"How close are we to getting eyes and ears into southern towns and cities?" asked Sedgwick.

"Gentlemen," said Martell as calmly as possible, "relieve me of all responsibilities, but the gathering of information in the South and I will give you what you want."

"How?" asked Sedgwick, glancing over the hallway noting the many small discussions like theirs among the pillars. None close enough to hear, eyes glanced their way. "If we cannot give these old fools hope, then we are all done for."

"Done for," said Martell, sick of the politics authored by the men standing next to him, but aware they represented a practical path to a solution. He could not imagine having to deal with Dowler. "You allowed this man to be in power. Now you lament your actions because the situation on the ground has changed significantly." Martell shook his head, steadied himself, and let his anger melt away. "You have in the past stood against a determined enemy in the field. Think strategically. The North will prevail, but only if I enlist the non-projectors into our efforts. I must be able to offer them something to get their allegiance."

"Isn't power over the South enough?"

"No." Martell knew what it took to get men to surge forward against an entrenched enemy. It took faith, something sorely lacking in the Northern cause. "Acceptance, gentlemen." Martell looked over his shoulder. "How many of these families have children they have tossed aside? We need these abandoned children to win. What will we offer them to make the sacrifice worthwhile?"

"I see," said Higgins. He scanned the room, feeling the passive energy from so many capable manipulators. "Give the forsaken what you think best." He sensed the power of his words, but not their potential outcome. Healing never went without great pain, especially after one hundred years of judgement and prejudice.

* * *

Colonel Martell stared blankly, thinking of the meeting with the Prime Minister. He liked the man. If asked, he could not say exactly why. In the field as commander, the Colonel knew he would more than likely kill Dowler before he got good men needlessly murdered. In those comfortable chairs, however, with high-quality liquor in easy reach and supporters in the discussion circle, the plans floated: a delightful fantasy. He now had to launch the fantasy in the real world.

"Something has defeated us." Martell's eyes flew over the room, noting its crumbling plaster, raised and rotten floorboards, and the smell. The non-projector headquarters lay near an overused cesspit. Martell raised the scented handkerchief to his nose. He intended to move the unit to Hempstead as soon as practical. "We do not know why. Our best guess is that our forces got caught unaware. What do you think?"

"I think," said Lakeland, "you don't know your enemy." Reginald Lakeland with Stan Folfox sat across from Colonel Martell. Their uniforms wrinkled, showing wear at the elbows and knees, and ground in dirt from weeks working with their battalion in the field.

"That Colonel Lakeland states the obvious," said Martell, aware either man would want to strangle the life out of him, given their current conditions. "And is only what we can see. I believe we are facing a much greater threat. I, however, cannot prove the point. Which…" paused Martell, "means we need you and your men. I cannot make up for the years of abuse, but, and I have this directly from the Prime Minister, non-projectors will no longer face isolation and ostracism. He believes you and men like you have rights and deserve better from your families and the government."

"You will excuse us," said Major Folfox, "if we think you are full of crap!" Stan would not complain if his death came fast and painless. Certainly, the chief spy for the Dowler government could end him with little exertion. He and most of the men under his command felt the same: murder us or support us. "Either end this fiasco that you need non-projectors or give us reasons to sacrifice spit for you, our so-called families, or any of your kind."

"I, with the Prime Minister's authority, have ordered immediate changes to you and your men's circumstances. You will move immediately to Hempstead, where you will find quarters in the best rooms, etc. I want to train your men in the arts of espionage methods and practices."

"What exactly," asked Lakeland, "do you want to know with certainty?"

"Is the slave war localized in the eastern regions or has it spread across the whole South?" Martell raised his hand and pulled down one of his fingers. "Are there more projectors than the fifty we know about that went south with Forrester? How are they able to keep their forces in the field and organized?" Two more fingers folded. "Are the unruly southern regions uniting behind a cause or a personality?" His last standing finger, the index on the right hand, remained. "Finally, who the hell is Jack Fox?"

CHAPTER 25

"Here are the battle formations from the fight at Avon a hundred years ago," said Robert Forrester, pointing to a large paper draped over two side-by-side chalk boards wheeled into the room. "No rifle companies, as you can see, held in the front." He considered the drawing, and the notes scribbled at the edges and among the separate units in faded brown, red, green, or no color. The riflemen with weapons over their shoulders were the latter colorless. "Since the groups in color have their hands in one or two unique positions and no weapons, they are projectors."

"Professor," asked Tom Haggard, "we stand between the proverbial rock and a hard place. The army continues to grow, with units from southern towns and villages. To be honest, time, an uncontrolled variable, sours my expectation for success. Give us your best description of the colors' meaning."

Forrester stared at the General. He knew the work with his assistants, Jack's, and Anna's provisioning actions, and last, what might come from the targeted gold mine could not happen fast enough. The leaves turned. *Do we have fifty projectors to counter thousands on the other side, or are there more? Do we have until the spring or will they come earlier?*

"It is interesting," he said calmly, "to note that the depiction shows no women in the ranks." Forrester pulled a large tome from a stack of books on a table along the wall. "My students have found the following diary of a staff officer that helps us decipher the meaning of the colors. It is not, however, definitive." Opening the book and flipping through the pages, he stopped and turned to the graphic. "The brown coloring shows projectors held in reserve. We base this in part on their position on the field. The green we think are the units providing shielding or defense. See how their palms face outward? The red units are the attack units, fists raised."

"So, the rifle units behind the reserves rarely engaged the enemy?" asked Haggard.

"A last resort, perhaps," said Forrester, considering the formation. "It makes sense."

"The only sure thing, Professor, is our rifle units." Haggard stared at the paper, highlighting the coming disaster. "We can't stand against projectors."

"No, General," said Forrester. "My team and I are working to bring along enough projector capability by the winter. Unexpected support from other quarters, about which I cannot comment, may be coming." The defeat sweeping the room born from the data scraped from long forgotten and decaying pages of history made Forrester reveal what he wanted to avoid: a greater power in which he did not believe might be at work.

"Professor?" Gracie, sitting to Haggard's right, leaned forward. "This is no time for hemming and hawing about this situation."

"Agreed, Gracie." Forrester closed the book and walked to the table, stopping in front of Haggard. "Let's have this discussion later, in private. You can decide if you wish to share it with the rest of the army."

"We will need regular reports from all units trying to solve these problems," said Haggard. "I and my command staff must go west and meet with the politicians ruling in other cities who might join Snakeport's fight. They are not all in agreement. We must persuade them."

The meeting continued going over eyewitness reports on the battles fought so long ago: the interaction of shields, energy bolts, and volleys of lead. In the end, betrayal had destroyed the southern army. Haggard took hope, since betrayal would not be a problem this time. The historical review ended.

"Gracie, a moment of your time," said Haggard, so only she could hear.

"Of course." She followed Haggard into her office and closed the door.

"You will not join me for the trip west," said Haggard, his hands clasped behind his back, "at least not until you do something for me." He looked Gracie in the eye and stated, "I need someone I trust to find out if there is any effort to send spies south. They would not be projectors: too easy to spot. They would be one of us or, more like, a northern non-projector who came south." He waved his hand at what he thought might be her disappointment and added, "We will meet up in Lancaster or Middleton when you have completed your work. Send a message."

"You are thinking of Lakeland or others like him coming south?" Gracie moved around her desk and sat. She had no time for anything other than the job at hand and smiled at Tom's awkward consideration of her feelings.

"Exactly." Haggard sighed. "There is also the possibility that such men might form a negotiating party for their masters."

Neither spoke for a time, caught up in the deadly possibilities. Gracie discarded the thought of any negotiation, any diplomacy. Its only value would be as a tool to buy time. Southern destruction clearly guided the northern action.

"Your teams in the trees and elsewhere have been our eyes and ears." Haggard collapsed into a chair. "Unless the boy could single-handedly destroy thousands of men like himself, I see no escape from the coming destruction." Haggard fought his defeatist attitude and took a deep breath, letting it out slowly. "We need them to come out of the trees and get into the border towns. What do you think?"

"There is only one crossing that will support a large troupe movement over the river. We can watch the towns around the bridge. Since the river is not fordable along most of its length, the only other way would be through the Western Mountains. The towns in the area fiercely support us." Gracie glanced up at the Jack's artwork. "Strangers cannot go unnoticed. Of course, in one of our uniforms, some might get through unchallenged."

"Have any northerners come that way in the past?" Haggard leaned forward and insisted, "We have to know. What about projectors building temporary structures across the Aquitaine to get their spies across or a simple rowboat anywhere on the river?"

"Tom," Gracie smiled. "You are thinking too much like a southerner. Remember, northerners hate their inferior offspring almost as much as they detest us." She watched as Haggard considered her words, then stood straight and rubbed his chin.

"You have a point, but we cannot assume they are all stupid."

"How many women," asked Gracie, "fought in the first small invasion in the summer?"

"None, of course." Haggard looked at Gracie and pointed his index finger at her. "Yes. You are right." Tom closed his eyes, took another deep breath, then said, "Let's do everything to make sure we are not the stupid ones."

"I will refocus my foot soldiers to seek any spies and pursue any river crossings in small boats." Gracie stood. "Now, we need to get Jack back to the Snake. He must train our newfound projectors. They are our wildcard in all of this. Who knew they existed?"

"Yes, I agree. I still do not know what to expect of Jack. What can he do? What can't he do?"

"Jack," said Gracie, speaking carefully, staring at the eagle sculpture, "grows into his abilities and then stretches those muscles he never knew he had. It makes me wonder if Mr. Fox isn't what the Professor wants to talk about in private."

"Too many variables and too many unknowns."

"Tom," said Gracie in a calm but direct manner, "stop. We will control what we can. The rest is out of our hands. Do not make yourself into a powerless leader undone by doubt."

"You have no doubts about what might happen, or how it might end?" Haggard crossed his arms. He felt angry at his subordinate's presumption, but knew in his gut she had it right.

"Doubt is a fatal disease in the Snake." Gracie returned to her seat. "Action, planned or not, saves lives."

"Let's get the Professor in here," said Haggard nodding his agreement, "and hear what he has to say in private."

"In short, Tom," said Robert Forrester in Gracie's office, "you have several hundred soldier quality projectors we can identify who are completely untrained and will need intense, possibly lethal, battle skills. There may be thousands more."

"How can this be?" Haggard could not believe his good fortune.

"I have a theory," Forrester's eyes looked to Tom, then Gracie. "The northern non-projectors tossed out by their families came south and started their own. Maybe… just maybe, projection is a part of all of us. It can go fallow for a time, one generation to the next, but will reassert itself at some point."

"Practically speaking, Professor," asked Gracie, "southern djinn escaped destruction. Not all headed north."

"Not exactly, madam." Forrester scratched his chin, thinking about what he observed in his classroom. "Northerners gathered up individuals with any obvious projector ability. They left behind those with less detectable ability, like late-bloomers. Southern djinn have always been here, and now we are finding strong projectors rising in the population after a hundred years."

Gracie looked at Forrester as if he spoke a foreign language.

"In short, the South may have the same number of projectors as the North."

"Can't be," stated Haggard, shaking his head.

"The southern culture profoundly absorbed the northern propaganda that they had stolen all of your djinn. You stopped looking for it. So, it wasn't there." Forrester leaned forward and stated, "Now I have evidence that it is here." He stood and knocked the desktop with a knuckle. "You general just got lucky."

CHAPTER 26

Every student in the room hailed from the Snake. Except for a few of the Professor's assistants and a few unexpected adults, the students looked to be Jack's age or younger. The fifth class of the day began. Jack lectured and projected non-stop training the new energy manipulators to be defenders or killers: both would be best. Many still had dirt under their nails from the fields they worked over the last weeks. The older Snakeport residents attended at the Professor's invitation because he wanted to know if there might be more surprises among the southern populace.

"Shields up!" demanded Jack of forty students.

"Wh-What?" called out a few. "What do we know 'bout…"

A stunning force came from above and fell like rain on each participant. All raised their arms in defense, but for some with their raised arms came the shimmering. The energy never touched these people. Others jumped around, slapping where the bolts landed on them. The attack stopped.

"Defend yourselves, damnit all!" Jack noted who projected successfully and who did not. One of the older participants never moved but raised his shield. "We have no time to bring you along slow and steady. We need everything you have now!" Jack walked among the class. Some continued to rub shoulders or thighs. "You loaded the earth with what the soil needed to grow the food we need. Now load the surrounding space with a powerful shield." He went back to the front of class slowly, letting the advice sink in. No one grumbled about the exercise. Children of the Snake knew better.

"The next attack will be stronger than the last! We don't need any weak ones in the Snake. Do we?... Shields up!"

The storm fell harder, brighter. When the energy dissipated, the room glowed with a continuous protecting layer, like a deep, clear pond, with the sun reflecting off the surface.

"Well, alright then." Jack clapped his hands, saluting the students' success. The smiles and grins born of his praise filled the room. He could see his students worshipped him, but he did not want this. He wanted them willing to do anything, no matter who led the way. These kings and queens of squalor unwilling to go down quietly but unsure of their newfound power demanded Jack stand with them, stand for them. Jack wanted them to fight for themselves.

"You three in the back," Jack pointed to the three adults: a woman and two men in their late twenties or early thirties. "What made you think you had some djinn?"

"Well, sir, if it please ya," said one man.

"What's your name?" Jack smiled.

"Samuel Gomper, your lordship."

"Okay, Sam," said Jack. "And I'm Jack, just Jack."

"I got near kill't by a runaway wagon," said Sam nodding. "Horse knocked me down and wheel come over m' chest." He kept looking at Jack, then looking away as if he did not have the right to address one so high. "Got the scar." He unbuttoning his shirt to prove he spoke the truth. The angry red welt showed the wheel's passing on the man's skin. "Should be dead, don' ya know, but ain't."

The other two adults, Sue and John, had similar stories. Each finding it hard to look Jack in the eye. Jack nodded, then stood silent.

"I am tired," said Jack finally. He bent at the waist, placed his hands on his knees, and took a couple of deep breaths. "It is your job," he stood up, "to kill me." Frowns and gasps as in the earlier classes swept across the room. "Kill me using all the power you can muster. I am everything you hate. I steal the likes of you for slave money," his finger pointed at the youngest. "I take and take and leave y'all with nothing. Kill me and you will be free."

The silence boiled with expectation. Jack powered up and unleashed a surprise. Something he had learned back in Hempstead as he brought enough light into his room to read at night. It was a matter of creating lenses manipulating air density and his shield. Light could be bent, blocked, reflected, or refracted. One night, with nothing new to read and bored, he played with the light. With a little effort, he painted a reasonable picture of Peppers in bright traces. Before his students, Jack projected a picture; a monster rose.

The shock at what came at them caused all to move back. Jack Fox had disappeared. A hairy giant with four arms took his place and towered over them with intent to kill. The first feeble balls of energy hit the giant, and the beast laughed. Large arms stretched out to take bodies and crush the life from them. Bolts flew with more energy and the monster stepped back, froze in place, then fell away piece by piece in a slurry of sparkling light.

"You cannot penetrate my shield! You little wimps are holding back. Unleash your power!" The iridescence around Jack vanished as he walked among the class. "What do you think the invaders will do to you?" He glared at a few and pushed a few on the shoulder. He stopped in front of the adults. "You ready to show these young how it's done, Sam Gompers?" he paused. Sue, John?"

"Sure as night follows day," yelled Sam.

"Again!" Jack returned to the head of the class. The giant came forth again. "Fire!"

The exercises continued for another hour. The children and adults had exhausted themselves by pouring power into their attacks. His pitting the older against the younger had the desired effect. The energy level rose so high that the wooden furniture smoldered. Jack called a halt when the sun had dropped below the rooftops.

"Go to dinner, the lot of you! You did well." Jack stationed himself at the door and touched every soul on the shoulder or arm. He congratulated them. "Those northern soldiers will laugh at you, but not for long."

When the last student exited, Jack gathered his assistants.

"What do you think?" Jack sat behind a desk while the four northern graduate students gathered in front.

"Your methods," said the one female, "are unorthodox and probably dangerous, but… the amount of energy released amazed me."

"Tell us about the big, ogre-like thing? Certainly, scared the hell out of me," said the young man next to her. "I have seen nothing like it."

"A simple manipulation of the force field we all use," said Jack. "Didn't you ever bring light into your room from a distant source so you could keep working?" Jack almost laughed at their dumbfounded expressions. He realized they never had the need with their own light sources at hand. Changing the subject, he asked, "Are they soldier-material?"

"Yes." All four spoke simultaneously.

The sky had turned black when Jack left the school, heading back to his and Spunk's rooms above the courtroom. He would report to Haggard that the South had projectors: soldier quality. All the talk about the North taking everything of value with them was wrong. With more training, this might turn a sure defeat into a chance for victory.

At these times, consumed with keeping up with the expectations, he especially missed Spunk. Overdue, he worried and wondered what should be done. He bumped into a woman coming from the opposite direction as they went around the same side of a pile of cut lumber blocking the sidewalk.

"Jack?"

After a few steps, Jack stopped and turned. A woman in a hooded cape faced him with her face partially hidden.

"It's been awhile. You been very busy, as I hear it." The woman pulled back the hood.

"Mom?" Jack just stared.

Lilly held his gaze a moment, then turned away to adjust a bag she carried over her shoulder.

"Gracie put me in charge of soldier's clothing, boots, and such." She smiled. "Seems I'm good for somethin' after all." Lilly glanced up at her son then as the silence went on, shook her head and turned to go. "I'm glad to see you're doing fine," she said sadly.

"Wait!" called Jack. "I haven't had time to eat. Would you care to have dinner with me?" She came close. Jack saw a smile light up her face. Confused, he did not know what to say or think. She stood not drunk nor angry railing against the world. Jack had never dealt with his mother in any other condition.

"I would like that very much," said Lilly.

"I'm staying in the old courthouse on the top floor." Jack walked in step with his mother.

"I always thought you and Spunk made a good match. Nanna did a good job with her and Mini." Lilly kept her eyes on the sidewalk, trying to ease the awkwardness. "I can't say I'm all that proud of what I done, but I'm sure as hell proud of you."

Jack nodded and mumbled his thanks. He feared what might be coming. Jack judged his silence a better defensive position. As the thought crossed his mind, he wondered why and what he feared.

"I been goin' cold turkey since Gracie put me in charge

of about a hundred people." Lilly chatted on about the job, the people, and how it would not be helpful to get drunk in her current position. She sighed and filled the silence, talking constantly as they walked down the street.

In his room, sitting across from each other over a well laid out dinner, they stared at each other.

"I'm so sorry," started Lilly. Tears started down her cheeks. "I been like a disease in your life. But we, Stan and me, didn't start out to hurt anyone."

Jack watched and listened as his mother laid herself bare. At first, feeling awkward as the confession progressed, a great sorrow overwhelmed him.

"Not much to be done about the past." As his words left his mouth, they felt lame. Jack shook his head. The silence extended, then Jack went where he did not want to go. The earth goddess told him it had to be done. He turned on her suddenly, finally allowing himself to free years of anger. "You were both complete and total shits! You lived in a shadow world where I had to take care of you and myself. My father," he said, the sarcasm dripping, "damned near committed murder selling me into slavery." Fury invaded every part of him. "You betrayed me."

"Yes," wailed Lilly. She cried and crossed her hands over her stomach, rocking back and forth. "Yes. I betrayed you and let the Snake have its way with you. Then, when you survived, I used you. I did that. I deserve… I deserve to… to be ignored and left to die alone."

Jack, unprepared for his mother's capitulation and ownership of her part in his life, found no words. What was it the goddess said?

"I abandoned you." Lilly choked.

Jack knocked his chair over, rising to his feet. He came around the table and went to his knees. He threw his arms around her, pulling her tight. Her arms gripped him like Mini. Holding each other for a long time in silence, wrapped like a blanket against the harsh cold of the past, would be enough for now.

"I ain't cured." She held her son tight. "I can't say for sure. I won't go back to the drink. But I'll try."

"I love you anyway," whispered Jack. *Regardless* went unspoken. He exhaled a huge breath he had held and with it went part of his anger and hate. *Yes, I am djinn, but my greatest power is being human.*

"I have much to tell you," whispered Jack, relaxing the hug and leaning back. He kept a firm grip on her hands. He told her about Anna and the earth goddess, the growing of crops, finding others like himself, and everything he had done. Hours passed.

Finally, with nothing more to be said, they sat across from each other and ate. Hunger, like no other they had experienced, seized them as every morsel evaporated from the plates.

"The sky lightens," said Jack. "I could have a room made up for you next door."

"A blanket and the floor will be good enough for me," said Lilly. "But… tell me of this Clay person."

"The Doc?" asked Jack.

Jack told the story of his wounds and recovery. The trials and training in Hempstead.

As the sun made its way higher in the sky, Jack finished his story. Both, by this time, could hardly stay awake. A deep sleep took them: Jack on the bed and Lilly on the floor.

Lilly awoke first in the early afternoon. Quietly, she gathered herself together and made ready to get back to her office on her day off. With her bag over her shoulder, she stood by the bed and looked down at her sleeping son. She wanted to laugh and cry, throw her arms around him. They had cracked their mutually fortified internal boundaries and spilled their pain, deceit, trickery, and faithlessness. She stifled a giggle. She and her son laughed after most of the ugly stuff spilled out. The door closed behind her with the slightest swish and click.

Lilly felt she had better control over herself, focusing on the immense work to do. Gracie told her there may be a large contingent of new soldiers from the western cities. Wool and cotton ran low. With her eyes fixed on the sidewalk, she gathered speed and thought about solutions. When she came to a gap in the line of buildings, she felt a tug like a youngster pulling on a parent's coat to pay attention and see something important.

The open lot looked like the one Jack described to her. Brown corn husk remnants lay here and there. Lilly stared at the dark earth, then stepped off the sidewalk. An idea, a hope, came to her. Looking over her shoulder to be sure no one noticed, she headed to the back corner where lumber and bricks lay piled. Lifting the bag's belt over her head, she set it next to the wood. Sufficiently hidden so no passerby might question a crazy person in the dirt, she prepared.

Lilly picked up her dress, so it would not get dirty, and planted her bare knees on the earth. As she leaned forward to set her hands as Jack described, a trick of the afternoon sun made the ground twinkle, or so she thought.

"I don't know if you can hear me or if I am doing this right, but if you can help my Jack." She pushed her hands harder into the soil. "Take me if needs must." Nothing happened. Lilly tried to remember everything her son had told her about the youngsters: imagine water flowing from their hands. "Won't work for me."

Lilly sat back on her heals and brushed her hands against each other to knock off the dirt. Placing her hands on her waist, she thought about giving up. "No. I always give up when it gets a little hard. Not today." *What do I know for certain? What am I good at?*

Her hands at the end of her arms worked like machines, creating wearable clothing from sheets of wool or cotton. She often found herself in deep conversation with her workers at the tables while her hands sewed, crimped, and cut on their own. Her gift, she thought. Now she needed these hands for something else and demanded with fingers straight and rigid like fleshy needles to sow the soil as deep as possible to pull together and provide a different seam. Lilly pounded her straight-fingered hands into the dirt and pushed her prayer for her son with them. She waited, still as a statue. She stopped breathing.

"You are long overdue, daughter."

Lilly choked, afraid to say anything that might break the connection. The words echoed in her head.

"It is not from him you need forgiveness."

What? Lilly begged to know a power better than she would look over her son.

"When you forgive yourself, you will find the strength to stand for your boy."

"Is this real?" whispered Lilly. This might be a hallucination in some painful shakes episode after a binge. It had happened before.

"Feel the truth of this and be ready to serve. You will have your chance: a redemption."

Her hands felt a sudden heat. It radiated up her arms and touched her, toes to head. She convulsed and rolled to the ground, ending the connection. When she could feel anything, Lilly found herself on her back. Every muscle hurt as she struggled to her feet. Grabbing the bag's strap, she dragged it across the dirt, trying to get her legs to work normally. Her knees buckled; she felt her body slide when a leg froze up. Like any child of the

Snake, she waited in the dirt for death or recovery. Minutes passed, and strength returned to her legs. Back on the sidewalk, Lilly stopped and hefted the bag over her shoulder. After a block or two of steady motion, her whole body worked. The pain and stiffness faded.

"I will be ready," she said to herself, completely unaware of the tears streaming down her face.

CHAPTER 27

"Gentlemen! Ladies!" called Tom Haggard. He sat at a long table on a raised platform with Gracie at his side and the representatives from several southern cities in the western parts. Gracie and Tom had come to the western city of Lancaster close to the western mountains but on the slaving routes north. The rank and file in the meeting hall expressed their opinions without reservation. He managed only a few words at a time before being shouted down. The leaders at the table did nothing to bring order.

"Do you want your children to be safe?" Haggard had stood up and cupped his hands around his mouth, so his words reached to the corners of the room. When the clashing voices went silent, he jumped into the opening and said, "The northern bastards can't steal all that you have! Not the food off your table! Not your kids!"

The crowd clapped but remained unexpectedly disengaged. Their tepid reaction angered Haggard. He read the mood in the room poorly: not one of his talents.

A uniformed soldier came up behind the table and pulled on Gracie's sleeve. She turned and leaned down to hear the report from the soldier. She slid off her seat and stepped off the platform, and raced with the messenger to the back door of the venue.

"What's in it for us?" yelled a woman in the front.

"Your children!" Haggard repeated fervently.

"The Snake never had much to share before." This came from a man near the middle of the crowd. "When the famine hit a few years back, not much help came from Snakeport!" Heads nodded around the man with mumbled agreement. "It's been dog eat dog fer as long as I ken remember!"

"It ain't been any different in Snakeport," called Haggard.

"Where was Lancaster when the cyclone hit the Snake?" The crowd went totally quiet. Haggard had touched a nerve. "We all just tried to survive. I make no judgement. You all did what you had to do, and we did too. Now…" Haggard looked over the men and women before him, "What price do you put on a united South? We help each other. Tell the slavers to go to hell. Fight for each other's right to hold his coin in his hand and not give it over for protection. Go steal someone else's children!" Haggard knew, as did everyone in the room, such extortion happened all over the western cities. "Snakeport crushed the slavers. What about Lancaster?"

"You ain't faced djinn!" came from one side of the room.

"Suicide if ya ask me to line up 'gainst them northern troops!" yelled another. "A few a' them ken wipe out all of us!"

"We already beat a hundred djinn!" yelled Haggard. "Y'all heard about it, and we got what they left behind if ya need evidence. And y'all are wrong about not having djinn." The people before him froze and Haggard smiled. As the silence grew, he looked down the line of the table, ready to reveal what they had found in the Snake. The representatives stared at Haggard, confused and eager to hear his next words. "In Snakeport we have found hundreds of untrained djinn. We have northerners who have joined and taken up our cause. They train these new djinn even as we speak. What we have done in Snakeport can be done in Lancaster!"

"Haggard ain't the name we been hearing beggin' your pardon," said a woman, stepping forward. She had two revolvers in her belt and several knives.

"What name is that good lady?" asked Haggard.

"Jack Fox." She turned to face the audience and added, "'Course we ain't sure he rightly exists at all." A low-grade rumble passed throughout the crowd. "What say you, Haggard?" she asked, spinning around and pointing at him.

"Jack Fox plays a part in all of our decisions."

"Bring 'im here and let 'im make us good enough to stand in a fight with them northern pissers." She rested her hands on the gun handles.

"I will have him here as soon as possible," said Haggard confident. He turned to one of his staff officers behind the platform and gave the order.

"His woman too! She won that summer fight ya told us 'bout."

"She once again has taken the field. I will make the arrangements when she returns." Haggard saw the heads nodding and fists in the air. He turned to a noise behind him as Gracie returned with soldiers carrying heavy canvas bags.

"We sent a force north!" called Gracie. "Jack Fox's woman led them!" Gracie leaned over and whispered into Haggard's ear, "no casualties. Tight and clean." She straightened and confronted the assembly. "Here is your proof!"

Four soldiers lined up along the front of the platform, each with a bag. At Gracie's signal, the bags opened. Their contents dumped. Gold coins rained down on the floor and rolled this way and that.

The people in front picked up the gold and studied the markings.

"This here is northern gold!" Voices yelled at the crowd behind them. "We beat 'em again."

"Where do we go next?" asked Gracie of Haggard. They watched the coins disappear into the pockets of the audience. The soldiers kept the rush forward under control.

"Memphis," said Haggard. "But word of this will get their ahead of us." Haggard smiled. "Will the Mountain people help us?"

"Some," said Gracie. "Spunk and her team caught the northerners by surprise again." Gracie sat in her chair. "Still, we may have some new, unexpected support in our fight."

* * *

"Are you sure about this Professor?" James his former student at Hempstead University shoved the last of four bags—as bags of gold coins poured on the floor in Lancaster—behind the rear seat of the horseless carriage used by Jack and Doc to return South.

"No… but something has to be tried." Robert Forrester leaned against the front wheel fender and fumbled around in the soft leather bag resting on the vehicle's hood. "We're long on raw talent but very short on trainers to turn that talent into something useful." Satisfied he had everything needed, he pulled the bag's canvas strap over his head and settled the pouch on his right hip. Looking at his three companions, James, David, and Katrina, he said, "Just a professor and students returning to school after the brief holiday." He accepted their nods and climbed into the front passenger seat. "Jack and Peppers took four days to get from Hempstead to the Snake. Let's see if we can beat that time."

* * *

"This proves with no doubt that you are a clueless academic or a crazy person, unable to comprehend the danger all about you." Doctor James Shephards considered Robert Forrester, who sat across from him in his Hempstead office. The late afternoon sun poured through the tall windows. "Government agents invaded Hempstead University months ago looking for you doing research or so Camden, the University President, informed department heads. So far, no one else knows of your presence with several former students." Shephards felt dangerously exposed.

"Since I am not in the gentle care of the government, I will assume you are considering your options," said Robert. He looked out the office window. "Me and my companions made the trip up here in record time." Turning back to Shephards, he said, "We have been lucky so far. No one has questioned us. Our landlord smiled when coins had dropped into his hand and left us alone. On the first night, we downed several bottles of cheap wine. If they did not arrest us in the next few hours, then I thought this meeting might actually happen." Robert raised his arms. "Here we are, and decisions have to be made or…"

"Or what?" Shephards stared out of the window while his fingers drummed on the polished desktop. "How do I assess this stupidity? The government agents returned in larger numbers just before you showed up. They are all over the place like ants on sugar cakes." He turned to Forrester and said, "You seem, however, to have a measure of luck. They are not well organized yet. Otherwise, you would be viewing the world through iron bars."

"Luck?" questioned Forrester. His left eyebrow arched as he said, "Luck or not, I had no choice but to act as I have done. Because we remain free gives me hope."

"And what exactly have southerners done, my friend?" Shephards drummed his fingers faster. He felt fearful of the coming request. "What have we missed about the South in all the latest turmoil?"

"Several key points," said Robert. "The slave trade has ended. An attempt to reactivate the trade left northern soldiers dead on the field or running for their lives. Non-projectors defeated projectors." He allowed the point to settle and corrode long-held beliefs of southern ineptitude. "The South is not the wasteland, full of hopeless imbeciles, only good for backbreaking work in northern fields, mines, or homes."

"Nice speech, but let's get to the point." Shephards leaned forward over his desk. "The government has reported no battlefield loss." He raised his hand when Forrester argued. "My intern at the remote clinic on the river treated the walking wounded and kept me informed. The government secrecy over this matter worries me." Shephards stood and pointed a finger at Forrester. "Now you lure students away from lucrative futures to a possible deadly end. Then come to me to disrupt lives for a dangerous dream."

"I have a letter for you from Claymore Peppers." Robert smiled, showing no concern, and reached down into the pouch resting on the floor, slid out a paper, and handed it over.

Shephards came around the desk and took the sheet, then returned to his seat, placing it on the desk. He glanced at Forrester, annoyed, then read. Sitting back after absorbing the message, he said, "I often wondered what happened to the boy we bought and how he and Peppers suddenly disappeared."

"Doctor Peppers said to tell you something to confirm that this letter is legitimate." Robert told the story of how Peppers and Shephards examined Jack at the remote clinic: things only Peppers would know.

"Yes. Yes. I recall," he smiled. "At the hearing the arrogant rube of a teenager stood, told us his name, then told us to go to hell." Shephards chuckled. "So, Jack Fox is the author of fate changing energy."

"You cannot comprehend what it is like to be in his presence."

"Tell me." Shephards sat back and rolled his eyes. He raised an eyebrow then said, "I am ready to disbelieve anything not data driven."

"He's a teenager, and his confidence and hope are clear."

Robert took a few deep breaths, crossed his arms over his chest, and took a moment to gather his thoughts. "Then he erupts into my senses with the most surprising level of control. It is amazing to watch the energy level rise and fall in him." He paused, then said, "Using every talent available to me, I have not discovered his end-point."

Shephards just stared at the old man. A projector's endpoint, the highest level of energy a projector can achieve, set the path for his or her future in the military, in medicine, and other professions. Soldiers possessed deep endpoints. Forrester, Shephards knew, a projector with deep endpoints, had served as a soldier in his younger days.

"No endpoint," whispered Shephards. "Five holes in the skull, unconscious, not likely to survive." He shook his head. "And now this." Looking at Forrester, he said, "I need to think and consider."

"Of course."

"There is a large contingent of non-projectors being trained for some kind of action. They are very secretive." Shephards rose from his chair and went to a window. "The students protest their presence." He observed a crowd forming at a distant intersection. "It is a laughable paradox. The students don't want non-projectors contaminating their idyllic campus." He turned to Robert. "Such prejudice runs deep and has been fertile ground for rabid adherents… until now."

"Interesting," said Robert. "Our plans will have to change." He rose. "I must go. Me and my team will stay in the shadows."

"I promise to say nothing of your visit." Shephards got to his feet and walked him to the door. "We may not meet again. I know what you want me to do." Shephards shook his head, the decision a heavy load on his shoulders. "You have given me much to consider."

The men shook hands. They parted ways, deep in thought.

Back at the lodging house, Professor Forrester brought his compatriots up to speed on the discussion with Shephards. They discussed their 'Plan B' if it looked like their mission might fail.

"So, Professor," said Katrina, "what next?"

"You will contact your friends, but keep an eye out for potential betrayal." Forrester sat with his protégés at the table in the center room. "Remember, Kat, you are no longer an equally valued member of the society, so to speak." He caught her eye roll. "You can't drive a man to the ground because of an unwanted advance. Expect unwanted interest." Scanning everyone at the table, he said, "Remember where you are." He let that sink in.

"Tomorrow, each of us will join the protests taking place at the old student union building. Stay in the background, but learn everything you can. I'll take the early hours."

"Non-projectors in Hempstead," said James, shaking his head. "The government must be desperate."

"Yes." Forrester stood. "It's a dangerous time for us all." He turned toward the door. When no government agents crashed through the wood, he sighed and asked, "Am I the only one hungry?"

* * *

"He did what?" screamed Anna Forrester.

"He and a few others went to Hempstead," said Peppers. He shrugged, sitting at his desk. "It had to be done."

"Who approved?" Anna paced the floor in Pepper's office.

"He and I agreed we had reached a wall. Simply not enough of us northerners to do all the training and healing, especially healing," said Peppers. "If we concentrated our resources in

Snakeport abandoning the other cities, we could make a stand and expect to survive, possibly win. Of course, the other city leaders would never accept it."

"He is old and no spymaster to sleuth deep into enemy territory."

"Him or me," began the doctor. "Right now I'm lucky to get four hours of sleep in any day." Peppers wiped the weariness from his eyes, then looked at Anna. "I don't want to argue the point further."

"When will we know if we have to mount a rescue mission?" Anna stopped pacing and leaned on the desk.

"He and his team are due back in three weeks. As soon as they cross the bridge, we will get reports." Peppers dragged himself to his feet. "I have patients to treat."

Anna stood in silence as the door closed behind the doctor. Something had to be done, but what? She lacked patience when worry over Robert consumed her. Maybe a connection through the earth could help. Anna was not hopeful. Robert's atheism blocked the level of open-mindedness needed.

"You old fool," she said to herself, picturing Robert's sardonic grin whenever she spoke of a living earth. "I'll open your eyes to save your sorry old butt, whether or not you like it."

CHAPTER 28

"So, you be Jack Fox," said Sally Riley, her hands resting on the handles of her guns. She stood before a group of leaders in the city of Lancaster: thirty men and women gathered in the space where Haggard had addressed a larger audience. "This here's your woman?" Sally nodded to Spunk. She noted how their hands, hips, and arms touched, but Sally thought their secreted smiles told the tale.

Jack and Spunk nodded.

"Well, ya don't look like much." Sally turned to those behind her. "What would ya have of these two to join this fight?"

"We heard a lot 'bout what ya done." A tall man in a long coat with the end of a sabre showing beneath its hem stepped forward. "Show us." He wore his black, silver streaked hair long tied back, as did many among the leaders. Clean shaven, he placed his hands on his hips. "Give us the truth, not a hocus-pocus lie that we have a chance."

Jack looked out at the crowd, then turned to Spunk. Their eyes locked and Jack grinned as he relived the bedroom scene from the night before: arms and legs intertwined, lips and hands searching, eyes probing the other's as two bodies became one in a steady rhythm. Jack leaned down and kissed Spunk.

The audience never saw the kiss since the two sitting before them vanished. Instead, the floor beneath their feet moved like a wave in the ocean with heads at the back pushed up, then down in a trough. The energy passed through the room and ended where Sally stood. The room suffered no damage.

"What more do you need?" asked Jack when he and Spunk popped back. He did not want to stop falling into Spunk's dark eyes.

Sally pulled both revolvers, held them at her waist, and pulled the triggers until they clicked against the exploded caps.

"Well, I'll be damned," called one witness. Voices across the room expressed disbelief in what their own eyes saw. Twelve bullets spun in place a foot from the two young people, still staring into each other's eyes like no one else existed.

"The lead," said Jack, turning slowly to the crowd, "will stay where I wish or go where I say." A bullet shot into the room, trimming a lock of hair, a piece of mustache, or patch of beard. Eleven rounds came together and started spinning about a center point, looking like a small tornado. The miniature storm of lead passed back and forth in front of the awed watchers. When it found a wooden chair against a wall, it chewed it up like raw wood digested in a lathe.

"So guns alone won't win the coming battle." Jack felt Spunk squeeze his hand. The time had come to teach these people the lessons learned in the Snake. "Shields up!"

"What!"

"We ain't no djinn. We can't…"

"He said," ordered Spunk, "shields up!"

A force hit the crowd as fast as Sally had pulled her weapons and fired at Jack and Spunk. Everyone went down: some to the floor unconscious, but a few to their knees with their hands over their heads, palms out. The room glittered with rudimentary shields. Jack walked over to Sally, who first felt the attack. Still conscious, he helped her rise from her knees.

"I…," said Sally, stunned and scared, staring wide eyed as Jack brought her shaking to her feet. Jack smiled at her.

"You are more than you think."

* * *

"I'm heading east and rejoining the army in the field," said

Tom Haggard. "I am not good at politics and grow weary of the show we must put on to drag others to our cause." He sat across from his second in command, caressing his glass of whiskey. They both sat back from the table with its white tablecloth and the remnants of a splendid dinner. Gracie sipped red wine from a long-stemmed glass. The city of Memphis celebrated their military exploits against the slavers. Citizens cheered them in front of their city hall. The power brokers, like those in the Snake, wined and dined the Slave War heroes with gold to hand out. Standing up to the North on a battlefield, the General knew was another matter altogether.

"You want to abandon the effort to enlist support from these other cities?" asked Gracie.

The two meetings in Memphis had not gone well when help with the coming battle came up. The people in this city felt comfortably far away from the Aquitaine. They never took part in the slave trade with few of their children taken. The war belonged in the east. Gracie salvaged the second meeting, reminding the good citizens what would happen when the north destroyed the eastern areas. With those cities and towns turned to ash, from where did they think they would snatch the children to feed the slave trade?

"No," said Tom. "This is a political action." He considered the contents of his shot glass. "You, Gracie, have a talent for the maneuvers, placing the right words, and the grit to make believers." He emptied his glass. "Those are not among my talents."

"Tom, these people need to see the man leading them to victory," said Gracie.

"No, my dear, they need to hear about victory from someone with whom they connect. You saved last night's meeting." Haggard placed his glass on the table and rose. "You will continue the meetings through as many cities as possible. I believe, maybe for the first time, with all the work by the Professor, his wife, and Jack, we might win. You, however, are the best messenger to bring allies."

"Thank you, sir," said Gracie, dumbfounded.

"We, when this is all over, will stand or hang together, eh?" Haggard headed for the stairway up to his rooms. "In the meantime, between success and the rope, I need you to bring the people together."

"Yes, sir." Gracie set down her wine and stood. "Tom," she called as he walked away, "it will be you at the head of the army that will bring victory." She watched him stop and heard him chuckle.

"My dear Mrs. Hargreaves, it will be the amazing Jack Fox, not me." He turned his head and said, "I will be a footnote to this history." Haggard paused, "As it should be."

Gracie's eyes followed him as he left the dining area and climbed the stairs. He had this one right, which only increased his stature in her eyes.

"A great man," she whispered.

* * *

"We must leave immediately," said Forrester to his companions the following evening after gathering what information they could at the Hempstead protests. Candles flickered around the room.

"I've only just reconnected, Professor." Kat frowned, disappointed. She and the others had stood their shifts on the street in the vocal crowd of protestors. "There are a few who might come with us."

"Kat, it may already be too late for us to escape. The patrols are out on the street, forcing college men into the army and ending the protests at the student union." Forrester sat in his usual spot at the table, his chin covered by his hand and his thoughts racing, trying to make the right decision.

"Forced conscription?" James sat back, stunned, and stared into space, imagining how such a thing would be done. "Projector against projector, right?"

"Yes," said Forrester, dropping his hand and looking at James. "They use military techniques not understood or available to academics. Students are defenseless against them."

"Only the males, though? The young ones?" questioned David.

"Yes," said Forrester. "Your age."

"Damn," hissed David.

"Worse. Our leaders need to know that a northern colonel, Martell is his name, is training non-projectors to infiltrate the South." Forrester shuddered. "He can be the epitome of reason, smiling congenially as he boils your blood."

"You know him," stated Kat.

"Twenty years ago, a Lieutenant Martell interviewed me at the government's behest. Obviously unhappy with my last treatise, he grilled me with questions on weakening of the gene pool: too much powerful family to powerful family consanguinity." He paused and stared blankly as he recalled the confrontation. "Martell said, 'I could continue to research all that I wished or die prematurely with the publishing of my findings.'" Forrester paused. "I published them, but the government made a joke of the conclusions and maintained a powerful counter campaign."

"Why didn't they make good on their threat?" asked James.

"Forrester, the man survived, but as a trusted purveyor of the truth, their ridicule overpowered me. I no longer held the trust of the public." He coughed and surveyed the room. "Get things packed up. We head south."

An hour later, they looked over the field of parked vehicles captured in the moonlight of a half-moon. They went to the four-seater in which they arrived, packed the back seat, and made ready to leave.

"Out late, aren't you?" asked a commanding voice.

Forrester and his team froze.

"Looks like trouble-makers making a hasty retreat, Sarge," said one of the four soldiers blocking the way. The air sparkled with energy around the uniformed men.

"Sergeant, Sergeant," said Forrester affably, smiling at the apparent leader. "My students and I are embarking on a field trip to study the nocturnal mating habits of the vampire bat." His outstretched arm pointed to the thick forest barely visible in the distance where they would start their study. "You are welcome to join us, if you wish."

The laughter showed they would not take advantage of the invitation.

"What say we take your two men here and you, old-timer, and your girl can go off and watch the bats screw?"

The silence could be cut with a knife.

"Oh, for shit's sake," stated Kat, frustrated with the lack of action. With two moves releasing low frequency energy through the soldier's shields, the sergeant and one other dropped to the ground.

The other two soldiers shot energy bolts at the four standing near the vehicle. James and David easily deflected the attack, but Robert, slow to raise his shield, took a direct hit. He dropped to his knees and fell forward onto his hands. The pain and power stole his breath, leaving him helpless.

Kat attacked again with support from her companions. The two remaining soldiers hit the dirt unconscious.

"Looks like we learned a thing or two from Jack Fox," grinned Kat. "Low frequency energy works."

"Professor!" David saw his mentor on the ground, went to his side, and placed a hand on his back. Energy immediately erupted from the contact, throwing him back. A sparkling field encased the man.

"Can't stay, but we can't leave," said David. He felt the radiated energy coming from the field around the Professor. They all felt it.

"David, James and I will stay with the Professor," said Kat. "You should grab one of those single seaters and get south fast as you can with the message about that Colonel Martel." She looked at the unconscious soldiers. "Let's hide these four first and hope no one comes looking for them for a while."

With the battle evidence secreted under nearby vehicles, Kat and James watched David race off, kicking up dust.

"Now," said James, sitting beside his mentor's shielded body, "we wait".

CHAPTER 29

Gracie sent out her riders the morning after her dinner with Tom Haggard to gather reports on any action along the western part of the river to sneak in spies. Shortly thereafter, Haggard passed through the dining room just as her lips touched the coffee cup. He gracefully refused Gracie's invitation to breakfast, shared his concerns about the army, then hastily joined his mounted entourage. Once in the saddle, he led the cavalry east. Gracie watched with a mix of sadness and pride: sadness that he would not get the credit he deserved and pride that he had given her the freedom to bring the southern cities into line. Her thoughts wondered over strategies to accomplish her goal. All of them required Jack to be successful.

"May we join you?"

Gracie jumped to her feet and threw her arms around Jack as he came to her.

"Just thinking of you." She let him go, then in a very un-military manner hugged her captain. "Spunk! It's good you two came together."

"Haggard left you to survey the western districts by yourself?" Jack glanced out the window as the last of the horse train passed.

"He does what is best for the South." She turned to the table and pulled out two chairs, ordering them to sit and eat. "Tell me about Lancaster, then I have a few questions about the mountain people."

Vanquishing their hunger, they exchanged stories about what they could expect from Lancaster and the mountain areas. Gracie described the push-back from the people of Memphis.

"So, I can pull back my resources around here and around the Lancaster part of the border and move them east."

"Yes, sir." Spunk confirmed the mountain passes would be

closed. "They may provide forces if we ask, but I wouldn't count on that."

"Did you see any of their hidden cities?"

"We saw only what they would allow." Spunk told of her travels through the tunnels. "I suspect they want a new governing power on their eastern border. They do not feel any connection to the North."

"Good." Gracie took it all in and tried to see the bigger picture of what they attempted with this war. "I need to ask…" She stopped abruptly when a messenger she did not recognize barged into the dining room. She waved her in. "Report."

"The Professor has sent a warning," said the sergeant who rode hard to get to Memphis from the Snake. She stank, her boots and pants mud encrusted. "You should expect a potent force of northern spies to infest our borders in a few weeks. He says our enemies are desperate to know how we defeated them twice." The woman looked at Spunk and nodded her respect.

"I did not know the Professor went north," said Gracie. "Under orders?"

"He and Doctor Peppers planned the action and executed it on their own."

"Ah." *Brave old goat*, she thought. *None of us would have agreed to let him go.* "He wants me to do what?"

"The Professor leaves it up to you to take action." The sergeant stood at attention but near exhaustion wavered, catching herself at the last second.

"Sit," ordered Spunk, who offered her chair. "Eat."

Gracie stood and waved to one of her staff officers at the door to the dining room.

"There will be a staff meeting here in thirty minutes." She sent him off to spread the word, returning his salute. "We need to think this through and come up with a strategy." Gracie looked at the sergeant, who finished a mug of coffee and downed a plate of ham and eggs. "Sergeant, go rest. You can use my room. I may need you in the saddle later today to get the word out all along the border." The woman nodded, then rose, holding tight to the plate: the only food she had seen in three days. Gracie smiled when the soldier failed to salute. *The sergeant has done enough.*

"What do you think, Jack?"

"If this is an action supported by the northern government, then we should expect a visit from Lakeland, my father, and their ilk. The bounty offered by the North to know what is going on here would be beyond their ability to refuse." Jack grinned. "Since they are so well known in the east, they will probably show up here in the west."

"Should we ask our mountain allies to open a path we can monitor?" Gracie caught Jack's excitement. Scores needed settling.

"It shouldn't be too obvious," warned Spunk. "The enemy is not stupid."

"What do you suggest?" asked Gracie.

"Jack and I will go talk to the mountain scouts and see." Spunk raised her hand, stopping Gracie from voicing her concern about the lack of time. The Professor's information implied a more important outcome to their army. "There will be no massive invasion until this effort either fails or delivers usable intelligence."

"We have until the summer, then." Gracie nodded and appreciated the analysis. "I will need the two of you to drag the locals into alignment with our goals. A repeat performance, as you described in Lancaster, should do the trick. I will need you on the border when we finish in Memphis."

"Yes, sir." Spunk sat back down.

"Lakeland," said Jack. The name hung in the air.

"Yes," said Gracie, thinking of Edward Blogger and her satisfaction with his end. "Reginald has much to account for."

* * *

Shephards at home reached up and pulled a snifter from the row of glasses above his bar. His students and fellow medical men knew of his penchant for collecting the high quality, expensive liquor and keeping it in his study behind a long bar with a brass foot rail along the floor. No one complained since Shephards freely shared his collection with his colleagues and graduate students. The head of the Hempstead University's Medical Department rarely drank. Tonight, he made an exception. He went behind the bar and returned with a dusty squat bottle of brown liquid. The long untouched cork crackled slightly when turned and pulled. Shephards filled the snifter and left the bottle uncorked on the bar. He downed half of it, refilled the glass, then went to the nearest high-back leather chair and collapsed into it.

"Damned Peppers!"

Shephards set down his drink on the side table and grabbed the paper he wanted to ignore or set ablaze. He read it again.

I need you. I know you are not aligned with the government. The situation in the South is nothing like they have taught us for generations. I have no expectations or have reasons good enough to prove to you that your abilities will help correct a long existing wrong. Come south. If you can come to Snakeport. You will be the doctor you have always wanted to be, helping those who desperately need your abilities.

In all honesty, based on all that I have witnessed while in the Snake, as the locals call it, the North can expect to win a battle or two but lose the war. I cannot tell you why I know this to be the case in writing. It is not safe. Remember Titus and the works of the messenger who handed you this letter. Recall the young man who should not have lived.

I will, of course, respect your decision whichever way you decide.

Shephards dropped the letter on his lap and took another drink. Titus, he knew, prophesied a coming of a savior of sorts. Forrester, who gathered family histories, birth rates, projector counts, and all manner of statistics, proved the North would lose power. The teenager, a data point, proved the South did not lose all of its projectors. This last point helped with his decision. He stood, downed the rest of the liquor, then went to the small fireplace in his study. Exerting a minimum but intense bolt of energy, the letter burst into flame. He let it fall onto the logs and watched it turn to black ash.

"I must meet this Jack Fox."

* * *

As Shephards considered his escape from Hempstead, Colonel Martell entered the Student Union to discuss strategy with non-projectors.

"We can expect fifty percent of your men to be captured in the first wave over the Aquitaine." Martell stood before Lakeland and his officers, showing marks on a large map where insertion could be possible. "None of you should expect execution. Death is reserved for projectors or djinn, as the southerners call us." Martell turned from the map. "What more do your troops need?" This would be the last session in the Student Union. Lakeland's teams would stand on southern soil soon. Details still required his attention.

"Thanks for asking," said Stan Folfox. "There are no bridges at the access points. Who goes where and how is not clear. Certainly, you do not want me or the Colonel," Stan looked at Lakeland sitting to his right, "to play coy anywhere in the Snakeport environs."

"Major, you are correct." Martell stepped to the side and picked up a folder from a side table. "There is an old slaver path at the far end of the river near the mountains. Anyone recognized in Snakeport will enter at that point." Martell closed the folder and looked out over the ranks of men. "You will be strangers. You are not djinn. I ask you," the Colonel raised his voice to make his point, "what are your cover stories?" He scanned the room, waiting for a response.

"Starvation," called one voice from the back.

"Getting away from the troubles back east!" yelled another.

"All good, I guess, but I look to all of you to discuss this among yourselves." No fool, Martell stated a simple truth about himself. "I am ignorant." He let the statement settle among the men. "You have lived in the south. That is your strength and my failing. You must help me understand how you escape detection."

"Start," said Lakeland, "by describing why you are so needful of us. What has brought you to what must be such a distasteful act?"

Martell spent the next hour describing the two defeats at the hands of non-projectors. He reinforced the prize money to be earned by each soldier involved in this action.

"Finally, after spending time with you, I can say you are not distasteful to me." He looked over the room. "I appreciate those who take the field regardless of their energy abilities."

"And we can stay in the north and not have to take low-level jobs?" asked a man in the front row. "We stand as equal?" Everyone in the room stared at Martell.

"Yes. Prime Minister Dowler promises equal treatment before the law." The Colonel saw the disbelief in their eyes.

"Current laws say our kind don't count!" yelled Stan, who rose and leaned across the table. "Don't think you can play us."

"Those laws no longer apply unofficially and will officially change in short order." No one in the room believed him. "That's the best I can offer."

"Let's just get on with it," said Lakeland, placing a hand on Stan's arm and turning to face the men gathered behind him. "What choice do we have?"

"Your training for the last four weeks provides everything you need. I trust your cover stories will stand. You," said Martell, "deploy in a week. You will have gold and silver in your pockets and our total support. Projectors will get you across the river where we say and bring you back."

"What about them loudmouth youngsters outside?" asked a man in the back. "Could be our move south may get reported in Snakeport." The man felt empowered to continue when the chuckling started. "Seems they do not believe we are on their side." The room became deathly quiet.

"There has not been a time when university students did not oppose government policies." Martell smiled. "They are about to experience, however, a policy that will let them know they are on *your* side." The response heartened Martell: the nodding of heads and a flurry of raised fists. He needed these non-projectors to believe as he believed, for now.

* * *

"Look, you've all seen what's going on," said Doctor Shephards the next morning to a mix of senior and lower-class students. Both men and women filled the medical school auditorium for a meeting called only an hour before. Word of mouth spread like wildfire. "Males, herded like cattle, go into the army." He ran his hand through his hair. "The female students should expect arrest for protesting or actively opposing the government. Most will go home. They think so little of you."

"And you don't?" called a female voice.

"Fair enough," said Shephards, "but I am leaving right after this meeting. You should all do the same. You can come with me to the South or…". He raised his hands and shrugged his shoulders, signaling he did not know where else they might go.

"Why south? That's where all the trouble is," called out another student.

"I have a friend in the South who says he needs my help." Shephards looked out over the two hundred men and women. "If you think you can avoid the gangs of soldiers grabbing the male students or want to be detained by soldiers who think females have only limited uses, then stay. I'm going."

With those last words, Shephards reached down and picked up his traveling bag. He exited to the right. At the field where the vehicles lined up and reflected the afternoon sun, he stopped and turned to see if anyone followed. Amazed, he saw the line stretched a long way. A sudden weight of responsibility fell on his shoulders. The decision to abandon a comfortable life would not be his alone. His followers chose for themselves.

"No one expects a move in broad daylight." He dropped his bag to the ground and waved his hands to bring everyone forward. "Get into the vehicles and get settled. I want to be in the lead in case we meet soldiers." He repeated his orders, stepped to the side, and watched the line file by. Following the last student in line, he stepped down the knoll to the tarmac, tossed his bag into the lead car, and took the passenger seat next to the driver.

"Go!" *We outnumber them.* This mantra or prayer eased his fears minimally if they came face to face with a military roadblock.

CHAPTER 30

FORRESTER KNEW HE TOOK A HIT. INSTEAD OF FINDING HIS wounded body bleeding out on the ground, he sat on a bench in a clearing surrounded by enormous trees: three feet wide trunks and branches high above. Titus smirked, dressed, and posed like the portraits of him on museum walls.

"So," said Robert, annoyed at the dapper, long bearded gentleman with smiling eyes, "Anna's goddess, I presume."

"Know this. I will not cause my daughter any pain."

"Why am I not dead?" asked Robert, confused by the comment and angry, feeling unjustly abused by everything.

"You will survive, old man. For the reason given." Titus laughed. "You will likely wish yourself dead when you return to your world."

"What," demanded Robert, "are you anyway and why hide?"

Titus smiled. "I have not hidden. You decided not to look even when offered the opportunity. My existence insulted your rational mind."

"Can't argue with that," nodded Robert, hearing the many echoes of Anna's admonitions to make the effort which he refused. "But I am seriously wounded and in terrible pain in the real world, and this," he waved at the trees and then pointed to Titus, "are hallucinations delivered to ease my way out of life."

"I will not argue the point," chuckled Titus, who became serious. "You will know for sure when you wake up, otherwise none of this matters." He took a seat on the bench. "So for now let's go with you'll live."

"Okay," said Robert, nodding at the logic. "What do you want?"

"I appear to you as one of my sons. I want you to be one, too." Titus opened his arms.

"Well, I'm not much for worship or sacrifices or the like. What exactly will you need from me?"

"Truth, my son, only the truth. It is far more difficult than you might imagine. I have it from an excellent source, however, you may be up to the challenge." Titus stood and walked the clearing, stopping to appreciate a flower or touch the smooth skin of a tree.

"Then tell me the truth," insisted Robert, raising his hands and demanding Titus' full attention. "Is this the great reconciliation described in your writings?"

"If you want it to be and will fight for that goal, it is."

"A typical politician's answer," said Robert, shaking his head.

"Jack has no complaints and fights for what he believes." Titus returned to the bench.

"Jack Fox," said Robert, "leads without leading."

"Quite," said Titus, looking up into the trees. A breeze moved the leaves, and they rustled while shafts of sunlight brightened the ground. He returned his attention to Robert and bent his head to the side, saying, "Will you embrace me, son, or at least take my hand?" He extended his right hand.

Robert stared at the hand, suspicious and fearful. The power before him could make him do anything, but it gave him the final decision.

Yes, I can believe in this if I wake up. Assuming he would, Robert reached forward and felt the power as the fingers wrapped around his. The touch launched Robert into his past and future: the passions and hopes. He cried for both and felt grateful to have long lost memories of his mother and father refreshed. The future, a more perfect union of all peoples, could be awash in freedom with a heavy infusion of doing unto others as you would have done to you.

"Welcome, my son."

* * *

Anna kept looking back at her Robert as he recovered in bed. His eyes never left her. When she left the room, his energy sought her out. She looked back over her shoulder at the doorway, finding his behavior something new and annoying. When he returned to Snakeport, seriously wounded but alive, she yelled and screamed at him, then held him tight and cried with relief. He only smiled at her with no defense offered. She loved and hated him at these moments: love usually won out.

"Is the pain less today?" she asked when she tired of his eyes boring a hole in her back. "Are you hungry?"

"I don't think I have ever been more wrong in my life as I have been with you." Robert propped himself up on an extra pillow. He felt weak. The energy blast took him down and left him an invalid. Recovery lagged, adding to his frustration.

"I've heard that before," said Anna. She stopped her puttering around the room and took a seat close to the bed. "Wrong about what?" She crossed her legs and arms, ready for his usual explanations, which angered and relieved her. Of course, such behavior was *so Robert* she could cry.

"My love, I talked to him or her." Robert raised a hand for Anna to take. "She showed me."

"Oh, my love," she said and snapped up his hand in both of hers.

"I think the goddess may have more to do with this war than any of us think."

Anna's eyes went wide. "What do you mean?" she asked quickly.

"Disconnected… we live alone in our power," said Robert. "We use power to enhance our individuality and wealth instead of… I can't rightly describe what she allowed me to see."

Anna kept silent and waited. Robert's eyes slid from left to right, then up. She knew he searched for insufficient words to allow a small comprehension of his experience.

"As trees and their neighboring trees' roots in a forest touch and intertwine, our abilities should do the same. We are not and should not be enemies outside our borders. We are all dancers hearing a different tune. This is so hard to explain."

"Shhh," whispered Anna. "I know, my dear." She raised her hand palm out and waited.

Robert did likewise, and when their palms touched, a light wrapped about them.

I know you, thought Robert. Every cell in his body filled with Anna and opened itself to her knowledge.

And I, you, she agreed.

Robert willed himself out of bed the next morning, ignoring the pain from his wounds. *I may be old, but I'm not dead yet,* he thought. Anna forced his surrender to the use of a cane. Complaining, he grabbed the brass handled support she left by the door and headed out. Ignoring the electric-like torture in his legs as best he could, he hobbled down the street. Fresh air invigorated him.

The end play in the war is coming. He limped along toward Gracie's place. The players, north and south, moved inexorably like the remaining pawns and power pieces on the chessboard in the last stages of the game: an ultimate confrontation. Whichever side had the better command of the details would likely prevail.

Anna worked in the field on some project with flowers and roots, or some such. It gladdened him to have his wife fully engaged in action, but he missed her and, not for the last time, wished she walked beside him. His recovery left him exhausted, so they never finished sharing what happened in the moments he fell to his knees wounded. He, she, or whatever saved his life.

"You earth… something," he said, frustrated. A string of insults went unsaid. Robert walked down the street, staring at the cracked pavement. "Could have made your point years earlier. I wouldn't have wasted…" He growled. The frustrations and fears escaped in the wind. *I woke up.*

Robert had to stop in the middle of the street as the pain made a sudden return. After a few deep breaths, he continued.

"Damn," he said. "Now I have to believe in a god, of sorts." Robert, without thinking, sped up. He hated the notion of the goddess and switched to thoughts of Jack Fox.

"Okay, my man, you seem to be in the lead. Where to next?"

CHAPTER 31

"We left the University several hundred strong. By the time we crossed the river, half of us survived." Shephards talked as though dazed. "We didn't, I didn't, expect the reinforced roadblocks just south of Hempstead." His energy charred clothes told anyone with sense this man put up a fight.

"Tell me," said Peppers. He grabbed the neck of the liquor bottle and reached over his desk to refill the glass in Shephards' shaking hands.

"They expected us." Shephards drank. "We tried to negotiate since we had the greater numbers. They kept quiet, gave the impression they understood and then outright murdered a young intern, Taunton: a damn fine doctor." He placed the empty glass on the desk and bent forward with his arms crossed at his stomach. "Got right through his shield." He rocked, reliving the moment, trying to find some slight relief.

"Then what happened?" This time when he refilled the glass, Peppers came around the desk poured, then placed a comforting hand on Shephards' shoulder. The man stopped rocking.

"We hesitated, and it cost us. Then one of us fought back." A grin flashed for a moment, then his eyes watered. "Kyle, not one of my best, but he stepped up. He probably saved us all." Shephards paused holding back tears. "Two soldiers close by turned white as sheets and fell. Blood pooled at their feet." Shephards drank. "Kyle used his medical knowledge as a weapon. When he turned to us and told us how to breach the shields, ten bolts struck him. He looked so shocked as he fell to his knees, his severed arms on the ground. He bled out from ..." Shephards sobbed.

Peppers who returned to his seat, remained silent. He waited as his former mentor collected his inner strength to tell the whole truth.

"Kyle's words quickly passed up and down our line." Shephard's stopped crying. He sat up straight and said, "We killed them all. Their screaming felt satisfying. Can't say I am proud of what I did, but…"

"They would have killed you all."

Shephards nodded.

"Here in the South, those were good kills," said Peppers understanding why his friend's action upset him so. "So, accept the fact and move on. What you came up against southerners have been fighting for generations. Expect little sympathy."

"The screams…"

"Deserved. Remember what happened to your student." Peppers watched Shephards nod his head in agreement. "Buck up, Doctor. The people you brought with you need you to bless what you and they did. Do you understand?"

"Yes." Shephards' introduction to violence cut him to his core. His relish at seeing his enemies taken to the ground embarrassed him.

"Good. Now tell me more about enemy actions in Hempstead. Afterwards, let's go to your survivors and forgive them so they can kill again if needed." Peppers filled both his and Shephards' glass. He raised his in a toast. "Welcome to the South, Doctor Shephards. It is all downhill from here."

The doctors drained their cups, then talked for an hour about Hempstead, medical matters in the South, training needs, and the unusual northern non-projector force.

"When we left, they remained with no evidence of obvious deployment." Shephards slumped in his chair. Kyle's death haunted him. "He laughed as he told us the easy way to do it," he whispered.

"What?"

"Nothing. They're dead." The doctor got up, filled his own glass one last time and silently raised it in salute. He composed himself and wiped the tears from his face. "I must meet this Jack Fox."

* * *

The wee hours of night erupted with sparkling light from energy, bridging the Aquitaine. The diaphanous structures spanned the river at key points in long arcs of varying colors. Over two hundred men crossed from the north. Over a thousand watched from the trees in the south.

"Well, Stan, this is it," said Lakeland, stepping from the energy platform to solid ground at the furthest west crossing.

"It?" said Stan Folfox. "I'm glad to be out of the North, but this is our end if ya want to know what I think."

"Already talking like the locals, are you?" Lakeland took a deep breath and looked around. "We will be the heroes when this all ends."

"Do you hear yourself?" said Stan sarcastically. "Stop the crap and tell me what ya plan on doin'."

In the dark, other men gathered around them. Lakeland looked at Stan and shook his head. Stan got the point and kept quiet.

"The major, me, and McGee," Lakeland nodded to a man walking up to them, "are heading to Lancaster. Do you have your targets?"

"Yes, sir," said a voice in the dark.

"Go. The sooner we separate, the better." Lakeland saw the men from his command disappear into the forest, heading to many locations in groups of three. Finally, only his triad remained. "McGee, what supplies do you have?"

"Just what they handed out," said the old man, looking down into the pouch he carried.

Lakeland's haymaker punch to McGee's face caught him completely by surprise. Before the old man could recover, Lakeland grabbed him from behind, placed his powerful hands on McGee's head, and snapped his neck. *The old codger will slow us down.* The body dropped to the dirt.

"Gather up his supplies," ordered Lakeland.

Stan did a quick inventory check as his commander watched.

"Now, we need to get a few things straight." Lakeland took half of what Stan found in McGee's sack. "When this is over, I want to rule down here." He emphasized the "down here." Lakeland placed a hand on Stan's shoulder and gave him a sympathetic look. "You and me can't go home. Our only home is the one we make where we stand."

Stan stared at the hand on his shoulder for a second, then into Lakeland's eyes. "McGee, don't bother me none, but you," he said, "can be scary." Stan smiled, then added, "I hope you never find me to be a burden." Stan pulled his arm from Lakeland's grasp and dragged McGee's body into the underbrush, then completed packing up.

"Finally," Stan said, confronting Lakeland. "For a time I thought ya had bought into Martell's life will be better crap." He watched as Lakeland gathered his pouch strap and pulled it over his shoulder. "My father will detest the ground I walk on, no matter what happens."

"What do you know about Lancaster? Any safe places to be?" Lakeland nodded at Stan's problem with his family. He had gone to the old Lakeland home while training in Hempstead. The pity in the gray-haired house slaves' eyes while he waited to be received in the library told the tale. When he felt sufficiently ignored by his family, he left: his leaving a final statement. He wondered, mounting his horse, how fast the fire might spread with so much paper fuel.

"Little about Lancaster," said Stan. "I heard 'bout a few men who bowed to gold."

"A few names will have to do."

Lakeland and Stan headed into the brush on a southern heading.

* * *

"Me and the boys been in the branches," said Jimmie Nicks. "Overlookin' the river as ordered." He stood at attention before Spunk and Jack. They returned to Lancaster to find and train as many projectors as they could.

"Relax, Mr. Nicks," said Spunk. She and Jack sat at a table in a small office to take the report. Echoes of "shields up" reached them from the training room. She smiled and, turning to Jack, said, "This soldier and his outfit played a big part in our success at the mine." Looking at Jimmy, who had not moved a muscle, she asked, "How's Heather?"

"Left her in charge as it should be, ma'am." Jimmy tried to keep his eyes fixed to a point on the wall, but kept stealing glances at Jack. He gulped, unsure what to do in the presence of… he could not describe what he felt. Not doing something stupid became incredibly important to him.

"Soldier," said Jack, who stood and walked around the table. He took Jimmy by the arm, pulled out a chair, and pushed him into it. Like Spunk, he smiled at Jimmy, who, once touched by Jack, could not take his eyes away from his face. "Report." He crossed his arms and leaned on the table.

"We saw maybe two dozen or more men cross a kinda bridge, all sparkly like." stammered Jimmy. "Groups a three made off into the forest where others followed 'em. The last three became two when one of 'em killed the third. Those two is now nearby. We got eyes on 'em."

"Did you hear anything?" asked Spunk.

"Too far away," said Jimmy, clearly intimidated by Jack so close. "Orders, ma'am?"

"Keep up your watch. Make sure Gracie gets your report. She has set up a headquarters in Memphis."

"Aye, ma'am."

"Then Mr. Nicks," said Jack, looking down on the boy. "Get yourself into training. You have djinn in you."

"What…?" Jimmy just stared.

"Shields up, Mr. Nicks." Jack returned to his side of the table as the commands from the training bounced off the walls down the hall.

* * *

Gracie prepared a written report for her commanding officer. She pored over the many bits of data received from the troops along the Aquitaine. The last scribbled note delivered that morning proved of particular interest. Doctor Peppers transcribed his conversation with a Doctor Shephards recently arriving from the Hempstead. Apparently, Shephards shared a kindred spirit with the Forresters. She read the pages three times and made critical deductions, needing Haggard's appraisal. The North built a larger army, it would need time to make it a viable force, and non-projectors finally received orders to deploy and gather intelligence on the South.

Based on these facts, she wrote, *the North will not invade until late summer or early fall. Our two successes have scared them. They will come with twice what they think they will need: twenty thousand or more. They are not so stupid as to deploy raw recruits after the South's two successes. The North will move slowly with great caution. This is our advantage. They do not know what they will meet, but have sent spies to find out. I will deal with these spies: non-projectors. It is best the northern forces believe all they need is to be more careful rather than come south with forty thousand men.. Our strength grows, as you know.*

She signed the document, folded it, and sealed it with wax. Calling for the courier, she watched as the young corporal loaded the pages into his pouch. Gracie returned his salute and reiterated that these pages go to General Haggard only.

Gracie, who had turned the hotel in Memphis into her headquarters, issued orders from the dining room. As the courier galloped east, another messenger arrived on foot.

With coffee mug in hand, Gracie walked to the front of the hotel to stretch her legs. Her fist worked the stiffness out of her back: too long bent over paperwork. She intercepted the boy in camouflage at the front desk. Dried mud covered his face.

"What have ya got, soldier?"

"From the Aquitaine, ma'am," said the boy, shocked to address the second in command directly.

"Wait here." Gracie took the papers from his hand and returned to the dining room, reading as she walked.

Her eyes studied the field report carefully; she tried to maintain her calm. She failed.

"Lakeland," Gracie whispered. She had no reason to believe the last of the teams to infiltrate from the river included her hated enemy: a gut reaction, a premonition. If it turned out not to be Lakeland, then a new evil would die and kept from spreading. She quickly penned a response and started making plans for moving to Lancaster. She smiled.

"We will let you see what we have built, my dear Reginald, but…," whispered Gracie. A knife appeared in her hand as if by magic and flew across the room. Her anger made sure it stuck deep in the doorframe. She pulled the blade free as she walked to where the boy waited. Handing her orders to the waiting soldier, he rushed out. "Wait!" she commanded. Gracie sent one of her assistants to get this boy a horse and an escort back to his outfit. She returned to her makeshift office, twirled the knife in her hand, and scanned the many papers needing her attention. Her thumb passed over the edge of the blade repeatedly.

"I so look forward to our next meeting, dear Reginald."

CHAPTER 32

"WHAT'S ALL THIS LOW FREQUENCY ENERGY ABOUT?" complained Robert Forrester. He, Peppers, and Shephards, with many followers, crowded Gracie's warehouse. "The first I heard of it. Kat named it. Is she here?" Robert swept the audience and finally caught a hand raised and waving in the back. "Come forward, Kat. Tell us what you learned from Jack."

Shephards leaned in. "Kyle, who died defending us, found another approach."

Forrester nodded. "Then we must hear of that as well."

Kat made her way to the front facing the table of men hardened in the southern cause and awaited their questions.

"Kat, you said, if I recall correctly, that Jack taught you about a particular attack?"

"In a training session," said Kat. "None of our attacks penetrated the shields. So, he told us to try something different." She stopped and thought a moment. "I started a bolt attack with very low luminosity. It got through my target's defenses. Knocked him flat." Kat turned to the audience. "Jack called it lower frequency." Turning back to the table, she said, "That's all."

"Have we included this in our training program?" asked Forrester, looking left and right.

"Yes, sir," said one of Forrester's followers, stepping forward. "It is a major target of our education among the many training sessions underway in the Snake."

Forrester smiled. The northerners he brought with him had acclimated to a new life. "Dr. Shephards, you had a question?"

"Attacks based upon a knowledge of bodily functions have delivered results. Have you discussed these with any of the new arrivals?" Shephards leaned forward.

"We are," said Kat, "trying to create a training protocol. It's complex."

"But very effective," followed Shephards. "We will provide any help you need." He watched her nod, then step back into line. Treating women as equals and, sometimes, superiors rankled. Shephards constantly reminded himself he no longer lived by the morays of the North.

"Anything further, doctor?" asked Forrester.

"Yes." Shephards stood. "I have consulted with Doctor Peppers and agree that we offer the progress made in Snakeport with health matters to other southern cities. I and many of my students head west to set up clinics and hospitals." He weighed his next words. "The South is not without its own projectors. These persons, male and female, can become doctors or nurses depending on their abilities." Shephards waited as the sudden applause abated. "Finally, I must extend my congratulations to Doctor Peppers on his nuptials, or should I say, his commitment."

Peppers rose, surprised and embarrassed by the lively round of applause.

* * *

"There ain't nothin' wrong with a bit of celebratin' now and again," said Nanna, hovering about the white dress made specially for Hattie. With a scissor, she nipped here and there. With talented fingers, she tucked the unfinished edges out of sight. Taking a step back and looking the bride up and down, she said, "You is a vision of beauty, you are."

Hattie stepped down from the small platform and hugged her.

"'Bout time you and Clay got together, as far as I can tell." The old woman stepped back, smiling at her charge. "Ready?"

"Willing and able," laughed Hattie. She and Peppers ignored each other religiously as they focused on the work of healing.

In one moment of exhaustion and respite, they had found each other and, like iron to a magnet, they became inseparable. Today's ceremony allowed the guests who wanted to laugh and cry over their obvious attraction to let off some steam and forget the coming battle.

"It's good the Professor will stand and tie the knot for the two of ya," said Nanna. She sorely wanted Jack and Spunk, but demands and circumstance took them away. "Who's putting your hand in his?"

"Shephards will play that part," said Hattie.

"Good. If ya can't be with the family ya started with, then best to go with the good ones you find along the way." Nanna turned to the door when the carriage arrived to take them to the courthouse. "Need any advice on… a woman's ways?"

"I think," laughed Hattie, "the subject needs no discussion."

Nanna nodded and blushed. "Ya've been a great help and I want ya to know I think of ya as a second daughter."

Hattie threw her arms around the old woman again and pulled her close. "Thanks, Nanna."

"Well, off we go." Nanna indicated the front door.

Hattie pulled a bright red shawl hanging from a chair over her shoulders and headed to the waiting ride. Nanna followed and, not for the last time, wondered how Jack and Spunk got along out west.

CHAPTER 33

"Goin' ta training, mister?" said a young boy dressed in the colors of the forest. He and others, young and old, headed down the main street of Lancaster. "Come along, ya might be djinn."

"Whose doin' the teachin'?" asked Stan.

"Jack Fox hisself, if ya can believe it." The boy ran on ahead as Stan fell back. He stepped away from the crowd and stopped in front of a store with the "closed-gone to training" sign prominently displayed. After the street cleared, he went the other way to find Lakeland in a back alley.

"We got trouble," said Stan. "My son is here and doing some kind of training. These people think they're djinn."

"We need to see what's going on." Lakeland gathered up dirt from the alley and rubbed his hands together. There had been no opportunity since he crossed the river to shave; the beard added to the disguise. The muck applied to his face masked him well enough, he thought. He demanded Stan do the same.

"My son will recognize me, regardless." Stan could not believe their bad luck.

"Paint your face cause you're coming." Lakeland pulled his revolver from his holster, spun the chambers, and checked the caps. "Stay in the back. I might need backup."

"What are ya thinkin'?" asked Stan. He gathered up a handful of dirt and stared at it not sure he wanted to follow Lakeland.

"Obvious, don't you think?"

"Kill my son?" *Didn't work before,* he thought.

"What else?"

"We won't come out of this alive is what else." Stan rubbed his hands together and dirtied his face. He pulled his own weapon more for show than to check its ability to fire. *Not a good idea.* "It would be better if we waited until he leaves or moves to another city. Make a plan, then get the information Martell wants easier."

"No. The enemy is here, and I intend to kill him with the chance offered." Lakeland headed out of the alley.

Stan followed.

"Come on, we'll miss it," shouted a voice. Several children sprinted down the street. "Ya old fogies best move faster than that." The young ones laughed and hurried to get to the training. Several looked over their shoulders at the two men hanging back.

Lakeland and Stan trotted to catch up, climbed the steps, and entered the crowded room. Lakeland surveyed the mass of people, looking for the best vantage point. He waded through the crowd to the right, taking up a position a few rows from the front. Stan went left and hung back, standing behind men taller than he. If he heard a shot fired, Lakeland could settle the affair on his own.

"Ladies and gentlemen!" a rotund, well-dressed man addressed the assemblage. "Jack Fox and his lady will join us directly. Remember, this here is basic training. Tomorrow in Butcher's Field just after the sun clears the trees, we will see if you can do more than what y'all learned today." The man smiled at the cheers and the calls to get on with it. He stepped back and, as he did, Jack and Spunk appeared. They walked into the crowd.

Stan grabbed glimpses of his son over the shoulder of the men in front. He looked good and acted like the smashing of his skull had never happened. Part of Stan cheered while the other part wondered whether he would shoot Lakeland or his son if the chance presented itself. He waited for his colonel to make a move.

The training started with many gasps and shouts of success. The air radiated with shields. Weak projections, as far as Stan could tell, but power. He wondered about himself. Lakeland had changed the plan when no gun shot interrupted the gathering.

An hour later, the training ended, and people filed out of the building. Stan came up on Lakeland's right. People gathered in small groups up and down the street, laughing and calling out their surprise to find they possessed djinn powers.

"They got projectors," said Stan, looking up and down the street. "They maybe got thousands."

"Looks like," said Lakeland, disinterested as though distracted. "Tomorrow will tell the tale. Then… we will get back to Martell."

"So… we get a room and somethin' to eat?" asked Stan. When Lakeland nodded, he started up the street where he saw signs for rooms for a night. "Ya might want to wipe some that crap off your face. Unless ya want to sleep in the street." Knocking dried mud out of his beard and off cheeks, he watched Lakeland do the same.

"His back was to me the whole time," said Lakeland, staring into space, giving up on cleaning his face. "He never would have seen it coming."

"Why didn't you do it?" He saw a child in the distance disappear around a corner.

"Too many shields in the way," said Lakeland, following Stan's gaze. "Even those damn kids from the street kept getting in the way."

"Ya don' think they're on to us?"

"Doubt it. Why let me get so close to Jack?" asked Lakeland.

Stan nodded. "It would be a very complicated game of cat and mouse to risk their hero like that." *If any risk existed*, he wondered. *What did we miss?* He turned quickly, feeling someone at his back, and stared back the way they had come. The empty street stretched into the distance.

Lakeland stared at Stan in disgust. "Hero? A southern

strategy?" he scoffed. "If your son is a hero, I'm the next Prime Minister in the North. Remember where we are." He again rubbed his cheeks; dirt like a waterfall fell. "Let's go. I need a drink."

The hotel they chose looked rundown, but perfect for their purposes. The bartender scratched his chin, looking the strangers up and down for how much he might extract from their pockets. He reached behind him and grabbed the neck of a bottle, then turned to fill their shot glasses.

"These here are on the house." He put the bottle on the bar. "Got a room for one up the stairs yonder and a place outback over the horses and such. Comfortable enough if you can stand the smell."

Lakeland looked at Stan, who nodded, agreeing to take the loft accommodations. The negotiated price laid stacked on the bar. Sniffing the air, he asked, "What's that cooking in the kitchen?" The aroma of roasting meat overcame the smell of whiskey.

"Well, that will be extra," the bartender winked. After another coin crowned the pile, the bartender smiled. "Take the bottle, no charge, over to a table and I'll have Lisa serve you, gentlemen."

"Want to clean up a bit," said Stan.

"There's a trough just outside the back door. Go dunk your heads," laughed their host. He reached down behind the bar and produced some burlap rags, which he tossed to his guests. "May want to dry up a bit."

"Thanks," said Lakeland sarcastically.

"No charge," said the bartender.

The food turned out to be very good: roast beef and vegetables. The whiskey flowed and Lisa, a not yet twenty, beautiful woman, brought them more of both before they could ask. She smiled and leaned into Lakeland as the second bottle emptied into their glasses.

"Well, my dear," said Lakeland, his hand moving from her

knee up her dress. "Enough. My friend and I need to sleep." His hand squeezed her buttock. When she smiled, he knew this would be a good night for him. Looking at Stan, who appeared to be on the edge of collapse, he said, "Go find the loft, Major." *Never could hold his liquor.* He reached over and lightly slapped his face. "Stan, go to bed."

"Yep," he said, smiling at nothing, and rose unsteadily. After a knocking into a few chairs, he looked to the backdoor and stumbled along. "Night, sir."

Lakeland removed his hand and abandoned the table, almost tripping backwards. He recovered, then took Lisa's hand and pulled her along to the stairway. His mission slipped from his mind, forgotten in the whiskey fog.

"You can clean this up later," whispered Lakeland, coming in close to her and waving at their dinner's collateral leftovers and spills. When she picked up the burning candle, then put her hand on his cheek, all of Lakeland's defenses melted. His desire flamed.

"This will be a night," said Lakeland after they broke and headed to his room.

"The bitch shot me!" yelled Lakeland again, leaning on Stan as they sought safety in the woods bordering the river. Daylight found Lakeland wounded, and both men hung over. Stan staggered, dry heaving on the ground, letting his human load fall. Lakeland hit the dirt on his shoulder and turned over on his back, groaning.

"Damn fool, let your pecker do your thinking," coughed Stan, wiping his mouth on his sleeve. The headache pounded behind his eyes.

"Shut up," grunted Lakeland. Stifling a scream, he still imagined Lisa's beautiful smile, which never faltered.

Once in the room, the woman, Lisa, had become hesitant. Lakeland spent an hour or more cajoling promising her anything. The dress finally slipped down ever so slowly over her shoulders, exposing her breasts. She stood and pushed it down further until it dropped to the floor. Lakeland stared as she turned away and placed her hands on either side of her last piece of clothing. Looking back at the man on the bed, she pushed them down, then stepped out of them. When she turned around, Lakeland just stared as the candlelight showed him paradise.

Still smiling, Lisa went to the end of the bed as Lakeland's eyes followed. She reached down under the mattress. The revolver appeared at her waist with the hammer cocked. A bullet ripped into Lakeland's shoulder. The second blast missed as he threw himself through the window. He bounced off a tin roof just below, then rolled off to the alley floor. On his feet and running on adrenalin, he burst into the barn, screamed for Stan, who just registered the yelling through a thick alcohol haze. They took off, Lakeland leaning on Stan, and let the dark of the wee hours hide them.

With no time to think, they ran for their lives. As the sun broke the horizon and their tide of alcohol induced poisoning receded, they concluded the enemy played them. Hunkered down behind a tree, they stopped to catch their breaths and gather what strength they could. The river roared close by with the promise of rescue. Blood continued to trickle from Lakeland's wound.

"Always surrounded by them kids," stated Lakeland, hugging his right shoulder with his left arm.

"Why didn't they chase after us?" asked Stan, staring back the way they came. "I think we're the mice and the cat's about to pounce."

"If we can give the signal at the river, maybe we can get some shielding and then escape." Lakeland stared at the sky, trying to ignore the pain in his shoulder.

"Then we better get movin'," demanded Stan.

"Could…," said a voice among the trees, "but I wouldn't advise it."

The two men froze as Lisa, revolver in hand, in her officer's uniform, stepped beyond the underbrush. A dozen armed soldiers, boys and girls, came from all sides. Stan recognized several from the Lancaster streets.

"You slutty bitch!" cried Lakeland, frustrated and frightened.

"Sure," said Lisa, smiling, "but you lose. Don't ya?" She looked back over her shoulder. "Come on up, boys."

Four adult soldiers entered the ring. One hauled Stan to his feet while two others lifted Lakeland to his. The fourth man with three stripes on his sleeve turned to the Lisa. "Ready, ma'am."

"You will now go to separate locations for questioning," said the young officer.

"How many of us did ya catch?" called out Stan. He watched as Lisa and her outfit of scouts holstered their weapons. He received no answer and hung his head in despair as the soldiers marched him away. "All, most likely," Stan said, then asked, "Where ya takin' me?"

"If I had to hazard a guess…" Lisa looked back at him as she disappeared into the forest and said, "your son wants a few words with you."

⋆ ⋆ ⋆

"The bullet's still in your shoulder," said Gracie. She passed around the room, gathering bottles, powders, and instruments. "Of course, you have lost a good deal of blood." She came up to Lakeland tied to a bed, his head raised on pillows. "You might not survive the procedure."

"Why don't you just get on with it?" Lakeland, pale from his pain, exertions, and blood loss, remained defiant.

"My dear, Reginald, I intend to, but I need to know a few things." Gracie studied the exposed bright red, swollen wound with a purple hole oozing blood, then stepped away and picked up a jar, poured some of its contents into a glass with a small amount of water, and stirred. "Drink this. It will ease the pain for a short period. We will talk."

"Poison more like," said Lakeland, eyeing the glass. Relief from the burning, bone cracking pain would be a greater good even if the proffered medicine killed him.

"Not long before that hole festers and the pain really takes hold. Which would be far more entertaining. Why waste poison?" Gracie swirled the contents once, then put the glass to his lips. When he opened his mouth, she tilted the glass, and he swallowed the contents. "It will take a bit of time."

Gracie crossed the room to a hot stove on which a pot steamed. Lifting it with a thick cloth, she went to a metal basin and filled it with the boiling water. The instruments she gathered earlier splashed into the basin.

Gracie caught Lakeland watching her.

"I dug out a few slugs in my time. But this…" Gracie pulled her knife and showed it to Lakeland. "is what I used to cut the throat of the cowards who send men to kill me in my warehouse. Of course, I simply blew the Blogger's heart in two." The afternoon sunlight reflected off its edge. Gracie smiled down at her enemy. "Reginald, I could use the doctor's tools, or I can use this to get out the bullet. The doctor's blades and such would be far less painful."

"Ask your questions." The drug began to work. He could think more clearly.

"You and Ed Blogger worked together to end me?" She sheathed her knife.

"When it became obvious that, you'd be a roadblock to our slave trade, then…" Lakeland nodded his head. "I provided some of the money, but it turned out to be a waste. Edward made the mistake. Underestimating you, Mrs. Hargreaves, will get a man killed."

"Tell me about the North," said Gracie, keeping to the business at hand, but the corners of her mouth twitched. "Your commanding officer? Why did they put you in command? How many men did you have in your battalion? What did they dangle before you?"

Lakeland stared at his shoulder, blood trickling out. The surety of great pain, if left untreated, provided all the incentive needed. He told her everything in as much detail as possible. It took a long time to cover all of it: escaping to the North then returning south to spy. Lakeland gladly gulped another draught of pain killer as the first wore off.

"Like you Gracie, the North grossly underestimated the South, and they paid a heavy price in those early encounters." Lakeland closed his eyes, feeling weary. "After what I saw here, the North is walking into a trap. They are men who wear blinders where the South is concerned." He felt the need to sleep take hold. "Martell saw it. That's why he sent us over the river… to find out."

"What are your thoughts about Jack Fox?" Gracie prepared one more glass of medication and set it aside.

"Lost a lot of money on him. Other than being Stan's son and having some djinn in him, he is nothing special from a northerner's point of view. Down here, it seems like he is the lynchpin to what will happen when the armies meet."

"What does this Colonel Martell know of him?"

"Like what I just said. But… he has eyes and ears everywhere. He might know more about Jack than you think."

"Well," said Gracie, "I have what I need, and that bullet needs to come out." She picked up the medicine. "You will sleep deeply with this last dose."

"Thanks," said Lakeland, having a hard time feeling his mouth or seeing clearly. "Thought you would…" His breath caught for a moment. "Thought you would skin me alive just to hear my screams."

Gracie smiled and saw her enemy lose consciousness. She left the room and gave orders to untie the prisoner. "He will give you no trouble."

Taking a seat at the worktable in the dining room, she wrote everything learned from Lakeland. Concluding her report, she added,

Please be advised, Tom. After careful consideration, I have settled the matter per your recommendations.

As the sun sank behind the building across the street, she signed and sealed the document. In short order, a courier stuffed it in his pouch and galloped east.

Gracie stood at the window wondering what she would do next with the goal at the top of her list achieved. Lakeland died in a drug induced sleep, no screaming or blood on the wall. Tom insisted. Surviving the oncoming assault and performing the due diligence so the bulk of her soldiers might live another year struck her as something in the distance. *What will I do with myself until then?*

An aide entered the dining room and lit candles and stoked the fireplace.

"Ma'am?" The graybeard with two stripes on his sleeve saluted. "The usual dinner?"

"No, Corporal." Gracie turned to face the man. "I am particularly hungry tonight. Steak, I think. Wine, too."

"Yes, sir," snapped the soldier. "Anything else? More light for working?"

"No." Gracie returned to the window and, in the candlelight, focused on her reflected features. "Send a message to Jack Fox and Spunk. As soon as practicable, they should report to me here."

"Sir." The Corporal saluted.

Gracie raised her hand in response, heard the man cross the floor, and close the door behind him. The reflection in the glass told a tale of missing meals and stressing over details for the good of her soldiers: thin in the face with dark circles under her eyes. With Lakeland out of the picture, she felt adrift.

"What now, Jack?" she whispered.

CHAPTER 34

Stan grudgingly realized his surroundings. They had tossed him on a field cot in a large tent and left him. The canvas wall at which he stared flickered from the candlelight behind him. He did not move, appreciating the pillow and blanket comforting him. Not one to question unexpected blessings, he wondered. *What's to become of me?*

Raising his head and turning to face into the tent, he stopped. Stan focused on the elbows on the chair's arms leading up to entwined fingers, and, finally, to a set of fiery eyes staring at him. The same eyes that bored into him after his son found him on his pallet with a hole in his shoulder. Jack sat with legs crossed in a camp chair.

"What now, Jack?" stuttered Stan, pulling back the blanket, sitting at the edge of the cot with his stockinged feet on the tent's floorboards. "Ya going to save me again?"

"Depends."

"I'm to be offered a ridiculous choice," nodded Stan, resigned to the reality of his situation and knowing how these negotiations went. "I die if I do or don't… what?"

"You will not die on this side of the Aquitaine." Jack let his hands drop away from his face. "But… before we get to that. Tell me your real name and what family I have in the North."

"Stan Folfox, but ya already know that. The Folfox family," he said, looking at the floor angry and disgusted, "has a long and glorious history in northern politics, military, and business, or so I learned repeatedly as I grew up."

"Are my grandparents still alive?"

"Very much so, and if this big battle happens, then you might meet your grandfather. He put up the gold and commands a force of a thousand men in answer to the government's call." Stan looked at Jack to see any reaction. Jack had none. "Your grandmother, my mother, never amounted to much. At least, in my eyes."

"Did you ever love my mother?"

"We…" he began, caught by surprise. "We had some good times and cared very much for each other." Reaching behind him, he lifted the blanket over his shoulders. "Then things went to hell over money and her drinking so much."

"What do you think my grandfather would think of me if we met?" Jack locked eyes with his father.

"He will test, try to kill you." Stan stared blankly as scenes played out in his mind's eye. His father, voicing his disgust, had left him on the floor broken but not dead. "The old bastard came close to ending me." Anger raged in his soul, remembering. "You will scare him. On one hand, he will smile and welcome you. On the other, he will hold the knife to do you in. He only respects power like most of his kind."

"Why did you give up on me?" Jack grimaced.

"Your ma and me went our separate ways when you was around nine or ten. I heard about you a few months after." He shrugged. "Thought you'd be better off without me."

"In the Snake?" asked Jack sarcastically.

"Well…" Stan counted the floorboards, then looked up. With the very real likelihood of being hanged as a spy, the truth seemed the best way to go. "I didn't want to carry the load. Had a messed up life enough without adding to it. Your ma looked not to be much help. I just didn't see the worth of it."

"Yeah. Like your father didn't see your worth, did he?" Jack stared down his father and said in a calm, threatening voice, "It takes a great effort not to blast you until you are nothing but a shadow on the wall."

"I ain't got much worth, son," whispered Stan. "The best thing I did was to put you in your ma's stomach. The worst thing… giving you over to Lakeland." A tear escaped his right eye. He wiped it away. "Go ahead, blow me away or hang me. I deserve it."

"Like I said," said Jack, controlling his righteous anger, "you will not die here." Jack pushed himself up in the chair while looking at the tent flap, like some outside commotion might interrupt the interrogation. "I have a proposition for you. Maybe what you deserve and what you get are two very different things."

His father stared at him.

"We are sending two survivors back to the North. A third will go if you will vouch for the other two. We need to know when and where the northern forces gather to prepare for the invasion. Maybe when you know, you could send them south." He paused, then added, "Come yourself. If you wish."

"I see. What else?" asked Stan. His son's silence and steady, angry stare made him cringe. He wondered what respect might look like in his son's eyes. "No matter. I will do it."

Jack nodded.

They spent the next hours going over the details. Other men and women joined them, providing updates that affected the plans. Jack introduced Stan to the two southern spies. The four men shared dinner, talking about themselves and the coming battle. After eating their fill, the focus went to the job to be done. Finally, Jack and Stan stood and watched their dinner companion's head to their bunks.

"I'm leaving in the morning," said Jack. "You and the others will pass to the other side of the river tomorrow night. You make the signal and then you are all on your own."

"You might not see me again, depending." Stan felt like he wanted to hug his son but held back.

"Don't get killed," said Jack. Without thinking, he placed a hand on his father's shoulder and smiled.

Stan saw what he needed to see in his son's eyes. Redemption might just be possible.

CHAPTER 35

"WHAT DO WE KNOW?" ASKED PRIME MINISTER DOWLER, suffering from a severe cough and runny nose. He pulled the heavy wool red cloak tighter as he sat at his desk. His small war cabinet assembled before him: Higgins, Sedgwick, and Martell.

"The survivors..." started Martell.

"How do they stand it?" whined Dowler. He turned to the windows and exerted just enough energy to remove the frost.

"Sir?" asked Martell.

"This blasted cold. Can't keep the fires burning high enough to warm up." The prime minister sneezed and shoved a kerchief against his nose. "Not having the lens is a misery."

"Yes, sir, I am sure, and the country will certainly appreciate your suffering for the good of the state." Martell waited for any further complaining; Dowler scowled but kept quiet. "The survivors, as I started, tell a story of a south with significant numbers of fighters and high spirits, but few with projector capabilities. Their reports point to the northerners who betrayed us, plus a few weak southern projectors. That's all."

"How do you know?" asked Higgins, sitting to the Colonel's right, "that you can trust these reports. Are these the men we sent south, or southern men ordered north to spy?"

"Hard to be certain, except that one man was Major Folfox."

"His debriefing left you thinking...?" asked Sedgewick, raising an eyebrow.

"First," Martell said. "I knew the Major from meetings with his commanding officer, Lakeland. His story and those of the other survivors were more or less consistent and credible based on what we knew when we launched those men over the Aquitaine. We should plan accordingly."

"Yes, yes," said Dowler waving his hand to move on to another issue, "the South continues to live up to our expectations. What about our strength?"

"Conscription has provided us with what we need," said Sedgewick. "We can field over twenty thousand trained men by spring."

"I received reports that the University in Hempstead revolted." Dowler sneezed again, wiped his nose, then wrapped his hands around a steaming mug.

"Inconsequential." Sedgwick leaned forward in his chair. "Most of the difficulty had to do with harboring non-projectors near projectors. Nothing else. Just so much whining."

"So, what's our timeframe?" Dowler sipped from his mug.

"We concentrate supplies at the river in early spring and build the bridges and roads. We will need to move a large force," said Higgins.

"Bridges?" questioned Dowler. "You there," he called to a corporal standing guard at the door. "Get that other fireplace going." He returned his attention to his Minister of War.

"Getting a few men over the river taking maybe ten minutes is one thing." Higgins took a deep breath. "Moving thousands of men and equipment over days is quite another."

Dowler wagged his hand again. Important details such as this belonged to his cabinet, not him.

"By early summer," continued Higgins, "we will move men, supplies, and equipment over pre-arranged paths and bridges into the South. Our depots and field hospitals will be just north of the Aquitaine."

"And?" Dowler watched as slaves set the second fire and stoked it.

"Expect a fight by late May or early June," followed Higgins. "Training continues even as we speak."

"Who's commanding this army?" Dowler wiped away the flow from his nose.

"At this time," said Sedgwick, "you are."

"I am?" Dowler froze, then shivered. "I cannot take on this burden." Wiping his nose again he said, "Gentlemen," he looked to his ministers, "I am not experienced in leading armies. We must have a single general in charge of this effort."

"We agree," said Higgins. "After careful consideration, we propose either General Cole or General Hammersmith."

"I know neither of these men." Dowler relaxed his hold on his cloak as the room warmed with both fireplaces aglow. "What's the difference? Should I flip a coin?"

"Sir, if I may," began Martell. "Hammersmith is an aggressive and a very charismatic leader. His men will follow him anywhere." The colonel paused, watching his prime minister consider the political implications. "Cole thinks strategically and has been repeatedly successful against our enemies in the north. No detail is too small. A quiet man, he leads by example."

"Higgins," said Dowler, "promote Cole. He reports to you and me only."

"As you wish, Prime Minister," nodded Higgins.

"Gentlemen, we are done," said the Prime Minister dismissing his cabinet with a wave of his damp kerchief. As his ministers exited, a stream of assistants flowed in with documents to be signed and ledgers on expenditures to be considered and approved.

Martell sat quietly as the Minister of War's valet drove him, Sedgwick, and Higgins to the Office of Ministries building. He had controlled his annoyance, satisfied their leader did exactly what he and the ministers wanted him to do. A private conversation to cover the irksome details that won or lost battles would happen in the Higgin's office.

Martell stared out of the vehicle's window. He had no data to counter the non-projector survivors' stories, but something did not sit right with him. To overturn a hundred years of belief in a weak, lawless South, he needed concrete proof. Dowler would never do more to increase the size of the army in response to a rise of southern power without viable evidence. Martell hoped time remained to discover the truth.

CHAPTER 36

"THEY AIN'T COMIN' SIR," SAID JIMMIE NICKS TO GENERAL Haggard. "Me and my boys went over the bridge at night. Looked 'round and saw nothin' of any camps. Damn near froze our butts off, sir."

Haggard considered the young man's report. He and his senior staff gathered in Middleton halfway between Lancaster and Snakeport and reasonably close to the Aquitaine. At the long table sat Jack, Spunk, Peppers, Forrester, and Shephards. On either side of Haggard, Gracie and Will held their usual positions. As the cold weather settled over the South, a council of war became necessary to comprehend their true strengths and weaknesses.

"Very good, Mr. Nicks," said Haggard. He remained quiet, considering Jimmie's words. "We can count on the invasion coming in the summer. Why am I wrong?" His question went out to all. Many of the northerners who had escaped south with Forrester or Shephards sat behind the many assistants to the senior staff. "You may take your seat, Mr. Nicks." He watched the outspoken veteran meld into the gathering of soldiers who had risked their lives to observe the enemy from cover or struck out over the river.

"Our people," said Shephards after a quick exchange with Forrester, "are hard to motivate if they must sacrifice comfort. We, therefore, agree with your assessment." The doctor saw heads nodding among the northerners. Silence ensued.

"Mr. Nicks," commanded Haggard, "you may pull your people back to a safer, warmer position. Send out patrols on a weekly basis, just in case."

"Yes, sir." Jimmy stood. "I will get the message out along the river, sir."

"Very good. Now…," said the commanding general as Nicks sat. "I must deal with an army with capabilities well outside my experience. Ladies and gentlemen, I am blind on how to use these projector units: these djinn powers. I understand how to deploy and use riflemen and cannon. Either we choose new leaders," he let that sink in, "or start intense training based on the details from the last war."

"General Haggard," said Jack, coming to his feet, "you have the confidence of every man, woman, and child in the field. We cannot replace you. It would be best if you and your officers attend private training and take what you can from hard experience found in the archives discovered so far."

"Tom," whispered Gracie, leaning into Haggard, "don't let this become more than details to be worked out. You command, period." She turned away, looked over the crowd of soldiers and civilians across the floor, and called for action. "The senior staff need all you can dig up on the forces deployed in the civil war. We will count on those former northerners to get this done as soon as practical."

"Not northerners, no more." The words carried in the quiet after Gracie's call for action. The applause and foot stomping brought smiles to all.

"Hear, hear," said Gracie, standing and slapping the table as the clapping faded. "We are all one fighting for justice and an end to slavery." Gracie raised her hand and commanded, "Jack. Your thoughts." The claps and stomps started up.

"What do we know?" Jack raised his hands for quiet, intent on keeping it simple. "No djinn exist below the river. Wrong! Southerners will never fight for their own. Wrong! The South cannot win. Wrong!" Jack passed back and forth before the many concerned but confidant fighters. "We have many with raw talent. Southern forces engaged the enemy and won. We have leaders," Jack raised his hand toward Haggard, Gracie, and Will, "who have a clear-eyed view of the death and destruction we face. So, let's get down to the way things are."

"We have some time. Push the training as fast as possible. We have the cities and towns closer to the river ready to join up. Get those cities further south who think they are safe to understand the threat." Jack stopped, raised a fist and a shield. "Who will work with me until you drop so we win?"

Everyone in the audience stood and raised a fist. Some created a shield. Jimmie Nicks had the rudiments of a shield pouring from his raised hand. Tears of joy and great pride rolled over his cheeks. Jack caught his eye, smiled, and winked. Behind him at the table, the leaders stood with hands raised in solidarity. The air sparkled in front of Gracie.

"I don't mean to say you're a crybaby or any such thing," said Gracie, sitting across from Jimmie Nicks. The meeting, like most, had ended as the sky grayed. She sought the young man who spent countless hours watching from the trees, needing to talk about what had happened. "Tears ran down your face. Why?"

"Never thought I'd amount to anything," started Jimmie, shrugging his shoulders, embarrassed to be addressed in this way by a general officer. "Always wanted to feel special 'bout somethin', ma'am." He glanced at Gracie, then looked away, studying the stains on the tabletop. "Maybe I can do more, a thing like Jack… I dunno." He put his hand on the top of the tankard of ale in front of him and squeezed the pewter rim tight. It helped him control the feelings, ready to rush out. His eyes watered. "It's mine, ma'am. Nothin' anyone can take away." He released his grip on the tall mug and quickly wiped his eyes.

"Tonight, Jimmie, I found out I have a thing too." Gracie lifted her second glass of whiskey and gulped half of it. "I don't know what to do with it."

"Well, ma'am," smiled Jimmie, who raised his tankard, "we take all we can get and make the best of it." Like most soldiers in the trenches, he had his doubts about the general officers, but this woman he would follow. "If ya take my meaning, ma'am."

"Like we always have, Mr. Nicks," said Gracie, also wiping away a tear and raising her glass. They drank together for a while, talking about the scouting reports along the river. "I have been meaning to inform…"

"May we join you?" asked Spunk, with Jack coming up behind her. She almost laughed when Jimmie jumped up to salute, knocking over his chair. "At ease, soldier."

"Yes, ma'am." The boy righted his chair but did not sit when he saw Jack: respect demanded it.

"Oh, sit down Nicks!" demanded Jack. As Jimmie settled, Jack sat and turned to Gracie. "Did you have any idea you had djinn in you?"

"No."

"A little training," said Jack, and you will put up a powerful shield in the field." He turned to Jimmie. "We already know what we will do with this soldier." He reached over the table and placed a hand on Jimmie's arm. "Our front line will need the likes of him."

"Jimmie has been very effective, manipulator or not," said Spunk. She looked at Jimmie. "Remember the mines?"

"Yes, ma'am."

"You will be something special out front." Spunk turned and addressed her commanding officer. "Jack and I are heading into the mountains."

"How long will you be gone?" asked Gracie.

"We will be back before the springtime. I have some work to finish up with the mountain people." Spunk noted Gracie's questioning lift of an eyebrow. "The Warden requested I return as we left the mountains with the wagons of gold. I agreed. It seems we have the time based on what Mr. Nicks and others have reported."

"When will you leave?" asked Gracie.

"We will take a day or two to make sure," said Jack, "that others support the critical energy training issues before we go."

Gracie nodded but felt the loss of these two who made all things possible. Knowing she could reach them if needed shored up her confidence like a warm blanket pulled close as the cold invades.

"We have a mystery to investigate." Jack smiled. "Here." He placed a paper wrapped gift on the table along with a locket holding a miniature painting of a young Gracie and Lilly within. Sliding the two objects across the table, he watched Gracie open the gold clasp and her finger brush lightly over the portrait.

"She has surprised me with her determination to fight her demons," said Gracie, remembering the teenage Lilly in the picture.

"Thanks for what you've done," said Jack, his fingers entwined with Spunk's. Gracie nodded. They rose together, said their goodbyes, and left.

"You are a marvel, Jack," whispered Gracie, uncovering the finished sculpture of herself.

"I seen nothing like it, ma'am," said Jimmie.

"No," she said. "Remind me to show you the eagle, Mr. Nicks."

"To Jack and Spunk, General?" Jimmie raised his ale.

Gracie slid her fingers around her whiskey, lifted the glass, and tapped Jimmie's tankard, then drank.

"Before any interruptions, Mr. Nicks, I promote you to lieutenant," stated Gracie.

CHAPTER 37

The council in Middleton broke up. Jack and Spunk had spent most of their time with the Northern volunteers who educated Haggard, Gracie, and other officers on the manipulator battle configurations; questions went answered or logged for research. They needed to sit down with Gracie and discuss their plans to go into the mountains. Jack nudged Spunk and tilted his head toward the group huddled around the Forresters, Peppers, and Shephards: first things first.

Anna placed her hand on Robert's arm when she saw Jack and Spunk approaching.

"There are not enough medical people to meet demand," said Shephards. "I do not see how we support the military and civilian needs."

"My wife," said Peppers, "has created a large contingent of mostly women who are quite talented when dealing with sickness. Hard experience has been their teacher. They may not be manipulators, but I have confidence in them. I will ask her to come west and do the same in other cities as fast as she is able."

"Not the best way, but…" said Shephards.

"We need 'good enough' doctor under the circumstances," interrupted Peppers.

"I understand…" started Shephards, who stopped. Jack had joined the group.

"I apologize for the interruption," said Jack. "I need a moment with Anna and Robert, if you do not mind."

"Of course," said Peppers, seeing the signs of stress and sleepless nights on his face.

"There is no description," said Jack as they settled in a corner away from the other groups, "of what you and I know to be a weapon. A division of barely capable djinn could enlist the Earth entity's help."

"What is this?" asked Robert.

Anna raised an eyebrow. She smiled when Robert nodded. "There is power in the earth."

"I have been in battles," said Spunk. "If what Jack has told me is true, then we have a way to catch them by surprise."

"You grow corn," stated Jack. "Can you grow a strangling vine through the earth, bypassing a shield?" He watched as Robert rubbed his chin, considering the possibility. "You should experiment with that." He paused. "I have to ask. Is she or he or whatever on our side and, if so, why?"

"I don't know," said Anna.

"Maybe we should ask?" stated Robert, who shrugged his shoulders in a 'just an idea' manner.

"You don't just question a goddess," said Anna, annoyed at Robert, who pestered her on the way back to Snakeport. Riding old, but surefooted horses, they plodded side-by-side in the long train of mounted soldiers.

"Why not?" Robert leaned toward her with a glint of mischief in his eye. "A goddess or god who cannot be straightforward in her or his communications must have something to hide, or is not much of an almighty power." It always bothered him from a young boy when the old religious texts never presented a god who would answer questions simply. Punished for not grasping the simple laws of Holy Scripture, he fumed and began his race to atheism.

Anna reached over and pushed him away. "You don't challenge a greater power. You show respect."

"All I'm saying is," said Robert, looking pained and rubbing his shoulder dramatically, "worship is earned. Could she intrude mysteriously from time to time to get what she wants?" His horse dropped its head and shook it, pulling the reins and Robert forward with a jolt. "Thanks," he said when Anna's fingers took a firm hold on his arm, keeping him from being thrown over the beast's head.

"Should have let you bounce on the ground, you old fool!" Anna spoke in frustration. "You don't know what you ask."

"Well, maybe I will do just that, go to the ground, shoot some power, call her up, and ask." Robert stared at Anna as though she insulted him beyond forgiveness.

"Disrespecting a goddess is not a wise move." Anna sighed. "You're going to do it, aren't you?" She gave him the evil eye, scrunching her eyebrows. Turning away, Anna gave in. "Alright… I will. If only to save you from yourself." She rode without speaking for a time. "When we get back home after the next training."

"Good," he said, trying not to grin but failing. Not thinking, letting his excitement run wild, he asked, "Do you want to discuss the questions and approach to…"

"No!"

The remaining ride back to Snakeport would be uneventful and silent. Anna wondered how she might confront a higher power. Her mind whirled, searching for the best strategy.

Robert floundered in his silence, needing her to forgive his thoughtlessness. Older, tried-and-true solutions came to mind, which sometimes worked or made things worse. The lifelong partners avoided looking at each other. The moment they did, their mutual irritation would melt away into smiles. Robert acted first. His hand reached across and took hers.

*　*　*

Anna addressed one hundred trainees in a large open lot near the Snake courthouse.

"Mole Weed when left untended grows voraciously up the side of a brick wall, a tree, or anything else in its path. It will, over time, crack bricks and crumble mortar or kill an oak. Fortunately for us, it has several insect enemies who devour the leaves or the roots when they find them." All had taken part in the crop growing and gathering. "This weed lies everywhere within inches of the surface. Aside from its voracious growth ability, it has a special feel you must recognize like you know corn or wheat. My assistants will pass among you with potted versions of this plant. Touch it. Let it register with your energy. Today we want only this thing to come forth from the ground."

The sun flared in a cloudless sky, but the cold held sway. Everyone stamped their feet, shoved hands into underarms or blew frosted breath into icy fingers or gathered close for warmth. It took an hour for everyone to touch the plant.

"I want ten rows of ten with room in front and back to contact the earth." Anna walked along the front and down one side of the formation. Satisfied, she stood at the front and pointed to a derelict building several blocks away: no doors or windows. A large crack ran up the side, separating bricks across the three stories. "I want you to devour that building with the weed." She pointed. Doubt rose among her students. "Remember what we did with the corn, so find the way with this new plant." She paused, then said, "Do it."

In the first ten minutes, the weed popped up among the trainees, but after several more attempts, the projectors on their hands and knees sent the attack to the target. Anna's assistants joined the effort. In thirty minutes, the building's wall facing cracked and fell beneath the burden of dark green leaves and ravenous roots pulling the wall apart.

"Enough," called Anna. She walked among the men, women, and children as they rose from the ground. Some staggered, their energy used up. "You did well. I am impressed." The smiles, the pride, and the hope, the unquenchable hope of these people, struck her. *You deserved better.* She let the thought go and said, "Can you do the same to men across a field and do it faster under fire? It has to happen in seconds, not minutes."

"We got the how, ma'am," called a man among the company. "Let us have another go."

"Do it!"

In minutes after her command, even the most weary went to the ground. The building's empty rooms became visible as the plant chewed into the guts of the structure: a large section totally collapsed in less than a minute.

"Very good!" Anna watched as a third-floor flat gave way collapsing into the one below. Satisfied, she sent the group and her assistants back to the classrooms in the courthouse to warm up and practice shielding methods and perform stamina building exercises. Hanging back, she waited until she stood alone. On her hands and knees, only a small amount of energy brought the goddess, as Anna knew her.

"*Daughter, you question my gifts?*"

"*No,*" thought Anna, her hands clawing at the dirt. "I… we question how we communicate." She tried to remember what Robert wanted asked, but the energy flow from the earth overwhelmed her. It felt like drowning, staring up through the water at the bright surface with salvation: air only inches away. Anna gave up. "*Do what you will.*"

"*Ungrateful child, you embarrass me.*"

"*I meant no disrespect.*" The energy diminished and her burning lungs desperately pulled in the air. She laid prone, her face in the dirt, her hands glowing buried in the earth.

"*We are not equals. You cannot bring me down to your level.*"

"*True. We are not equal in power.*" Still breathing hard, Anna managed a chuckle, hearing Robert's words about what he thought might be worthy of worship. *"Is it might makes right? If so, kill me. If not, share with me."*

In an instant, Anna sat in her garden at home on a summer's day. Across the white stone path, on the opposite bench, sat Robert with the same look of mischief as on the trail to Snakeport.

"You want to talk. So, talk." Robert stretched his legs, crossed his feet, and laid his head back with eyes closed. The sunlight graced his face.

"You are helping the South. Why?"

"Ha!" said Robert. "I cannot answer your question without revealing myself." He opened his eyes, raised his head, and began, "I am the earth guardian. All living things born of the earth are mine to manage. What you call the South lives in harmony with my charges. The North destroys them and works actively to deny my existence."

"How long have you existed?" Anna no longer feared for her life and relaxed. Looking to her right, she recognized the white roses in full bloom. Her garden from twenty years ago flourished wherever she looked.

"As the first dry land emerged from the sea, I came into being. I became self-aware when the first fur clad beasts roamed this land. In short, I am very old." Robert stood up and clasped his hands behind his back, stepping along the path.

"Are you a god?" Anna watched as this version of Robert stopped, reached out to touch a rose, then chuckled.

"To anything of less power, I am. Your species is the exception. You have the most annoying habit of questioning authority. You and your kind will die before you give in." He turned around. "Using your definition of god, the answer is no. I am not all knowing nor all-powerful: a demigod, perhaps."

"What is greater than you?" Anna placed her arm along the top of the bench. "Do you fear anything?"

"The sea might be, but I do not know of a power among the waves." Robert came and stood before her. "The sun is certainly more powerful. It does not, however, talk to me either. I fear nothing of which you are aware." Leaning slightly and looking deeply into her eyes, he answered her next questions before she asked.

"I do not have the power to wave what I dislike out of existence. I choose not to bring what I do into the sunlight for all to see." He returned to the bench across the way, relaxing in the sun's rays as they once again fell on his face. "If I had my way, the land would be all forest from the sea to the tree-line on the highest mountain. Your kind would build your cities amidst the forest: you, your homes, everything part of a living whole."

"What value do we offer you?" Anna's heart skipped a beat as this Robert turned from the sun to her and smiled.

"Become managers of the earth, believe in me, and I will believe in you." The fantasy Robert sat up straight and faced her. "Love me and I will love you. I protect those who protect my charges. I give life to those who support life."

"But… we must take life to win," stated Anna. "How does that work? How…" Her garden disappeared. On the ground, dirt in her mouth and nose, she raised her head, spitting.

"I am sure, daughter; you will work it out."

"Can we count on this?" asked Robert, excited, eyes wide. What would have started an argument and flashes of unresolved anger now existed as a minor irritant. He continued to test everything having to do with the earth goddess, but he did not have to control everything. "If I press too hard, I'm sorry."

"I tried the weed growth. Experimented with some new

arrivals and it works," said Anna. She sat collapsed into the soft cushions, her eyes closed and her head resting back.

"You're shaking," said Robert, kneeling close. Among the cushions and enfolded in a heavy blanket, Anna's eyes looked glazed to him as she stared into the flickering yellow-orange glow. He worried about finding his soulmate this way. Her hands usually warm, felt ice cold. Robert held her left hand between his two, trying to warm it. "What have I done to you, my dear?"

"You," said Anna in a deadpan voice, "have taken a goddess down a few pegs, but then raised her up in my eyes. The goddess opened the door to questions and answered." Anna opened her eyes and faced Robert. "She came to me disguised as you."

"Me?" Robert laughed.

"You are hardly," started Anna with more enthusiasm, "worthy of worship, but I can talk to you." Anna described all that happened.

"A little sketchy on the saving and taking life thing," said Robert. "But I agree with you. We need to respect this power. I will do what I can."

"Which is?" Anna grinned with a suspicious look.

"I will stop arguing the point and start loving the dirt."

CHAPTER 38

They stole over the bridge in the early morning and started cutting down trees. Wide, straight trunks for the foundation with other trees cut into planks: hard labor.

"No better than slaves," said the recently promoted Major Potter.

"No surprise," said Stan, now Colonel Folfox. Martell raised him up to take over the Lakeland regiment. "We are what is available." The work to provide building materials strategically placed along the path of invasion proceeded without interruption. Stan expected no trouble. He and Potter walked among the crews. Several times, Stan removed his uniform cloak, took up the harness, and dragged a trimmed tree to the river's edge. His men appreciated a commanding officer willing to share their burden.

"Colonel! Need to take a dump, sir," called a corporal who escaped the leather straps.

"Don't need my permission. Just go, soldier." Stan monitored the corporal, disappearing into the forest underbrush. The southern observers, always close by, would get what they needed from their spy. "Easier than I thought," he whispered as he put his shoulder to the harness with the other men and dragged the two-foot thick trunk another ten feet. Sweat darkened his shirt front and back.

Near sunset, his men crossed to the north and went to their camps. Fires burned, meat cooked, and exhausted men collapsed into their bunks. Near midnight, Stan went to the cook's tent, usually abandoned with cleaned pots and pans stacked on the floorboards. Ten men sat around a table with mugs steaming: five sergeants, three lieutenants, and two corporals.

"At ease, gentlemen," said Stan when he entered the tent and the men rose and saluted. "Is the coffee fresh?"

"Aye, sir, fresh." A soldier with three stripes on his sleeve got up and poured a mug full. He handed it to Stan and returned to his place.

"What's the word from the men?" asked the Colonel. He drank his coffee and took the empty chair at the head of the table, then reached into his coat's inner pocket and produced an unopened half pint bottle of dark brown liquor. "Sweetener, gentlemen?" The familiar twist and snap as the cap came off brought a smile to the faces around the table.

"If not for you adding your shoulder to the effort, Colonel, there would be open revolt," said the sergeant who finished the liquor passed man-to-man down the table, then tossed it in the pile of garbage by the table of pots. "They expected more to join up. Some think the southerners might treat them better."

"I think we here feel the same way." Stan noted the nods from every man. "I believe we are sacrificial lambs." He let the silence stretch, placing his mug on the table. "I want you men to prepare."

"Strategy, sir? What of Major Potter?" asked a lieutenant.

"Potter expects to get very rich," confirmed Stan. "He is a threat, but not a serious one." The Colonel commanded two separate groups of five hundred troops. Potter took charge of one. Stan paused, considering his answers, then addressed the first question. "I will arrange for our men to be placed at the front on the left or right flank. I will concentrate our faction on one side. If the North tears through the southern troops, then we support the North and our northern masters will be none the wiser of our strategies." Stan looked over at the corporals, who nodded. *They understand the commonsense strategy.* "If not, we fire on the northerners." Stan felt the weight of the silence fall as every man saw his death in a blast of bright energy. "Shake it off gentlemen. I don't believe in suicide."

"The attack," he continued, "if it comes to it, on the northerners will be a total surprise. A quick but controlled retreat will keep us alive, but we must move fast, reload on the run, and fire volleys until we are away. We may become the least of their troubles with the southerners attacking."

"I agree this might work, sir, but," said a lieutenant, "it will be a matter of luck depending on what the southern soldiers do."

"Remember, gentlemen, every battle plan is perfect until the enemy is engaged, then all bets are off." Stan reached and picked up his coffee. Just before he drank, he said, almost to himself, "Too bad we do not have a way to let the other side know what we might have to do."

The corporal who slipped the straps to relieve himself earlier in the day smiled at his fellow corporal, then addressed the Colonel.

"Yes, sir," he said with a grin. "Too damn bad."

CHAPTER 39

After a week of travel from Middleton, Jack and Spunk, with their small entourage of soldiers passed into mountain country. Spunk retold the story of the action into the mine, pointing out key sites along the path. Late the following morning at the fork in the road where months earlier a stone wall blocked their progress, the Warden and members of the ruling class waited. Jack and Spunk approached on horseback.

"We welcome the return of the Captain." The Warden spread his arms in welcome as the others behind him, richly dressed men and women, bowed their heads in respect. To Jack, he said, "we open Our hearts and homes to the Source."

Jack leaned toward Spunk and asked in a whisper, "What is this source business?"

"He never explained it." Spunk nodded to the Warden. "Dismount. Let's go find out."

Before a word could be spoken, the mountain people moved to the side; a path opened into a tunnel. The Warden pivoted on his heel and led the way. When he, Jack, and Spunk stood close together in a small room, he reached over and pulled a lever cleverly camouflaged against the stone wall. Two doors closed, trapping them.

The Warden smiled broadly as the room rose. "Do not be afraid. We call these shafts and rooms elevators."

After an interminably long time to Jack and Spunk, the room stopped moving, and the doors opened. Cheers greeted them as they stepped into an avenue of intricately carved stone columns stretching into the distance. Sunlight poured in from openings in the rock ceiling high above, with every other column having a flaming brazier attached.

"Source, source!" came from the crowd of people: men, women, and children pushing forward. Doors, other elevators, opened. Others from the welcoming party poured onto the floor.

Still awed by his first ride in such a contraption plus the unexpected grandeur of the hall beneath the mountain, Jack could not make any sense of anything, especially the people's reaction. Energy suddenly poured from his hands, enveloping all those close to him in a colorful whirlwind.

The people froze for a moment, then exploded in a frenzy of laughter and tears. Some went to their knees; their arms raised in supplication. The call of "Source" became louder.

"Warden," commanded Jack, "get us out of here."

"Drop your shield." As the colors melted away, the Warden stepped forward and addressed his people. "You are all witnesses!" He smiled as they cheered. "The Source has come to us and we have much to discuss." Quietly, the crowd spread apart. The Warden stepped forward. Jack and Spunk followed.

"What is all this?" Jack confronted the Warden in a side-chamber as he shed his hooded robe, tossing it over a chair as he headed to a desk at the back of the room with colorful tapestries covering the stone walls.

"You are the Source, the solution to many of our troubles," said the Warden in an isn't-it-obvious tone of voice. "Something to eat or drink after your long journey?" He went to a sideboard with many dishes of meat, fish, and vegetables. The empty plate in his hand filled quickly. The silence caught his attention.

Shocked and confused, Jack and Spunk froze in place and stared at the old man.

"Are you familiar with Titus?" He returned to studying the various foods available, as though the reference ended any misunderstanding.

"We know of Titus, but not much about the details of his

writings," said Spunk, recalling something Robert Forrester had described. "What exactly did he write about this solution you mention?"

"See for yourself." The Warden pointed to his left.

In the far corner, a table with a large tome opened, rested on a pedestal. They approached, hoping they read well enough. The book looked ancient and fragile. They bent over the pages together and whispered the words on the pages.

He or she, the Source, will foment a righteous war. Earth, wind, and fire will know the Source. Water and stone will play their part. The Source will reestablish the balance among the peoples. That which could not be resolved, will be.

The writing went on in the same vein, calling out the mythical abilities of the Source to bring about great things.

"The Professor should see this," said Jack.

"Not much on specifics," called Spunk over her shoulder. "How do you know this refers to Jack?" She stood up straight and addressed the Warden, who had found a seat and happily ate.

"We who live in the western mountains have waited patiently." The Warden licked his fingers, then lifted a fork and hoisted a piece of meat. "The Slaver War, as you call it, is the first of its kind in living memory. It is indeed a righteous endeavor to end a great evil." Half of the forkful disappeared into his mouth. Chewing, he said, "Do you know why the Eng, those you call projectors, who could easily overwhelm us have not?" He finished the meat, swallowed, then said, "Their shield projection does not work well in these mountains. Yet you projected a strong one, easily. Therefore, the people reacted as they did." He got to his feet and returned to the sideboard. "You must try this spiced chicken. It is exquisite."

"So, if we force them to fight in the mountains, our guns will hurt them?" Spunk, excited by the prospect, moved close to the Mountain leader. "We could win." She watched him sigh and set down his plate.

"First, you could never maneuver them into such a battle unless you give up all the land south of the Aquitaine." He picked up an empty plate and shoved it into her hands. "If they have the land north and south of the river and you're bottled up in the mountains, they win." A second plate he tossed to Jack, who came up behind Spunk. "Now stop talking nonsense and eat. Afterward, you and your people should rest. We prepared your rooms. We have much to discuss and people you must meet."

"Who?" asked Jack, finally giving into his growling stomach and filling his plate.

"The far northern enemy of your enemy." The Warden winked. "They've read Titus too."

CHAPTER 40

"I simply got curious," said Will Biggs, who spent the last few months patrolling the sea lanes looking for a surprise attack. With nothing to show for his efforts and the winter storms churning the seas, he and his crews abandoned their ships for action on dry land. He painstakingly lined up divisions of paper soldiers. "I will keep this simple and use phalanx order."

Around Will, at Gracie's place near the office, his team erected a three-tier amphitheater. The general officers and staff had spent weeks at their desks absorbing a new language on battle formations and energy weapons. Many complained of headaches after marathon sessions. Behind Will's setup, frayed leather-bound books formed a wall across four tables. Little by little, the tapestry of battle formations from one hundred years ago became comprehensible to the southern military.

"Tell us again, Will. What caught your interest?" asked Gracie. Dark circles because of the long nights of training aged her. The weariness weighed down everyone. Not one officer, however, abandoned the effort to learn how to survive a fight with projectors.

"Easy," said Will. "How many times did we run out of candles over the last weeks after sunset?" He continued to make corrections to his model. "When the candles burned out, did we run out of light?" Will turned around and studied his audience. He smiled at their confusion and then stated, "No. Did magic light keep us at our work?" Will raised a hand to quiet the annoyed voices demanding he get to the point. "Our northern teachers used lenses to put the light from every available source on the chalkboards. They do the same, on my model."

"I never noticed," said Tom Haggard.

"Lensing, as they call it, is subtle and not easily detected unless you trace the light from the target back to its origin, which I did a few sessions ago." Will waved his hand to the northern expatriate assistants standing by the piles of books. "Our new brothers and sisters thought nothing of it. It was something they did to study when lights went out in the University dorms or library. I, however, got to thinking about the lens over Dover. Talked it over with the Professor and his supporters and here we are." He stepped back away from the model. "Let's begin."

The light in the room faded. A single ball of light, looking like a small sun, appeared near the rafters. Beneath that sun, a ray shot toward the paper army. The ray became a tight beam and struck. Half of the model burst into flame. The beam disappeared.

"Quiet!" ordered Will when the questions erupted. "Watch!"

One northerner approached the table next to the unburnt sample. The beam struck again, but this time it looked like each paper soldier held up a mirror shield. Such shielding deflected the attack. A stack of paper burst into flame. Uniformed men and women ducked below their desks. The fire extinguished quickly.

"Sorry about that," said Will. He studied the officers, then looked directly at Tom Haggard. "We have a weapon and a potential defense if they use it against us, which, I suspect, they will."

"And you got all this just because you got curious?" asked Haggard, very impressed with the presentation. "We need the details on how this is to be deployed. How many projectors to start? What configuration?"

"The battlefield-scale details have yet to be worked out," said Will.

"As of this moment, Will Biggs," commanded Haggard, "you are to make these regiments a reality."

"Yes, sir," responded Will. "I would strongly recommend

that all training include the mirror shield creation. It is a simple variation on Jack Fox's manipulation technique."

"See to it, Will." Haggard stood, gathered a few papers: his notes. "Gentlemen and ladies, we need to rest and gather our strength. I call a halt to this session. We will start fresh tomorrow morning."

"Tom, a moment?" whispered Gracie. They stepped off the platform and went to Gracie's office.

"I have news from our spies." Gracie poured amber liquid into two glasses. "Stan Folfox is playing true with us."

"What are the specifics?" asked Haggard, taking the proffered drink.

"There will be a non-projector force on one flank ready to fight for us if we hold the field against the northerners."

"Suicide more like." Haggard stared into his glass, considering the pros and cons. "It will certainly be a surprise and may offer an opportunity." His brow furrowed. "If we can't hold our own, I guess their aid does not matter."

"We should have a sortie party ready on that flank, prepared to throw up shields," said Gracie.

"Do it," said Haggard, who downed his drink and set the glass on the desk. "What are your thoughts on taking all of this classroom learning into the field? We must be very familiar with these tools before we place our troops in harm's way."

"Before the cold breaks. Before Jack gets back." Gracie watched Haggard stand, tip his hat, and head for the door. "Our success should not wholly rest on his shoulders."

Looking back, Haggard said, "It does, Gracie. We must be prepared to sacrifice and support him to do whatever he will do. I expect it to shock this world."

CHAPTER 41

"I care little, Colonel Martell," said General Arthur Cole, "for mixing military matters with political needs. I am not, however, so foolish as to believe I can ignore politics." Cole set up his central command in Hempstead. He and his staff took over the library after Doctor Shephards and his followers went south. The general sat at the head table, reviewing reports on the most urgent issues needing his attention. He addressed the North's spymaster, seated at the first table to the general's right. "You, it seems, have the Prime Minister's ear, as well as the support of his key ministers. I cannot command, but I will request that you keep me informed of the politics while you strive to block their influence on my command."

"I will do anything to support this action," said Martell. The Colonel considered Cole with some admiration. Tall, thin, in a uniform unadorned with the usual gold braid. Martell observed the General kept up their conversation while reading the paper before him. Cole wore a full beard cropped close: forty years old, he looked younger. He had charisma and looked the part of a confident leader of men. "I am at your service."

"Excellent." The North's commanding general let the page he held slide onto the smaller of two stacks. He leaned forward and commanded, "Tell me about your spies, what has happened in the South, and what we might be up against. Since I am having this discussion at all, it is a concern, Colonel. Are we facing a capable force that might defeat us?" Cole looked toward the back of the room. "Captain Troy!" An officer appeared instantly. "Tell those fools at the Commissary," he tapped his index finger on the paper he just put down, "to stop counting their gold and start stockpiling at strategic points along our route. I will not tolerate their graft. I will hang many of them if I have to make an example!"

"Yes, sir." The officer dashed off.

"I expect you to approve any hanging I must order. Some of these men have friends in Dover."

"Of course." Martell relaxed, surprised by Cole's sudden outburst. "Traitors are traitors."

"Now, what about these southerners and the spies you sent over the river?" Cole sat back.

"What we know is that we are outnumbered by two or three to one. We guess they have only a few hundred projectors, if that many. The spies who survived and returned described a society in disarray. We will face muskets more than shields."

"Then why haven't they sued for peace?" Cole stared at Martell.

"They would rather die than submit to our demand for workers."

"Do you suggest we kill the vast majority?" Cole scanned another report in his hand, allowing Martell's inability to answer to stretch. "No? Do the powers that be expect our honorable soldiers to murder the vast majority of southerners who want to protect their children?" Cole looked up from the report and set it on another pile. "I have no intention, Colonel, of sending the best of my soldiers to commit atrocities so our pampered citizens can maintain their… what? Self-centered lifestyles." He stared at the Colonel. "What is the real threat to our country?"

"You enter the realm of politics, sir." Martell weighed his next words. "I have no data to confirm my concerns. I think, however, you may face several thousand projectors of varying capabilities with limited training. Certainly, their officer corps will be inexperienced in how to use such forces. You will experience losses, but you will prevail."

"Colonel, without solid intelligence, this is wishful thinking." Cole rose, extracted another few sheets from the taller pile, and walked down the line of library reading tables. "I must assume, Colonel, that I will meet a force at least the equal to my own." The general, surrounded by aides, spoke to one unseen, made a half-hearted salute, and waited until footfalls faded. He turned and returned to his seat. "The only difference will be command experience. That, Colonel, will be our edge and my men will fight to defeat this enemy because otherwise they will invade and lay waste to our country."

Martell's mind went into overdrive, evaluating any other plausible scenario. Finally, he said, "It is the only logical course open. I will make sure my superiors comprehend it in the capital."

"Good." Cole rustled through more pages. "I have some notes from a conversation with Camden, the university president. I take it, you know the man?"

"Typical academic, rebelled against military intrusion," said Martell. "He finally caved to my settling the non-projector outfit here."

"Under house arrest for advising students to fight… what exactly, Colonel?" The General found the notes and reviewed the list.

"Doing their duty for the country that has given them so much." Martell had not expected to discuss the near draft riots among the students with the university president's approval.

"A draft, Colonel? More forced indenture." Cole closed his eyes. "In my long experience, these troops are of no use to me. Either they are out front to be sacrificed or in the rear guarding supply lines. Both will run when the fight gets tough. My officers are releasing these men."

"Do not release them, sir, is my recommendation. Hold them in reserve to be called up if needed. Double the training effort."

"Colonel, I have ordered my recruiters to play to honor but cajole and plead when love of country is not enough. Sometimes, if money is an issue, to buy participation. I agree hard training will instill loyalty to an outfit and to the men in it. I will consider keeping some reserve units." Cole placed the list flat on the table and started tapping it with his finger. "I have one concern, however, Camden discussed at length. Who is this Jack Fox?"

* * *

Jack leaned against the wall outside the rooms he and Spunk shared. The mountain people never failed to surprise: their machines and stone mastery. The observatories, however, made an indelible mark on Jack: the climb to the highest chambers near the mountain tops, the tree-sized telescopes with their huge finely polished glass lenses, and the vistas these tools opened for him. Jack felt small after hours in the observation chair learning about things every school age mountain child knew. What could be on the globes nearer the sun and the ones far away?

Jack and Spunk had enjoyed mountain hospitality for four weeks. They spent hours with either the Warden or his aides learning the mountain culture, politics, and survival. The embassy from the Far North territories, the aides advised, ran into foul winter weather but finally arrived. Tonight's dinner would be the first time either Jack or Spunk or any southerner since before the civil war met a citizen from the Far North.

The Warden's latest request, however, brought lofty stargazing to an abrupt halt. Delay did not help. Jack pushed off the wall, opened the door, and sought Spunk. He wondered how she would react. It came quickly.

"He wants you to what?" she yelled.

"Apparently, to avoid insult to his people, the Warden expects me, the Source, as he calls me, to impregnate one of their women."

Jack dragged himself into the spacious living quarters and dropped onto the fur covered bed. "I refused, of course, as gently as possible."

"We must explain to him how we are!" Spunk joined him on their bed, barely controlling her outrage.

"He offered to return the favor by having one of his men impreg…".

"Hell, no!"

"Agreed, but we need to discuss the politics of…"

"There is nothing to discuss!" Spunk jumped to her feet. With her hands on her hips she said, "We should go home now!" Jumping to the floor, she pulled clothes from a dresser drawer. "What other perversions do these people practice?"

"Adding insult to injury will not help. They may not let us go," said Jack, staring at the chiseled stone ceiling. "We need to get the Warden alone after dinner and talk this out."

"Damn," said Spunk, sitting on the bed throwing the things in her hand at the open dresser drawer. "If not for this man and his people, me and my crew would not have succeeded at the mines." She frowned, felt ungrateful. "I won't share you. You are mine and I am yours, but we can discuss how to work around it."

"Let's get ready and go meet these other northern people. We will see how things will play out." Jack rose from the bed and wrapped his arms around Spunk. "Committed," he whispered softly.

The state dinner came and went with little excitement. The six far Northern ambassadors entered the large anti-room, where the dinner invitees congregated to great fanfare. One of the six sought Jack and demanded to know the southern strategy. The Warden stepped in and handled the situation adeptly, guiding the errant ambassador back to his team.

In the wee hours of the morning, Jack, Spunk, and the Warden sat before a cold fireplace. Each with their own thoughts.

"Let's get a fire going now that our frigid guests have retired," said the Warden. "It is interesting how little comfort they take from warmth." Footmen flooded in with wood, kindling, and a flint. It did not take long for tall flames to rise in the hearth and erase the cold. "Now, what seems to be the trouble?"

"How can you make such a request?" demanded Spunk.

"Oh," nodded the Warden. "A similar request to your enemy posed no problem. I would call them eager. We thought you might be the same."

"Spunk and I have stated we commit to each other." Jack saw the confusion on their host's face. "We will have no others. We are one."

"Ah," said the Warden. "I see the problem and I apologize." He thought for a moment. "We have other ways to deal with this situation. We will absolutely respect your commitment to each other."

"Other ways?" questioned Jack.

The Warden smiled. "One of our doctors will speak with you." He cleared his throat. "What did you think of the ambassadors?"

"Have you made offers to those people too?" asked Spunk. "Do you have children from these… exchanges?"

"First, we, like you, deal forcefully with matters of survival. This strategy is one of those." The Warden raised a hand. "Some mulled wine, if you please." Like the fire, a tray of three tall steaming goblets appeared quickly. "Please, drink. It will help you sleep and settle any stomach grumbling from tonight's meal." He patted his stomach.

Leaning forward, the older man lifted his cup and swallowed, closing his eyes in delight. He remained silent for a minute then said, "You, Captain, have worked closely with some of those born from these tristes. They are Eng when outside these mountains. You had an extra shield or two during the mine excursion, though I doubt you noticed."

"Far northerners," said Jack, changing the subject. He warmed his hands, cradling the wine, "are very direct." He found their soft voices not in concert with their muscular frame, large brow ridges, and thick brown hair. The males sported thick, well-trimmed beards and thicker hair on their hands and wrists. The women, built similarly, possessed a predator's charm but with less body hair.

"Their eyes," whispered Spunk. "The intensity I found disturbing, as if I stared at a wolf having found its next meal."

"Feral," said the Warden. "Many of their kind died defending their homes from the army you will face this summer. They have an interest in your success but are not sure how to help or if they should."

"If you will pardon my impudence, Warden," said Jack. "Considering the coming battle, the success of the mine skirmish, and the inability for Eng to function in these mountains, what power is yours to use as needed?"

"Cut to the chase, hey Jack?" The Warden finished the wine and set it down. "We live in stone, but the earth sustains us. I live surrounded by rock, but pay homage to the dirt, as do you?"

Jack nodded. "We share this and have the same enemy, but you will not join us in the coming battle?"

"I realize," said Spunk, closing her eyes feeling the effects of the wine, "that they cannot. It is our fight, as it is the far northerner's fight."

"And if we win," said Jack, addressing the Warden.

"It is our most solemn prayer…" the old man paused, "that you will hear us, the far northerners, and, yes, even your defeated enemy."

"Hear what?" asked Jack.

"To avoid an effusion of blood over generations, if you should win." The Warden looked from Spunk to Jack, then said, "Listen carefully. You should not rule four kingdoms as one."

CHAPTER 42

"This is not working. They are too vulnerable." General Haggard standing on high ground with his senior commanders watched as one thousand soldiers, five groups of two hundred, executed exercises that presented a shield defense, energy bolt offense, and a weed attack through the earth. "The Weeders cannot be on their hands and knees. Tell them to take off their boots. See if bare feet work."

"Never thought of that," said Gracie, studying the field through binoculars.

"If it works," commanded Haggard, turning to an aide, "have them project shielding and drive the weed at the same time."

"Yes, sir," called a young officer. He mounted a horse and charged down the slope.

"Ladies and gentlemen, what would a northern army do in the time it will take for my order to reach the right persons?" Haggard followed the aide on horseback, who pulled up in a cloud of dust and passed on the orders. Other runners dashed up and down the line, keeping all officers informed. "Imagine there are fifty thousand troops." He paused, shaking his head. "Poor communications hamstrings us. What do you suggest?"

"Tight beam light signaling might work better." The suggestion came from one of the northern expatriates. "We would send orders to the regimental officers in this way. Mounted messengers could handle the messaging at the company level."

"You have a code and people who know it? Who and how many understand the method?" asked Haggard.

"General, some of us former Hempstead engineering students developed it and know how to use it. It's how we kept up with the latest news or gossip."

Haggard turned to the voice. "You are a trainer, I see." The man he addressed wore civilian clothes. "You are now an officer, a colonel, and it is your job to build this capability. I want to see it working in a week, Colonel...?"

"Smithfield, sir."

"See Miss Lilly about your uniform first, Colonel Smithfield. No soldier will pay much attention to you without it. Get to it."

"Yes, sir. Immediately, sir."

"It is rare, madam," said Haggard, studying the field, mindful of Gracie's earlier comment, but smiling, "that I out-think you on any level. Look!" Haggard pointed to the barefoot unit to the left. Weeds popped up a distance in front of it and the air rippled with shield energy. The other Weeder companies soon showed the same capability. "What of the Folfox riflemen?"

"All arranged," said Gracie. "Stan Folfox and his men will have an eagle head badge. The other group will have something else. Once identified, our flanker regiment will steal away on that side of the field, get positioned behind the line, and support those men."

"I find it hard to accept how easy it is to get these actions arranged." Haggard turned to Gracie and asked, "Are you sure we are not being deceived? Could this be a trap?"

"I am confident the trap is ours to set." She paused. "Stan shows himself dedicated for his own reasons, from what my spies report."

"You are telling me that Stan Folfox, a back stabber from long before this war, has discovered dignity and honor?"

"Stan's interests are best served by us, if we win," said Gracie. "Dignity and honor?" She shook her head. "I can only hope." She gazed up at the sky, then said, "Self-interest has driven all of us with no consideration of dignity or honor."

Tom Haggard continued to observe the soldiers' actions.

Occasionally, he glanced at Gracie. She had opened his eyes to the evil of the slave trade and gently nudged him into action. Finally, he said, "I take your point, Mrs. Hargreaves."

"Might I recommend," said Gracie, "that we double the size of the units every few days? We need to see how cumbersome it becomes with Smithfield's new signaling to move tens of thousands. We will need warming stations, so our bootless units endure no damage during practice sessions in this cold weather." She leaned toward Haggard and whispered, "You are the better man, Tom. Always have been. I am not innocent either. We have done things to better our own position. There is, however, strength in redemption if we are open to it."

"Feels like it might snow." Tom looked up at the sky as the sunlight failed. "Redemption? Maybe." Haggard shook his head, not sure he could count on such a thing, then said, "We are done for today… but we cannot afford to interrupt practice because of unfavorable conditions. See to the warming stations for tomorrow. Snow or no snow, get the next battalions ready to work just after dawn."

"Yes, sir," replied Haggard's adjutant. He turned to the other staff waiting close by and gave orders. Horses galloped off in all directions.

"Gracie, if it is not too much of an imposition, join me for dinner."

"Of course, Tom." Gracie smiled

"I want to discuss the unthinkable." He turned and led his officers down the slope. "What do we do when we win?"

"I know," said Mini, excited. "I been in and among the northerners since the Professor brought 'em here."

"Oh," stated the new Colonel Smithfield, who looked at Mini

doubtfully. "You know the code?" Smithfield stood on a crate while Lilly made measurements.

"Yeah. I learnt it from the northern girls." Mini scribbled down the measurements called out by Lilly. "They said I best learn it cause you boys were kinda dumb when it came to girls and such." Mini stepped over to the rack of coats. "We have a fit, Ms. Lilly. It will need some piping, but that won't take long."

"Very good, Mini." Lilly looked up at the northerner. "Do not, young man, underestimate that girl. Creating ways to communicate comes natural-like to her."

"Hey there, missy," called Smithfield. "What do you make of this?"

Mini smiled, then frowned as the pinpoint light flashed a foot in front of her face. "I am not a silly girl playing at grownup!" Her fingers suddenly twirled and rifled through a response.

"Such language," admonished Smithfield, bringing his hands to his cheeks in mock exasperation. "You vile little creature…" He stopped and laughed so hard the measuring stopped. "Miss Lilly," he said, wiping a tear from his cheek, "if it is not too much trouble, outfit Miss Mini with a lieutenant's uniform. If…" he stepped down from the crate and put a hand on Mini's shoulder, "you are ready to serve under me?"

"I'll be in the field?" asked Mini.

"Where else?"

"You do this, Mini," said Lilly. "I have others to pick up the slack."

Mini looked from Lilly to Smithfield, then raised her right hand in salute to her superior officer.

CHAPTER 43

"THE QUESTION BEEN ASKED, GENTLEMEN, AND WE NEED AN answer!" yelled Jimmie Nicks. He stood fifty yards away from three soldiers in the practice field.

In Middleton weeks earlier, finishing their last round of political gatherings, Gracie had wondered out loud if there might be a point where a bullet given a larger powder charge might pierce a projector's shield. Jimmie took her question as an order to find out. Working with his troops back in the Snake, the experiment started.

"Wouldn't want to see you wounded or nothing, Mr. Nicks," responded Corporal Cousins as he checked the sun behind the trees. Spring came as the days grew longer.

"You just keep an eye out for where the bullet heads after it hits the shield," shouted Jimmie, not quite comfortable with his recent command. Many of his troops stood taller and had more years under their belts. "Now, Jenkins," he pointed to the man on the left, leaning on his rifle. "Take your shot."

"Any of you," whispered Jenkins, "want to take a bet on what happens first: the rifle cracks or the bullet takes a piece of him?" Jenkins, raising his rifle and pulling his long hair back from his face, nodded toward their commanding officer.

"Our dear Jimmie ain't been this stupid a'fore," said Baldy, the white-haired old man standing on Jenkins' right. "But..." he huffed, "I don't like the risks, but... our Jimmie goes down first, and I have a silver piece to back that up."

"I'll take some of that action," said Cousins, his brown uniform as frayed and worn as the others. He pulled two paper wrapped cartridges from his pouch. "Baldy, you be careful with packing three. Don't ram the powder down too hard. Never tried to blow up one a these here rifles and I don't want ta lose the bet or have to search for your face in the dark if the barrel gives way."

"Fire dammit!" yelled Jimmie. The air sparkled with the shield he put up.

Jenkins aimed at the Captain, praying the boy knew his business and fired. The bullet hit the shield, penetrating less than an inch before its kinetic energy went to the right and down into the ground.

"Okay, Corporal. Your turn."

Cousins brought the wrapper to his mouth and tore off the top. He poured the powder into the muzzle, then discarded the paper-wrapped bullet. The powder from the second cartridge and the single bullet went down the barrel. Cousins rammed it home. He placed a cap on the firing pin, then shouldered the weapon. "Ready, Mr. Nicks?"

"Fire!"

The bullet reached the shield and sank half a foot, an inch from Jimmie's shoulder, before it gave up its forward motion to the shield and dropped to the ground.

"Your turn, Baldy!"

The old man's rifle held three times the gunpowder. He shouldered the rifle and took aim, then stopped. He lowered the gun to his waist, pointed, and said, "This here is a bad idea. If it blows, you boys be gentle with me." He fired.

Jimmie kept the power going into the shield at the same level for all three shots. He could have easily reinforced the shield to stop the third ball. He didn't. The lead passed through the shield and tore a hole in his coat just under his arm. If he had not moved at the last second, his right lung would have welcomed the bullet.

"Well, gentlemen, that settles it," said Jimmie, walking forward sticking his finger in the hole.

"Dammit all, Baldy," shouted Cousin. "Didn't I say not to pack it tight?" The three soldiers ignored Jimmie staring at the rifle on the ground. The barrel cracked just in front of the hammer.

Jimmie came forward and inspected the weapon. "You okay there, Baldy."

"Yes, sir. Just a little rattled. Might a been kilt." Baldy pulled a cloth from his pocket he used to clean his rifle, but wiped the beads of sweat from his forehead instead.

"So," said Jimmie, "if we get desperate and all we have left is you lot with your rifles, then a triple powder charge from a thousand soldiers might buy us some time and… probably kill some of us."

"Looks that way," said Cousins.

"Good." Jimmie smiled and pulled some coins from his pocket. "Looks like no one wins the bet… near thing, though." He tossed the silver to each man.

"Ya heard that?" asked Cousins.

"Heard nothing." Jimmie winked at his men, kept the ruined gun, and walked away. "You men are dismissed. Baldy, get yourself a new rifle." After a few steps, he turned, "I would have bet on the lead too." He again stuck his finger in the coat's hole to make the point and laughed.

"That's why he's a leader and I ain't." Cousins, Jenkins, and Baldy followed Jimmie off the field. "Ol' Jimmie, can fight and don't forget where he's from… the Snake."

* * *

Jack Fox, hand in hand with Spunk, pushed through the doors into the dining area of the Old Courthouse in the Snake. They had returned from the mountains a few days earlier, updated Tom Haggard and his command on the Mountain People's intentions, and described the far northern people. Tonight, however, they celebrated their grand homecoming.

The hearth flared and the table with white linen stretched with place settings for fifty. No one else had arrived. Jack and Spunk walked the length of the table and took their seats, as ordered by the name cards at each setting.

"Off yore, sorry butts, ya two sneak-aways," yelled Nanna from the doorway. "Come and give us a hug." Her eyes teared at her happiness to see her granddaughter and Jack. She stood without the aid of a cane and walked forward to fall into their arms.

"Your unarmed," said Jack, expecting to feel the handle pressed into him.

"Today we's safe and I don' need it." Nanna stepped back and grasped Spunk's cheeks in her hands. "Ain't never seen so happy a look on ya." She looked up at Jack. "Been doin' yore job, I'm thinkin'." She laughed.

"Almost," whispered Spunk, blushing. She told her grandmother what the Mountain people requested. "Seems Jack had to…"

"Provide a sample in a jar is all." Jack's cheeks blossomed a flaming red.

"A sample for them," Spunk caressed Jack's cheek, "then he provided a few samples for me… it all worked out."

"Then," pronounced Nanna, "no need ta hash over private business." She turned when loud voices interrupted the awkward moment.

"About time you showed up!" Peppers strode into the room, arms wide. He took Nanna's place, grabbing Jack in a tight hug and lifting him off his feet. "Sonofabitch, but I've missed you." He released Jack and said, "Let's talk later." He then went to Nanna, who gave him a chase kiss on the cheek.

Hattie kept close to her husband but reached out to Jack with a hand on his shoulder. "Glad you're home." She felt Jack take her hand, then pulled her into a hug.

"Congratulations," said Jack, "on your wedding. Sorry we missed it." He released Hattie and watched Spunk put her arms around her. He placed his hands on Pepper's shoulders and said, "We wish you happiness."

Invitees arrived; a receiving line sprang up from which Jack and Spunk would not escape until Gracie pushed to the front of the queue.

"Rank has its privileges," she said, pulling Jack into her embrace. "Let's talk later. Our army is on the move." She stepped back and looked her protégé up and down, then did the same to Spunk. "You look ready for a fight." Gracie leaned toward Spunk. "You will stay close to Jack. Understood?"

"Yes, sir," whispered Spunk. "Of course."

The rest of the dinner guests showed up, greeted the honorees, and found their seats. Servers started swarming. The wine glasses never went unfilled for long, one course after another filled the table, and the occasional special request found satisfaction.

"How the hell did ya get invited?" asked Jimmie Nicks fresh from the training field. He stared at Mini in her pristine uniform. "Looks like they ain't particular about who sits at this here table."

"You could have washed up a bit Jimmie Nicks," said Mini. She had heard about the crazy Nicks who had his men shoot at him. She watched as he ran his hand over the hole in his uniform. "Not much on the courtesies, are you?"

"Well, Miss Mini," said Jimmie, smiling. "I only had time to wipe the important parts, if ya know what I mean?" He liked this girl immediately, just as he had Spunk who sat next to his hero: Jack Fox.

"Ladies and gentlemen," called Doctor Shepherds, tapping

a spoon against a glass. "We are here to welcome home Jack Fox and Spunk." Shephards waited for the applause to subside. "There is much to fret about, but not tonight. We will sing, dance, I hope, and have a damned good time. On with it!" He raised his glass and emptied it.

Doctor Shephards got his way. A fiddler and a thumper with his large, tight skin handheld drum provided a rousing series of rounds and other music. Legs moved and kept time with the beat. Before too long, the floor before the hearth filled with dancers.

It was a celebration for the history books. Exhaustion slowly engulfed the participants and, though no one wanted it to end, after midnight, people made their apologies and left. The last of the diners pulled chairs into a circle before the dying hearth. With after-dinner drinks in hand, Jack, Spunk, Peppers, Hattie, Shephards, and Gracie gathered before the ebbing fire. Jimmie Nicks and Mini carried their chairs from the dinner table to complete the circle.

"To business," said Gracie. "The northerners are massing along the Aquitaine, and we will set our pieces upon the board in a field of our choosing." Gracie looked around the circle. She wished the Forresters had graced their gathering. Their surety of success infected all. Haggard, however, commanded their presence this night. "We bring over fifty thousand to this fight, none of which should be projectors, but they are." She winked at Jack, who had trained so many. "Projectors make up near thirty thousand, and the enemy suspects nothing."

"The field hospitals are well prepared," stated Peppers. "Hattie and I will be close to the front to care for the wounded as quick as possible. We expect more burn wounds than puncture wounds."

"To be honest," followed Gracie when the conversation died, "I am hopeful." She took a deep breath and let it out. "Of course, what can go wrong will, but our enemy's prejudices blind them."

"Gracie," began Jack. "We have our plan." Jack knew the measure of those in the circle. "We stick to it and adjust as we must." He paused a moment, then said, saddened, "The dead will probably pile up."

"Enough," called Jimmie. "When has there ever been any worries 'bout dying in the Snake? Only the doing counts now."

"So be it." Spunk turned to Gracie. "Tell us, what has improved our chances, what has happened?"

"Killer weeds, shields, bolts, and beams." She smiled. "Bullets getting through shields." Gracie nodded at Jimmie, who blushed, then provided the details as Jack and Spunk listened intently.

* * *

"We move tomorrow." Tom Haggard's fingers drummed on the table. The commanders of the southern army filled the floor of Gracie's warehouse the day after the celebration of Jack and Spunk's return.

"Everything that can be done to prepare for battle has been done," said Professor Forrester.

"They do not know about the earth attack," interjected Anna Forrester.

"We do not know about their attacks," stated Haggard. "How many will we lose? Are our shields and energy bolts the equal of theirs?" He shook his head. "No one can answer that question."

"Our losses...? It depends," said the Professor. "You have many shielders. They look adequate for the job. Clearly, they stop bullets."

"Does that really matter?" asked Anna. "You are children of the South... many are survivors of the Snake? You are facing another fight for survival. What else is there to say?"

The applause and catcalls from the rank and file erupted. Death posed no problem. Life often did.

"Kill them all," came from the floor.

"So, we shall," called Haggard. "We cannot fail!" Haggard stood up. "We have the earth, we have Jack Fox, and we have all of you. No surrender, no prisoners!"

The applause and foot stomping lasted for minutes.

"Do not make me a liar, Professor," whispered Haggard to Forrester.

"The enemy's certainty will be their undoing, Tom."

"From your mouth to any listening gods' ear, Professor," whispered Haggard.

CHAPTER 44

"We have better weapons and methods," said Martell, responding to the Ministers of War and the Interior. They met at the Interior Minister's home outside the capital. Reports lay stacked across the floor of a small room with only one window. A cold, iron pot-belly stove stood in the corner and a long table covered with maps on one end filled most of the room. After a day of studying what might go wrong, looking for any better strategy, and the best defense when dealing with a confused Prime Minister who thought he knew more than the generals, they broke for an early dinner. The late spring sun poured through the window, warming the room.

"You don't mean the non-projectors?" questioned Higgins. His lips curled in disgust at the very thought.

"No, of course not," responded Martell, insulted by the idea but controlling his irritation. "They are the lambs to be sacrificed at the opportune moment."

"Tell us what Cole plans and what more he needs," said Sedgwick.

He called the meeting with the war minister and his head of intelligence and set it where he felt safe. The estate sprawled over one hundred acres, with a tall, thick wall encircling the house, stables, and abandoned slave quarters. The slaves went to work in the mines or fields months ago, where many would likely die. Their survival did not concern him. His political survival, however, played heavily in his calculations. Sedgwick used paid staff to maintain his opulent style of living: he could afford it.

"The General is a whirlwind of action with no detail too small," began Martell. "He expects to be met with a competent projector enemy." Footmen scurried around the table refilling drinks, removing, and placing new plates of food before the diners.

"And the likelihood of such a competent force is… what?" asked Higgins. He sat across from the window and raised his hand to block the glare. Light filtered through new leaves on branches, moving in a soft breeze. "Summer," he said, "is coming on fast."

"The reports from the surviving spies say it is not a high risk, but…" Martell's mind raced with the many variables for which he lacked details. "Few made it back. I think Cole has it right."

"Since intelligence is sparse, as you say. Does he have enough men?" asked Sedgwick.

"Trained soldiers facing non-projectors could easily destroy a force twenty times their size. Cole's strategy starts with the assumption that he can handle only two times the force he brings to the field." Martell, obsessed with the coming battle, barely touched the food on his plate. He stared at the bright colors refracted on the white tablecloth through his crystal goblet and fingered the stem. "A reasonable, conservative estimate, in my opinion. It will guarantee a victory." These last words collapsed into a skeptical silence. "So," said the Colonel, finding surety, "Cole has thirty thousand now with another five thousand in training, but not ready for the field. They will be reserve units." The Colonel looked to his superiors, who nodded, but they did not look especially uplifted by his words. "The southerners will not be ready for our Hammer Offense."

"What?" asked Sedgwick, who sat upright eagerly.

"It is a new, shield breaking attack used on the northern border vaporizing the enemy or leaving them open to a nominal energy attack." Martell leaned forward, warming to the subject. "A thousand men source the energy. Enemy shields break, and many soldiers fall in the initial attack. A regular attack sweeps the field of any able to fight."

"How long does it take for these one thousand to recover and aren't they vulnerable?"

"Well… yes," said Martell, "but the shock to the enemy has and will give us time to make adjustments before the enemy can act. Such an attack could remove two or three thousand from the fight."

"Do you, Colonel, still expect to be confronted by riflemen largely?" Higgins studied the officer.

"Yes," said Martell, "the enemy will have three riflemen for every one of our projectors, but neither the riflemen nor their few projectors can match us. Furthermore, their force is a mix of men and women and teenagers with children in support." Martell glowered at the impudence of the South to meet hardened soldiers with women and children in their ranks. "No surprise this time."

The three men picked at the meat on their plates, gulped their drinks, and found the confidence to believe in an easy victory. The southern successes over the last months stung like pins pushed under their fingernails, torturing their prejudices. They would not lose to those low people. The silence stretched. Then Sedgwick rose with his empty glass and went to a tall, narrow cupboard next to the room's closed door. From the cupboard, he retrieved a dusty bottle. He returned to his seat and with a knife cut away the wax over the cork, then removed the stopper with a corkscrew. He poured the thick amber liquid into his and Higgins' goblets. Martell waved him off when the Minister raised an eyebrow to offer the officer a taste.

Higgins finished two full glasses of the liquor with Sedgwick not far behind.

"It is time, Colonel, to share everything you know about this Jack Fox person." Higgins' fingers tapped impatiently on the table. "The name keeps coming up in the reports." The Minister of War waved his hand at the stacks of papers littering the floor. "What of him?"

Martell stood up, grabbed an empty goblet, then went around the table. Sedgwick looked up at him when he stopped beside his chair. Without asking, he filled the crystal from the bottle. He drank, then paced the room.

"Jack Fox is one of several unknown variables that will influence the outcome."

"Like?" asked Higgins.

"Like the Forresters and the several hundred northern students who followed Forrester or that Doctor Shephards from Hempstead. A hundred years ago we wiped away southern projectors… but apparently not the potential."

Martell stopped to stare out of the window. The sun touched the horizon.

"As to Jack Fox, he is a southern teenager from Snakeport. Captured last year to be sold as a slave. Somehow, he ended up in Hempstead, where he apparently caused a mild level of destruction as an untrained projector. He received some training. His instructors told me he excelled. Then, he disappeared with a resident physician."

"A slave is a projector who then magically disappears?" asked Sedgwick, turning to address the Colonel's back.

"Drove away in a stolen vehicle." Martell turned to the ministers and returned to the table. "Before you ask, the answer is yes. The boy figured out how to move our transports but, I would guess, he is the only projector displaying significant power born south of the Aquitaine."

"So," said Higgins, "taking all of this into account…"

"We win!" called out Sedgwick.

CHAPTER 45

"The bridges are placed, General Cole," said an aide, flipping through the engineers' report. "We've identified the best field of operations."

"There were no attempts by the South to destroy or slow the building of these bridges?" Cole scanned his notes, waiting for a response.

"No sir. The work progressed without interruption."

"So," said Cole, looking up from his notebook. "They offer an open invitation."

"Sir?"

"It means they are not overly concerned or, more to the point, confident." Cole shook his head. "Too late," he whispered.

"Start moving the army to the other side of the river," commanded Cole. "Make sure we have scouts out in front and on the flanks. I want no more surprises." The General quickly signed several sheets of orders and handed them to his orderly. Another aide helped him with his coat, then stepped back. Cole left his Hempstead command center, stepped into the waiting bus full of his staff. He sat in the back and gave the command to get moving.

"Sir," said a lieutenant standing in the aisle and leaning forward, "horses will be available once we are over the bridge. We have raised a tall platform on the field for your observations."

"Horses," whispered Cole derisively. He had not taken to the saddle in years. *Stupid animals…,* the General thought. *Not too bright and difficult at the best of times, but they know when to get out of the way.* Cole nodded and returned the officer's salute, then watched the scenery pass by on the way south. He forced himself to stop thinking and relax. Nothing more could be accomplished until he stepped on the field of battle.

* * *

The children, like squirrels in the trees, slid down the trunks to the ground to join their support units as they sensed the energy rise. The advanced northern units crossed the bridges. When the enemy closed within fifty yards, the southern troops dropped their shields to avoid detection and bounded out of the woods like deer fleeing a raging fire. They poured over the ridge, some with a rifle held high in one hand and the other keeping their hats on their heads. The advanced regiments in the field below waited with rifles aimed and shields up to protect the retreating scouts.

Several hundred yards back on a rise, Tom Haggard and his officers watched the forest units return. The southern army filled the field to the base of the ridge. From his position, he would have a clear view of the enemy units stretched out along the face of the ridge. The battlefield was an amphitheater with Haggard center stage able to observe the audience, his enemy, deployed along the curving ridge. When the northern men constructed the platform at the highest point along the hill, he sighed in relief. There would be time to get units where they needed to be. The northern caution played into his hands.

"Order the regiments forward." Haggard watched Smithfield, his signal officer, turn in his saddle and flash the coded order. Disciplined lines of men and women strode forward on either side of Haggard and his officers. Tens of thousands took the field. Tom watched. The ranks failed to stir martial snap and awe in their worn uniforms, but the enemy would not easily knock down the well fed, trained, and determined force.

"Will Biggs and Gracie Hargreaves, all of our plans and

strategies make perfect sense until the battle begins." Haggard glanced at the men, women, and children passing them. None would die in vain if he could have his way. "You have my trust. Make sure we respond appropriately to what happens on the field as this day progresses."

"Yes, sir." They called out together.

Stupidity will get us all killed, he thought to himself. Haggard fretted that he might not have enough reserve units and wondered not for the last time if the young man's shoulders were big enough. "Good luck, Jack," he whispered.

* * *

As the southern units moved to the front, Lilly Fox followed them from the most forward hospital station after delivering piles of extra blankets, barrels of salves, and countless stretchers. The hundred wagons and their crews under her command who delivered the supplies would become the ambulance drivers and field corpsmen dragging the wounded out of harm's way on those stretchers. She wore an officer's uniform as required for the number of people she controlled and the job: a rank out of place among the foot soldiers in the usual military scheme.

A beautiful summer's day. Taking a deep breath, she studied the ground and the slow rise of the grass like a thick green carpet along the ridge ahead. *Harm's way.* Not Haggard nor Gracie or any other commanding officer expected Lilly to take part in the fighting; she demanded it of herself. *Jack will be here.* Imagining massed men blanketing the ridge intent on delivering death, she felt the need for a drink.

A regiment of shielders, bolters, and weeders marched up behind her, passing by on either side taking up their position in line. Another thousand soldiers took positions to the right. Lilly turned around and headed to the rear of the formation. Sitting, she removed her boots and socks, taking up a place in the last line among a weeder unit. The weeders seemed happy to have her; she returned their smiles then focused forward.

Pushing what energy she could into the soil, she thought, *I am here. I am ready.*

So be it, came the response.

CHAPTER 46

"Colonel Folfox," called Colonel Martell, smiling as though happy to find him. He rode next to Stan, whose unit marched behind the projector battalions moving up and over the ridge. "You will get in behind our forward units on the far left. Be ready to deal with the southern riflemen as they engage. Do you have questions?"

"None, Colonel. The Eagle regiment knows the job that is expected," confirmed Stan loud enough for the men marching nearby to hear.

"Good. I will be with General Cole during the early part of the battle. Expect me with further orders after the first exchanges." With that, Martell used his spurs and hauled on the reins. The horse leaped forward, then galloped to the right, heading to Cole.

"Major Rodgers!" called Stan. He watched the officer marching with his men step out of formation. Only the colonel received a horse. "Are we ready, Major?"

"Yes, sir," saluted the officer. "All units are ready, fully armed with either double or triple charged muskets. Every soldier carries an additional revolver. They know their job, sir."

"Major, when we take up our positions, you will pass a musket to me with some extra rounds. Is that understood?"

"Yes, sir."

Stan returned the salute, then added, "Send out flankers to the right, just to be safe."

The major turned to the nearest soldiers and gave the order. Ten men trotted off across a field of tall grass to get into the trees bordering the army's path south.

Stan pulled to the side of the trail to watch his men pass. He had one thing on his mind: the disgusted look in his son's eyes as he lay on the pallet half dead after Gracie put a bullet through his shoulder.

"Time for the fix," he whispered.

* * *

"Disgusting, unruly beasts." Cole hated horses and complained to his staff all the way from the river. His aides kept quiet: any response would take on the general's anger or, worse, give him the notion that they thought he needed help. An explosion of obscenities would follow immediately and a demotion more than likely.

His army traveled from the river in five streams of sky-blue-clad men. He kept pace with the center column of marching soldiers. By the time he dismounted, most of his army would have taken up positions: a long ridge sloping down to an open field where he expected to find the massed enemy ready to be destroyed.

"Gentlemen," said Cole, happy to relinquish the saddle, tossed the reins to an aide. His officers and aides gathered behind as the commanding officer climbed the ten steps onto the platform placed halfway between the distant forests that bordered the battlefield on either side: fifty men could comfortably observe from the wooden deck. "Today we will…" He came up short, losing his train of thought, looking out over the terrain. "My impression," he stated in anger, not seeing what the scouting report said he should expect, "was that grass stretched for miles ahead of us and side to side." An expanse of thick tree cover blocked any view of the field below the ridge.

"No such forest grew here a day ago, sir. I stood with the engineers when they constructed this observation post," said a Major with binoculars pressed to his eyes, studying the thick fir trees along the front. "I suspect they are not real."

"You suspect?" asked the General obviously annoyed. "You, Major, will go down there and make sure. Be quick about it." He watched the officer join the flow of men down the grassy slope. His army formed ranks across the ridge. They would need another hour to be ready, but the enemy, thought Cole, would not be so accommodating.

Just then, a single enemy soldier appeared just ahead of the unexpected tree line and walked calmly to a point directly opposite the command platform.

Cole turned around when a horse complained loudly. Martell pulled hard on the reins and kicked up dust. He slid out of the saddle and ran to Cole.

"Hammer that man! Do it now, General, or all is lost!"

Jack Fox stepped onto center stage. He popped up as if by magic in front of the tangle of trees and halted at the bottom of the slope. The northern forces still poured over the ridge, forming up along the slope.

"Many of you and many of us will die today!" Jack's voice carried across the entire slope, magnified by his projected energy. "Why?"

He waited. "We, like you, love our children. We fight today to protect them. What are you fighting for?" Jack paced along the line of trees, then back. "What wouldn't you do for your children?"

Still, no reply came. "We outnumber you. We southerners have no fear of death. Do you?" Jack raised his hands.

Seconds later, the forest curtain disappeared and the army facing the northern invaders became visible. Forty thousand stood against twenty thousand in similar configurations, giving the lie to the southerner's ignorance of military strategy. Haggard sat on his horse alongside Gracie, Will, and the other officers, looking for the flash of shields or a coming attack along the slope. They felt the sudden buildup of energy in the air: fear gripped them.

Jack felt it too and faced the sudden release of energy off to his right. Bright light exploded from the northern regiments onto Jack's position.

Shields failed. Human beings vaporized, exposed to the huge amount of power. Fine ash rose and mixed with the dark smoke from burning grass. It rained down across the front like heavy gray snow.

The wall of trees, like a curtain swept across the southern front, corpsmen raced forward to remove the wounded or dead from the field, and replacement units dashed to the empty positions. Several searing energy beams targeted the northerners and sliced back and forth across the ridge. Bolts of energy targeted the source of the attack on Jack while two thousand riflemen fired volley after volley until the northern shields reasserted themselves. In minutes, the exchange ended, and all went deathly quiet.

Haggard waited to lift the curtain until the corpsmen moved the wounded to the rear. The frantic dash of replacement units to the front ended, and Jack's survival confirmed. He and his officers focused on where Jack had stood and fretted, waiting.

"On your feet, soldier," ordered Spunk. She stood over a smoldering Jack Fox. At the back of the formation, as prearranged, the explosion had knocked her down; her legs could not recover fast enough, but she fought to her feet and stumbled to the center of the blast site. Hands slapped at Jack's clothing to smother embers and small flames.

"That…surprised." Jack flat on his back tried to sit up but failed. He grimaced as the pain of many small burns made themselves felt. "Help me." He raised his hand and Spunk locked on his forearm as he did hers.

"What…" Spunk hauled Jack up into a sitting position.

"Didn't you understand…" She got behind him and grunted with effort to lift him up with her arms under his. "I can't live without you." With Jack wavering on his feet, she stepped back. "You ready, soldier?"

"Go," said Jack. He wanted Spunk back where they agreed she would be safe but close enough to be there at need. "How many?"

"Thousands turned to dust," said Spunk. "More than that wounded." As reinforcements came up, Spunk placed her hand on the back of Jack's neck and tipped her head forward so his forehead touched hers. She wanted to grab his hand and take him far away, but stepped back.

"I need some of that salve," said Jack, pulling off his coat. Through the holes in his shirt, the skin showed red with small blisters in places. He watched her dash away. Stiff and aching, he stretched his arms out and rolled his head to unknot the pain in his neck.

The curtain opened.

"Is he dead?" demanded Martell. He and others scanned the field, frustrated by the pseudo-forest blinding them. Thousands of men responsible for the attack filed to the rear exhausted, as their replacements rushed to the front.

"Get me the number of our killed and wounded," ordered the General Cole. "Send a message to the rear for the troops in Hempstead to be ready to move." The minutes passed, and Cole whispered curses.

"Order all reserves at the river forward," said Cole. He remained calm but knew the North could lose this fight. "We have made the first moves on the board. As soon as the wounded have been moved, make ready for round two." The general scanned the exhausted units moving to the rear: men used up for no obvious gain.

"Sir," said an aide, looking over a written report scribbled on a scrap of paper, "the regiment delivering the Hammer attack has suffered twenty percent casualties. We could not get shields up fast enough to deflect the southern projector attack plus the bullets which tore through that part of the field."

"The enemy's beam attack?" asked Cole.

"Shields failed to stop that, sir," commented the aide. "We do not have a full report. We lost fewer, but…"

"How many?" demanded the General.

"Another five hundred killed or wounded."

Cole nodded. "This is no rifle totting army of non-projectors." He looked at Martell. "I suspect we came out ahead in this attack, but…." A fury rose in him. "In an even exchange," he hissed, "we lose."

"Sir!" interjected the aide. "On our far right, there are reports of men disappearing. They drown in raging vines."

Cole shook his head and looked over to the right. "Colonel, I order you to our far right, where you will find a solution to whatever this might be. I want those useless non-projector units out front to absorb this attack."

"Sir," snapped Martell.

General Cole leaned on the platform rail, collected himself, calmed, and returned his focus to the enemy. "Gentlemen," he said, addressing his staff. "Our plans are useless. We need a new one with better options. Get it." The General watched half of the men on the platform leave to carry out his order.

"Damn!" cursed Martell out loud from horseback. "Damn, damn, damn!"

The enemy had raised their curtain.

Cole studied the lone soldier in the charred field. Southern replacements on the run filled the gaps. The air shimmered with shields.

"Jack Fox," whispered Cole, "I presume."

"Can't see help to our left," said Major Rodgers. He handed Colonel Folfox an unloaded rifle and a full cartridge pouch.

"Not supposed to, Major," smiled Stan. "Rest assured, they are there and ready." He took the pouch by its strap and hung it over his shoulder with the rifle over his other.

The battle settled into a threatening calm. The Wolf brigade on the northern right and the Eagles on the left took up positions on the front line, as ordered by Cole. No shielders joined them. Stan knew he and his men would dangle in the open as bait to be sacrificed.

"Sons of bitches," he hissed.

"Sir?"

"Your job major when things happen is to keep as many of these men alive… especially if I go down." He looked up and down the line of riflemen. "All double loaded?"

"Yes, sir." Rodgers stared at his commander. "Just walking dead, sir," he said so only Stan could hear.

"Not if we do our jobs." Stan thought a moment, then said, "I will hang back as part of the rearguard." He felt the younger man's eyes on him. "I will need fifty volunteers to join me."

The Major nodded. Everything rehearsed over and over beneath the nose of Martell, who congratulated Colonel Folfox on his men's discipline, tactics, and esprit de corp.

"Watch for the signal," commanded Stan.

The sudden burst of light and energy bolts emanating from the ridge onto the southern field made them jump. The attack landed on shield-shimmering air and dissipated across the front in flashes of green, red, and blue.

"A probe?" said Major Rodgers.

"Probably," said Stan, his teeth grinding. "They don't tell us anything."

The southern response erupted with twice the amount of energy but equally deflected by northern shields.

"There's your answer, Major, just looking for weaknesses and…"

The energy beam flashed from the center of the southern line and vaporized everything it touched along the ridge. It never came near the northern left flank, but wreaked havoc on the center. Stan dashed to the right and walked among the projectors to get a better view. He expected a lens focused by many projectors and powered by hundreds. His son, alone, controlled the beam. He wanted to scream, "That's my son that did that!", but kept quiet. He turned aside, beaming, and returned to his men and stood by Rodgers.

"Major, we are on the right side of this fight."

CHAPTER 47

"Corpsman!" A hand latched onto the teenager's ankle as he raced about, performing triage on the wounded as fast as possible.

"What'd ya need?" He stopped among the burn victims laid out in the open next to the stack of stretchers.

"Get me back up there." The corpsman looked at the man. More than half his uniform burned away, showing angry, blistered skin.

"Look, you ain't in any shape to fight."

"Get me som' a that medicine and help me up!" The man released the hold and pushed himself up. "They got mi' Maggie. She was there and then…," he choked as a tear flowed over his cheek. He wiped his face and got onto his hands and knees. The corpsman helped him to his feet. "Get me the damn medicine. I'm goin' back."

The corpsman left and returned with two tubs: one of salve and the other with painkilling jelly. The man sloshed some of both over the damaged skin he could reach.

"Hey, you two!" came from another stretcher bound victim. "Get me some."

"Give me these," said the man, taking the tubs. "We goin' to need some new clothes."

The corpsman nodded, too amazed to find words or deny this man anything. When he returned with as many uniforms as he could carry, six men and three women covered with the unguent helped others.

"Need more medicine, corpsman." The man scraped the last of the mixture from the tub and applied it to the feet and legs of a woman, cursing the North and demanding to get back to the fight.

"I'll bring more barrels." He trotted back to the supply tent and stacked two barrels onto a wheelbarrow and rolled it back with extra clothes.

"What's going on, corpsman?" asked Hattie, stepping out of the hospital tent.

"Seems like ya got fewer patients." He nodded to the part of the field where soldiers, men and women, pulled off their burnt clothes and applied the mixtures. "They're goin' back."

"Well, I'll be damned." Hattie shook her head in disbelief. "You make sure they all drink as much water as they can."

"Aye, ma'am."

"Corpsman," she called as he rolled away with the supplies, "what happened to Jack?"

"Smoking some, but standing as I hauled away the wounded around 'im," called the corpsman over his shoulder. He heard her gentle reminder, "Never give up, Jack."

"Well, Professor," asked Tom Haggard, "what do you make of that first attack?"

"I have never seen the like." Forrester, happy to be out of the saddle, stood next to his horse and surveyed the battlefield with binoculars on Haggard's left. Gracie and Will Biggs did the same from horse back. "The strength of their attack surprised us, but they were not ready for our response. I suspect they are rethinking their strategy."

"Meaning?" Haggard turned back to Forrester.

"It would appear they unleashed a huge amount of energy to kill Jack, failed, then took casualties." The Professor dropped the binoculars, then added, "In an even or near even exchange, we win."

Haggard nodded, then said, "We learned a hard lesson." He waved over the signalers. "Order all front regiments to double their shielder count. Use reserve units if necessary." As the communications began, Haggard leaned down and said, "What will happen next Professor?"

"Let the northerners," recommended the Professor, "make the next move then signal the Eagles."

"No," said Haggard, straightening up. "We have to be sure of our advantage when we order them to sacrifice themselves." Tom turned to Gracie and ordered, "Take up a position on our right and do what needs doing to shorten the northern line and tighten ours. Give the signal when you are certain the time is right."

"Yes, sir." Gracie addressed the Professor. "I would most appreciate your advice. Mount up and join me." She looked left and right, then said, "Tom, bring up more shielders to cover this position. No one here will survive a similar attack."

Haggard nodded and watched Gracie with Forrester, unsteady in the saddle, trot to the southern right.

"Will Biggs, see to more shielders supporting our center." The southern commander scanned the field. "Take your unit to the left flank. Anna Forrester started her attack over an hour ago. Something is happening in that quarter if the amount of dust tells us anything. Reinforcements might be needed."

When Martell first reached the North's right flank, he handed over his orders and attempted to sooth the ruffled feathers of the brigadier, commanding this part of the northern line. The brigadier crushed the paper and tossed the crumpled orders back at the Colonel and waved an angry "Do what you must," dismissing him.

On the front, Martell observed the seven-foot high hedge. It looked like it might be another illusion, but up close the flowers turned out to be hands or pieces of light blue uniforms: elbows or a shoulder. Approaching from above, he noted the hedge grew about ten feet wide, and blue uniformed men held ground beyond the hedge hopelessly isolated from the rest of the force.

Martell dismounted. Orders flew along the line and among the units. Thousands of northern troops focused on preparing to execute a modified Hammer Attack. An hour later, they were ready.

"Fire," said Martell, who joined the first ranks in releasing energy. "Into the ground! Destroy the roots!" As the first ranks weakened, the next set moved up and repeated the procedure. Dark ash and smoke rose into the air along with some gray.

"Sir," called out a lieutenant, "we may kill our men trapped on the other side of this hedge."

"What regiments?" demanded Martell.

"The wolf badged riflemen mostly," yelled the young officer.

"Wages of war," stated Martell. "You don't want your men swallowed up next."

"No, sir," agreed the lieutenant. He turned and signaled. The next ranks of men marched forward and burned out the killing weed.

Colonel Martell, satisfied with the results, climbed back into the saddle. The attack cleared the ground of the hedge and cauterized it to a depth of six feet; the weed attack stopped. He sent a quick note to Cole on the best response to the weed attack. The kill zone included hundreds of northern troops butchered to stop the attack from the earth. It bothered him, but duty demanded he stop the weed that crawled up a man's body, freezing him in place, then slowly choking the life out of him.

"Damned Wolf Pack… good for something after all," he whispered, wondering if the northern left needed to prepare for a hedge offensive. Martell turned his horse to return to Cole and provide a detailed report when the energy beam tore through the soldiers. Shields collapsed, and gaps appeared in the line where men once stood. The last of the energy sliced the hind legs off his horse. Both horse and rider crashed to the ground.

"Return fire now!" yelled Martell as he pulled himself out from under the wounded animal. He ended the animal's life, then demanded, "Get me another mount!"

Energy bolts flashed from his hands, joining the fight. Once exhausted, he surveyed the field. No further action came from the enemy.

"I am off to the left," stated Martell in the saddle of a fresh mount. "to prevent such an attack there. Send a message to Cole to that effect." He nodded as junior officers saluted and executed his order.

Good god, we are wrong... the price... the price, kept running through his mind. Digging in his spurs, the horse leapt forward.

Anna Forrester felt deflated. The initial success of the Weeders on the far left of the southern line cut off. The northerners seared the earth, destroying the land's ability to produce. Weed and human became ash in the response ordered. A northern brigade carrying rifles became dust under friendly fire. The rifles fell in a long line sprinkled by a gray ash.

"They can't lay waste to everything." Anna looked on in horror as human dust and bits of blue uniforms filled the sky. He shook her head and prayed the battle would end soon.

"Yes, madam, they can," stated Will Biggs, arriving with his energy beam unit. "Pull the weeders back and push the bolters and shielders forward." He scanned the ridge with binoculars. "In fact, double the shielder count." This last order, Will's aide, scribbled into a notebook. "If they pound us with an attack like the one on Jack…" We all die, did not need to be said out loud.

"So, will they?" asked Anna, controlling her outrage at the northern attack. "I think they will use that attack only in an all-out offensive. They used up too much energy to kill off the weed. Such an offense will leave many with their energy used up. They will be open to our guns and bolters."

"You are right, of course. We will win or fight to a stalemate with many dead on both sides," said Will, dropping the binoculars.

"There will be no stalemate," said Anna. The anger in her voice surprised Will. "Robert is on the right, Jack in the center, and I am here on the left."

"Mrs. Forrester…?" Will, his view clouded by his own prejudices, could not conceive of these two elderly people able to do much. He chuckled and would have patted her shoulder like he might pet a doddering, old dog ready to pounce on a porcupine's quills. His opinion evaporated as the octogenarian woman stepped forward, formed a lens, and sent an energy beam of her own into the enemy projectors.

"Shields up!" she called to the regiment around her as her reserves ran out. The air became opaque. Her attack had not been as enduring as those after Jack went to the ground, but it made a point on the northern soldiers to her front. The ones who did not explode into dust poured energy into shields protecting themselves. The energy bolts fired in response, fell on southern shields and dissipated, doing no harm.

"I hope," Will said awed, "that you accept my apology."

Anna smiled.

"There may be ten or twenty projectors on the other side who could do this, but they will not dirty their hands." Anna returned to Will's side and winked at him. "I intend to get very dirty."

"No, they're not," responded Hattie to a corpsman's question about the bodies filling this part of the field. She returned to the hospital tent after a quick check on the fallen. "They're not dead, just used up. Wrap them in a blanket. Keep them warm."

"Aye, ma'am." The corpsman hefted several blankets then noted, "We got our colonel out there. She fought with the Weeders. Miss Lilly seems worse off than the others. If you could take a closer look?"

"Bring her in," said Hattie.

"She's drained," said Peppers, examining Lilly. Her body collapsed on itself, looking like a dried-out husk. "She will die without some infusion of energy." The doctor ran his hands above the woman's body, doing what he could. The skin color improved, but the damage was too great. "Get ten projectors here now!" Peppers would have collapsed, but for Hattie supporting him.

"There are many like her outside," said Hattie.

"Then get a hundred ready to share their energy." Peppers staggered to a field chair with Hattie's help. "I am needed for the burn victims."

"You need to rest a bit, my love." She left the tent to give the necessary orders, then returned to find Peppers with his head on his chest, asleep.

Cole calculated the variables, the dead, the wounded, and the missing, then decided. All attacks would cease. The current strategy led to defeat. Their assumptions all wrong made fools of this army.

"Bring all forces forward from the rear. Get all the units in Hempstead to the river." Cole stepped off the platform. "The next attack will settle the issue. Leave a minimal force to hold the ridge."

CHAPTER 48

Haggard watched the enemy turn around and march up the slope. He had studied the old books and knew this maneuver offered no admission of defeat: a temporary end of the hostilities. He sent messages to his right and left flanks to pull back and make camp. His forces had suffered more losses than the North, but he could afford it. The invaders could not.

The sun dropped below the trees, but ample light remained to charge up the slope in pursuit. Such an attack, however, could not succeed against an army of projectors, or so the ancient books reported. Riflemen would simply cease to exist as energy consumed them. His projectors would exhaust themselves running up the ridge, leaving them unable to attack with any strength. Haggard imagined such troops running down the slope, putting as much power into their shields as possible. Rest the army. He nodded.

"We surprised them today," stated Haggard to the officers and aides around him, "but we won't tomorrow." He turned his horse about and ordered, "Find my generals, Jack, and the Forresters. Have them join me in my tent. Keep several thousand troops in the field but relieve them every four hours."

They desperately needed more options—something unexpected—to destroy their deadly dangerous, wounded enemy. Haggard studied the enemy token force along the top of the ridge. "We cannot abandon this field," he said. "We are the wall protecting the South. The enemy prepares and will return."

"Sir?" asked one of his aides. "Further orders?"

"We will not become white ash on a summer's breeze."

* * *

"We sent her to Snakeport. Doctor Shephards will do everything he can," said Peppers, working by candlelight. He labored hard to address the burn wounds of a soldier on the table in front of him. The sleep of the dead captured him for an hour until Hattie got him back on his feet. "To my eye, Lilly came in consumed and in a deep coma, but with no signs of trauma."

"I don't understand. She shouldn't have been anywhere near the fighting," said Jack.

"She was not the only one in that state." Hattie offered the doctor a fresh bowl of ointment. "Go easy with this," she said to Peppers. "It's more potent." Hattie turned to Jack. "Shephards can do more for her at the hospital than we can here."

Jack nodded. He stood there wanting more, but they could say nothing further. As Peppers and Hattie moved from table to table in the tent, he realized he impeded their efforts. He left and walked among the campfires toward Haggard's tent. Smiles, fisted salutes, or thumbs-up greeted him.

"Get 'em tommorra, Jack!" or "Just you wait, Jack, they be running real soon!"

He acknowledged their confidence with an exertion of energy. It felt like a slap on the shoulder claiming, "Damn right!"

Jack stepped into the firelight and walked across the circle of men and women to an open seat next to Gracie. She threw her arm around his shoulder and pulled him close.

"You did good today," she said.

Everyone in the circle rose when Haggard joined the circle.

"I am surprised," said Haggard, taking a seat, "that we did so well." He studied his team, going face to face. "Why aren't half of us dead? Why haven't they matched our lens attack?" Haggard focused on Robert and Anna. "Are they that stupid?"

"Stupid," said Robert. "No. Willfully blind, yes. But learning fast."

Jack nodded. He felt used up like he walked in knee deep mud and another forward step became impossible. It was an effort to stay in the moment. Spunk, always consuming his thoughts, remained at the front talking to the soldiers, building their confidence, and gathering details about how the troops saw the fight.

"Have we cured their blindness today, Professor?" asked Tom Haggard. "Will they find an attack we cannot survive?"

"They already have that, Tom." Robert snorted. "They used it at the outset, but they believed that these rabble southerners would run. Our response brought them up short. They know they cannot win exchanging attacks."

"If I commanded those blue forces," said Haggard getting to his feet and pacing around the fire, "I would pull back to the other side of the river, setup a strong defensive position, and pull all the manpower available in the North." He pointed at Robert. "Why won't they do that?"

"We hurt them," began the Professor. "The South does not have their respect, but the soldiers in this field do, if grudgingly." He watched Haggard continue around the circle and take a seat. "They will return to the field reinforced and determined to destroy us southerners who lead miserable lives of soulless people counted on to lie, murder, and steal: the lowest level of humanity." The Professor stared at the fire. "I think because there is not enough time," he said slowly, searching for the right words, "they will hit us with the same attack as the one on Jack. It will be, however, twice, maybe three times as strong."

"I saw how they adjusted to our weed attack. They will sacrifice their own to win," said Anna. "They will stay on the offensive, bringing projector energy to be used up. We will, I fear, have to kill them all."

"What say the rest of you?" Haggard turned, looking for more from the gathering.

"Stand. Never give up," called out many voices from all sides. Hours later, they stayed with the current strategy. The group broke up.

"Jack?" Gracie nudged the boy who had fallen asleep, his head on her shoulder. "Time to go." She pulled him to his feet and guided him toward his tent. When he fell onto his cot, she pulled a blanket over his shoulder.

"Sleep well, Jack," she whispered.

At dawn, the southern forces faced an empty ridge. Northern units remained along the top, but the enemy had not taken up positions on the slope. There would be no fight this day.

"I'll be damned," said Haggard on horseback. He laughed out loud. "They're throwing the dice." He turned to his aide. "Have the army stand down. Get me Hargreaves."

"Gracie," said Haggard back in his tent, "I want four regiments on the right to cross the river undetected where possible and be ready to attack north of the bridges."

"Tom?"

"They are going on the offense with every troop they have. It takes time to get the men in place." Haggard could not hide his glee at their luck. "Use our reserves. Tomorrow at sunrise they should deploy far enough away not to arouse northern interest but close enough to move and engage the enemy."

"And the rest of us should…?"

"Stick with the plan, but with more shielders and a different start." Haggard went to his field desk and wrote out the orders. "They will hammer us."

"Survivors will then," said Gracie, "destroy the exhausted."

"Yes." He smiled as the pencil scratched on the page. "When that happens, they will run. A surprise at the bridges will truly end this."

"Casualties?" Gracie frowned, thinking the worst. The attack on Jack had taken out fifty percent of the surrounding regiment.

"I need to confer with Jack, the Professor, and his wife. They will determine the outcome of this battle." Haggard put down his pen and sat back. "We need a bit of djinn magic. Send the Professor, his wife, and Jack to me."

"This is foolish," stated Colonel Martell, reporting to Cole's tent. "We should pull back."

"Surrender?" Cole sat aghast at the suggestion. He drank wine from a crystal glass. "We will use a total hammer attack, taking advantage of the untrained projectors' energy. Kill the bulk of the enemy and scare the rest into scampering away as fast as they can."

"If they don't scamper?" asked Martell. He scanned the table of general officers dining with Cole. "Based on the battle so far, they are not likely to."

"We shield, recover, and attack again," said an angry voice. Brigadier Folfox, Stan's father, had arrived from Hempstead with fresh regiments. He brought a fork with a slice of fruit to his mouth.

"Do you not know what we face? We did not win yesterday." Martell's faith in the obvious led him to supreme frustration dealing with such imbeciles. "General Cole, this strategy will not work. Recovery time alone will hamper our plan."

"Colonel," said Cole calmly, "we will have another twenty thousand fresh troops. We will win this battle tomorrow." "How many of these twenty thousand have completed the training?" Martell stared at the two men, sure they knew well they could not count on the new, unseasoned troops.

"Go back to your spying, Colonel," said Folfox smugly. "Let

the army do what it does best. The new troops are trained well enough for this action."

Martell snapped to attention and gave a dramatic salute. *Damn fools.*

CHAPTER 49

"Illusion," insisted Haggard, his breakfast untouched. "The first few minutes of the next action will inform us." Haggard leaned over his field desk, studying the position of his regiments.

"General?" asked Anna with her husband, Robert, Jack, and Gracie.

"Perfect illusion," said Haggard. He looked up at them and said, "You have this higher power. Time to ask for more."

Jack smiled. "Tell us what you want."

Cole sat in the saddle surrounded by his officers and considered the troops passing by over the ridge and down into positions along the ridge. He noted the curtain still down on his enemy. *No matter. Today ends this.*

Cole returned to the field with thirty thousand fresh troops. He and his entourage walked their mounts to the platform. Cole climbed the steps, took his usual place, and waited. As his men filled the ridge, the enemy soldiers poured onto the field below.

Brigadier Folfox joined him.

"You," stated Folfox, "will have a high place in our history books."

General Cole did not respond. He scanned the enemy soldiers with his binoculars. The grim-faced men and women in shoddy uniforms, some barefoot, stood in their ranks. The air shimmered everywhere he looked.

"Sir?"

"Report," commanded Cole. He continued to study the enemy.

"All is ready, sir."

"Signal the Attack," said the General. "Let's end this." He put the binoculars away.

Fire hammered the massed southern forces in squares as if giants wielded huge, blazing mallets. Three thousand troops evaporated with each release of northern energy. A patchwork of burned earth and surviving units filled the southern field. The onslaught continued until only the scorched earth remained.

"Glorious," shouted Brigadier Folfox standing next to Cole on the platform. "They will not survive this."

At mid-morning, the northern soldiers fired off their energy, then straggled to the back, exhausted. Countless untrained projectors in support lay unconscious on the ridge, their energy depleted. Fresh units moved up to continue the pounding, they stepped over or around the used up.

"Why aren't they running?" asked Cole, surveying the enemy formations further back.

"Too stupid," snorted the elder Folfox.

Cole focused on his counterpart, Haggard, on horseback at the back, surrounded by what he took to be aides. No soldiers stood behind him in reserve.

"They made a total commitment of their forces."

"Like I said, General. They're stupid." Folfox laughed as the repeated assaults removed southern forces so efficiently. Black smoke obscured parts of the battle.

"This is not right." Cole turned to an aide. "I want the line officers up here now!" He looked over the replacement units. "Hold all regiments in place except those already on the field. Clear the dead or near dead used up projectors to the rear. They are in the way."

"This is going as expected," argued Folfox. "We're winning."

"General," said Cole, "it's too easy. Not right."

"The field is almost cleared of enemy forces," pointed out Folfox. "Finish it."

"What, Folfox, did you expect the enemy to do once we started our attack?"

Folfox studied the enemy forces as the air cleared of smoke and debris from the attacks. "They would turn to dust or turn and run for their lives."

"How much white or gray ash do you observe? How many are running, General?" Cole turned to Folfox, waiting.

Brigadier Folfox scanned the field with his field glasses. None of the southern units moved, as if they were waiting patiently to be annihilated. No haze of vaporized humans amid the dark smoke of burning grass flew through the air. The sudden blast of gunfire to his right diverted his attention. "What the hell?"

Cole left the platform as officers gathered at the steps.

The expected signal finally came. The Eagle Unit stood and formed ranks.

Stan, very much aware of his father's presence on the ridge, hating the man, ordered the maneuver. It would take time for the northern forces to respond with fresh troops. The damage, however, would be done.

His thousand-strong regiment of non-projectors stepped back from their position on the front and, like an opening fence, swung to face the exhausted northern soldiers heading to the rear. Three hundred men fired, knelt, and reloaded. The next three hundred stood, aimed, and fired. A second line went to their knees as the third line of men poured their fire into northern units. Again, the first line stood; the conveyor of death began again.

Pale blue-clad men fell dead or near dead with bullet wounds. Stan ordered his men forward to find new targets quickly and start the practiced sequence again. When gaps showed in his line as the new northern troops sent bolts of energy into the ranks of riflemen, he ordered a controlled retreat. His men fell back, stopped and turned to fire a barrage, then reloaded as they retreated. A line of fifty men spread out and took a stand with their commander.

"Go!" ordered Stan, waving to the rest of his battalion. He watched, satisfied, as the bulk of his command ran. The air shimmered not too far away. "We hold here for as long as we can!" he demanded of his fifty-man rearguard. "Load to break shields! Ready… aim… fire!"

The lead tore through shields with some deflected by fresh oncoming forces. Gaps appeared in the northern line of projectors coming to eliminate this minor annoyance. He and his men reloaded quickly and poured their fire into the advancing line. Fewer enemy, however, dropped. They had adjusted. Stan ordered his small unit to step back double quick.

"Get to the shields!" ordered Stan. He and his men broke and ran.

"Cowards!"

Major Stan Folfox stopped and turned. He tore open a round with his teeth, poured the gunpowder down the barrel, then tossed away the bullet. Alone, Stan stood with his triple charged musket. Another round of powder and finally the bullet he rammed home.

Surprised, Martell and the projector company he led halted, facing one man. He looked left and right, expecting trickery.

"Just enough time," whispered Stan, then he screamed, "For my son!" He aimed carefully. As the bullet exited the barrel, his unshielded body absorbed the energy bolts raining down. The rifle's breach exploded, unable to hold against the extra exploding gunpowder, but the shrapnel found no flesh to slice through only white dust.

The bullet crashed through Martell's shield, giving up its energy, ruining his uniform as it passed between his ribs through his right lung, tearing up a small clod of dirt behind him. Martell's hand shot to the sight of sudden pain. He stared, confused, at his fingers dripping with blood. Shock took him to his knees. The soldiers, Martell led, stared frozen in place.

"Get me a doctor," called out Martell. He coughed up blood. His order thawed his troops, releasing them from their torpor. They pulled back, carrying the Colonel to the rear, allowing the traitors to escape. The explosion of energy erupted behind them.

* * *

Jimmie Nicks, a hundred yards in front of two regiments of southern projectors, gathered up the retreating eagle badged units according to plan as they ran to his line. His one hundred men and women put up their shields, expecting an attack. It never came.

"Why not?" whispered Jimmie. He stood in the tall grass, camouflaging his unit on the northerner's far left. "Inform the commander, Raymond, with all due respect," Jimmie said to his sergeant, "he should advance on the enemy position with the expectation of rolling up their front." He watched as his sergeant and message disappeared into the trees several hundred yards behind.

Raymond found Jimmie in short order as his troops filled the space on the northern left behind Nicks' troops. "What's the situation, Jimmie?"

"Plain as the nose on your face," said Jimmie. "They are

done in. We can get a good twist on 'em if we move quick." He prayed Haggard also recognized the opportunity.

As they carried Martell from the field, Raymond ordered the all-out attack on the northern left flank. The energy from five thousand southern soldiers exploded among the northern veteran units and destroyed them. Dust filled the air. The eagle badged troops alongside the southern riflemen fired on the enemy with significant effect.

"It's a lie!" Cole ordered all available fresh troops forward. "We've been attacking phantoms." The unexpected attack on the northern left erupted. Cole ignored it, focusing on his center.

"Phantoms?" questioned Brigadier Folfox as Cole returned to the platform after conferring with his line officers. The northern front exploded as energy bolts and concentrated beams eviscerated Cole's forces.

The commanding general watched as the southern units curtained off behind the southern general officers, magically appeared, and washed into the field like an unrelenting tide: their shields strong, their energy fresh. His left disintegrated as his center labored under the constant attack from thirty thousand rested troops.

"Gentlemen," said Cole calmly, "it is time to fall back. The field is theirs."

Tom Haggard observed the northern units retreating up and over the slope. He also noted that Jack, Robert, and Anna had to be carried to the rear. Grim-faced, unhappy he had cost his supporters so much, Haggard whispered, "Our luck has held."

Let the hammer fall on illusions, he had argued. Neither Jack, Robert, nor Anna had thought the fake soldiers would look genuine enough. They, however, saw the logic of Haggard's design and had stepped out onto the field barefoot. They could project the fake units, but the earth had to help fill in the convincing details. She did.

"Get the message to Gracie Hargreaves that her forces north of the Aquitaine should expect a flood of northern soldiers at the bridges. We will hound the retreat as we are able."

CHAPTER 50

WHEN GRACIE RECEIVED HAGGARD'S MESSAGE, ANOTHER THREE regiments hurried forward to join the one on the northern bank of the river. Gracie sent Spunk to the bridgeheads to lead the men and women on a flanking maneuver.

"You lead this regiment?" asked Spunk two hours later. She handed the gruff, scarred commander Gracie's hastily written note giving her command. The man frowned, she noticed, then he looked up and smiled.

"Spunk, isn't it?" he said, "the names Blackman. How do you wish to proceed?" He folded the note and stuffed it in his chest pocket and looked out over the ground to their front.

"In an hour we'll have the additional four thousand troops plus your two thousand." Spunk pointed to the two nearest bridges. "Ten or twelve thousand retreating northerners will pour over those bridges. Their energy mostly used up. Our riflemen should do substantial damage if properly shielded."

"What do you think about a bayonet charge?" Blackman grinned. "They won't expect that. Surprise seems to be a winning proposition." He winked at Spunk.

"I like it." Spunk slapped Blackman on the back. "Go scare the hell out of them."

Spunk and Blackman worked out the details of their strategy. She had the overall lead, but Blackman would command an independent force.

"We'll either end 'em or die trying," said Blackman. He shook Spunk's hand. "Good luck." He moved off to gather his officers and form up the units.

Spunk nodded and watched him move further to the right into the tall grass.

"Ma'am?" asked Spunk's aide. "Our action will be…?"

"We will allow the northerners to cross, then sweep the field of the enemy with bullets and fire. Get the company leaders together for orders."

"Sir," saluted the sergeant, who ran back into the trees.

Jimmie Nicks gathered up about five hundred troopers and shadowed the retreating northern forces up and over the ridge. With a mix of shielders, bolters, and riflemen, he made sure the air rippled to keep the enemy fearful of attack; the enemy shied away to the west. Jimmie wanted a clear path north. The old bridge had to be captured intact and held.

"We run like the slavers are after us," stated Jimmie when they reached the water's edge. "You stay on this end with a hundred." He pointed to a sergeant not much older than him, who nodded. "We will hold the north end." Jimmie looked out over the river, seeing a few men in blue uniforms on the new bridges waving their hands and screaming something he could not hear. Jimmie reacted. "Go Now!"

The four hundred dashed across the old bridge. Unchallenged, they formed a line along the road leading north.

"Shields up!" called out many in Nick's company. The air shimmered with defensive energy.

"Suppose ta be som' help this side," stated a trooper ramming a bullet down with a double charge of powder in her rifle. She felt exposed with enemy soldiers only a few hundred feet away, watching them.

"Rest easy, trooper," said Jimmie, passing among his thin line of men and women. "They be just out of sight." Jimmie placed his hand on her shoulder, and she looked up at him, revealing the burn marks on her face.

"Aye, Jimmie," she said. "Just don't want to be alone right

about now. If ya know what I mean." She nodded to the enemy, forming their lines. Their troops stretched beyond the southerner's line.

"Rifleman or bolter?" asked Jimmie.

"Bolter, but ready to pull the trigger." She patted the rifle affectionately. "Think they'll try to flank us?"

"They're beat, but some don't know it yet. We will settle the matter." Jimmie smiled at the trooper.

"Well, damn!" The yell startled the troopers who heard. "I can't say I approve of your promotion, Nicks." Spunk stood over Jimmie as he gave confidence to his soldier.

"Looks like they made a big, useless girl a commander," said Jimmie with a wink at the trooper. He stood and clasped Spunk's upper arm, his relief clear in his broad smile. Southern soldiers came from the woods adding to the Nick's numbers. "Always show at the last possible second."

"What's your situation?" asked Spunk, suddenly all business looking over the enemy formation along the road.

Jimmie provided a quick report, then suggested, "As far as I can tell, we hold and wait for Haggard."

"Might wait," nodded Spunk. "Might not."

* * *

Jack Fox recovered quicker than Robert or Anna Forrester. He sat up on the cot, pulling the blanket from his shoulder. His eyes sought Spunk, but found his fellow illusionists unconscious. These old people, like Nanna, had grit. Jack stood felt the floor slide but stayed on his feet. The headache throbbed with his pounding heart. Still barefoot, he exited the tent and absorbed the sunlight, glad of the warmth.

"Well damn, Jack, good to see you on your feet!" Peppers came up to him and started a quick medical assessment of his friend. "Thought you might not make it back. I have never seen life levels so low as I did with you three." He released Jack's wrist, satisfied with the strength and steady beat of his pulse. "So, what happened?"

"I felt used up as the northern blast attacks eased up, but then energy poured into me from the earth. Don't know why, but it got pulled back." He grabbed his friend's arm desperate. "Where's Spunk?"

"Hargreaves ordered her north of the river to take command is what I heard." Peppers looked Jack over but concluded, "You seem to be okay. A headache bothering you?"

"Yes." Jack grabbed Peppers by his shoulders, begging. "Where is she now?"

Peppers shrugged. "Probably preparing for action against the retreating northerners."

"We won?" Jack stared at the doctor, then shut his eyes to the pain.

"Took them completely by surprise." Peppers pulled a packet of powder from his pocket. "We had a good many weeders complain about headaches. Hattie did a bit of her magic and came up with this. Swallow it."

Jack tore the paper, threw back his head, and poured the powder into his mouth. He gagged on the bitter concoction.

"Now, I would like you…," started Pepper handing Jack a ladle of water he retrieved from the barrel just outside the tent, "to stay put for further evaluation…", he took back the empty ladle, "but… of course… you won't take medical advice."

Jack felt a moment of disorientation as the drug took effect. The pain became something trying impotently to claw into his awareness, so he ignored it. He smiled at Peppers, who pressed a pair of boots into his hands.

"You'll need this too," said the Doc, who bent his head toward the saddled horse, waiting.

"Against all reasonable medical advice, you are going back to the fight, as did so many of you crazy southerners." Peppers smiled. "I love all of you crazy people. Go!"

Jack pulled on the boots, stamped his feet, then mounted up. "I owe you, my friend, in so many ways."

"We will settle accounts later." Peppers shook Jack's offered hand, placing his other over Jack's. "Find Spunk and take care, Jack Fox. We are not through with you."

"I missed you," said Jack, his arms around Spunk. Their world collapsed to a small space of grass surrounded by a field of soldiers who stared for a moment at the couple, grinned, then looked away to give the two some small sense of privacy.

"You and the lady take care," said a gruff voice of a nearby shielder. "We'll finish this, Jack." Agreement came in a hundred voices up and down the line. Jack stood with them. How could they lose? Hope and certainty of victory infected all.

"You be careful," insisted Jack, focused on holding Spunk's loving eyes.

"Always," she whispered, annoyed that he came to keep her safe, but happy he sought her out. "You must do something useful." She kissed his cheek. "I'm busy."

Jack nodded, hugged her tight one more time, then headed back the way he came. It occurred to him he needed another surprise. He spun around and headed to the old bridge. Still weakened from creating the illusion of forty thousand well-formed soldiers, he hobbled forward to get on the southern side of the river.

CHAPTER 51

"We lost," complained Brigadier Folfox. He followed Cole, badgering him as they crossed a bridge recently constructed by northern non-projectors.

"Yes, damnit, we lost." Cole crossed the bridge on foot. "Form up a rear guard," he called to surprised reserve soldiers on the northern end of the bridge. He watched officers jump to action. "You and I, Folfox, plus several others, are the only offensive soldiers not used up as far as I can tell." Cole gathered his staff and any other older officer, like Folfox, to form up. "We will destroy any advanced southern force and delay them long enough to make an escape."

"What?" demanded Folfox, stopping dead in his tracks. He never expected to dirty his hands. "I don't put myself in harm's way to deal with this riffraff."

"If we want a viable force," said Cole through gritted teeth, "and fight another day, then we need to keep as much of this army intact as possible." The General turned and grabbed Folfox by the throat. "Make ready to do all you can with the energy at your disposal or, I swear, you can join our dead." Cole looked at the air blown gray dust cloud drifting over the Aquitaine.

"Yes," choked Folfox, afraid.

Cole released him.

The generals watched as thousands retreated over the bridges, falling into the tender mercies of officers determined to make a stand. Some soldiers formed up in line, while others ignored orders and kept going north. Their leaders vaporized the deserters in front of their fellows: the action stopped the retreat. The men got the message and gathered into ranks amid the chaos.

Cole commanded a small contingent of one thousand

experienced, energy savvy, high-ranking projectors. These older men grasped the situation. Back home, they ranked high as community leaders, raised because of their abilities. A few led assaults, but none fought at the bottom of the ridge, leaving the battle's trench work to lesser men. Around them waited several thousand panicked soldiers, still able to shield or attack but obviously not at full strength. Some showed burn marks, like the southern enemy. Many had uniforms torn with bloodied wounds caused by hot lead breaking through a shield. Disoriented, some wanted to run. The General had to take the officers in hand. The foot soldiers needed trusted leadership to get ready for another fight.

"We have enemy units on our left at the old bridge." Cole addressed captains and lieutenants. "You did well to defend our flank. Go back to your men and tell them to hold until I send new orders. Let them know that we still outnumber them on this side of the river, but not for long. Give them as much confidence as you are able."

Cole closed his eyes, calming himself, then added, "I will do everything in my power to make you successful." He exclaimed. "I expect every man to do his duty. You will have some time to recover, but not much."

"What, sir, is the desired outcome?" asked a captain, his uniform ragged.

"We want the river to stay the boundary between our countries." Cole gave vague orders, allowing the line officers to interpret them as needed as the situation changed. "Destroy the bridges. We will do what we can from here." He watched the men quickly return to their commands.

Blackman arranged his troops in the tall grass. After two hours, the first bolter attack from Spunk's position signaled him to move. Two thousand soldiers screaming and howling ran from the tall grass into the northern line.

The Colonel took full advantage of what seemed like shock, causing the northern troops to hesitate. Sharp steel got through the weak shielding. His soldiers thrust deep into a stomach, turned the blade, pulled back, then hunted for the next enemy. Bodies piled up as blood made the grass slippery.

Suddenly, energy bolts came over the top of the front line into Blackman's crew. Unprotected, the air filled with ash.

"Pull back!" ordered Blackman, intent on saving as many of his men as possible. He ran with his men, panting. "We would appreciate a little help," he mumbled.

"Folfox, time to fight." Cole walked away saying, "All of us get our hands dirty or…" He stopped suddenly as thousands of men groaned. Together, they watched a lone person step from the trees on the southern side of a bridge.

"Jack Fox," echoed across the front from choked and desperate voices. Sergeants called for steadiness to hold the line as the exhausted wanted to be anywhere else but here.

To the west, beyond a bend in the Aquitaine, columns of black smoke rose: bridges burned. The span a quarter mile away exploded, but the closest one to Jack and the old bridge survived the hammer attack from Cole and his remaining fresh men. Even in his weakened condition, Jack easily blocked the attack by syphoning energy from the thousands of southerners coming up behind him, hidden among the trees.

The demolition of the bridges ended. Strong shielding crackled over the last two spans over the Aquitaine. Jack set an easy pace, strolled with hands in his pockets, and stopped to kick bits of debris into the river. On the other side, he faced the front line of the enemy: some angry and cursing with pointless, single combat challenges, some with pleading eyes, and those silent, just staring, waiting for the end. Jack's quiet confidence and smile had unnerved them. With only a slight energy push, the entire front backed up a step from the bridgehead.

"You will reap," yelled Jack, "what you sow! Stay here, you die!" He looked up as the bolts passed over his head from behind, then more arced from the right into the northern formation. Dust exploded into the air. Chaos crept into the ranks, forming the front of the depleted northern army.

The enemy fell back. Jack crossed the bridge at an easy gate as though enjoying an outing on a summer's day. A phalanx of northern soldiers, mostly officers, did not fall back. They returned fire and slowed the southern advance, coming up behind Jack. Weeds sprang up at Jack's urging among the enemy rearguard, forcing them to deal with the green cables trapping their feet and clawing up their legs.

Jack strode forward, deflecting the shower of bolts aimed his way. The enemy continued to give ground. Concentrated energy flew over his head from the southern troops: beams and bolts. White ash filled the air. Jack turned to the many regiments following him, determined to destroy the enemy. These regiments stalled on the bridge. He faced forward, strengthened his shield until it became opaque, and walked forward fifty feet.

Energy bolts fell like rain on him, but with no effect; the enemy gave up ground. Jack watched the southern units scurry off the bridge, going left and right, building a beachhead along the river. The attack on him eased when southern soldiers returned fire on those northern troops. He eased his shield into a shimmer and studied the situation.

The northern troops had retreated as he advanced. They stopped, turned, then linked their shields. The firing of bolts stopped as the southern counterattacks devastated the attackers.

Jack considered his options. Southern strength grew by the minute with the lull in the battle. Men poured unimpeded over the bridge. He knew they expected him to lead this next attack. The line of soldiers in light blue uniforms still retreated a few steps at a time.

The sudden explosion of energy at the old bridge eight hundred yards to his right made him duck. The units at his back attacked the blue line to their front.

Energy bolts crashed into the shield wall, driving the invaders back further. Jack added his power to the assault and signaled the army to move forward. With each step forward, another barrage hit the weakening shield wall.

"It's over," stated General Cole to the surrounding men. "Drop shields. We must surrender." The battlefield became silent. He stepped out in front of his line and walked up to the young man, now surrounded by his commanders.

"Gentlemen and ladies," said Cole, tipping his hat. "My name is General Cole and I command the forces of the North. I wish to discuss terms of surrender."

"General, I am Jack Fox, and this is General Will Biggs." He listened to the battle still raging. "Can you order those people over there to surrender?"

"Unfortunately, we are cut off," admitted Cole. "I can send runners."

"Do so." Jack took Will's arm and walked away a few paces. "I have to get over to our right. Take their surrender."

"Of course," said Will. "You can ride my horse." Will nodded to the riverbank, where a few horses milled about. "Tom crossed the old bridge to support Gracie. You'll find him there."

Together, they faced the northern general.

"I have sent my orders," said Cole as they approached.

"General Biggs will set the terms. I am needed elsewhere." Jack spun around abruptly, pushed through the ranks, mounted up, and raced to where the ash clouded the sky.

CHAPTER 52

G RACIE HAD CHARGED ACROSS THE OLD BRIDGE AND STRAIGHT up the road. She had not expected to be pulled into a desperate melee but did not hesitate as Blackman's charge met resistance: energy bolts reduced and stopped his forces. His line fell back. Gracie, with her forces projecting shields, stormed up the road, passed Spunk's forces engaged with the enemy, and got in behind Blackman's front. The sudden concentration of power on her, however, forced Gracie to pull her shield in close for self-preservation. Energy rained down: it found weaknesses. Her uniform smoldered in places, but she and her troops held. In the brief respite offered by the added shielding, the riflemen regrouped, then pointed their razor-sharp bayonets at the enemy. Gracie felt her legs weaken as her shield faltered, but refused to give in to the weariness.

"If you can manage it, ma'am," said Blackman, who pulled her deeper into his ranks, "they are firing at a ranking officer… you, to be exact. Your troopers have got out in front, weakened the enemy, and gave my riflemen the opportunity to do their jobs. You, if I might make a suggestion, should retire until you recover."

Gracie understood and ignored Blackman's suggestion.

She rose to her feet and joined her soldiers, stepping out along the line. Ugly hand-to-hand combat erupted with the northerners. Too close for shields to offer much protection, Gracie attacked with knives in her hands. With her blades and hands blood soaked, Gracie glowed as the enemy continued to light her up. Pulling her blades from a northern officer's chest as he fell to the ground, she stopped and focused, pouring the last of her energy into her shield.

So many have made the ultimate sacrifice crossed her mind as she collapsed. *My turn.*

"Ya damned woman!" A hand gripped her shoulder as she hit the ground. "A stupid death will not be much help," cursed Blackman. He once again dragged Gracie back into the hands of her aides.

"There are times, Mr. Blackman, when a commander's life does not matter. I lead by example," said Gracie, feeling herself fade.

"Forward," Blackman ordered, a revolver in hand, "double quick!" A wall of steel charged, glinting in the sunlight. The young, least trained, exhausted northern troops saw determined bolters, shielders, and most fearsome, long, sharp blades coming for them. They broke and ran.

Gracie recovered enough with ten minutes rest to trail the enemy. With a few troopers, she advanced to the first paved road beyond the bridges. The smooth blacktop road amazed the southerners. Gracie knelt and ran her hand over the surface, as did her soldiers.

"We stop here," she ordered, coughing, not fully recharged. Her hands brushed at the smudges of charred material all over her uniform. She wanted to look more presentable, like she expected northern officers to seek her out to negotiate a surrender.

In the distance, horseless carriages drove away with the remains of the northern rearguard. Expecting a formal surrender made no sense. She stopped tidying herself, looked over her shoulder and called, "signal all forces to stand down. We hold here." Her orders signalled to distant companies. "Over to the left are the northerner's camp and supply train." Gracie raised her hand, showing where her scavenger and supply units should make their efforts. She ordered a field chair and collapsed into it when it arrived minutes later.

Jack and Spunk, hand in hand, found Gracie in her seat recovering as row upon row of southern soldiers held defensive positions along the paved road leading to the mountains in one direction and to the northern capital in the other. Gracie stared up the road heading north, wondering about a counterattack.

"So," said Jack. "We won."

"Now what?" asked Spunk.

Gracie turned to her long time protégés, cleared her mind, and said, "We rest first, then work like all hell not to lose the peace." She gathered their hands in hers. "You made this possible. The two of you."

"And thousands of others," insisted Spunk.

Gracie nodded. "Now, however, it will be all politics and the usual manure that comes along for the ride."

"And I cannot find a better person than you, Gracie, to carry us forward." Tom Haggard strode up to them. Gracie stood. "You have my total confidence when the negotiations begin."

The General had crossed the old bridge followed by thousands, met up with Jack, and joined Spunk's forces to outnumber the enemy and end the northern ability to fight. He surveyed the area around them and found a line of abandoned silver vehicles. "Do you know how to make those things go, Mr. Fox?"

"The Doc and I have some experience along those lines," said Jack, smiling.

"If it is not too much trouble," said Tom, "we will need a student driver program unless you and the doctor want to do all the carting around?"

"Jimmie Nicks," said Spunk, "should be first in line along with a few others I could recommend."

"Make it so," said Haggard. "We will need to go to Dover once they make an overture."

"If they don't?" asked Gracie.

"We invade," said Haggard. "Hempstead would be an easy target. They would likely welcome us. Dover will be a rare fight, I would imagine."

* * *

"I heard it clear as day," insisted Jimmie standing in his tent with Jack and Spunk sitting in field chairs sipping hot coffee. Jimmie's tent lay among a sea of tents in the field bordered by the paved road. His men slept in the early morning quiet.

"Will you ever relax, Mr. Nicks, for goodness' sake? I'm not king or saint or anything," insisted Jack. "You are commander in your own right now."

"We won cause a you, sir," stammered Jimmie. He sunk into an empty chair.

Jack shook his head, knowing he would never change the young man's view. "Okay, Jimmie, tell me about the eagle badged colonel."

"He ran to our shields, but stopped. This enemy officer picked off a few of the colonel's men, calling them cowards." Jimmie closed his eyes, recalling all that happened. "I saw him load his rifle. He must a known he was a dead man." Jimmie stopped, opened his eyes, looked at Jack, and said, "He raised the rifle aimed at the northern officer, yelled 'For my son', then fired. He stood stock still. No escape running from the energy. He was too far in front of our shielders to help."

"Understood," said Jack calmly but feeling the rush of pride and tears. His father kept their agreement to spy for the South, then stood tall in the face of certain death.

"The bullet dropped the northerner, but the eagle badged colonel simply ceased to be. His rifle exploded. Must 'ave been four times the powder since the breach exploded." Jimmie drank from his cup, then said, "Don't know who the son might be, but

I wouldn't mind havin' a dad willing to do that. If you know what I mean?"

"Yes, Mr. Nicks," said Jack, allowing a tear to escape down his cheek, "I know what you mean."

CHAPTER 53

"KNOW'D THE TWO A YOU WAS BUSY, BUT I'M A MIGHT GLAD TO see ya," said Nanna, accepting hugs from Spunk, Jack, and Mini. They met at the Snakeport hospital's entrance as the sun set. A week had passed since Gracie stepped on the paved road watching the enemy retreat. "Look at you, girl!" smiled the old woman, looking Mini up and down in her uniform. "Come a ways," she briefly caressed the cheeks of all three, "so we have?"

"How are you holding up, grandma?" Mini looked concerned but relaxed as Nanna grabbed her hand and held tight.

"Can't tell ya how good it is to hear ya talking, my girl." She released her granddaughter and saw the same worried looks on Jack and Spunk. "I be fine, fit as a fiddle: no cane if ya hadn't noticed. Just a little worn. I'm old 's all."

"My mom, Nanna?" asked Jack.

"Come along, come along." She shuffled toward the stairway and placed her hand on Jack's shoulder. "Doc Shephards is a wonder, don't ya know, but… there be healing and then there be a deeper healing. Yore ma needs the deeper sort, if ya take my meaning." With a little help from Jack, she climbed the steps and took them down the corridor to the right. Lit with candles in sconces along the wall, Nanna led them to a room with one patient.

"She ain't e't nothing in a while. Can't last that much longer." Nanna went to the bed's side table. "Doc Shephards said somethin' about this here puny plant and some djinn magic. He said he saw it work a while back." Nanna headed out of the room and nudged both Spunk and Mini. "Family business, my girls. Seems she needs a key ta open the lock, if ya understand rightly." The door closed quietly as they left.

Night darkness invaded the room. Jack stood alone in the shadows, looking down at his mother. Skeletal flashed through his mind, but strangely peaceful. A lone candle provided the only light in the room. He turned his attention to the side table.

"Well, old friend," he said, lifting the pot. "We seem to keep running into each other." Jack placed the plant on the bed next to his mother's hand. His finger reached under the green leaf, which immediately wrapped around it. Jack carefully lifted his mother's finger to another leaf.

The flash of light happened instantly. Time stopped.

Jack, flat on his back on the floor, stared up at the ceiling. His head hurt. How and why the connection broke, he did not know nor had he any memory of what took place.

"Damned earth... can't make anything easy," Jack complained. He reached up to the mattress to pull himself up. Sunlight blinded him and made the pain worse behind his eyes. "Sonofabitch," he moaned, blocking the sunlight with his hand as he climbed from his knees to his feet. "Better be some good come of all this."

"Maybe a bit," said a small voice.

Speechless, Jack looked down at his mother, clear-eyed and smiling. He took several steps back, then turned to the door, opened it, and called out, "Need some food here, now!"

"You look worn," whispered Lilly, the dark circles under her eyes prominent.

"Yes, the both of us," said Jack.

"She said you would not remember what happened while we connected, but I would." She turned to the sunlit window and said sadly, "Stan is dead."

Jack nodded. They went into a mutual, agreeable silence.

The food arrived. Jack helped his mom sit up and then took

the spoon from her hand when her hand shook too much to manage it.

"You saved me," he said, taking a napkin and wiping the dribble of soup at the corner of her mouth and sopping up the spilt soup, staining the sheet. "You and about fifty others."

"Give me your hand," whispered Lilly. She pulled it forward and placed it on her belly. "You can help me now by projecting a shield." She glowed a bit; Jack felt the draw she absorbed. The dark circles beneath her eyes faded. "Much better." Lilly smiled. Her hand grabbed the empty spoon in Jack's hand and pried it away. The other took the bowl, and she fed herself. "Now, you have done enough."

CHAPTER 54

The northern overture arrived in the Snake four weeks later as southern forces gathered and prepared to move north on Hempstead. Cole and the other northern general rank officers rolled up in one of the horseless vehicles and waited. They stopped at the end of the smooth road. Southern guards waved them on. More soldiers ordered them to stop and abandon their silver carriage. They gathered at the edge of the field where the first northern force met their demise.

Haggard, Hargreaves, and Biggs, with many southern city leaders, approached the northern contingent on foot. They surrounded the northern men, then waited in silence.

"I am General Cole." The General tipped his hat in recognition of the southern success. "May I shake your hand, General Haggard?" He stepped forward.

"Gracie Hargreaves first, sir," said Haggard.

Without hesitation, Cole extended his hand to Gracie, who took it.

"General Biggs," said Cole, shaking his hand. "The last of my wounded?"

"Expect them home in another week or two," confirmed Biggs. He had allowed the northern soldiers able to walk to leave the field and agreed to treat their wounded and bury their dead.

"We are enemies in the field no longer," stated Haggard as he grasped the ungloved hand. "Still in a state of war until we settled the peace."

Cole smiled. "When this is all settled, General, I would be delighted to have you at my home for two old soldiers to recall the battle."

"I would like that, but..." Haggard released the hand and

turned to Gracie. "Gracie will receive and act on any message from the government of the North."

Cole nodded and said, "If it is agreeable, a negotiation will take place in our capital with our leaders in two weeks. This is contingent on all hostilities ending now."

"Agreed," stated Gracie. "We will advance no further. Please provide the number allowed for our negotiators, plus the reasons we should be confident that a sudden death does not await us at this meeting or another invasion."

"First, two weeks is not enough time to rebuild and re-outfit such a force." said Cole thoughtfully. "Second, you still care for several hundred of our wounded officers and foot soldiers."

Gracie nodded. "We will keep our forces ready."

"Madam," bowed Cole in agreement. "Come with as many men," he looked at the southerners and added, "and women as you think necessary."

"Thank you, General." Gracie returned the bow, bending slightly at the waist.

"Our government makes one special request." Cole's eyes scanned the immediate area. "Perhaps it is a foolish thing… but our prime minister wishes to meet Mr. Fox."

* * *

"The arrogance of these people!" Prime Minister Dowler stood at his office window, surrounded by government ministers. His complaints and finger pointing began after the first string of screamed curses ended when news of the defeat reached Dover. The officer delivering the news a month ago blessed his lucky stars. He did not wind up a bloody spot on the rug. If Dowler had his way, Cole, Sedgwick, Higgins, Martell, and a host of others would dangle at the end of a rope in the public square as traitors or for gross negligence.

The northern generals, the ministers, and others confronted the apoplectic leader and threatened his removal from office. The Prime Minister knew his popularity had plummeted among the power brokers. His tune changed, expressing great sorrow for the thousands lost. He saw the disbelief in their expressions.

Quietly, Dowler invited men who shared his prejudices to the peace negotiation.

The Prime Minister huffed with a hand resting on the window's glass. "Using our own vehicles to arrive in our capital."

Higgins rolled his eyes. "The point Dowler is that they can use our abandoned transports, which means they have arrived with well rested, battle hardened projectors."

"I am not replaced yet, minister," he shot back. Dowler rankled at Higgins' cursory nod. "Why not just destroy those few?"

"Because there are tens of thousand ready to lay waste to this city and…" Colonel Martell watched from another window as a uniformed woman stepped out of the second carriage surrounded by southern bodyguards from the first and third vehicles. "I doubt, very much, we can win against those arriving." Martell returned his attention to the street, examining the young man climbing the steps just behind the woman.

The men stepped away from the windows and gathered in front of the desk. Dowler waited next to Cole, a half-step ahead of him.

"I find it hard to believe, Colonel, that we cannot simply wave them away. Our Dover forces just need the order to act." Dowler disgusted, pointed at the southern representatives and said, "we have to deal with a woman."

"I will forgive your ignorance this time. You were not at the battle," whispered Cole in the Prime Minister's ear, "so you do not know. This is how it will be. Stop whining." He straightened up and said, "We might have won with women such as she on our side. Be respectful."

"I do not have to…" he began haughtily.

"Shut up, Dowler," hissed Sedgwick, "or so help me. I'll vaporize you myself."

The knock echoed in the chamber, and the door opened. A brief pause ensued, then the southern negotiators, projectors, poured into the room. Gracie led the way, her hat in her left hand, followed by Jack, with Robert and Anna Forrester on either side. Behind them came twenty-five southern officers and city counselors, quickly elected from a variety of southern towns for this task.

"General Cole," said Gracie, bowing slightly. "I believe introductions are in order, then down to business."

The northern general stepped forward and made sure that all knew who held sway on the northern side. Gracie did the same for her team. After Jack's introduction, Sedgwick, Higgins, and Martell studied him, ignoring the other participants. In the sudden quiet after the introductions, the northern ministers moved to the large table where their war plans came together the previous year.

"Your commanding general is not taking part?" asked Cole, searching for his counterpart.

"General Haggard surveys the new boundaries and performs other important work," said Gracie, smiling. "Besides, not being a projector, he felt he would incite prejudices and become a distraction."

"I understand," said the general, genuinely disappointed. He joined the others, taking a seat at the table.

"Wait," called out Dowler, "new boundaries?"

Jack pulled back a chair intending to sit, then stopped. "Energy levels are rising," he said, taking a step back.

"What new boundaries?" Dowler exclaimed angrily. "This is just too much. Who of you support me?" A self-satisfied grin curled his lips as several older men rose, including the elder Folfox and others. "Rid me of these cumbersome persons," commanded Dowler.

Sedgwick pushed back his chair and stood. He moved quickly to the Prime Minister, whose smile disappeared an instant before a burst of light and a haze of dust filled a shielded space where Dowler once stood. The minister's projected field kept the room from contamination by the Prime Minister's remains. The Minister of War faced the other men on their feet, frozen by the quick murder of their leader.

"Dowler was our tool, useful at the start, but a dangerous impediment in the current situation. Those who choose to be constructive will sit. Those who wish to obstruct today's business should remain standing." Like children scrambling to look innocent when caught in the act, the old men found their seats. "So, no further time is lost. I put forward General Cole as the Prime Minister Pro Temp." He nodded to the general. Not a single voice objected.

Dowler's dust contained by the shield settled to the floor as if it exploded in a glass box. The shield dropped, and an aide stepped forward. The young officer removed the ash covered chair while another swiftly swept the floor.

"I will take the silence as a unanimous agreement." Sedgwick surveyed his side of the table and those grouped behind. "Prime Minister," he addressed the General, "if you would carry on." Turning to the southerners, he said, "My apologies ladies and gentlemen, but this had to be done to reach an agreement." Sedgwick returned to his seat.

"Where to start," said Cole, startled by Sedgwick's violence but glad to be rid of one fool with the others cowed for the time being. "What is your intent?"

"Simple," started Gracie, sure she would have ended all the gray-haired men standing for Dowler in Sedgwick's place. She weighed her words. "We in the south want to be left alone. Your country is yours to rule as you see fit and ours is for us to move forward as we wish it."

The discussions, arguments, and agreements passed back and forth across the table for hours. The Northerners, relieved the Southerners did not want to rule them, listened carefully, and agreed to reasonable requests. Soldiers hauled in several desks where clerks readied themselves to record several copies of an accord. Food and drink appeared on a long sideboard. Southerners and Northerners mingled over the hours and found they had much in common.

"What of the mountain and far northern people?" insisted Martell.

"We did not," said Gracie, "allow their issues with you to affect our actions. Nor did they send forces to fight with us." She checked with Jack, Robert, and Anna, who nodded. "You will deal with them as you see fit, but…"

"We will defend them if they ask for our help," said Jack.

"I see," said Cole. *With a weakened army, he thought, we must talk with both.* Out loud, Cole stated, "We will seek peace with our neighbors."

"Of course," said Jack, winking at Gracie, "of course." Jack went to the sideboard and filled a plate. Nothing more needed to be said on the issue.

"Damn these weaklings," whispered Folfox to a small group gathered around him. They stood nibbling food from plates or drinking from cups. "Higgins, Sedgwick, and Cole betray us with every breath they take." The old man failed to notice the southerner approaching his circle of adherents.

"Well, grandad, that is no way for a civil man to act." Jack chewed on a piece of meat and examined his plate, deciding what to sample next. "You should know better."

"You are not related to me," hissed the old man, stepping forward to confront Jack.

"My father," said Jack, holding Folfox's gaze, "was Stan Folfox who committed to my mother Lilly." He set his plate down, then stepped close to his grandfather. "You will keep very, very quiet, grandpa, and be civil. If that is not possible…" Jack smiled. "I will end you." He watched rage pass over his grandfather's features and felt the attempt to attack. Jack, in response, overwhelmed his grandfather's defenses, draining the energy. Folfox lost the color in his face and blinked. "I think my father would approve of your death. Don't you think?"

"You know," said the elder Folfox, the corner of his mouth twitching, "the man who killed your father sits next to Cole?" He grinned feeling gratified when Jack glanced over at the table.

"I expect he and I will have words." Jack paused, became serious, and studied Martell. "Have you always been a small, cowardly man?" Without looking at his grandfather, he smiled when he received no answer. Jack pushed the old man out of his way reaching for a napkin, then picked up his plate and turned away intent on discovering the other food delights found along the sideboard.

Energy lamps provided light as darkness fell and the clerks scratched furiously to provide the final copies of the agreement. The groups mingled, staying with safe subjects as they waited.

"I suspected you might be a Folfox, but was not sure until that moment," said Colonel Martell. "You might have sprung from any number of powerful families." He had purposefully moved into an empty corner of the room and nodded to Jack to join him.

"Did you kill my father?" A strange calmness hugged Jack. This man he no longer consider his mortal enemy.

"I might have," said Martell, looking down, remembering that moment. "Hard to tell with so much energy converging on him. I wanted him dead to be perfectly honest." Martell looked directly into Jack's eyes. "He and his troops killed many of my soldiers."

Jack nodded.

"He damn near killed me, but sacrificed his life for his men. I respect that. He and all those others like him deserved better of us. I… am especially guilty." He shook his head and looked away then said, "I am a small-minded man, Mr. Fox, but…," he took a deep breath, "I hope to improve."

"I have been told," said Jack, "that my father yelled out just as he fired."

"Indeed. I heard him clearly." Martell with a bitter grin said, "That is when I learned about you." He pointed his finger at Jack. "'For my son!' he called out." Lost momentarily in the memory staring at the floor, the colonel added, "It stopped me for an instant." He looked up at Jack. "Who says such things when their death is at hand? Then I knew."

"That I was his son?" asked Jack.

"That and… he was a better man than I."

They said nothing more for a long moment.

"You are recovering, Colonel?" asked Jack, breaking the silence nodding to the sling Martell still wore.

"I am, thank you." Martell considered the young man, commanding a great power, yet so much older than his years. "I believe your Mrs. Hargreaves has been very generous in her conditions for our surrender."

"If you learn nothing else from these negotiations," said Jack with a big grin, "know that she is three steps ahead in her thinking and seeing the future through a lens of practical experience."

Martell nodded, then asked, "With the end of hostilities, what of you, Mr. Fox?"

Jack suddenly grew tired being the 'Jack Fox' and discovered a strong desire for time alone and quiet.

"Haven't decided yet," he said finally. "Maybe find a place for a fresh start."

Martell nodded. "I wish you luck."

CHAPTER 55

Alone, Jack sat on the overturned, rotting tree trunk and took off his boots. *Time a wee human settled things with a god.* He slid down the trunk to sit in the dirt and buried his feet into the earth. The sun rose above the horizon and threw shadows everywhere. Energy flowed into the earth. The earth responded.

"About time, Jack Fox." The feminine voice, full of laughter, welcomed him.

"Thank you. I would not be alive if not for you."

"You are welcome."

Jack felt a momentary twist in his stomach as the world turned and swirled, then settled on a hill topped by an old oak tree with thick clusters of dark green leaves moved by a warm breeze. With legs stretched out and his back against the tree, he surveyed the landscape. Below the hill ranged a deep valley of fertile fields and sparkling streams.

"You have questions?" The voice shifted to male. Stan Folfox appeared and strode up the hill. He sat next to his son, leaned back against the trunk, and turned to Jack.

"You are using me," stated Jack, mildly upset.

"You want truth?" Stan frowned. "Get over it."

"I want the truth," Jack nodded. He ignored the figure of his father and began, "What happened to my mother at the first attack?"

"She made the same choice as did your father. I used her energy plus a few others who believed in you to save your life."

"Okay, I survived, and the South defeated the North." The sun felt warm. Birds flew through the valley. The streams in the distance beckoned and promised a cold, clear resolution to any thirst. "What do you want?"

"Do not forget or ignore me," said Stan.

"I know you. You are always in my thoughts," stated Jack.

"I appreciate your belief, but you won't live forever," said Stan.

"You got it all wrong," insisted Jack. "Aside from me, Anna, and Robert, to whom have you revealed yourself?"

"Over the centuries?" Stan sat forward and looked over the valley. "Many more." He faced Jack. "Then a weariness overtook me as well as a resentment. The North, in their arrogance, forgot and the South, worried about simple survival, stopped believing." He looked up into the tree as the soft wind continued to rattle the leaves. "I am not without fault."

Jack considered the revelation, then said, "You sound almost human." Climbing to his feet and stretching, he added, "Seems you want to be courted."

"You could see it that way."

Jack realized no straightforward answer would come. He changed the subject.

"Why don't I remember the time with my mother in the hospital?"

"Lilly wished it so." Stan rose to his feet and looked down at Jack. "She is not cured of her need, but I have fortified her with some strength to resist. Time will tell."

"So, again, what do you want? Churches, worshipers, priests, what?"

Stan laughed out loud. "A sure way to insignificance and resentment." He paused. "I want considerations and steps taken to preserve the blessing of the land. I only want a few in the dirt burying their hands or bare feet to make requests, seek advice, or say thanks. I want to be relevant."

"Like a god?" asked Jack.

"Like a power greater than you that cares about the wellness of the earth." Stan scanned the field and appeared to be considering his answer. "Care about what I care about."

"After what you did at the battle," said Jack, "I want to."

"Yes, Jack, and I love you for it."

"Love me?" Jack considered the image of his father wishing he still lived. Question upon question crowded his thoughts. "I will miss him," he whispered. Stan melted and reformed as Lilly.

"Yes, you will and rightly so," said Lilly, who knelt next to Jack. She wore a white smock and smiled at her son. After a few seconds, Lilly frowned and said, "I am not a ghost, Jack." She placed a hand on her son's leg. "You believe because I am real in your life. For only a few, it is not a matter of faith."

"Then be real to everyone who calls on you," demanded Jack, who felt frustrated with the obvious solution about which they danced. "Make yourself known to the farmer suffering with poor weather or the children playing, running barefoot among the trees. Hidden gods are no gods at all."

"You, my boy," nodded Lilly, "are my priest and Anna Forrester, my priestess. I call on you to do nothing."

"Nothing?" asked a skeptical Jack Fox.

"The right thing when needed, I am sure, will occur to you." Lilly, still on her knees, leaned in close, and kissed Jack on the cheek. Her right hand caressed it.

Everything went black.

* * *

"Spunk and I are going back to the mountains," said Jack Fox, sitting across from Gracie: the same office, the same old warehouse, and the same desk. Both shared mugs of black coffee as they had so many times before. Two days passed since his talk with the earth. Dinner, ignored, waited beneath metal covers on the edge of the desk. A late summer's sunlight lit the office from the windows high on the walls.

Gracie nodded. "Any particular reason you want to leave?"

"Many," said Jack, taking a sip and collecting his thoughts. "I will be a problem if I stay. You and Tom must sort out what we will become. If people don't get what they want from you, they will come to me to tip the balance. I don't want to deal with that."

"The next few years will need leaders willing to act regardless of the sacrifice for a greater good." Gracie stared into her mug. "We will, I suspect, be hated for a time." She looked up. "What else?"

"I," said Jack, his cheeks suddenly red, "might have a son or daughter on the way if the mountain people follow through on their plans. I want to meet that person when he or she comes forth."

"How does Spunk feel about that?" Gracie smiled, wondering how she might react to such a thing: a child born outside a commitment.

"This mountain child, if he or she exists, needs a playmate, is what she says."

"Ha!" laughed Gracie, spilling coffee on the desk. Spunk never failed to impress. With superior control, Gracie calmed and said, "I see."

"I…" started Jack, who set down his mug on the desk and sat back. "I need to tell you something… should have said it a long time ago. Now that I'm leaving." He paused and took a deep breath. "You and me and those things you did. You never gave up on me and I…"

Gracie raised her hand to stop the rush of emotion, likely to leave her crying like a baby. "Good business, Jack. Nothing more. Don't ya know? But…" She leaned forward and said, "If I could have had a son…"

Gracie stood, unable to finish. Choking back her feelings, she turned to the shelves. When she sat, she gently set Jack's eagle before him. "You're a marvel, Jack."

"Me and Spunk head west. You and Tom will start a major campaign to unite the South. The Forresters go home to help the North if they're allowed." Jack stared into his coffee cup, feeling the loss of good friends. "Even Will Biggs talks of exploring to the far western oceans." He drank. "How does this end?" He watched as Gracie sat back, grinning broadly.

"It doesn't."